DAWN
WARRIOR SERIES

Also by Melanie P. Smith

Dawn

Warrior Series

Book Three

by:
Melanie P. Smith

MPSmith Publishing

Dedication:

To my mother…

Who has always supported my independence

And my many adventures, no matter how wild

And crazy she believed them to be.

Thank you for all you do.

Chapter One

Samantha stood in front of the large oval mirror ignoring the enormous crack that spread like long boney fingers down the left side of the old glass. A loud sigh escaped from deep within her chest. She didn't notice. She was focused on the reflection of her small, uninviting apartment looming in the background. Sam hated this place. That's why she rarely spent more than a few minutes here these days. She just couldn't stand to be alone anymore. She shook her head trying to stave off the gloom, picked up her brush and pulled her long red hair into a tight pony tail. She wasn't going to dwell on her lack of a social life or inadequate living arrangements tonight. She had more important things to do. It was futile anyway. She didn't have time to hang out in clubs or date some brainless jerk that only had one thing on his mind. She'd tried dating, but there were always so many questions when she went out alone late at night. Questions she couldn't answer. Until she reached her goal, she couldn't allow complications in her life. She wouldn't give up hunting for anyone, not even a guy. She glanced around, picked up her black ball cap and placed it securely on her head; pulling her large ponytail through the small hole in the back. Hunting was her life. She had accepted her fate long ago. There was no way she'd turn back now.

Sam adjusted her hat one more time making sure it was tight and secure. Then, she walked to the kitchen and retrieved two small transceivers from the table. She always carried the tiny devices when she left the apartment these days. They were almost perfect now, the slight alterations she'd made earlier would almost double their reception. Maybe she'd get a chance to test one out tonight. She didn't use them on many vampires but occasionally they came in handy. Like with Lilith. It was always best to have a couple on hand in case of an emergency. Sam casually glanced around the room again and frowned. It really was time to move to a better place. The apartment was small and felt dirty. No matter how many hours she spent cleaning the tiny space, she could never get the haze off the windows or the grime off the walls. It was sparsely furnished and extremely impersonal. She'd rented in the Bronx on purpose. When she first came to New York, she didn't know much about vampires and their habits. She believed they would hang out in slums and target prostitutes or the homeless. Sam had rented the rundown apartment because she thought she needed to live where she hunted. She'd been wrong. Vampires hung out everywhere and targeted anyone. They didn't seem to care if the people they killed would be missed or how the loss would impact their surviving family members.

Sam took a deep breath and closed her eyes. She was terribly lonely without her family. Work helped, but she missed the closeness she had shared with Michael growing up and the support her mother always gave her no matter what. She wasn't close to anyone like that now days. She hadn't been since their death. What would her brother be like today if he'd survived that violent attack?

At twelve he had already developed such a strong, fun personality. He'd been so innocent. She immediately stopped herself. She wasn't going to dwell on that tonight. Thinking about Michael always made her depressed. She was happy and successful now. Being alone hadn't handicapped her. She'd done okay without her family's support. Her recent promotion to Executive Manager at D-Tech proved she could make it on her own just fine. Wasn't that what she had always wanted? She was only thirty-five, but she'd already achieved her lifelong dream. Well, career wise anyway. Sam slowly settled onto the old couch, studying the awful pattern in disgust. She was definitely going to move. She needed a better place, a place she could personalize. Somewhere she could buy a nice couch and not worry about getting robbed blind. Her thoughts drifted to the Realtors' office she walked past every day on her way to the lab. Maybe she'd buy her own place this time. She could definitely afford it, especially after her recent promotion. and she wasn't going anywhere. She loved New York. Maybe it was time to put down roots.

Sam sighed as she laid her head against the back of the sofa. She didn't plan on hunting tonight, but she was so bored. If she hung out here, she'd just sink into a deeper depression. Her thoughts flashed back to work. Today had been so productive she didn't have any projects to bring home to keep her occupied. She was excited about the new transceivers, but she'd completed the draft proposal this morning. It was now in R&D's hands. Hopefully the work she'd been doing on the side to aid in her vampire hunting, would pay off in her pocketbook. Time would tell. The only other pressing issue at the lab was the droid line. D-Tech needed to increase production and fast. The orders were backing up. Sam had spent the entire afternoon brainstorming and developing a new production plan. She couldn't implement any of her changes until she got the okay from Alex though. After such a long stressful day, she needed a break from work anyway. She wanted the thrill of the chase. So why was she procrastinating? Well, not anymore. She reached over and slid the transceivers into the pocket of her leather jacket, pushed into her boots, jumped to her feet then headed for the door. She paused long enough to lock up then left the apartment, anxious to start her evening out.

It was cool and dark outside, perfect weather for hunting vampires. The construction cranes and city lights sprinkled throughout the borough were somehow comforting. Sam hoped the growth would continue. Over the last couple years, several new residential buildings had replaced vacant lots throughout the neighborhood. The Bronx was slowly improving. It wasn't stable yet but she hoped with time it would be productive again. As she walked casually down the sidewalk, her thoughts returned to Alex. Her current boss wasn't happy about her extracurricular activities. Sam liked Alex but she wasn't willing to stop making those monsters pay for what they did to her family, not even to make her boss happy. The more vampire's Sam killed the better as far as she was concerned. Vampires had killed her parents and her brother, her uncle and his family and her maternal grandparents. Sam was alone in the world thanks to those blood sucking fiends. She didn't have any family left now at all. Her paternal grandparents had done their best to fill the void after her parents and brother were killed. Unfortunately, they died in a car crash a couple years ago leaving her completely alone. The closest thing she had to family was Luke Deveraux and he was dead now, too.

Sam stepped onto the subway out of habit. Her thoughts drifted back to that awful night. No matter how hard she tried, she couldn't stop the scene from forming in her mind. Her mother had locked her in a small cupboard determined to save her life. But Sam still saw everything in vivid detail. Michael had already been discovered. There was no hope for him. Sam still hadn't found the vampire responsible for their deaths. Until she did, any vampire she encountered was going to pay for her loss. She would never forget those cold, violet eyes as they stared vacantly at the lifeless bodies of her family. One day she would find that killer and make him pay. She wouldn't stop hunting until she found him. He couldn't hide. His eyes would give him away. Most vampires had mystic green eyes similar to a cat's. The vampire that had killed her family had violet eyes. She'd never seen another vampire like him.

Sam shook off the old memories and concentrated on the night. She was surprised to realize she was already in downtown New York. When did she get off the subway? She took a deep breath and forced all thoughts from her mind, she needed to be alert. After one more calming breath she silently crept into the darkness of a nearby alley. There was no doubt in her mind, at least one vampire would be hiding in the shadows. There were always vampires back here. It was close to a busy club. If a vampire arrived at just the right time, they'd stumble onto a smorgasbord. In this secluded back street, vampires could feed as long as they wanted with very little effort or interruption. The thought enraged Sam. If she did her job right, no humans would die back here tonight.

Sam slid further into the shadows. She needed to get to the ladder that led up the fire escape before the vampires noticed her. A slight noise echoed through the darkness. It was a bone chilling sound that resonated from the abandoned space ahead. Sam froze. She wasn't going to make it. She quickly pulled her knife from the sheath on her belt and prepared for battle. It was best to avoid hand to hand with a vampire if possible. Most of them weren't very smart, but they were strong and fast. It was extremely difficult for a human to hold their own against a vampire in an even fight. Sam could usually get up high and take them out from a distance with her arrows, but occasionally she was forced to engage her enemy up close and personal. Unfortunately when that happened, she usually went home injured. She took another deep breath and focused on her surroundings. The night was not getting off to a good start. Maybe she should have stayed home after all. Oh well, too late now. She slowly pressed her back against the brick wall and waited.

A large vampire charged from the back of the alley. He was fast. Sam gave her shoulders a little shake and hoped for the best. She concentrated on the vampire, waiting for just the right moment to plunge her knife into his chest. She would only have one shot at this. If she missed, she was dead. Sam waited a second too long. Before she could shift away, the vampire reached out and latched onto her arm. It was like a vice grip. He began violently swinging her around the small space. Sam clung to the vampire with all her might, but she was having a hard time holding on. He was just too strong. If she lost her grip, she'd be flung against the wall for sure. The force would most likely knock her out and she'd be dead in seconds. She needed to act fast, but he was flopping her around like a rag doll. Sam heard a loud pop then grimaced as pain shot through her small body. She had to strike now and hope for the best.

Luckily her knife hit its mark. The vampire dissipated into thin air. Sam instantly fell to the ground with a thud. A slight breeze drifted down the alleyway scattering the remaining vampire dust in all directions. Sam tried to move her arm and gritted her teeth. She was in a lot of pain. The vampire had yanked on her arm with enough force to dislocate her left shoulder. She couldn't hunt like this. Almost as soon as her night had begun it was over. She took a deep breath as she slowly slid her body against the brick wall. She had to get out of this alley. She was too vulnerable here. Any minute another vampire could enter the dark hideout looking for food. This spot was too popular to stay vacant for long. She'd have to head for the hospital, again. Good thing Deveraux Industries had excellent insurance. She spent entirely too much time in the ER. Sam sighed and stumbled to her feet. She'd need to come up with a good story. The doctors were getting suspicious and they asked too many questions, especially that female doctor that was always so serious and intense. When she stared at Sam with those deep hazel eyes, it felt as though she had a direct window into Sam's soul. With any luck, that doctor would have the night off tonight.

* * * *

Sam sat in the small sterile emergency room tapping her foot against the metal bed frame as she impatiently waited for someone, anyone, to return. She hoped that nurse hadn't called the police. But even if she had, Sam would stick with her story. They couldn't prove she was lying. Timmy had been playing on the stairs with that truck this morning. Chances were good he had left it there. He always left his toys on the stairs. She didn't have a new bag of groceries, but it was too late to fix that mistake. They couldn't force her to show them her apartment, could they? No, she was pretty sure she didn't have to let them inside her home if she didn't want to. She was a victim, not a suspect. Sam looked up as metal rings clanged across the circular bar. A well-groomed woman brushed aside the white curtain and entered her small room. Sam groaned inwardly, it was that female doctor again. What was her name? She glanced at a small tag pinned to the tidy scrubs. Oh yeah, Dr. Quintana. This definitely was not her lucky night.

Sam conjured her most winning smile. Dr. Quintana wasn't moved. She was scowling openly and just stood there quietly studying Sam's face. Okay, fine. Sam could hold her own against this woman. She'd done it several times before. "This is kind of painful doc, how much longer before someone pops it back into place?" Sam asked.

"I've requested a couple nurses. They should be joining us shortly," Kylee Quintana paused. She knew Samantha hadn't tripped on a truck left on the stairs by a neighboring child like she claimed. Someone had done this to her. Someone was assaulting this woman, Kylee just wished she could prove it. "We need to talk about your injuries," she began.

"Okay, what do you want to know?" Sam said, trying to sound casual.

"What really happened to you tonight?" Kylee asked.

"I told that nurse already. I was carrying a sack of groceries home and tripped on a truck left on the stairs. I know better. There are so many kids in my apartment complex. They're always leaving things on the steps. I should have watched where I was walking," Sam explained.

Dr. Quintana sat in silence. She wanted Samantha to know she didn't believe her, but she had to be careful. She could be in a lot of trouble if she accused a patient of lying.

Sam knew what the doctor was doing. She thought if she left an uncomfortable silence, Sam would confess. This doctor didn't believe Sam, but she couldn't prove her story was fabricated. Sam could wait her out. She wasn't about to confess anything to this woman. If she told the good doctor what she thought she wanted to know, they'd lock Sam in the loony bin for sure. She just needed her shoulder fixed so she could get home and go to bed. Tonight had been a disaster and she was going to have to face Alex in the morning. Compared to her boss, dealing with the nosy doctor was a piece of cake.

"Okay fine, we'll stick with that for now," Dr. Quintana interrupted Sam's thoughts. "I just want you to know you don't have to deal with this alone." Kylee pulled a business card from her pocket and held it out to Sam. "I know this detective personally.

He can help. Whoever's doing this needs to be stopped." Kylee paused waiting for Sam to take the card.

Sam hesitated then decided if she took the card, maybe the doctor would think she'd won. She slowly reached forward and accepted the information. Detective Rand McBride was boldly printed across the front. Sam shrugged, then winced and placed it in her jacket pocket.

"Think about calling him. He's a good man. You've been here..." Kylee glanced down at her notes, she didn't need them but she didn't want Samantha to know she'd taken a personal interest in her case. "You've been here five times in the last six months. That's excessive. The injuries keep escalating," Kylee looked pleadingly at her patient. "If you don't get help, next time they might be wheeling you in here on a stretcher. Just think about it, that's all I'm asking," she pled.

Sam slowly gave the doctor a nod. Of course she wouldn't talk to this detective, but the doctor didn't need to know that. She'd just play along and get out of here. Next time she'd need to go to a different hospital. She should have thought of that before. Going to the same place every time was drawing attention to herself. Oh well, that was easily rectified.

Two men walked into the small room. "Hey, doc," the largest one said enthusiastically. "I hear we get to pop a shoulder back in place tonight," he glanced over at Sam and sobered. "Not exactly what I expected. It's more fun when they're men," he whined. "New York has a lot of bar fights. I like hearing tough guys cry," he grinned. "Fixing up a woman won't be as entertaining."

Dr. Quintana watched Samantha exit the hospital and disappear into the night. She wasn't going to let this drop. She liked Sam. She wouldn't let some guy abuse her this way. Kylee was afraid the attacks against Samantha would continue to escalate until the wounds were fatal. It had happened too many times before. She pondered her options. She had plenty of vacation leave saved up. Maybe it was time to use a little of it. If she pretended to take a break, the hospital administrator would stop nagging her about a private life. He was sure she was going to burn out any day now. If Kylee made up some exotic vacation plan, she could use that time off to follow Samantha. She needed to see what was going on, then she'd know how to help her patient. Kylee smiled inwardly. She'd fantasized about being a private investigator when she was younger. Once in college, she realized she was better suited to medicine. Maybe she'd start a bucket list and playing detective would be her first task. She glanced at her watch, just enough time to send her boss an email. He'd get her vacation request first thing in the morning. She slid Sam's file under her jacket and slowly walked through the revolving doors.

Chapter Two

Alex walked through the winding hall of D-Tech. She needed to talk to Sam. Their robot project was a bigger hit than anticipated. They all knew the robot maid would be hot, but supply wasn't coming close to keeping up with demand. They needed to step up production in a big way. They also had a small defect that needed to be fixed immediately. So far the tech guys hadn't figured it out. Alex was prepared to hire additional personnel if needed. She smiled inwardly, that was Sam's problem now. She came around the corner and stopped. Sam was clearly in pain. There was something wrong with her shoulder. Alex sobered. Had the woman been out hunting vampires again?

Sam turned and saw Alex scowling at her. "Hey, what's up?" she asked casually. Maybe if she pretended not to notice Alex's displeasure, they wouldn't have to talk about her injury.

"What happened to your arm?" Alex asked, clearly concerned.

Dawn

"I dislocated my shoulder last night. It's no big deal and it's not going to interfere with my work. I promise. Was there something you needed to talk to me about?" Sam asked. She needed to talk to Alex about the droids, but she was curious what had brought her boss to the office this morning.

Alex studied Sam. Pressing her wasn't going to do any good, but she wasn't ready to drop this yet. "Did a vampire do that to you?" she asked trying to sound unconcerned.

Sam sighed. "Look, I know you don't approve of my off duty activities. But after hours, once I leave the office, that's my time. I get to do what I want during my free time. If that means recreational skydiving, motorcycle racing or vampire hunting, you have no say in the matter. I'm going to spend my free time the way I want. Don't press this Alex. I'm not changing my life for this job."

They stood in silence for a long moment. Alex knew if she kept pressing she might lose Sam as an employee. She definitely didn't want to lose her. Sam was good at tech work. Alex had never met anyone better. She needed to keep her happy, but vampire hunting could be fatal. "Let's head into the office. I have a couple things I need to talk to you about," Alex finally said. She turned and headed for the closed door.

Sam swallowed the lump in her throat and slowly followed Alex. She was nervous now. Had she pushed things too far? Was Alex going to tell her to find a new job? Sam loved this place. She didn't want to leave. She would never leave voluntarily. She'd been bluffing, sort of. She wasn't going to stop vampire hunting, but she would be more careful. She might even tone it down and go out less often if her job depended on it. Did she need to apologize to Alex? She could do that. She'd do whatever she had to. She was determined to keep this job. It was a dream come true.

"We need to talk about the robots and production," Alex began.

"Oh," Sam answered, relieved.

Alex smiled. "I'm not going to hassle you about vampire hunting. You know how I feel about it. I like you Sam. I don't want to lose you. Vampire hunting is dangerous. I shouldn't have to remind you of that," she paused. "Other than family, you're the only one that knows how Luke died. When I say I don't want to lose you, I mean to a vampire or to another company. We need you," Alex confessed.

Sam smiled back. Good, this was about work. She might tone things down a bit anyway. If she was injured every time Alex stopped by, she might change her mind. "I've been thinking about our options. Demand is far outweighing supply right now. Let me show you my preliminary plans. They're really rough but it should give you an idea of what I'm thinking and you can see which direction you want to go."

The two women immediately put their differences aside and got to work.

* * * *

Dimitri walked silently through the kitchen door and stopped. Alex was adding the final touches to a large platter of appetizers. He was still astonished at the intense love he felt for her. He had finally found the perfect woman. It had taken him more than four hundred years, but she was worth the wait. Spring couldn't come quick enough for him. He understood the need for such a big elaborate wedding but he wanted her to be his wife, now. He wanted to give her so much, but he couldn't. Dimitri sighed, things had been beyond hectic lately. He wished he could whisk Alex away on a luxurious vacation tonight, but that was going to have to wait for their honeymoon. Right now they had to focus on this war. Leaving town, even for a weekend wasn't an option. The vampires were changing tactics. It was hard to know what was coming next. Radek was becoming desperate. He wanted to rule the fae and vampire communities. His hunger for power was making him reckless and dangerous. Worse, it was making him unpredictable.

He smiled when Alex turned and noticed he was standing there. She'd worked so hard the last few days. "How's my kitchen master?" he asked as he walked toward her.

"I wish Marta was here," Alex sighed. "She's so much better at this than I am. Did Jake say when they'd be back in town?"

"Not really," Dimitri admitted. "Jake was evasive and secretive about his plans. He never did give me a clear answer on when they would return." Dimitri gently wrapped his arms around Alex's waist and pulled her against him. "Thanks for all your hard work today. I still think we should have thrown together some potato salad and maybe some beans. Once I grill the steaks that would have been good enough."

"Maybe next time," Alex agreed, "but not tonight. We haven't had any time to relax for weeks. Tonight needs to be special. Our big night to kick off our new plan."

Dimitri picked up one of the trays and headed for the door. "The warriors are growing restless. We need to get upstairs before they start eating the furniture."

"Somehow I don't think they'll eat the pool chairs. Your man cave is safe for now." Alex picked up a large bowl of pasta salad and headed for the door.

Dimitri slowed until he was standing beside Alex. "You already look tired. I wish you had let me help you set things up today. The BBQ was my idea."

"I'm fine," Alex answered smiling at Dimitri. "I'm going to veg all day tomorrow. Tonight I'm going to socialize with a great group of guys and meet whatever flavor of the week they brought with them. I assume we already have a full house?"

"Yeah," he admitted. He was amused. Alex already knew the warriors so well. "I told them to go up and make themselves at home. I hope they didn't take me too seriously. I think they're getting cramped in the mansion with Thomas. If we're not careful, they might move into the guest rooms before we can stop them."

Alex stopped and looked over at Dimitri. "Are they having a hard time getting along?" she asked concerned.

"Nothing too serious. They're just having a hard time coordinating their schedules. I know Ty is extremely frustrated. He's behind schedule on his new game and can't find the peace and quiet he needs to make the final touches. He's already threatening to move back to his ranch up state. That reminds me, did you talk to Thomas today? Are we still on schedule if Ty's agreeable? I want him to head out in a couple days if possible?" Dimitri admitted.

"Yeah," Alex smiled. "Everything is all set. We have a delivery coming tomorrow but that's the last one. Afterwards the house is ready and completely habitable. I even had the maid service stock the refrigerator in anticipation of company. I do need to talk to you about something though. Let's go welcome our guests and then we can sneak away for a minute," she said mysteriously.

Dimitri followed. He hated it when she did that, but he knew Alex wouldn't share until she was ready. He also knew it wouldn't be long. He opened the large door that led to the roof and held it for her. It was like entering Victor's club, Dimitri observed. "I hope the neighbors don't call the cops. Maybe we should lower the volume on the stereo," he suggested.

"Its fine," Alex countered. "It's not that loud and our two closest neighbors know we're having a party tonight. The Nelson's are out of town and the Petersen's had plans. They won't be home until later. Let the guys enjoy themselves. It's been a long time since they could relax. They all deserve it."

Dimitri studied the room. Ty was missing. He walked to the table and put down the platter. Then, he approached Thomas. "Where's Ty?" he asked.

Thomas frowned. "He wouldn't join us, no matter how hard I tried. He promised he'd stop by later," Thomas answered. "He said he had work and he couldn't play until it was done."

Dimitri frowned. "I need to talk to him," he grumbled.

"Dimitri this arrangement is not working," Thomas scowled. "Ty can't work. He's frustrated and ready to move home. It's not like Ty to miss a party. That should tell you how desperate he is for quiet time," Thomas paused. "The house is a mess. I can't get any of those guys to clean up after themselves. I don't have the time or the patience for this and you took my housekeeper. Well, I guess Jake did but she's still gone. I'm at my wit's end."

"I know," Dimitri confessed. "You've actually lasted longer than I expected. Alex said the house will be ready tomorrow. That takes care of Ty if he's up for it. If he agrees to head out to the fort, he should have the peace and quiet he needs to finish his work. I know Marta's not around to help. Jake seems to have her preoccupied lately," he smiled. He was happy for Jake and Marta. Maybe this arrangement was the push the two of them needed to finally get together for good. "Why don't the other warriors rotate their maids through your house? They have to be out of work now that these guys are never home. It's a win for everyone."

"You suggest it. Anytime I bring up housework they just think I'm nagging," Thomas requested.

"Don't worry, I'll talk to them. If they won't hire their maids to help, they're going to have to do something. I know you're swamped trying to handle the business. I'm sorry I forced this on you," Dimitri apologized. "I need to talk to Ty tonight, then I want to have a meeting with everyone tomorrow morning. Alex and I will come to your place if that works for you. We can work something out then."

"Sure," Thomas agreed. "Just don't complain about the mess. You can see for yourself how out of control this situation has gotten."

Dimitri put a reassuring hand on Thomas' shoulder then made the rounds to the rest of the warriors. Once he talked to everyone, he tracked down Alex. "Let's go to the library. We can't talk here with all this noise." If Ty didn't show by the time he finished with Alex, he'd head over to the mansion and talk to him there. They needed to get a start on the project at the fort and Ty was the only one that could do it.

Dawn

Ty quietly walked through the door and stepped onto the rooftop patio. The music was loud and so were the women. Everyone was in the pool having a good time. Ty smiled inwardly. Normally he'd have his own date to share the evening with, but not tonight. He stepped up to the small table and poured himself a cup of coffee. After doctoring it to his satisfaction, he strolled over to a pool chair and attempted to relax. It had been a long day. His game still wasn't finished. There was a glitch he just couldn't locate. Marketing was getting impatient. His customers were getting impatient. He needed to find the flaw and fast. Dimitri wasn't going to be happy when he found out Ty was moving back home but he didn't have a choice.

Ty glanced down when he felt something rub up against his leg. He laughed. "What do we have here?" he asked as he reached down and set the black and white ball of fur on his lap. He gently ran his hand over the small puppies head and down its back. The puppy rolled over and presented his stomach for a good rub. Ty laughed and began rubbing the young dog's belly. He never could resist the innocence and exuberance of a puppy. He glanced up when he heard a noise to his right.

"I see you've met Cane," Dimitri grinned.

Ty raised an eyebrow. "Cane? Is Abel running around here somewhere? Or has this monster already killed him and buried him in the back yard?" he asked, grinning.

"Very funny," Dimitri scowled. "It's short for Hurricane." Dimitri leaned forward and picked up the small fur ball that was now jumping up and down on Ty's lap. "This little guy is a daily disaster waiting to happen. He runs through the house destroying everything in his path," Dimitri admitted.

"Did you do any research on breeds before you decided to get a Border Collie?" Ty asked amused.

"Of course I did," Dimitri countered.

Ty studied him skeptically.

"Okay, you're right. I didn't," Dimitri admitted. "I was doing a job for a lady and she had this one puppy left. She was desperate to find him a home and kept asking me to take him. I wasn't sure if that was the dog I wanted, but he followed me around for hours. I guess he grew on me. By the end of the day I knew I had to take him home. Alex has been wanting a dog, so I thought it was fate." The puppy had climbed up Dimitri's chest and was trying to give him puppy kisses all over his face. Dimitri was dodging the small tongue and grinning.

Ty grinned, too. Dimitri was definitely hooked. He'd never seen the mighty warrior leader this tolerant and mushy. He laughed out loud when the puppy won and slathered a huge kiss across Dimitri's mouth. "You two need some privacy?" he teased.

Dimitri gently put the dog on the floor and sat down next to Ty. "Don't start. I've seen you with your dogs," Dimitri shrugged. "It's impossible not to love the little shit."

"True," Ty admitted. "But you are going to have a challenge on your hands. I wouldn't recommend this breed to anyone for their first dog. They have too much energy and they're smart. You can't give a bit. One slip and you'll be sorry forever. Don't underestimate his intelligence. What are you doing with him while you and Alex are gone all day?"

Dimitri laughed. "He goes to work with me. We tried leaving him home at first, but it only took us one day to figure out that wasn't an option. When we got home, our house was a disaster. It looked like a hurricane had touched down in our living room. I'm not sure Alex has forgiven him for destroying her favorite shoes. He definitely earned his name."

"Is that working out okay?" Ty asked.

"I think we're finally getting a groove. When I'm outside working, he can usually wander around with me. While I'm in the house, I can put him in the bed of the truck. Right now he can't get out. I may have to rethink that once he's older and can just jump out and follow me."

"If you start now and train him to stay in the back of the truck when you put him there, he'll stay. Like I said, these dogs are smart. You can't leave him alone for hours though or he'll get bored and start to destroy things. But I think you can make it work as long as you give him plenty of activity throughout the day," Ty advised. He studied Dimitri. It was time to tell him he was moving back home.

Dimitri was watching Ty. He could tell the mood had changed. He knew Ty was thinking about moving back to his ranch, but Dimitri needed him at the fort. "I hate to pull you away from the party already, but can I talk to you in the library?" Dimitri asked.

Ty took a deep breath. That would be better. If he upset Dimitri when he told him he was moving, at least no one else would hear him rant. "Sure," Ty stood and followed Dimitri out the door.

* * * *

The two men walked into the library. Dimitri immediately moved to the big comfortable chair and sat down. Ty sat casually on the leather couch. "Alex, Thomas and I have been talking about our current situation with the vampires," Dimitri started before Ty could begin. "They're changing their techniques. With all the different explosives and devices of war the humans have created, this is the first time in history the vampires have actually used those as weapons against their enemies," Dimitri paused.

"I've been thinking a lot about that too," Ty admitted. "I'd know if any of the other vampires were using bombs. I have friends around the globe. We keep in touch and share information. The vampires in other parts of the world aren't following Radek's lead. Those vampire kings aren't declaring war on the fae either. This problem is local, thank goodness."

"That's what I've heard as well. The other communities never had a treaty to help them keep the peace. They just have an informal, mutual agreement to leave each other alone. The warriors might be part of the problem here. New York and the surrounding area is the only fae community that has protectors. Over the centuries the others have just figured out a way to occupy the same region without conflict. Somehow they're able to coexist. I'm grateful for that too," Dimitri said sincerely.

"If this was a global war, it would be much more difficult to win. It's already hard enough to coordinate with all the local species. Regardless of what Radek does, we still have to keep our existence a secret," Dimitri continued. "Right now that's a handicap for us. The vampires don't seem to care if the humans discover them. I think that's a mistake. If they continue to act this reckless,

Dawn

I believe the other vampires might get involved. If the humans can provide proof vampires exist, it's going to endanger vampires worldwide. Radek may not care about that, but the other king's will," Dimitri said confidently.

"I agree," Ty said studying his leader. He still didn't know why Dimitri had called him in here. "So what does that have to do with me?" Ty asked as he walked over to pour himself another cup of coffee. "You want one?" he asked.

"I'd love one," Dimitri answered. "I don't think we're ever going to have another treaty," Dimitri admitted. "I think we need to do what we can to fix this problem. If we can, kill Radek and see who takes his place. If Lilith somehow convinces the vampires to accept her as their queen our problems will continue. I'm afraid we'll eventually have to kill her, too."

"I agree," Ty put in. "Alex and Ariel said Lilith was responsible for the bombs at the ball. All the bombs I've dealt with were made by the same person. That means Lilith was also responsible for the bombs at the panther and shifter communities. I'm afraid Lilith may be more dangerous than Radek."

"Maybe," Dimitri conceded. "That's where our new plan comes in. Well, actually I think it was Luke and Marlena's plan. Alex found some paperwork and several maps of the Seneca Army Depot. With Thomas' help we've been able to piece things together and figure out what they were up to. It's actually a brilliant idea."

"The Seneca Army Depot?" Ty said confused. "Wasn't that closed years ago? I think that's the military facility where the humans protested for days at its closing?"

"It is," Dimitri admitted. "That was back in 2000. I was shocked to learn Luke already had a plan in the works to lease the property from the military. He has the connections, but he never said anything to the warriors. Which makes me wonder if it was actually Marlena's plan. Anyway, Luke had an agreement with the government to lease the property if they decided to close it. He agreed to hold off for a few years to let things settle before changing anything. He and Marlena didn't alter the property until the year before Marlena's death. They also purchased a large farm on the north side of the property. Alex and I flew out there a while ago. The house was in fairly good shape. So, here's the basics." Dimitri proceeded to outline the new plan for Ty.

Ty listened closely. It was a good plan. Dimitri wanted him to head out to the depot or the fort as he called it and set up a training camp for the fae and warriors. The young, upcoming generation needed to be prepared for all the changes that were taking place in their community. Eventually Dimitri and Alex wanted to offer training to the shifters as well. It was going to take a lot of work, but it was right up Ty's alley. He was starting to get excited, but sensed there was a hitch. "So far I'm game but what's the downside?"

"Well, like I said the house is in really good shape. Alex and Thomas have been working on making a few improvements and stocking everything you will need to get the job done. I think the computer equipment will be delivered tomorrow," Dimitri stalled.

"What don't you want to tell me?" Ty pressed.

"Samantha," Dimitri stated.

Ty furrowed his brow. He vaguely remembered Alex mentioning someone named Samantha, but Ty couldn't remember anything about her. "Who is that?" he asked.

Dawn

"Sam is a tech wiz that works for D-Tech. Alex wants to relocate her to D-Tech's Romulus plant, which just happens to be next door to the Army Depot," Dimitri began.

"No way!" Ty exclaimed. "I'm not babysitting Alex's human. If I do this, I'm going to be busy. I don't even know this woman and you want us to move into the same house together? I can't work with a human around," he said incredulously.

"Just hear me out," Dimitri pressed. "I know you're not big on humans. But Sam is going to be just as busy as you are. You won't have to babysit."

"How am I supposed to work on the security and get the training facility up and running and keep our secret with a human in the house?" Ty asked.

"Well, that's the good news. You don't have to keep anything from Sam. She already knows," Dimitri answered.

"What? How does a human know about us?" Ty asked. "Isn't that against the rules or something?"

"Well, since Alex sets the rules I doubt it," Dimitri provided.

"Not funny," Ty countered.

"Sam is the one that found all those photos of Luke and his vampire fighting. Remember, we were all in the pictures. We thought Sam was going to be upset and require a long explanation, but she didn't need one. Apparently vampires have killed her entire family. Alex is still trying to find out why, but regardless Sam is completely up to speed. She was in that alley with Alex and Ariel when they were battling the newborns and Lilith. In fact, Alex and Ariel joined the fight to help Sam. So, she knows about Alex, she knows about Ariel and she knows about the vampires. We haven't talked to her about the warriors, but she was also at the ball the night Lilith bombed us, so she has to know something is up there too. You don't need to keep secrets from Sam."

"Why does she have to go? I can handle this on my own. Or...Alex is great with tech stuff. She can go with me," Ty suggested.

Dimitri smiled. "Not a chance. Alex and I will come out as often as we can, but Alex has enough on her plate. She can't do it herself. We need Sam. Bottom line, Sam's going to be relocated. It would just help if she could stay at the house but I'm leaving that part up to you. If you really can't have her at the farm, she'll have to stay somewhere else."

Ty didn't like it, but he wasn't that unreasonable. He wouldn't make Sam stay in a hotel instead of having the comforts of a house just because he didn't want her there. He would be busy, with any luck maybe they wouldn't even see each other. "She's going to be as busy as I will?" Ty asked. "I won't have time to entertain her."

"At least. We need Sam to start building the sparring droids. We want every kid attending the camp to have their own personal droid in addition to the trainers. They need to be able to practice the moves we teach them in class. Plus, Alex has a great idea for a simulator. She thinks Sam might be able to rig something up there as well," Dimitri told him.

"Simulator? What kind of simulator?" Ty asked.

"Apparently D-Tech makes some kind of simulator for police and military personnel. The police ones are shooting scenarios and driving techniques. They also make flight Sims and other top secret stuff for the military. Alex wants Sam to develop one for our training program," Dimitri stated. "That's going to keep her busy."

"Is this woman really good?" Ty asked.

"From what I hear she's the best," Dimitri said. "Why?"

"Well, I think I could help with the simulator. I have a couple ideas that I use in my games that might be great for a battle Sim. But I don't want to waste my time if she's a novice," Ty answered.

"So is that a yes? You think you and Sam can work together and stay at the farm?" Dimitri asked, excited.

"I'll give it a try, but I still think there's something you're not telling me," he accused.

"Well, I kind of hinted but you didn't pick up on it. Alex is sending Sam out for all the reasons I told you. We really need her to get this place up and running in a timely manner," Dimitri paused.

"But?" Ty asked.

"But there's also a side benefit of sending her to the fort," Dimitri admitted.

"And what's that?" Ty asked.

"Sam has been vampire hunting at night alone," Dimitri told him.

"What?" Ty exclaimed. "Why would a human go out vampire hunting?" Ty paused, thinking. "Because they killed her parents," he answered his own question. "But doesn't she know how dangerous it is out there especially alone? We don't even do that and we're better equipped to handle a vamp," Ty argued.

"Alex has tried to talk some sense into her, but so far she's not getting anywhere. It's not like Sam can invite a friend to go with her. Most humans don't even believe in vampires. They're not going to stay out all night killing them. Anyway, this will keep her out of trouble for a little while at least," Dimitri confessed. "Alex believes in Sam 110% but she's also trying to save her life."

"I'm not going to babysit her," Ty reiterated. "If she goes out at night, that's her business. I will work with her on the Sims and I will take care of the security and other needs at the base but that's it. This should also give me the time I need to finish my game. I'm going to be extremely busy. She'll have to take care of herself," he paused. "When do you want me to leave?"

"As soon as you can. Go back and enjoy the BBQ. Stop worrying about your game and breaking the news to me that you're moving back home," Dimitri smiled at Ty's surprise. "Yeah, I know about that. The fort is going to keep you busy, but it should also give you the solitary life you need for the next few weeks to fix your game," Dimitri smiled.

"Do the rest of the guys know about this plan?" Ty asked.

"Nope," Dimitri answered. "I wanted to talk to you first and make sure you were willing to take this on. I've called a meeting for tomorrow morning to go over everything with the warriors. You'll also get more details at that time. I'd like you to head out as soon as you can. How long do you need to prepare for the trip?" he asked.

"I can probably take care of everything I have to do here in the city tomorrow. Then I'll need to head out to my place and pack. I can be ready the following morning if that's soon enough for you," Ty said thoughtfully. Dimitri obviously wanted to get started right away.

"Perfect," Dimitri said relieved. Getting Ty to agree to Sam was easier than he originally thought it would be. It was always nice when he could make his future wife happy. He already knew Ty would jump at the opportunity to work on the fort. Between Ty's skills and Sam's, this plan might be a reality sooner than they originally thought. Dimitri stood to signal the meeting was over.

Ty followed suit. He could relax and enjoy the BBQ now. He'd have the time and solitude he needed to figure out the glitch in his game and he was going to enjoy working on the fort. Sam might be a problem, but with any luck he wouldn't have to deal with her much. Humans were so fickle. He really didn't have any patience for the species. He'd just have to put her in her place from the beginning. He had plenty of practice in that area. The pompous, arrogant humans he'd been forced to deal with while working in the family oil business had soured him for good. Okay, he had to admit the guys he worked with at Tyson Electronics were great guys. Maybe the oil industry just produced intolerable humans. Ty didn't know, but he'd done his best to avoid dealings with the species as much as possible for the past fifty years. Sam would be no different.

Chapter Three

Radek sat silently watching the light flicker across the walls of the damp cave. He was hoping the small fire would help him relax but so far it wasn't calming his nerves. The heat did nothing for a vampire, their core temperature never changed regardless of the season. The drunk man lying on the floor let out a loud groan. Radek scowled as he glanced down at the annoying lump. His mind was going in a million directions. How was a vampire supposed to concentrate when his food wouldn't shut up?

Radek rarely drank from an intoxicated human, but he was at his wit's end. Nothing was going right for him lately. He still didn't have control of half his empire. The fae community was remaining loyal to that brat Alexandria and the council was following her lead. He had been so sure the fae would cooperate as soon as his mother was dead. Part of him assumed they would welcome his protection and embrace him as their new leader. This was all the warriors fault. Somehow he had to get rid of those warriors once and for all. The rest of the vampire world didn't have these pesky obstacles to overcome.

The drunk on the floor groaned again. Radek impatiently reached down, pulled him up by the lapel and sunk his teeth into the man's jugular. His sharp fangs effortlessly ripped through the human flesh as easily as a hot knife through butter. Radek started to relax as the intoxicating blood rippled through his system. Finally, the alcohol was having an impact. He closed his eyes and enjoyed the moment. "Awe," Radek sighed. "Good to the last drop." He grinned as he carelessly dropped the lifeless body with a thud. "Finally, peace and quiet!"

Radek reclined in the large comfortable chair, his mind continued to sporadically shift between the fae and the warriors, Lilith, Hector's death, back to Lilith. What was he going to do about Lilith? He shifted slightly in his recliner finally as relaxed as he was going to get. While he was sober, he'd avoided thinking about his dilemma. If Sammael was right, Lilith would have to be eliminated. He expected loyalty from his minions. He would not tolerate anything but complete loyalty from his lover. Radek knew it was unnatural for a vampire to have only one partner but he still insisted on it in his relationships. Maybe it was his fae side, but Radek had no desire to have more than one partner at a time. He also expected his lover to conform to his wishes. He didn't care if his subordinates thought the practice was strange. If Lilith had been unfaithful with Hector, she was going to have to pay for her betrayal. The thought depressed him. When he met Lilith, he thought he had found the perfect mate. She was so much like himself. Lilith had vision and ambition. She understood the importance of expanding his kingdom to include the fae community. Like him, she wanted complete control of the surrounding area. Radek had thought they would make a perfect royal couple, especially once he had an heir.

Radek's mind changed gears as he thought about the shifter community. He was still determined to mate with a shifter. His son would be the most envied and feared vampire on earth. Once Radek controlled the shifters, he'd have countless women begging him to pick them as his mate. He was sure of it. It was difficult to wait, but until he resolved the warrior problem he couldn't think about creating an heir. Maybe that was the solution to his other problem. He didn't want to believe Lilith had betrayed him but if she had, maybe he would replace her with a shifter. Until then, he'd keep her around until he determined the truth. With Hector dead, that might be impossible.

His mind shifted to Hector. He wasn't exactly upset that Hector was dead. He was just disappointed he hadn't done it himself. He should have had the opportunity to kill Hector and make an example out of him. He needed his people to know insubordination would not be tolerated. Whoever had killed Hector and taken that opportunity away from him, would have to pay. He still didn't know for sure if the shifters had killed him or if the warriors had somehow helped. Until the fiasco at the shifter camp, he had been confident the shifters were responsible. He had believed the shifters killed Hector while rescuing their two women. Now, he just didn't know.

His mind shifted once again back to Lilith. What to do about Lilith? She was becoming too independent. He had told her to use enough explosives to blow that shifter camp off the face of the earth, but Lilith had gone against his wishes. She'd been conservative so she could remain nearby and watch the destruction. If she had obeyed him, some of the warriors would be dead now too and at least part of his problem would be resolved. Radek closed his eyes and slowly drifted off to sleep thinking about the many problems he was facing.

Dawn

The Warriors sat in the large room relaxed and waiting for Victor to arrive. Other than Dimitri, he was the only one that didn't live at the mansion. They all heard the front door close and turned their attention to the doorway. To their surprise, Marta and Jake followed Victor and Ariel into the room.

"Is she part of the plan?" Bastian asked Dimitri upon seeing Ariel. "I thought warrior business was restricted to Warriors."

Dimitri glanced at Victor and quickly answered before the meeting started off on the wrong foot. "I asked Ariel to join us today because she will be involved in this new project." He glanced over at Jake and grinned. "Welcome back. I trust you enjoyed your vacation?"

All eyes turned to Jake. For the first time Bastian noticed the change in Marta. He jumped to his feet and stalked across the room, stopping to stand over Jake who had just sat on the large couch next to Marta. "How could you?" he demanded. "How could you risk her life like that?" He was breathing heavily and barely kept his temper under control.

Dimitri placed an arm on Bastian's shoulder. "Bastian," he said sternly. "I need you to go back and sit down."

Bastian turned and glared at Dimitri. He was furious. Jake had no right to risk Marta that way. The two men stood, silently watching each other.

"Now," Dimitri finally said sternly.

Bastian closed his eyes and tried to regain his composure. After a couple deep breaths, he slowly turned and walked back to his chair.

Alex was confused. She didn't understand what Bastian was so upset about. She glanced at Dimitri momentarily then returned her attention to Bastian. He was still visibly upset. She stood there watching him for several seconds, trying to understand but nothing came to her. She refocused her attention on Marta and smiled. Her friend looked wonderful. Actually, she looked younger and more rested than Alex had ever seen her. She crossed the room and gave Marta a big hug. "I'm so glad you're back! I have missed you so much."

Marta grinned. "I've missed you and Thomas too," she admitted. Thomas had moved to the back of the couch and placed a hand on Marta's shoulder. Marta glanced behind her and gave Thomas' hand a quick squeeze. "I have news," she admitted. "While we were in St Lucia, we decided to get married." She glowed as she held her left hand to show everyone her large diamond ring.

"Oh, Marta!" Alex exclaimed. "That's wonderful."

"Congratulations," Thomas said sincerely. "To both of you," he added as he firmly shook Jake's hand. "Obviously that's not the only decision the two of you made while you were in the Caribbean. Not exactly my idea of a beach vacation," he sobered. "Did everything go okay?"

Jake gave a firm nod as he looked back toward Dimitri, then over to Bastian.

Dawn

Alex was confused. Obviously they had a secret that everyone in this room except her understood. What were they talking about?

Ariel was watching Alex. She knew Alex thought of Marta as family and she wondered how she'd take the change. It didn't take long for her to realize that Alex didn't understand. She didn't know what Jake had done. Well, that made sense. Alex had been shielded from their world for so long. She cleared her throat and addressed her friend. "Dimitri?"

"Yes," he answered.

"I know there are mixed feelings about this whole situation from various members in the room, but before we discuss this new development any further I think someone should explain the situation to Alex. She's new at this and I don't think she knows exactly what decision Marta and Jake made while they were away."

"Oh," Dimitri looked toward Alex and realized Ariel was right. He crossed the room and sat in the large chair next to the one Alex had moved to. "Sorry, honey. I keep forgetting there are things about our world that you still don't understand," he turned his attention toward Jake and Marta. "Do you want to explain it or do you want me to?"

Marta quickly answered, "I want to explain." She shook her head slightly as Jake started to object. "I want Bastian to understand as well."

Bastian stood and walked toward Marta. "I'm sorry," he apologized. "I just can't stay and listen to this." He turned to Jake, "you risked her life for your own selfishness. No matter what the excuse, you didn't have that right." He turned to Dimitri, "I can't stay here. I need to leave. I'll get with you later and talk about the rest. I'm going to work on that helicopter project we talked about." Bastian turned and left the room.

"Please, will someone tell me what that is all about? Why is Bastian so upset? I've never seen him like this before." Alex looked around the room in concern.

"Alex," Marta began. "As you know, Jake and I have been spending a lot of time together lately."

"Yes," Alex agreed.

"I took your advice and risked my heart to find out how Jake really felt. To my surprise he was in love with me, just like you said." She grinned at Jake then looked back to Alex, who was also smiling.

"That's only news to you Marta. Everyone else here already knew that," she answered.

"Well, when we realized we felt the same about each other and had wasted so much time, we also knew we wanted to be together forever," Marta explained. "There was only one way for that to happen."

"I tried to discourage this," Jake insisted. "I told her how dangerous it was and I begged her to be satisfied with the time we had with her as a human. But Marta is persuasive and I finally had to agree this way was better. Not only for me, but for both of us."

"I don't understand," Alex furrowed her eyebrows in confusion.

Dimitri cut in. "Let me explain this part," he said in request as he studied Marta. "As you know warriors live for a very long time," he said concentrating on Alex.

"Yes," Alex answered.

"You also understand humans do not," he continued.

"Yes," Alex said rolling her eyes. "Stop explaining the obvious and tell me what's going on."

"Okay. Okay," Dimitri took a deep breath. "Well, there is a process warriors can use to turn a human into a warrior. Marta went through this process while she and Jake were in St. Lucia. That's why she looks so young and will for many years to come," he explained.

Alex's head shot back to Marta. She did look younger, but Alex had assumed it was just all the relaxation and the marriage. Marta almost glowed. Alex hadn't realized it had been a physical change, not an emotional one, that made Marta look so good. But now, knowing Marta had experienced some type of physical change, it was obvious. She was younger. Then she remembered Bastian's reaction. "Bastian said this could have killed Marta. Is that true?"

"Yes," Marta answered. "The process is very painful and very dangerous. But I knew that going in. I knew the risks and I believed it was worth it if I could have a long, happy life with Jake afterwards."

"But Marta!" Alex argued. "Why would the two of you take such a risk so far away from home? It was irresponsible. What if something had gone wrong? I was too far away. I couldn't have gotten to you in time," she pressed.

"There was nothing you could have done anyway," Jake said soberly. "This process is dangerous. If something goes wrong, not even a healer can fix it. Once we agreed to the transition, we also knew we had to take the risk alone. We couldn't put our friends and family through the agony of waiting for the results."

"Well, that's easy for you to say. It wasn't your life you were risking!" Alex said angrily.

"Actually," Dimitri said calmly, "it was."

Alex looked at him in shock. "Jake's life was at risk? Not Marta's?"

"They both could have died during the transition," he admitted. "The procedure is just as risky for the warrior as it is for the human. Just as many warriors have died in the transition as humans."

"Oh," Alex looked back to Jake. "Sorry, that wasn't fair."

Jake stood and walked to Alex. "I know how much Marta means to you," he waited until Alex was looking him in the eyes. "But do you think for one minute that she is any less important to me?"

"No," Alex conceded. "I know how much you love her, Jake. I guess I just lost it when I realized you guys did something that could have resulted in Marta's death. It's just as bad that you risked your own life. I still think it was irresponsible for the two of you to handle this on your own."

"I agree," Dimitri said sternly as he glowered at Jake. "You know better. What were you thinking? Isn't Bastian reminder enough? You shouldn't have handled this alone?"

"I still don't understand Bastian's reaction," Alex admitted but was completely ignored by everyone in the room.

Dawn

"We didn't do this alone. I'm not that idiotic, Dimitri. And frankly your lack of confidence is insulting. Tianna helped us," he admitted. "And before you get upset, she was sworn to secrecy. We insisted on it. Otherwise we wouldn't tell her where we were. I don't want her to have any repercussions for helping us."

"Well, your lack of confidence in my leadership is also insulting," Dimitri said then smiled at Jake. "You should know Tianna wouldn't suffer repercussions for helping someone. I'm grateful you involved her. Before we move on, I want to add my congratulations to both of you. On the marriage and the success of the transformation. I am honored to add you to our warrior family, Marta. Does this mean I can have my favorite desserts every night for all of eternity?" he asked winking at her.

"I can't promise them daily, but I promise to provide your favorites regularly," she laughed. "I can't believe how good I feel. I haven't felt like this for years! Actually I never have felt this good in my life."

Everyone in the room laughed. Dimitri put an arm around Alex's waist. "Okay, now let's get down to business. We have a lot to discuss and I need Ty to get to his ranch before the end of today."

Jake cleared his throat, "I don't mean to delay your meeting, but there is one more thing."

Dimitri raised one eyebrow.

Jake continued, "I'm afraid Marta is going to have to quit her employment with the Deveraux's. We've decided to open up a bakery."

"Before we get into that we need to fill everyone in on the new direction we will be going. It's important," Dimitri continued as Jake started to interrupt. "I'm going to ask each of you to make sacrifices for the good of the community. That includes you and Marta, Jake. The bakery may have to be put on hold for now."

"Thomas, Dimitri and I have discussed this at length," Alex interrupted. "I think our plan is a good one. However, we could use input from each of you to fine tune it. Everyone in this room is going to be asked to contribute to this huge project. I believe our survival depends on it," she glanced over at Ty and smiled. "Ty has already agreed to the first step."

"I have," Ty grinned back. "But I'm not sure it's a sacrifice for me. I get to escape the bachelor pad Thomas has going here and live in luxury while I play video games and develop technology to keep you guys safe," he paused and shrugged. "A dream come true. Where's the sacrifice in that?"

"Samantha," Alex said simply.

"Oh that," Ty sobered. "I hope Dimitri explained I won't babysit for you. I'll share space and work on the Sims with her, but I won't babysit. Not even for my queen, who happens to be my hero," he finished with a grin.

"I understand," Alex answered. She couldn't help it. She grinned back at Ty. He was too charming for his own good.

"Okay then," Dimitri continued. "Let's lay out this plan and see how you guys feel about it."

"Finally," Dante mumbled. "A guy can only handle so much suspense in one day."

The other warriors snickered, even Dimitri although he tried to hide his amusement.

"Who is Samantha?" Dante asked. "And what does she have to do with your plan for us?"

"We'll get to that later. First I want to explain how this came about," Dimitri answered. "All of you pipe down while I go through it."

Everyone in the room was immediately quiet.

"This isn't really our plan. It's Luke and Marlena's," Dimitri began. "Thomas," he paused while Thomas unrolled a large set of plans then pinned an elaborate diagram to the wall. The warriors were silent as they studied the map and surrounding area.

"Isn't that the old Army Depot? I forget the name," Ariel paused. "Give me a minute, and it will come to me. It's the one the human government closed down a few years ago."

"It is," Dimitri answered. "It's the Seneca Army Depot. We've been referring to it as the fort." The room continued to silently study the large diagram. Dimitri walked to the detailed set of plans. He picked up a pointer next to the wall. "As you can see, these are large bunkers." Dimitri pointed to a square area on the diagram. The bunkers ran in sections down the center of the base. "Each section has nine rows of 12 bunkers. Luke has leased this entire area," Dimitri paused to run the pointer across the far south end of the diagram. "That means we have four sections of bunkers. The one remaining is still under control of the US government. We have the warehouses, apartments and all the buildings at the north end of the Depot," Dimitri paused. "The downside is that there are others using the south end. Over here is a Trooper Station so there will be law enforcement officers coming and going all day and night. In addition, the Coast Guard has leased this tower. It gives them a perfect view of the lake, but they will also have a clear view of our operations as well. Luckily they are only there during the daytime. The army is still using the runway as a training airfield. Luke did work the airfield into the deal though. We actually lease it, but had to agree to share with the army. We have access to the garage area over here, but we don't plan to use it for more than one plane at a time. Luke included another hanger at the north end to house another plane as well as a helicopter. I want to leave at least four rows of empty bunkers as a buffer between our operations and theirs. I'm going to let Thomas explain the contract to you in more detail."

"It's pretty simple," Thomas began. "Dad had two contracts. The first one is classified. He finalized that deal with the government before they even closed the place down. That contract stipulates that dad wouldn't occupy the base or make any changes for seven years. Neither party wanted the public to think Deveraux Industries had anything to do with the closure. It was already controversial enough. Dad would have insisted on that clause. He wouldn't want anyone to think he was responsible for the loss of so many jobs. He wasn't, he just took advantage of a great opportunity. The depot officially closed in the fall of 2000. Five years later the second contract was developed. That contract is the only one the public will ever know about. Dad and Marlena obviously knew bad times were coming. They've planned well for this war," Thomas paused as he pinned up another diagram. This one was a close up of the north end of the property.

"They basically leased the property forever, the government can't terminate it. Only we can. I still can't figure out how dad managed that. I think he's the only one in the world that could have pulled off such a stunt. Our government just doesn't give up control like that. Anyway, in addition to the depot, they also purchased the old farm house across the street." Thomas pointed at the property to the east. "This warehouse over here is D-Tech's Romulus plant. To the west is state park land and then Seneca Lake. Dad was also able to extend our property into part of the forest. He has plans to develop a large obstacle course over here in the woods. Ty you should check that out once you get there and get settled in. We need to know if the course has been built or at least started, or if we're building it from scratch."

"No problem," Ty answered quickly. "I'll be going over the entire area anyway. Dimitri wants me to survey the property for security issues. Once I check it out, Dimitri is going to install a high tech security system out there. While I'm surveying for threats, I'll check out the forest."

"Great," Thomas continued. "Alex and I have been focusing on the farm house since we discovered these plans. We thought that way we could house someone out there permanently to begin work on the camp. Ty, while you're there, you're also going to have to go through all the bunkers and make sure they are empty and ready to furnish. Alex and I will come up with furniture to turn each of them into personal living quarters for those attending the camp. I do know dad hired a crew to turn several of the bunkers into bath and shower facilities. Looking at the invoices, I think that project's complete. Based on these plans we can house three hundred people in the bunkers plus the seventy-five that were turned into private bathrooms. That leaves us nine extra bunkers for more students or even large storage areas. The bathrooms are disbursed throughout the bunkers for convenient access. They're not in the rooms, but everyone will have their own private bathroom."

"Who are we housing out there?" Dante asked. "What will three hundred people be doing at the fort?"

"Good question," Dimitri answered. "This is going to be a training camp. Because of the treaty, young kids haven't been getting the training they need to defend themselves. To begin, it's going to be mandatory for all prospective warriors to attend and graduate from this private academy before they can join in the fight. We also want all the fae between the ages of fourteen and twenty-five to attend the camp. Once we're up and running we'd also like to extend an open invitation to the shifters. The alliance we've developed with them is getting stronger. We want to nurture that and make sure they are prepared for this war and the future, too."

"I realize we're only in the beginning stages of this project, but are you guys working on instructors?" Victor asked. "Three hundred kids will be a handful. We'll need a lot of adults to keep them under control. Then there's kitchen staff and how are you going to handle laundry and maid services?"

"I have a couple ideas," Alex answered. "Marta, we were wondering if you would be willing to take on the job as Domestic Administrator. Don't answer now. I want you to think about it. You'll also need to talk it over with Jake, I know. But we're going to need someone out there that can handle the supervision of the maid service as well as food preparation. We're going to make the kids do their own cleaning and laundry but we'll hire a service to clean the offices and classrooms."

"Okay. We'll talk about it," Marta agreed.

"Jake," Dimitri said seriously. "While you're discussing that, I would like you to think about moving out there as well and becoming one of our instructors."

Jake studied Dimitri seriously. "What would I instruct?" he asked.

"Weapons," Dimitri answered. "There's nobody that knows more about weapons than you do. Just think about it. Talk to Marta and the two of you decide if this is something you are willing to take on together. I can give you two weeks to decide. Then we'll need an answer."

"We'll let you know before then," Jake promised.

"Victor?" Dimitri looked to the corner where Victor and Ariel sat.

"Yeah?" Victor answered.

"I hate to ask, but I need your help with the apartment complex." Dimitri walked to the diagram. "It's over here," he pointed to the east side of the complex. "I know you're busy with rebuilding the garage and expanding the shelter but you're the only one that I can trust with this. You know apartments. If we're going to ask the best in our community to come out here and teach, they're going to expect high class accommodations. Those apartments have been vacant for more than ten years and I have no idea what shape they were in while they were occupied. I won't lie to you, it could be a huge undertaking," Dimitri finished soberly.

"We've finished the garage and the expansion is going well. I can't relocate permanently or even stay for extended periods, but I think I can swing it if you give me a little time," Victor assured him. "Not that I care, but is there a budget I'm supposed to use for this or am I on my own?"

Dimitri smiled. He knew if they asked, Victor would foot the bill without hesitation. "Luke and Marlena covered that side of the operation as well. They have a lot of investors. The pot is large enough that we're not worrying about cost right now. Thomas also has a long list of potential backers once we start accepting students.

They sold this as a private academy. Humans love that. They think they are keeping kids out of trouble and off the streets. They get a tax write off and we get the money we need to prepare our people for their future. It's a win/win for everyone."

"I should have known," Victor replied. "Luke and Marlena always thought of everything. How are you using Ariel?"

"For now she can help you with the apartments. Ariel has a wonderful knack for decorating," he smiled at Ariel. "Your father is an aristocrat. Since you've been back, you've visited a lot of the households in this community. Once we start getting commitments to participate, Ariel will know how to make each apartment feel like home to our members."

"I can do that," Ariel assured him. "But if you tell me you're bringing stuffy old Charlotte Walker out here, I will not decorate an apartment for her. It would literally kill me to decorate a room to match her taste let alone an entire apartment. Her house is awful!"

Everyone laughed in agreement.

"I can assure you Charlotte will not have any part in this project," Alex promised.

"Then I'm in," Ariel said enthusiastically.

"So we know what Ty, Victor, Ariel and Jake's assignments are," Nick commented. "But what about the rest of us? How are we going to help?"

"We're all going to have to spend time out at the fort," Dimitri answered. "Except Thomas. For now, I need him here in New York handling the business side of the project. Jake if you're up to it, in addition to teaching, I need you as legal counsel for the academy.

Once we're established, wealthy human parents are going to want their children to attend. We'll have a screening process but there are bound to be lawsuits when people who believe they are entitled are turned away. You're an attorney. You can help us develop criteria for screening that minimizes lawsuits. Regardless of your decision on the rest, I really need you to handle all court actions against us."

"Done," Jake said immediately. "I'll get started on a screening plan right away. I'll also handle any lawsuits that come our way," he turned to look at Marta. She nodded and Jake continued. "We don't need two weeks to discuss the rest. We're game. Just give us a little time to take care of things at home and I'll need to spend a few months in New York preparing the legal stuff for Thomas."

"Thanks," Dimitri said sincerely. He knew he could rely on the warriors. He turned back to Nick. "We can't send everyone out to the fort all at once. We still have a job to do here in New York. Radek's not going to sit by quietly while we take the offense. Some of us need to stay here to protect our people. For now I need you and Dante in New York. Bastian will also stay here off and on. He's working on obtaining a helicopter for the academy. He will also need to develop a facility to house blood and I want a scientific lab at the fort. These kids need to learn everything we can possibly teach them. Once we have reliable transportation in place, all of us will be spending a lot of time going back and forth. I know I'm spreading the team thin, but I can't think of any other way to accomplish this."

"We'll manage," Dante assured him. "Don't worry about us. We'll do whatever we can to help get the academy up and running. We can't leave the city vulnerable. Nick and I can handle the patrols for now. The rest of you focus on the fort."

"I agree," Nicholas chimed in. "Dante and I can handle things here. The sooner we get the academy going, the better. If we can help with anything out there just let us know."

"Thanks," Dimitri was grateful for such a wonderful team of men. "I knew I could depend on all of you. You always see the big picture and not one of you hesitates to jump in and give your all. I want you to know how much I appreciate all you do. That means everyone in this room as well as Bastian. Each and every one of you make me look good as your leader. You make my job easier. I can't express to you how much that means to me."

"Awe shucks," Ty said. "You're not going to go and get mushy on us are you? I might have to take that puppy away," he laughed out loud at the horrified look on Alex's face. "Don't worry Alex, I'm just kidding. Your dog's safe. I have my hands full with those two rascals of my own."

"I still have one more question," Dante said reluctantly.

"What's that?" Dimitri asked.

"You haven't explained who Samantha is and what she has to do with the fort," Dante replied.

"Oh," Alex answered. "I'll take this one," she turned to Ty and grinned. "Samantha is one of my employees." She proceeded to outline Samantha's involvement.

"You're serious?" Nick asked horrified. "You are actually going to include a human in this plan? Do you think that's a good idea?"

Ty tried to hide a smile, but failed.

"Don't start," Alex warned Ty.

Dawn

"It's perfect!" Ariel answered for Alex. "You guys haven't met her, but I have. I've also seen her in action. I agree with Alex. Samantha is the perfect addition to handle tech issues. Sending her to the fort may also save her life. She's so stubborn and reckless."

"What do you mean?" Nick asked.

"Samantha is human, but she has this bad habit of hunting vampires," Alex confessed. "She's relentless and keeps getting injured. I admit, that's a second reason for sending her away from the city."

"What?" Dante exclaimed. "A human vampire hunter? How has she survived this long?"

"That should tell you how good she is. You should see her," Ariel answered. "She has phenomenal aim with a bow and arrow. I was impressed the first time I saw her. Ask Victor, he was there."

"I arrived late," Victor told them. "But yes, she is definitely talented and fearless. I'm afraid I don't think her reckless hunting is an asset though. Sending her to the fort is a great idea. Alex is right, it might save her life."

"Once you guys get to know her you'll see why I'm so sure this is the right thing to do," Alex assured them. "She already knows about vampires so we don't have to keep our world a secret from her and this way I can keep her safe. It also gives me time to find out why her family has been targeted by vampires. That's unusual and there has to be a reason," Alex said still perplexed by Sam's family history.

"So Nick," Dante snickered. "I think we got the better end of the stick this time. Ty gets to babysit a vampire hunting human and Victor over there gets the shit job...literally." He glanced at Victor with a huge grin on his face. "I'd say it's about time. Victor's been hanging out in bars, partying all night, riding Harley's and driving fast cars for way too long. To top it all off, he even got the girl. But I guess karma's finally caught up with you my boy. You get to fix toilets while Nick and I go out and kick a little ass." Dante finished off by adding a karate kick and full body twist, landing back in the direction he was originally standing, both hands simulating a jab to a vampire with a knife or a stake.

Victor couldn't help himself, he had to laugh. Dante was always good for entertainment. "As always Dante, you do have a unique perspective on the situation." He was still grinning as he turned to Ariel. "You ready to go babe? We have that meeting with the contractor over at the shelter. He has yet another crisis I need to handle," Victor turned back to Dante. "You might want to curb the enthusiasm. I wouldn't want you to pull a hamstring while you're out there playing superhero. I'm not going to be around to come to the rescue. You know, karma and all?"

"I've gotta head out too," Ty stood and headed for the door. "I need to get out to the ranch, pack and take care of a few things before I leave. I'll head to the fort early tomorrow morning. Don't worry about arranging transportation, Dimitri. I'll use Frank. It will be a good opportunity for me to talk to him before he retires. If anyone hears of a good pilot let me know. I'm going to be losing Frank in about a month. I'd like to find someone new before he goes in case they need additional training."

Victor turned to Ty. "I sure wish your father wasn't so busy. This contractor he recommended is going to drive me insane. He can't make a decision on his own. With this new project, I'm afraid we'll never get the expansion finished."

Dawn

"I'll give him a call on my way out this morning," Ty offered. "Rhett's okay. I think dad just shook his confidence. He told him if he didn't make you happy, his company's rep would be on the line. I'll talk to him and see if I can settle him down. It wouldn't hurt for you to give him a compliment here and there. Dad can be a little over the top sometimes and I think he has Rhett afraid to pull down a wall without your approval. If you try to put him at ease, I think you'll be surprised at what he really can do. Other than dad and my uncle, he's the best there is."

"I didn't know your dad put that kind of pressure on him. I'll see what I can do. Hey, since you're heading out to the fort I was wondering if you could do me a big favor," Victor inquired.

"Sure, what do you need?" Ty asked.

"If you could take a camera and check out the apartment complex that would really help me out. Take tons of pictures and email them to me. If I had pictures of the place while I was here in New York, I could get a head start on the planning. That would give me an idea of what I'm up against and what material's I'm gonna need once I get out there."

"Great idea," Ty agreed. "I'll get them to you within a couple days."

"Good luck out there," Victor called before he opened the door for Ariel and climbed into his truck.

* * * *

Samantha sat in stunned silence staring at Alex. She had mixed feelings about this assignment. "I need an honest answer,"

Sam paused. "Is this your way of putting a stop to the vampire hunting?" she studied Alex. She needed to know if her boss was being honest with her.

"I'm not going to lie to you Sam," Alex answered honestly. "That is a side benefit, but it's not the primary reason for the move. We need to increase production on the droid line. You know that. I need you at the Romulus plant to head up the project personally. That's essential for the company. But my personal request is just as essential. I need hundreds of the combat droids you developed in a very short period of time. I also need the Sims immediately. You're the best Sam. I don't know anyone else I can depend on to handle so many projects simultaneously. Nobody else can do this. I realize this is a big decision and I'd like to give you time to think about it, but I don't have time. Ty's flying out tomorrow morning. If you're willing to take this on, I'll need you to go home and pack so you can head out by late morning, early afternoon at the latest."

Samantha had a million thoughts running through her mind. As manager, John went out of town frequently. Since Sam took over D-Tech, she hadn't had to deal with an out of town project. This would be her first. She had known she'd have to travel, but this wasn't what she expected. She thought she'd be leaving for the weekend or maybe a couple weeks at the longest. This project could take months. She was the best person for the job. The Romulus Plant was the perfect solution to the production shortfall with the droid line. Plus, she'd be working on the private stuff. Alex was right, there would be a lot going on at the same time. Sam knew she could handle it, but she still didn't trust her bosses' motives. She was going to have to give up vampire hunting. Could she do that for such an extended period of time? Should she put her hunting on hold for that long? The thought made her uncomfortable. Then there was this Ty guy. She had no idea who he was or what his skill level would be.

Dawn

"Are you sure this Ty person is up to the challenge? I'm not going to have time to carry the weight for someone else. If I agree I'm going to be busy," Samantha pressed.

Alex laughed.

"What?" Samantha said defensively.

"That's pretty much the same thing Ty said. He's not willing to babysit someone that's not up to the task."

"Babysit!" Sam said incredulously.

"I assured him you can hold your own. I think you're the best in your field Sam and I told Ty as much. Now, I'll tell you that Ty is the best in his field. He can hold his own on this project. I'm excited to see what the two of you can come up with once you put your heads together. I'm sure it's going to be far beyond my expectations."

Sam hesitated another moment then agreed. "Okay, I'm game. I'll give this a shot. You might get your side benny for a short time, but don't think it's going to stop me from hunting once I get back to the city."

Alex studied Sam. She was hesitant to bring it up, but Sam needed to be prepared. "Sam, I can't guarantee the vampires won't follow you guys out to the fort."

Sam visibly brightened and Alex rolled her eyes.

"As soon as they find out Ty is out there, the king is going to wonder why. I suspect at the very least they are going to send scouts out to try to discover what he's up to. I don't want you hunting, but I also don't think you should let your guard down. This assignment could be more dangerous than you think," Alex warned.

"I never let my guard down," Sam assured her. "This job sounds better already."

"Could you at least pretend to take a break for my sake?" Alex gave Sam her most stern look then sobered. "Samantha, Ty will be living at the farmhouse with you, but he's going to be extremely busy. He's not going to have time to watch out for your safety. You're going to have to be careful and take care of yourself. Please promise me you won't do anything reckless. I need you to focus on these projects. I'm not sending you out there to go hunting," Alex pressed.

"I can't promise I won't go hunting, but I will promise I'll be careful." Sam hurried on before Alex could interrupt. "Alex, vampire hunting is what I do. If I see a vampire lurking around, I won't just walk away. I'm going to take care of it. I would think of all people, you could understand that better than most. I will not give up until I find the vampire that killed my family. I'm sure you and Thomas feel the same about the vampires that killed Luke. Thomas is still out hunting. We're not so different you know."

Alex studied Samantha. She did understand, but knowing Sam was out fighting vampires made Alex nervous. Samantha was human. It wasn't the same as Thomas out hunting, but she couldn't explain that to Sam right now. Plus Thomas had already killed Hector, but if she told Sam that story it would only encourage the girl. Alex would just have to be satisfied with sending Samantha to Romulus and hope for the best. "Okay," Alex conceded. "I've got to get out of here. I have a ton of things to do before tomorrow. You should also go home early and pack. Settle things here in New York, you may be gone awhile. You have my number if you need anything. Call me anytime and good luck." Alex stood and headed for the door.

"Alex?" Samantha also stood.

"Yeah?" Alex stopped and turned back so she was facing Samantha.

"Thank you for giving me this opportunity. I know you are placing a lot of trust in me and I promise I won't let you down. The Sim is going to be out of this world! I can't wait to get started. See you when I get back." Sam gave Alex a sincere smile, she was actually getting excited for the new challenge.

"Oh. You'll see me before then," Alex assured her. "I plan to stop by the fort occasionally. In fact, I guess I should warn you there will be people coming and going frequently at that facility. But, just like Ty, we are all going to have plenty to do while we're there. This is a huge project. It's going to take a lot of people to get everything up and running. The jet will be waiting at the hanger in the morning. If you need extra time, call me. Have a safe trip and I'll see you before you know it," she turned and walked out the door.

Samantha stood motionless, she was already thinking about possibilities for the Sims. She'd helped develop the simulators for the military and law enforcement. Alex should cut her a little slack about her extracurricular activities. It was going to help her create a kickass vampire hunter simulator. She had firsthand knowledge of vampire techniques. I love my job, she thought to herself as she quickly moved to her desk and powered down her laptop. She had a lot to do if she was going to be ready to fly out in the morning.

* * * *

Ty felt good. Better than he'd felt in weeks. His body instantly relaxed the moment he left the main road and drove through the wooden gate that signaled the beginning of his property. His ranch was only a few miles out of the city, but it seemed like a world away. He missed the serenity he always felt here. He climbed onto the large sable stock horse and gave a loud whistle. Bo and Ace raced to his side. His dogs were certainly happy to see him. They'd gone nuts when he climbed out of the truck last night. He'd been gone longer than usual this time. He felt guilty about that. Sure, his staff took great care of them but it just wasn't the same and Ty knew it. Seeing Alex and Dimitri's new pup the other night had reminded him how much he missed these two companions. Bo was a three year old tri-colored Border Collie, Ace was just over two and a mix between a Border Collie and an Aussie Shepherd. That made him a little smaller than Bo, but his size gave him more agility. Both dogs were full of energy and excellent cattle dogs. Moving the herd was a snap with these two.

He sauntered towards the large pasture, dogs on his heels. They were excited for the game. That's what it was for them, a game with their pack leader. He was glad he had enough time to move the cattle himself this morning. At least they'd have this time together before he had to leave them again. Okay, so Dimitri was right. He was just as mushy when it came to his dogs. These two were special. It was going to kill him when he lost them. A definite downside to living so long. He crested the hill and spotted the cattle. There were just over a hundred head. They needed to be moved to the south pasture. The dogs were circling him now. They'd spotted the herd as well. They were waiting for his signal, circling in anticipation. He hesitated only a moment, taking in the cool air and the peace of the morning. He loved this life. The rest of the warriors didn't understand it. They loved the fast pace of the city. Their loss, Ty thought as he gave his horse a gentle kick. The horse began to trot and the dogs shot forward. Ty laughed out loud, the game had begun.

Dawn

* * * *

Sam entered the large farm house. It was a beautiful old home. She smiled as she thought of her dingy apartment. Alex, who had met her at the airport, had apologized over and over for the living arrangements. Her boss had made several excuses for the haphazard decor and lack of character. Sam disagreed. She thought this home had plenty of character. Alex didn't know what a step up this was for Sam. Nobody would have guessed someone in her position would be living in such a dump. She hadn't made it to the realtor's office yet. Walking into this quaint country home made her even more determined to buy her own place as soon as she returned to New York.

"Hello?" Sam called out. According to Alex this Ty person should already be here. No answer. Oh well, she'd just put her luggage in the study and head to the kitchen. She was starved. She hadn't had time for breakfast. Hopefully the fridge was stocked. Maybe she could make herself a sandwich or something before she looked around the house and settled in a room.

Sam entered the kitchen and froze. The hot guy she'd seen with Thomas that night at the ball was sitting at the kitchen table. "You're the bomb guy," Sam exclaimed.

Ty looked up uninterested. He studied Samantha for a second, then raised one eyebrow at her statement.

"Why did Alex send me out here with a bomb expert?" she asked. "I thought we were supposed to work on a Sim together. I'm not going to have time to bring you up to speed on electronics. This doesn't make any sense," Samantha said perplexed.

Ty now raised both eyebrows. "You bring me up to speed? Hardly," he shook his head. "Humans are so arrogant," he mumbled as he stood. "There's fried chicken and potato salad in the fridge. I'll be in my room. I'd appreciate it if you didn't interrupt me. I have a lot to do tonight. Meet me in the library tomorrow by nine and we'll discuss the simulator," he proceeded out the door.

Samantha was dumbfounded. She hadn't really thought about the kind of reception she was going to receive from Ty, but that was certainly not what she expected. It wasn't that he disliked her, it was more like he was completely neutral. He didn't seem to notice her. She didn't think he could be more indifferent. She wasn't sure why, but his lack of interest annoyed her. She had no interest in a relationship at this point in her life so why did his response, or more to the point lack of response, bother her so much? She didn't really know why. It just did. She walked to the fridge and pulled out the bag of chicken and bowl of potato salad. Maybe it was because she wasn't indifferent to Ty. He was hot. She'd watched him for over an hour diffusing bombs at that large ballroom. He wasn't like this with Alex and Thomas. They were obviously friends. So why was he so indifferent to her?

She laughed a short self-conscious laugh. Hadn't Luke told her she'd done the same thing to countless men in the lab? Luke used to make fun of her, frequently. He told her she was cruel and heartless. She hadn't understood what he was talking about back then. Now she did. She'd blown Luke off when he teased her like that. Now that she knew how it felt to be ignored, she'd never do that to anyone again.

Sam sat at the table and began her meal. Her mind was on the simulators she'd been sent there to build. Ty clearly thought Sam was inexperienced and insignificant. She'd show him. She needed to stop by the Romulus Plant this afternoon but no matter how long it took there, she was going to work on the sim tonight. She wouldn't go into their meeting cold. Regardless of Ty's skill, Sam was the one with experience building simulators. She planned to blow him away in the morning.

* * * *

Ty entered his room and firmly closed the door. Finally, time alone. He had several hours to shut out the world and work on his game. He had a lot to do at the fort. The sooner he could resolve the problem with the new game, the sooner he could start concentrating on things that needed to be done here. He'd focus on his game tonight and first thing in the morning he'd walk over and see where things stood at Seneca. He flung off his shirt, slipped out of his jeans and pulled on a baggy pair of sweats. He'd set up a small table with a coffee pot in the corner of the room earlier that afternoon. He started a pot brewing then flipped on his computer and got to work.

Chapter Four

Ty slowly walked through the front door closing it silently behind him. He'd worked well into the night but still couldn't find the glitch in his game. He was beginning to lose patience with it. He had honestly believed that with a few hours of peace and quiet the glitch would be history. Everyone from his marketing department to his customers were getting impatient. Tyson Electronics was starting to get bad press over the delay. He had warned his marketing director not to announce the release until the game was actually ready, but the man wouldn't listen. Now Ty was dealing with a publicity nightmare. If it took much longer to find the problem, customers were going to lose interest and move on to other games. If that happened, Renegade II would be a flop. Ty had to prevent that, he had to find the problem and fast.

He sipped his coffee and tried to enjoy the vibrant sunrise. One thing about running a ranch, no matter how late Ty was up the night before, he always rose with the sun. He enjoyed this time of day. Few people were out and about this early in the morning. Ty stopped and glanced back at the farmhouse, then took a deep calming breath. There was a slight nip in the air, but that only added to the serenity of the moment. Ty smiled. Sure he was still frustrated about his game and the delays, but he wasn't going to let that ruin such a perfect morning. If he couldn't be home running his own ranch, this was a very close substitute. Ty crossed the street and stopped in front of the large gate made of chain link fencing. He punched the five digit code into the electronic pad and watched the gate swing open. It was time to get to work on the Fort. Before he began his extensive security sweep, he wanted to walk through the abandoned buildings. Thomas, Dimitri and Alex had flown out to give the place a cursory inspection once they found the lease. But they spent most of their time at the farmhouse not the fort. Everyone understood Luke and Marlena's plan pretty well, they just didn't know how far they'd gotten on development. Ty wanted to figure that out first. Once he knew where things stood, he could prioritize. There were a lot of projects that needed attention, Ty was anxious to get started.

Hours later Ty was still surveying the area. He had checked out the hanger already. Luke did a great job of remodeling the building and he had even added a large landing zone for the helicopter. Ty had a couple suggestions to improve structural integrity in case of an attack, but very little needed to be done on that building. There were three small buildings that stood vacant just outside the warehouse. These were intended for the simulators he and Samantha would be developing. He was excited to get to work on those, but for now they would have to move to the back of the list. There were other more pressing projects to worry about. While Samantha worked on acquiring hardware for the Sims, he could focus on securing the rest of the complex. Luckily, the small buildings were stable and perfect for simulators. He wasn't sure what the military had used them for, but whatever it was they were in good shape. The large warehouse was going to need some work. His father was too busy, but maybe Uncle Steve could help. They would need a crew of about three or four to reinforce the foundation and repair the water damage on the roof. Other than that, the warehouse was in excellent shape and was going to make a great facility. Once the outside was finished, the crew could section off the classrooms and outfit the rec room and the cafeteria in about a week. Walking the grounds had also given him a great idea for Jake and Marta. His next stop was going to be the old apartment complex. He wanted to get plenty of photos for Victor. Then he was going to check out the small building to the north of the apartments. He wanted to see what condition the place was in. If the structure was in good shape Marta might be able to have her bakery after all.

The idea had hit him immediately when he saw the shop. It was on the north side of the complex so the troopers, coast guard and pilots in training would all have easy access without compromising the academy. He was sure Marta would get plenty of business once word got out. The students would have the cafeteria, but Ty was sure some of them would occasionally venture into the bakery for snacks or a quick breakfast as well. It was perfect, he just needed to make sure the building was stable.

A short time later, Ty stepped back outside and smiled. It just might turn out to be a good day after all. He sighed as he shot a glance back at the dilapidated apartment complex. That place could only be described as a huge disappointment. Victor was going to have his work cut out for him there. Ty had taken a ton of pictures, especially of the damage. Victor needed all the information he could get if he was going to turn that dive into luxury homes for their instructors. Ty didn't envy his friend. The project was going to take a lot of time, but Victor could handle it. No worries there. The intended bakery on the other hand was in great shape. It looked like the military had used it as a PX or general store. Marta would have to check it out of course to see about set up, but the building needed very little work structurally.

He was about to head over to the bunkers when he noticed the time. He'd better get back to the house for his meeting with Samantha. That should take about an hour, then he could head back out to the bunkers. He wanted to see how far along the bathroom facilities were and if anything had been done to make the bunkers habitable for the kids. He also needed to call Dimitri and get his okay to enlist his uncle, but Ty was sure Dimitri would like the idea. They'd need somewhere to house the crew of course. No more than four men would be needed. Ty thought taking over the bathroom and the bunkers closest to the warehouse would be perfect. So far he hadn't found any furniture though. The crew would only need the basics, but he was sure finding the bunkers furnished was too much to hope for. He'd have to wing it. If possible, he'd like the crew out here by next week.

* * * *

Samantha awoke slowly as the sun filtered through her large bedroom window. She'd been up past midnight working on the plans for the simulators. She glanced at the clock and sighed in relief. It was just after eight. She forgot to set the alarm last night and for just a second started to panic, thinking she may have missed her meeting with Ty. It really bothered her that Ty treated her like she was insignificant. She knew she wasn't a raving beauty, but men had always found her slightly attractive. Having such a hot guy completely ignore her was unnerving. She couldn't be late to their first meeting. That was not the impression she wanted to make on the man. Sam caught herself. Why did she care if Ty ignored her?

Hadn't she told Alex she would be too busy to entertain or educate anyone while she was here? She quickly climbed out of bed and jumped in the shower. If she hurried she'd have just enough time to grab something for breakfast before heading to her meeting.

Samantha walked casually into the study with her second cup of coffee and stopped. It was nine o'clock on the dot but Ty wasn't anywhere to be seen. She'd sat in the kitchen waiting for just the right time to make her entrance and the man had disappeared. Where was he anyway? Still in bed? She took a deep breath and began to lay out her plans. At least she'd have time to set up for the meeting before he got here. If he didn't show, she'd finish the diagram she'd been working on last night and then head over for her meeting at D-Tech. Only one of the managers was there yesterday afternoon when she'd gone on her first tour. He'd assured her they would get the word out about the eleven o'clock meeting today. She needed to meet everyone and go over the changes that were going to take place. Alex assured her Romulus knew she was coming and they were probably anxiously awaiting her arrival. She didn't want to keep them waiting long. Unknown changes always seemed to create anxiety in the workers. She sat in front of the diagram and began to fine tune her plans.

Ty walked silently through the front door and into the study. Samantha had plans and diagrams scattered everywhere. She did know Alex and Thomas were staying in New York didn't she? Humans were so predictable. They always wanted to impress the boss. Well, this human was going to be disappointed. Her boss would probably never see her hard work. Ty was sure Samantha had spent hours on all this. He hoped it helped her in some way. Otherwise it was just a waste of time.

He surveyed the room and then walked up behind Samantha. She was working on a diagram of some sort. It looked like the inside of the simulator if he had to guess. "How do you plan to get the simulator into the building?" he casually asked.

Samantha jumped. She hadn't even heard him come in. She glanced at the clock, it was seven minutes after nine. "You're late," she accused still focusing on the diagram she was working on. "I thought you said we were meeting at nine."

Ty raised one eyebrow. Another annoying habit humans had was clock watching. Maybe when you only had eighty or ninety years to live, time was more important. Ty didn't know. Warriors had all the time in the world, literally. Ty ignored her accusatory demeanor and focused on the project at hand. "The door is just a normal sized door, probably thirty inches or so, maybe thirty-two tops. How are you going to get something that big into the room?"

Samantha closed her eyes and took a deep breath. She wouldn't lose her temper. She didn't need an explanation of where he had been. They'd get this meeting over with and then she could head over to D-Tech. She still wasn't sure how an explosives expert was going to help her with the simulator, but Alex had insisted Ty participate, so Samantha would indulge them and see what Ty had to offer. "I don't plan to build the simulator and then move it into the building," she said with all the civility she could muster at the moment, which wasn't much. "The building is the simulator," she turned around to face him. "I assume you know which buildings we will be using for the Sims. If you can somehow find the time in your busy schedule, I need to get precise measurements. If you just point me in the right direction, I can handle the rest," she added.

Ty wasn't really listening. He was studying the diagram more closely. It was a great idea. Use the entire building as the Sim. Once you walk through the door, the game is in play. "Is that possible?" he asked. "Do you have the technology to make the whole wall an active screen?" Ideas were running through Ty's head and he was getting more and more excited to begin work on the scenarios. If they pulled this off, a partnership between D-Tech and Tyson Electronics could move both companies' light years ahead of any competition out there.

This man was infuriating. "We don't have anything in production right now if that's what you're asking. However, the technology is there. A few tweaks and I'm confident we can make it happen. I won't know for sure until I get the building measurements though. Maybe you could just give me a general idea of where on that huge base the simulators are going to be located. I can just wander around aimlessly this afternoon until I find them," she said sarcastically. She was getting pissed now. Nobody had ever ignored her this way. He didn't even have the decency to answer a direct question.

"What?" Ty caught the tone and realized he had somehow upset her. Humans were so emotional. Another reason he did his best to avoid them. Alex was going to owe him big time for this. He didn't have the time or the patience to molly-coddle this woman. "Look, I have a lot to do around here in a short amount of time. I'm sorry if my schedule is inconvenient for you. But don't think that my apology is going to change my behavior. You try to stay out of my way and I'll stay out of yours. We'll meet occasional y to go over the simulators. I like this plan. I think it's going to be perfect for our needs. If you wanted to see the buildings to get measurements, all you needed to do was ask. We can walk over right now, just give me ten minutes to make a phone call and I'll meet you outside." Ty turned and walked out the door.

Samantha sat in shocked silence as she watched Ty leave. She blinked, then blinked again. "Okay," she said to herself. "I can handle this. We'll stay out of each other's way." This arrangement could work for her. She'd go with Ty to get measurements on the building then she'd head over to D-Tech. With any luck she wouldn't see the man for the rest of the evening. She had plenty to do herself. While they were checking out the buildings for the Sims maybe she could get him to show her where the kids would be training. She'd need an idea of the layout before she could start programming the droids for their workouts. She'd also need to see the private living areas and get dimensions on the individual workout space. The droids would need to be programmed to remain on the mats and not extend into the living areas. Alex wouldn't be happy if she was constantly having to replace lamps and chairs because training got out of control. Samantha glanced out the window and decided to take a jacket. Fall was in the air and it might be a little chilly outside. She stood and headed to her room.

Ty just completed his call to Dimitri when he heard Samantha's bedroom door shut. He looked at the clock and thought he might have time to call his Uncle Steve. Dimitri agreed to have Steve's company handle the construction work, just as Ty had known he would. Ty ran his idea to set up a couple bunkers for the crew by Dimitri and was also given the go ahead for that project. In fact, Dimitri took it one step further. He wanted Ty to pick out four of the bunkers and one of the bathrooms to use as guest houses. Those wouldn't be equipped with exercise mats, they would have a sitting area instead. Dimitri wanted a place that parents, or dignitaries could stay when they came out to visit the academy. They still didn't know what they were going to do about furniture. Luke and Marlena had left that out of the plan completely. That wasn't like them. Ty suspected the problem had already been solved, he just didn't know how. He glanced one more time up the stairway and made the call to his uncle.

"Ty," Steve said enthusiastically. "How is everything?"

"Great, and with you?" Ty asked.

"Busy," Steve admitted. "I'm not having as many unexpected delays as your father, but for some reason the jobs are stacking up lately. Ken said they finished the repairs on the shifter homes last week. Can I assume no news is good news on that front?"

"So far," Ty agreed. "Radek's been too quiet though. We're all a little nervous about what he has planned for us next."

"I hear you," Steve agreed. "The bombs were unexpected. We're lucky to have you in our camp. I've never met anyone with your ability when it comes to defusing explosives."

"Thanks," Ty said humbled by his uncle's compliment. "I hate to ask but I'm looking for a favor," Ty began.

"Oh, what can I help you with?" he offered without hesitation.

Ty quickly filled his uncle in on the project at the fort and their need for a three to four man team to work on construction as soon as possible.

"I see," Steve finally answered. "Well, I'd love to be the one to help you myself, but Pearl called and they have an emergency out in Texas. It's not something I can delegate. I'll probably be there for several weeks," Steve paused.

"Nothing serious I hope," Ty asked concerned.

"No, a couple of wells seem to be collapsing and she needs me to check them out. See if I can stabilize them or if we need to shut them down. It's going to be a lot quicker for me to check it out myself than try to explain the process to someone on my crew Gavin's done all he can himself, but it's getting too dangerous and they need my help."

Dawn

"Well, make sure you give my love to Aunt Pearl and give that worthless brother of mine a hard time while you're there. I don't want Gav getting too comfortable in my absence. With everything going on here I haven't had time to get out there for a visit. Unfortunately, it looks like it's going to be awhile before I can swing some time off. Will you explain things to them while you're there so they don't think I've forgotten them?"

"Will do," Steve assured him. "I can probably send Jack out there to help if you want."

"Are you sure?" Ty didn't want his uncle jeopardizing his other work to help out the warriors. "If you're going to be out of town won't you need Jack to run things in New York while you're gone?"

"Actually, he's trying to teach his son the ropes so to speak. Justin's catching on pretty quick. I think leaving him in charge of things for a couple weeks might be good for him. He knows he can always call Jack or myself if he gets in over his head. Plus, Jack knows all about us. Remember he got attacked by that vampire a few years back. I think it's the perfect solution. I'll let Jack pick his own crew. He'll know which men to bring on this kind of project. You can be completely open with him, he'll control what information is relayed to the men. Don't worry, our secret is safe with Jack."

"I know. Sounds like he's dealing with the supernatural a little better now, huh?" Ty asked.

"He's accepted it," Steve replied somberly. "He doesn't like it, but he's accepted it. He's thrilled about the warriors though. After what those monsters did to him, he can't say enough about you guys. I'm grateful, too. Oh, don't get me wrong, I enjoyed my own fighting days. But I prefer construction over battle at this point in my life," Steve gave a little laugh. "So how soon do you need them? Jack's busy on a job this week, but I could probably have him there in ten days or so."

"That would be perfect. I need time to get their living quarters set up anyway," Ty said relieved. He thought he was going to have to find someone else for the job. Steve was right, Jack would fill in just fine. Ty preferred family, but Jack was the best alternative.

"I'll call Jack this morning and set everything up. Do I need to arrange for the materials, or is that already taken care of?" Steve asked.

"I'll work with Jack on what we don't already have. Luke and Marlena took care of most of the preparations and the plans. Once Jack gets here I'll go over everything with him. Thanks for helping me out on this Steve. You have no idea what a relief it is to have someone I trust working on this project," Ty said sincerely.

"I'm happy to help in any way I can. I'm just sorry I can't come out myself. I'll give your love to your family. Try not to wait too long before you get out to see them. They miss you, too. Well, business is calling. I'll be in touch. Expect a call from Jack in the next few days. He always likes to check in before he starts a job," Steve said.

"Okay. Thanks again, talk to you soon." Ty hung up and turned to see Samantha sitting on the top stair, waiting patiently. "Sorry, that took a little longer than I planned."

"I understand," she answered casually. "You ready to go now?"

Ty nodded and walked to the front door. That was a surprise. He'd expected another lecture on timeliness. Maybe Samantha wasn't going to be as annoying as he originally thought she would be.

* * * *

Samantha entered the empty house grateful for the solitude. She didn't know where Ty was, but she was glad. She wasn't up for company right now. She'd gone over to D-Tech planning to meet with management. To her surprise, the entire workforce was there. She'd been right, they were nervous about what changes were coming their way. The rumor mill at Romulus was worse than in New York. The entire plant was sure she was here to shut them down.

Things had been slow since the military closed the Seneca base. Romulus had been built to support the fort while it was up and running. Oh, they'd been thrown a project here and there over the years, but for the most part they ran day to day wondering if they'd still have a job tomorrow. What a way to live. Sam had no idea and she was sure Luke didn't know either. He'd probably assumed, like she had, that John had kept them in the loop. It had floored her when she discovered how little they really had to do. What a waste. John was such an idiot. New York was always so busy. Employees up there were working overtime while these guys were begging for something to do. Well, that all stopped now. Once she had calmed them down and explained the situation, the employees had been excited. She'd given them free rein to make improvements to the droid line. They had so many brilliant people working at the plant. They were bound to come up with ideas she had never thought of. She was actually excited to see where they went with this. She'd give them a week and then check back.

Once the project was out in the open Sam had met with top management. She assured them she wasn't there to micro-manage or watch over their shoulders. She was there to help. In fact, with the other project she was working on at the fort they probably wouldn't be seeing that much of her. Solving the production problem with the droid line was up to them. She was counting on them. They knew she'd stop by periodically and she gave each supervisor her business card so they could contact her anytime day or night in the event of a problem. It was fun to see the excitement in their eyes. It had obviously been a long time since they'd felt like a productive part of the company. Once this project was over, she was going to remember that. She was in charge now. It was her job to ensure the company was running efficiently and the employees were happy. No more assumptions. She was going to need to visit every plant to make sure the others hadn't been neglected by John as well. Luke would be furious if he knew so many people had been neglected for so many years. It made her proud to know she was the one that was going to fix it.

She settled onto the large couch and relaxed. She was so tired. Dealing with Ty this morning and then the crew at D-Tech had emotionally drained her. Maybe she'd take a little nap and then get started on the alterations the academy droids needed. Plans began forming in her mind as she slowly drifted off to sleep.

* * * *

Ty was almost completely through the bunkers now. So far, they were all empty. They had a lot of work ahead of them to fix this place up. Luke and Marlena had gotten off to a good start, but every bunker would need to be painted and the living area was going to need carpeting. The large exercise mats would take up the back half of each bunker, but where were the mats? He knew Luke too well to believe he'd made the plan but hadn't followed through. Maybe he had a warehouse somewhere they didn't know about. Ty ran a frustrated hand through his hair and glanced around the large complex. It was starting to get dark, he would need to head back to the house pretty soon. He'd spent more time analyzing the bunkers than he originally planned. But it had been worth it. He wanted to know everything there was to know about them. If parents were going to send their children to this academy, Ty wanted to make sure they were absolutely safe while they were here.

One thing he'd discovered was that the bunkers were one hundred percent sound proof. He'd set off a fire cracker in one to test the noise. Once outside with the door shut he didn't hear a thing. Dimitri would be happy to hear that. They'd been worried about the bunkers on the north side. That's why Dimitri insisted on leaving four rows of them empty. He wanted the noise buffer between the academy and the humans. Ty didn't think that was necessary now. He had an idea of how they could use them. What if they set up at least one additional row of bunkers and used those for employees at the bakery. Okay, Marta still had to agree to open the bakery, but he wasn't worried about that. Anyway, Marta's employees could work in the bakery and have access to training at the academy in their free time. Marta, Alex and Dimitri would have to work out the details, but Ty thought it was a great idea. He was sure they'd agree.

Ty opened the first bunker on the final row of the third section and hit the jackpot. It was full of exercise mats. They would need to be cut down to size but Ty was thrilled at the discovery. He knew Luke wouldn't put off something that important. He opened the next bunker and found more mats. The entire row was filled with them. He moved onto the fourth section and let out an excited whoop. This row was filled with furniture. After checking out a couple more bunkers he was confident they were all filled to the brim with everything they would need to set up the rooms. He'd have to check with Thomas, but he thought Marlena must have remodeled every hotel they owned and brought the old furniture here to equip the academy with bedding, desks, microwaves, chairs, lamps, everything they needed. He couldn't wait to get back to the house and call Alex. She'd been so stressed lately a little good news might be just what the doctor ordered.

Ty quickly secured the bunker and headed back to the farmhouse. He was starving. He'd call Alex, grab a bite to eat and get back to work on his game. He had to find the problem with that program fast, for the sake of his company as well as his community. Once he got that monkey off his back he could devote all his time and energy to making the fort safe. He also wanted to get started on the simulator scenarios. While he had Alex on the phone he'd run his idea for a partnership by her and see what she thought. They could work the details out later but he was excited at the prospect. He hadn't been this excited about an idea for a very long time. Radek might be on the attack but among the chaos, Ty's world was shaping up nicely. He pulled out his phone and dialed Alex.

* * * *

Ty entered the house and spotted Samantha in the study. Workaholic, he thought to himself. "Did you eat?" he asked as he stopped in the doorway.

"Yeah," Samantha answered, not looking up. "I grabbed a sandwich a couple hours ago." She'd come up with a cool alteration for the sparring droids and didn't want to lose her concentration. If this worked, the program was going to be brilliant. Alex would love it. She didn't notice Ty shrug and head for the kitchen.

Dawn

"She's definitely a workaholic," Ty mumbled. For an instant he wondered if she did anything for fun. Not likely, he decided. Alex said she worked long hours at the lab and it sounded like any free time she had, she spent hunting vampires. Ty grinned, okay that was fun. It was for him anyway. Could it be as much fun for a human? Or was it just another job. He had no idea. He'd never heard of a human vampire hunter before. He remembered his conversation with Alex. Samantha hunted to avenge her family. He thought about Thomas after his father's death and Luke just after Marlena had been killed. Watching their relentless pursuit of justice had been difficult. Ty doubted that kind of vampire hunting could be anything but more work for Samantha. Which brought him back to his original thought, she was a workaholic and probably didn't know how to have fun. Oh well, that was her problem. He opened the fridge and rummaged around for something to eat.

Hours later Ty was in his room concentrating on the complicated code that scrolled across his computer screen. He was methodically searching for anomalies when he heard a soft knock on his door. He looked at the clock and noticed it was after midnight, again. Time to shut this down for the night. He closed the lid on his laptop and walked to the door.

Sam stood nervously outside Ty's bedroom. The light was on, but that didn't mean he hadn't fallen asleep. She was just about to leave when the door slowly slid open. Ty stood there in nothing but a loose pair of shorts. Her stomach did a little somersault as she forced herself to keep her eyes on his face. A lump formed in her throat and she subconsciously swallowed hard.

"Yes?" he asked.

"I know it's late. Did I wake you?" she asked hesitantly. "I guess I should have waited until morning," she paused. "Yes, let's wait until morning. Sorry to bother you," she started to turn.

"You're not bothering me and no, you didn't wake me. I was just finishing up. What did you need?" he asked again.

"First, I know you are an explosives expert but do you know anything about electronics?" she asked hesitantly.

That was the second time she brought up explosives. What exactly had Alex told her about him? "What makes you think I'm an explosives expert?" he asked casually.

"Because I saw you at the ballroom. I was there the night that Lilith planted those bombs. The night the building blew up?" she pressed further when he didn't say anything. He was just standing there watching her.

"I know what night you're talking about," he finally answered. He'd been trying to think back to that night. Had he met her? He didn't think so. "I remember hearing someone was chasing after Lilith and I think they shot her with an arrow. Was that you?"

Samantha's face transformed into a huge smile. "Sure was," she said proudly. "If Alex and Ariel hadn't stopped me I think I could have taken her out that night. Her wounds were pretty serious. I soaked the arrows in holy water," she paused when Ty raised one eyebrow. "It was just an idea I had one night when I went out hunting. That's the night they killed John," Sam sobered. That night was a terrible night. John's death had been so quick. Before she knew what was happening he was dead. She couldn't save John, but she took out a lot of vampires that night. She had to admit she was in over her head with Lilith though. No human could hold their own against that vampire. Lucky for her Alex and Ariel showed up. She still hadn't asked Alex about Ariel's powers. That had thrown her. She'd had more than a few sleepless nights over that discovery. She'd accepted the idea now though. There were probably a lot of things in this world she didn't know about yet. "Anyway, it worked so well on Lilith that night I thought I'd soak the arrows in it and see what happened. Kind of my ace in the hole so to speak. I need any advantage I can get. They're so much stronger than I am."

Ty was still wondering why this woman was knocking on his door at midnight, but he decided to let her get to it on her own.

"Anyway, back to my original question. Alex didn't tell me what you do. She just said you are the best in your field the same as I'm the best in mine. I'm wondering if she was talking about explosives, but I can't figure out how that would help me with the simulator. So, I need to know if you have any electronic experience. I've hit a roadblock and I'm looking for someone to bounce off of."

Ty smiled. "Well, at least you're humble."

Samantha looked at him in confusion. "Oh," she exclaimed when his meaning hit her. "Well, I am the best. Anyway, electronics? Do you have any skills?" she said determined to get an answer from him this time.

Ty was amused. "I might be able to help. What's the roadblock?"

"Do you mind coming downstairs so I can show you my plans?" she asked, a little hesitant. "I've just found it's easier for people to understand where I'm going if they can actually look at my ideas. I guess it's true what they say about people being visual creatures," she shrugged and started for the stairs.

Ty followed. He had to admit he was a little curious. What problem was so big she was willing to venture upstairs to see if he was still awake so late at night? They entered the study and Ty stopped in surprise. Samantha had put a lot of work into this. Her diagrams were far more elaborate than they had been this morning. She was hastily shuffling papers, apparently looking for the right drawing. Ty sat in a large chair and watched her curiously. To his dismay, he was beginning to find her intriguing. He definitely hadn't seen that one coming. No human had ever interested him before. Even his casual hook ups had never been with a human.

"Okay," Samantha finally straightened and walked towards his chair. "This is where I'm stuck." She held out a diagram of one of the buildings. "These are the exact dimensions of the first building, first being the closest to that large warehouse."

"Okay, I'm with you so far." Ty studied the diagram closely. It was basically the same as it was before, only more detailed. "What's the roadblock? These dimensions look good. It's just like we talked about this morning. You walk in and the entire room is the sim. You said the walls won't be a problem so I don't get it." Ty looked at her for clarification.

"Okay, here's my idea..." Samantha sat down. "I want the entire building to be the Sim. They walk in and bam they're immediately in the game."

"Um-hum," Ty agreed as he continued to study the floor plan.

"We're going to have to find somebody that can work on the scenario part. I plan to call Alex in the morning and suggest she enlists a gaming expert. I've handled the basics in the past but this is beyond anything I've ever created. Those game guys have experience in the kind of world we're trying to create here. I'm sure Alex will know the right man for the job, but first I need to overcome the bigger problem," Samantha said obviously frustrated at something.

"And what would that be?" he asked. He was amused. They wouldn't be calling Alex for a gaming expert. They already had one.

"What's the trigger?" Samantha asked.

"Say what?" Ty asked, still not understanding.

"The Sims I've developed in the past are specific. We do firearms and EVO training for law enforcement," she paused at Ty's expression. "Emergency Vehicle Operation. They train in pursuit driving, stuff like that. Or we give them possible shooting scenarios. Active gunman in the strip mall, crazed ex-husband chasing down his estranged wife, things like that. In the shooting Sims the trigger is literally the gun trigger. In the driving Sims it's the steering wheel. We want these kids to walk in and the game begins as soon as they step foot into the building. What's the trigger? What will they be using to activate the game and then how are we going to simulate the fighting?" Samantha questioned. "I just can't come up with anything."

"Oh. I see," Ty looked back at the diagram. "We'll use the floor," he suggested.

"How?" she asked.

"Do you ever play video games Samantha?" he asked in exasperation.

"Sure," she answered. "But I use a game controller like everyone else," she said sarcastically.

"Ever heard of Wii?" he countered. "More specifically ever used a Wii Board?"

Samantha's eyes widened in understanding. "We put sensors in the floor. When the player hits a sensor something jumps out at them. I get it. I wonder..." she broke off, clearly concentrating on something new. She started measuring dimensions and then looked up at him enthusiastically. "I think that might work!" She smiled again. "I'll work on it more in the morning, but we still didn't resolve the other issue. How do we simulate the fighting?" she asked.

"Well, before you go and call Alex to summon a gaming expert let me give it a try. I have a few ideas of my own. I think I've already overcome that problem. I just need a couple more days to work out the kinks," he grinned at her skeptical look. "Trust me, I am an explosives expert, which will help me come up with some killer traps. But, I told you I also know a little about electronics. I think we can manage on our own for now," he assured her.

"I'll give you a couple days, but if you don't have something tangible by then, I'm calling Alex." She stood and let out a big yawn. "I'm beat. I think I'm going to call it a night. Thanks for your help. I must be tired. How did I not think of that on my own?" she shook her head, embarrassed. "Sorry I drug you downstairs for this. I've been concentrating on outfitting the walls and ceiling to make things seem realistic. I completely ignored the floor. I just assumed it would be an empty concrete slab. Your solution brings in a completely new avenue to explore." Samantha let out a deep breath. "Goodnight Ty, maybe I can use you after all." She turned and left the room.

Ty watched Samantha leave and then studied the diagram again. She was good. He had to admit Alex was right when she said Samantha was the best. She had things planned for the Sims he never would have considered possible. He grabbed a pencil and a clean sheet of paper and began working up the schematics for the floor. It was two-thirty before he finally went to bed. He would have stayed up longer but he just couldn't keep his eyes open another minute. It had been a long day and he knew he'd be up early again. It was nice to end on a positive note instead of frustration for a change. He still hadn't worked out the flaw in his game. What if he never found the problem? Naw, that wasn't possible. He'd eventually find it. He always did. He just needed time, but time was something he no longer had. Ty climbed into bed and immediately fell into a deep sleep.

* * * *

Samantha walked into the study the following morning ready to tackle the simulator floor project. She'd slept in, showered and then grabbed breakfast. She now sat in the large recliner and relaxed as she slowly savored her second cup of coffee. Her gaze shifted out the window where she began to watch a bird carelessly flutter from tree to tree. It was a wonderful morning. She was a little out of her league when it came to designing a sensor reactive floor, but she'd give it a try. She wasn't fooling herself. A gaming expert was going to be necessary to complete this project. She just didn't know enough about how those things worked to come up with a decent plan on her own.

Samantha set her mug down and reached for her diagram, then froze. She snatched up the elaborate drawing and studied it carefully. How long had Ty been up last night? She understood most of what he had on here, but was this really possible? She laughed a little. How many times had Ty asked her that very thing as she designed the other components of the simulator? She lowered the diagram and stared out the window again. Clearly she had underestimated Ty's abilities. She still didn't know how they were going to simulate the fighting, but this floor design was brilliant.

Samantha assumed Ty was still in bed. That floor plan must have taken hours to produce. She saw a slight notation to the side of the page, 'material' with a question mark. Samantha smiled. She knew what material they should use. Luke had developed it for NASA. It was a hard rubber type substance that was pliable but extremely reactive when used with sensors. Alex wouldn't have any trouble getting whatever they needed. Sam would send the measurements over right away. She decided to put the simulator aside for now and work on the droids. Once Ty woke up they could talk about the simulator again.

It was after noon and Samantha still hadn't seen Ty. She needed a break. Maybe she'd walk over to the Fort and study the buildings a little closer. She also wanted to orient herself and get to know the layout of the place a little. She'd already checked out the farm earlier this morning. Now it was time to get to know the fort. Sam slid on a light jacket and headed across the street. The fresh air would do her good.

* * * *

Ty only had a couple hours of sleep last night so he was beginning to get tired. He woke up with the sun, as he always did, and once awake couldn't get back to sleep. Instead he got up, showered, grabbed a cup of coffee and headed to the fort. It was now after noon and he didn't feel like he'd made much progress. He didn't want to tackle security on so little sleep. He was afraid he might miss something. So, once at the fort he'd decided to get the rooms ready for the construction crew. He'd gone through all the bunkers and discovered a few additional furniture items. The last bunker contained couches and small kitchen dinette sets. He transported those first. Each room would need one. Then he focused on finding bed sets. When he came across a bunker of desks, he decided to grab four of those as well. If Jack was coming out he'd need work space and Ty couldn't imagine him coming with less than three additional people. He'd confirm the count once Jack called, but for now he was going to set up housing for four and call it good. He still hadn't found any carpeting though. Before he could arrange anything he had to find the carpet.

Samantha strolled across the open space taking in the scene before her. This place was huge! The layout was pretty simple though. There were hundreds of bunkers running in sections down the middle. On the south end was the warehouse, the buildings that would house the simulators and what looked like an airport hangar. She wondered what was in there, but assumed it was empty. They'd probably use it later on to transport students to and from the academy. She hadn't seen any buildings to the west, only what looked like a large forest. If she didn't find Ty to the east she'd check out the forest, but for now she wanted to see the fort and what it had to offer.

It took her a long time to get to the end of the bunkers but as she approached what she thought was the last section, she heard a loud noise. As a new row of bunkers came into view she saw the chaos and knew she'd found Ty. She headed up the row until she stood in front of the bunker where the noise was originating. "Hello in there," she called. "Anything I can help you with?" she asked politely.

Ty hadn't expected company. He jumped at the sound of Samantha's voice and hit his head on a bedpost teetering precariously above him. The post swung upwards and then tumbled onto Ty's head.

Samantha heard what she thought was cursing and realized something had fallen on Ty. "Are you okay?" she asked. worried he might have been seriously injured.

"I'm fine," he answered grumpily. Shoving the furniture off him, he slowly worked his way towards the door.

"Oh, you're bleeding," Sam exclaimed as she rushed towards him.

Ty quickly raised his hand to his head and wiped away the blood. "It's nothing. Really, I'm fine," Ty assured her. "Just a little bump."

Sam studied him for another minute before she let it drop. "What's all this for?" she asked curiously.

"The furniture to outfit the bunkers," he said as he began throwing items back into the building.

Samantha studied Ty for a moment. "You look tired," she pointed out. "Here, let me help you." She helped with the small items while Ty took care of the larger ones. Once Ty shoved the door closed he turned and looked at her. "You really do look tired," Samantha repeated. "Maybe you should go take a nap," she suggested.

"Thanks," he answered absently. "You certainly have a firm grasp of the obvious, but I can't sleep during the day." He was frustrated at the lack of carpeting. How was he supposed to set up the rooms if he couldn't find the carpet?

"Tired and grumpy," Sam mumbled. "Such a winning combination."

"Was there something you needed?" he asked impatiently.

Dawn

"Just a break," she said nonchalantly as she shrugged one shoulder. "So I thought I'd go for a walk and check things out."

Ty was staring down the rows of bunkers trying to figure out where Luke would have put the carpet. It just didn't make sense. Luke would never buy the mats, store the furniture and ignore the carpet. Where could it be?

Sam cleared her throat to get Ty's attention. "I was thinking about cooking lunch, I'm starved. I found an old BBQ in the barn and some charcoal that might still be good. We also have plenty of burger in the fridge and some potato salad left. I'll cook if you'll join me." Samantha paused, she wasn't sure Ty was even listening to her. She silently watched him for a few more seconds. "You seem to be searching for something and you really do look tired. Can I help you find it so you can go relax before you fall down?"

Ty rolled his eyes. "I've never been so exhausted I've fallen down in my life. And I assure you, I've been far more tired than I am right now." He started up the row towards the apartment building.

"Okay, you're not tired. Have it your way. Don't get all weird on me now. What are you looking for?" she asked again.

"Carpet," Ty answered. "I can't install the furniture until I find the carpet."

"It's in the barn," Sam said casually. "There are several large rolls of it and it looks like someone started to cut it into smaller pieces but abandoned the project for some reason."

Ty stopped and turned on her. "You've known where the carpet is all along and you haven't mentioned it? Why not? You think it's funny having me search all over the fort? I guess you got your kicks watching me wander around aimlessly all day?' he was annoyed. He'd wasted a lot of time today searching for nothing. "This might seem like a game to you, but I don't have time for this!"

Samantha glared at him. Was this guy nuts or what? "Well to begin, my crystal ball is on the fritz so I had no idea you were even looking for the carpet," Sam snapped. "Plus, you're long gone every morning before I even wake up so how was I supposed to know you hadn't been in the barn. In addition to that, exactly when is it that I was supposed to mention carpet to you? Let me think back to all those casual conversations we've had over the last couple days. Oh yeah, we haven't had any because you are far too important to speak to someone as trivial as I am." She turned and stalked off in the direction of the house. She didn't need this. The man was insane.

Ty sighed deeply. Okay, she was right. They hadn't had any casual conversations. Not because he thought her trivial, boring and stuffy maybe, but not trivial. But that wasn't even the reason, Ty had been busy. He didn't have time to sit around socializing. He had work to do. He too began walking towards the house. "Samantha," he called.

Sam stopped abruptly and turned to face Ty. "What?" she asked coldly.

Ty stopped in front of her, watching her curiously. He felt guilty, which was strange. He didn't usually care if he offended humans. They offended him all the time. "You're right," he admitted. "We haven't had any casual conversations and I shouldn't have lost it back there about the carpet," he paused. "Can I still have lunch?" he asked, flashing her his most charming smile.

Samantha didn't move. She wanted to stay mad, Ty was so infuriating, but she couldn't. Especially not while he was standing there so sexy and charming. She couldn't help it, she smiled back. "You're forgiven just this once," she finally told him. "Anyway, it's not like I've known where the carpet was for days. I found it this morning while I was looking for a BBQ." She turned and headed for the house again.

Ty silently followed.

They'd only gone a short distance when Sam slowed so she could talk to him. "I wanted to apologize for last night," she began.

"Apologize for what?" he asked.

"I have a bad habit of getting so engrossed in what I'm doing that I lose track of time. I never would have knocked on your door if I'd realized it was after midnight. I'm sorry I drug you out of bed so late."

"Don't worry about it. I told you I was still up," he assured her.

"Yeah, that's what my grandparents said too. But I know they were lying," she accused.

"I'm not lying," Ty laughed. "You got your grandparents out of bed after midnight? Don't you know old people need their sleep?" he teased.

"That's what made it so horrible," she admitted. "I was working on this big project for Luke and I completely lost track of time. I was so thrilled when I got to a stopping point. I was thinking about heading home when it hit me. It was my grandparent's anniversary. I panicked, grabbed the phone and dialed their number. Grandpa answered groggily and obviously annoyed. That's when I looked at the clock and realized it was after two in the morning.

They didn't appreciate my happy anniversary call and I felt terrible for weeks," she admitted.

Ty laughed. He'd almost made a similar call to his parents. Fortunately, he looked at the clock before he dialed the number and stopped himself. How many times had he become engrossed in a game or some other project and completely forgotten everything else.

They continued to the farm house in silence, each lost in their own memories.

Chapter Five

Kylee Quintana lowered her binoculars. She wasn't sure what to make of the exchange she'd just witnessed. Was this the guy that was hurting Samantha? No, it couldn't be. "Why not Kylee? Because he's a good looking guy? You know good looking men can be control freaks," she chastised herself. But that wasn't really it. It didn't feel right because Samantha and this guy didn't act like a couple that had been together for over six months. Whoever was injuring Sam had been in her life at least that long, maybe longer because that was Sam's first visit to the ER. These two acted like they were just getting to know each other. Plus, this guy was obviously angry at Samantha for something but he didn't lash out at her or try to hurt her. Kylee was sure the guy that had been hurting Samantha wouldn't restrain himself if he got angry. The abuse had been going on too long. Maybe Samantha had finally moved on.

Kylee stood and gathered up her things. She was hungry. She was here to watch Samantha, but Sam was headed back to the large farmhouse. That would give Kylee time to head back to the cottage and grab a bite to eat. Maybe she'd come back in an hour or so and watch for a while longer. She had planned to stick around to make sure this guy wasn't her culprit, but now she was also curious what they were doing at the old military base. Whoever that guy was, he had pulled an awful lot of furniture out of that bunker. Clearly they intended to house people out here. Kylee was sure there hadn't been anything in the news about this. She couldn't leave now until she knew what was going on.

Kylee silently slipped through the forest and headed toward her car. When she first arrived in town she had no idea where she would find Samantha. All she knew was the plane had landed at the Depot. Just getting that much information had been difficult. People were obviously dedicated and loyal to the Deveraux family. Kylee smiled, employee loyalty didn't stand a chance against cleavage and a little flirting. Kylee decided to rent a small cottage on Seneca Lake just south of the army depot for a month. She couldn't stay any longer than that. She would need to get back to the hospital. The lake was pretty close. It wasn't in walking distance, but Kylee could park the car just off the highway and move through the forest unseen. She thought it was the perfect place to conduct surveillance. Now that she knew something else was going on here, she was even more determined to find out what.

* * * *

Samantha and Ty walked into the house and straight to the kitchen. Sam pulled two beers from the fridge and handed one to Ty. "Go relax," she urged. "I've got to go drag that BBQ out of the barn and then the coals will have to get hot. You have time to put up your feet and enjoy your beer."

Dawn

Ty leaned against the counter and took a long drink. "How about I go dig out the BBQ and prepare the charcoal and you can cook," he suggested.

Sam studied him for a long moment. "It's a deal on one condition."

"And what is that?" Ty asked.

"You go relax in the study while you finish your beer, then you can dig out the grill and get the coals going. I'll run take a shower and change. It's getting a little too cool for shorts now." She watched him. She wished he'd go take a nap, but there was no way she'd bring that up again. Anyway, what did she care if the guy relaxed or not? He was nothing to her. Funny, she did care though. He was probably the hottest man she'd ever met, but Sam wasn't that shallow. There was just something about him that she couldn't resist. No matter how much he annoyed her. The more she learned about him, the more she wanted to know. Nobody had ever affected her this way before. The realization was a little unnerving. She hardly knew the guy. And clearly he had no interest in her. "Deal?" she asked.

Ty studied her momentarily. For the first time he realized how extremely attractive she was. How had he missed that? Her long red hair gently shaped her face and made her beautiful blue eyes stand out like sapphires. They were actually the color of deep blue sapphires. He'd never seen eyes that bright before. "Okay, it's a deal," Ty said quickly. He was becoming uncomfortable with the direction his thoughts were going. Samantha was human. There was no way he was getting involved with a human. "I'll be in the study."

Samantha was relieved. She headed for the stairs. A hot shower was going to feel so good.

Ty entered the study and sank into the large couch. He was extremely tired and stressed. The pressure was beginning to take a toll. He needed to get that blasted game finished. When Dimitri asked him to come out, he honestly believed within one night he'd have the game completed and on the way to New York. But he'd been here several days now and it still wasn't working. He shouldn't be sitting here relaxing, wasting time. He needed to work on the game. He stared out the window absently, he just couldn't force himself to get off the couch. Ty leaned his head against the cushion and within seconds he dozed off.

Samantha finished her shower and strolled into the study. She'd expected to see Ty watching TV or working on designs. Instead she spotted him asleep on the couch. Good, she thought. Can't sleep during the day my butt. She quietly slipped back out the door and headed for the kitchen. She was still hungry. Maybe she could find something to snack on for now and they could have burgers for dinner. She rummaged through the contents of the large refrigerator and smiled. How had she missed the cherry pie? She loved cherry pie! Sam cut off a large slice, poured herself a glass of milk and wandered out onto the porch. It was beautiful out here. She settled into the small patio chair and relaxed. Too bad the barn was full of carpet instead of horses. She'd always loved horses.

Her mind drifted back to her childhood. Her family had lived in the country back then. Her parents had a large piece of property and several horses, a few cows and some chickens. She and Michael had gone riding almost every day. Sam missed the freedom of galloping through the open countryside. When Uncle James got married, he and his new wife moved onto the property adjacent to theirs. Her mom and her Uncle James had always been so close. Sam was only two when James married Lana so they'd been a part of her life from the beginning. She'd taken it almost as hard as her mother when James and his family died. He was a wonderful uncle, almost like a second father.

Then there was little Lexie. She had been such an adorable child. There were seven years between them, but for some reason they had always had a special connection. Aunt Lana was so beautiful and sweet. That was the only word Sam could think of to describe her. Lana had been reserved and insecure in the beginning, but Sam saw a stronger more independent woman beginning to emerge as she got older. Then they were killed. Sam's eyes began to water. She missed the life she could have had. Little Lexie was only five years old when those monsters butchered her. Michael shut down for weeks. He and Lexie were beyond close and he'd always been so protective of her. For some reason Michael had also developed a closer relationship with his uncle than he had his father. Maybe because they were so much alike. Sam's family was never the same after that horrible night. Then three years later her own family had been attacked.

Sam pulled her legs up to her chest and laid her head on her knees. The tears were flowing freely now. She'd held them back for so long. She just didn't have the energy to regain her composure anymore. Sam usually avoided thinking about her past, but for some reason today she couldn't put her family out of her mind. Maybe it had to do with her living arrangements and this farmhouse. Staying here with Ty also made her feel so alone. Sure, things had gotten a little better, but not much. She didn't know what was wrong with her. Why was he so indifferent to her presence? She'd watched him interact with Thomas that night at the ballroom. He seemed friendly, even fun. Not with her. She just didn't understand why.

Sam jumped when she heard a scraping sound and quickly looked around. She was embarrassed to see Ty standing next to her, watching her intently. She brushed her arm across her eyes and started to stand.

Ty gently put his hand on her arm. "Sorry," he said sincerely. "I didn't mean to interrupt. Don't leave on my account."

Samantha sat back down but didn't say anything.

"Want to talk about it?" he asked.

Sam gave her head a little shake and closed her eyes. She hated getting caught like this. She rarely cried. She wouldn't allow it. It made her feel weak.

Ty was at a loss. He had no idea what to do. Should he leave? He couldn't just walk away and leave her here like this. He wished she'd talk to him, but she'd been right today. They'd been here for days and he'd made no effort to get to know her at all. In fact, he'd pretty much lived in his own little world as if she wasn't there at all. He'd been so focused on his problems and the work that needed to be done that he hadn't stopped to think how his actions might impact her. "I was thinking about going for a walk," he finally said. "Would you like to join me?"

Samantha studied him. Was he inviting her because he felt sorry for her? She didn't need his sympathy. She'd wanted to spend some time with him, that's why she asked him to join her for the BBQ, but not out of sympathy.

"Samantha, I've been preoccupied since I got here. I know I haven't made any effort to get to know you. I'm sorry. I'd really like it if you joined me for a short walk," he asked again.

Sam wiped the last of the tears from her eyes. "Where are you going?"

Dawn

"I need to check out the forest," he told her. "Luke has an obstacle course planned for out there. I need to see if the course has been started or what the status is. If work hasn't begun, that's one more project I'm going to have to coordinate." He was feeling a little overwhelmed himself.

"Are you asking because you want company or because you're feeling sorry for me?" she said hesitantly.

Ty smiled. "I think I'd like the company," he said taking her hand and pulling her to her feet. "It's scary out there. What if I run into vampires? I need a fearless vampire hunter to keep me safe." He laughed at the look on her face.

"Now you're making fun of me," she glared at him.

"No. I'm not," he promised, giving her shoulder a little push. "Come on let's go. The sooner we get back, the sooner you can cook me dinner."

"Who said I'm still cooking dinner?" she said forcing herself to sound serious.

"That's okay, I'll cook dinner. Women can't BBQ anyway." He knew that would get her going.

"What?" Sam exclaimed. "I had no idea you were such a sexist. I'd put my skill in vampire hunting and cooking up against yours any day," she countered then scowled when she realized he was teasing her. "Not funny," she said angrily.

"Sure it was," he laughed. "Lighten up, Sam. Life doesn't always have to be so serious. Do you even know how to have fun?"

"Me?" she shot back. "What have you done for fun the last few days?"

"I've been busy," Ty defended himself shrugging off her accusation.

"So have I," she countered.

"Okay, so what do you do in New York to have fun?" Ty pressed.

"Lots of stuff," she told him.

"That's not an answer." Ty wasn't going to drop this. He believed she was a workaholic, but he wanted to know. He'd made enough assumptions about her since they'd met. He was beginning to wonder if he'd been wrong. "Do you visit clubs? Dance the night away? Get drunk every night? Belly dance? What? Specifically," he demanded.

"Why?" Samantha asked. "You've barely talked to me since we got here. Now you want me to tell you all about my life," she was annoyed. Was she mad at him or herself because she didn't do anything for fun? Her whole life was working and hunting.

"That's what I thought. You don't know how to have fun," Ty shrugged. "Don't feel bad, most people don't."

"Okay, big shot. What do you do to have fun?" Sam demanded.

Ty smiled. "Lots of stuff," he said sarcastically. Clearly she wasn't amused. "Okay, I spend some time at my friend's club. I hunt vamps. I play video games. I hang out with the guys. I have a beer and relax and watch a good movie every once in a while. I play with my dogs. I..."

"Okay, okay. I get the picture," she interrupted. "I hunt vamps," she said defensively.

Dawn

"True," Ty conceded. "But do you have fun while you're doing it? Or is it all about vengeance and justice? Once you find the vampire responsible for your families death will you still hunt or will the job be done?"

Samantha was silent for a long time. "I really don't know. I hadn't thought about that. It's been a part of my life for so long I can't imagine quitting. But I don't know if I want to do it forever. I don't know," she said honestly.

"We're here," Ty stopped and looked around. It was strange, he had a feeling they were being watched.

"What?" Sam asked.

"I'm not sure," Ty admitted. "I just get the feeling someone is watching us."

"Vamps?" she asked anxiously.

"I don't think so." Ty surveyed the area again. He couldn't see anyone but he was almost positive someone had been watching them. "It's possible for vampires to survive in the forest during the day if they can find enough shade or tree coverage but it's unlikely. They don't typically risk it. The sun is fatal for them, and from what I understand it's very painful. Maybe it's just a nosey neighbor. I haven't exactly been secretive about my activities the last couple days. Maybe someone saw me here."

Samantha studied the area. She wasn't prepared to encounter vampires right now. "What if it is a vampire? I didn't bring anything to fight with," she confessed.

"Don't worry. I think they're gone anyway," he assured her. "If not, I can handle it. I'm always prepared for an encounter."

"I don't want you to think I'm not," Samantha began. "It's just..."

"I didn't mean it that way," he cut her off. "I'm just saying you don't need to worry about leaving your fighting stuff at the house. I've got it covered. Anyway, like I said they're not vamps."

"How can you be so sure?" she asked.

"I just am." Alex had said Sam knew about the vamps, but he didn't want to explain how he could smell them. Sam hadn't asked anything about the warriors, so Ty suspected she wasn't aware he was different. She probably thought he was just another human. "Here's the trail. You ready to check this out?" he asked.

"Now's as good a time as any," she decided.

They walked silently into the shadows of the forest. Samantha was nervous at first, but once they were a few feet into the trees, she was dumbfounded. "Wow!" she exclaimed. "Luke created this?"

Ty smiled. The obstacle course was awesome. Luke had rearranged logs and constructed a marshland to create what looked like a challenging course. The kids were going to love this. "So," Ty turned to Sam, "you up for a little competition?"

Samantha grinned. "You want to race, hot shot?" she asked.

"Love to," he agreed. As he tried to take in the entire scene before him, he had a brilliant idea. He wondered if it was possible. Sam would know. Maybe he'd run it by her over dinner. "You ready?" he challenged.

"On three?" she asked.

Dawn

"Okay. One, two, three," they both said at once. Then they each shot off down the course.

* * * *

Initially Ty was into the competition, but then he held back. Luke had outdone himself. The obstacles were perfect. Ty followed Sam as she leapt over large logs and ducked to avoid others that were swinging from the trees. Luke had rigged up a system that was motion activated, it was great! It would teach the academy students to always be on the lookout. Ty continued to watch Samantha. She was so graceful as she ran through the course. He'd never met a human like her before. He was wrong when he told her she didn't know how to have fun. She was having a blast. The look on her face demonstrated that clearly enough. She was glowing and grinning as she jumped, twisted and ducked to avoid the next hazard.

Ty found himself enjoying the view. Samantha was fit. He guessed it was from all the vampire hunting. As a human she would be at a disadvantage. He remembered Victor saying when he arrived in that alley, Samantha was up on the roof with Alex. That made sense, she'd want to get up high and take the vampires out from above. He was so engrossed in his thoughts he almost ran right into Samantha who had stopped abruptly and was glaring at him.

"This is supposed to be a competition," she accused. "I don't need you to hold back and let me win. I can win on my own. Stop holding back."

"Me?" he tried to sound innocent. "Hold back? Never."

"I mean it," she squinted her eyes at him. "If I win, I want to win fair and square. If I lose, I lose." She turned and sprinted up a large deck like structure. "What do you think this is?"

Ty sobered. He noticed another motion sensor at the top of the platform. Luke would have designed this with the fae and warriors in mind, species that heal quickly if they get injured. He didn't think, he just took off at a dead run. He hit the top of the platform and leapt towards Samantha.

Sam didn't know what hit her. She was approaching the center of the platform when two things happened at the same time. The floor disappeared. She was sure she was going to fall through the trap when Ty's body slammed against hers as he wrapped his arms tightly around her waist. They flew off the back side of the structure. Ty was holding her so tight, it almost knocked the breath out of her. They hit the ground hard and Samantha heard something crack. Her eyes widened. "What was that?" No answer. "Ty are you okay?" she said in a panic.

Ty was gritting his teeth. He didn't want Samantha to know he had just broken a couple ribs. How would he explain the quick healing? They had hit the ground with so much force he couldn't avoid the enormous rock. Now he just had to regain his composure and pretend like everything was okay. "I think it was a large twig." He tried to sound normal. He could hear the pain in his voice, but could she? They really didn't know each other. Hopefully she wouldn't notice.

Sam rolled off Ty and onto her back. "What was that all about?" she asked. "I doubt falling through that trap door would have been any worse than your graceful save." She turned her head to look his way. He still hadn't moved. "Are you sure you're not hurt?" she asked concerned again. "I mean we did hit the ground pretty hard."

Ty took a deep breath. The worst of it was over. He was still a little sore but for the most part, his ribs were healed. Just a few more seconds and he could move again. Unfortunately, he was going to need some blood. He was feeling a little weak. Broken bones always took a lot out of him. He could handle anything else, cuts, gashes, whatever but broken bones always seemed to be a problem. "I'm a little sore, but nothing serious," he told her. He turned to face her, propping himself up on one elbow. "How about you? I didn't hurt you did I?" he asked. He hoped she didn't realize he was stalling. He knew he had done the right thing. Once he hit the platform he'd glanced down and realized just how deep the hole beneath the trap door was. Sam would have been seriously injured, possibly killed, if he hadn't reacted in time.

"No," she assured him. "I'm fine. I just don't get why you did that. It seemed more dangerous than the trap."

Ty reached over and brushed a lock of hair away from Samantha's face. She really was beautiful. Then he stopped himself. What was he doing? For a minute there he forgot she was human. He'd been lost in the moment and almost kissed her. That wasn't going to happen. He would not get involved with a human, no matter how irresistible she was. Their life span was just too short. He sat up to give them some distance.

Samantha was confused. She had been sure Ty was going to kiss her, which had been a shock after the last couple days. But she was even more surprised at how disappointed she'd been when he sat up and pulled away. Now she didn't know what to say to him. She straightened and looked away, focusing on the forest. It was a great course, she'd been having fun until she realized Ty was holding back. "Well, it looks like the course is complete. You won't have to add one more thing to your plate right now," she offered trying to casually fill the silence.

"Looks like," Ty agreed.

"But?" Samantha had heard something in his voice, but she didn't know him well enough to understand his tone.

Ty stood and held out a hand to her. "Come on. let's go barbeque that burger."

Samantha took his hand hesitantly. She was getting tired of him avoiding her questions. Well, she didn't know if he was avoiding them or just ignoring her all together. Ty pulled her to her feet so hard she almost fell over.

Ty hadn't meant to use that much force. He was frustrated and hurting and didn't think. He immediately reached out to steady her. Once he was sure she had her footing, he pulled away again and began walking back towards the house.

Samantha hesitated a couple seconds, then quickly caught up to him. They walked side by side in silence half way back to the farmhouse. She didn't like it, but didn't know how to make small talk with this man.

"I've been working on something for the Sims that would also take this obstacle course to a whole new level," he paused.

Samantha didn't say a word. She didn't want to ruin it. This was the first time Ty had ever initiated a conversation with her.

After a quick glance in Samantha's direction he continued. "I can't do it by myself though. I'm going to need your help. Are you up for a new challenge?" he asked casually.

Dawn

Sam heard excitement and maybe anxiety in Ty's voice. She was always up for a challenge. "Do I get to know the idea, or do I have to go into this blind?" she asked.

Ty smiled. He liked her sarcasm. How strange was that? "I thought we'd get out the BBQ and discuss it over dinner."

They had reached the house but instead of heading towards the entrance, they veered off toward the old barn. Ty pulled the large door open and was relieved to see several large rolls of carpet. Sam had told him someone was cutting the rolls into small pieces, but he didn't realize how far along they had gotten. There were probably a hundred sections of carpet ready to install in the bunkers. Luke wouldn't have been cutting these himself. He would have hired someone to take care of it. Ty wondered why they hadn't finished the job. They would probably never know.

Once the BBQ was going, Ty sat in the large patio chair and began to explain his new idea to Sam. He wanted to develop some VR goggles to go with the Sims. Now he also thought they could incorporate them into the obstacle course.

"They have to be small and lightweight though," Ty insisted. "I don't want them to be much larger than a pair of sunglasses."

"You're not asking for much, are you?" Samantha's mind was racing. Could they pull this off? If they could, it would take the simulator to a whole new level. D-tech could make a bundle on this. Samantha sobered. "I'm here working for D-Tech so they own anything new I come up with. Before we tackle this, you might want to talk to Alex and Thomas to see if you can capitalize on your design. If we succeed, D-Tech's Sims will be in high demand," she warned.

"I'm not worried about that," Ty assured her. He wasn't. Alex and Thomas would be fair. He wanted to get working on the scenarios, but he needed to know Samantha was willing to accept the challenge. "So?" he asked. "Can you do it? I was thinking we could develop different scenarios and store them on mini SD cards. That way we could have several copies and the students could just check them out or something. It would also give us a means to develop new scenarios in the future."

"How would the cards fit in the glasses?" Samantha wondered.

"I was thinking the glasses would be stationary, no hinges. What I mean is they won't fold up like most glasses do. Most of the electronics can be housed in the temple of the glasses. The side panels will have to be wider than most to accommodate the components. The SD card will slide into a slot on one side. We'll need to balance out the weight," Ty thought out loud. He'd finished cooking and the two of them were now continuing the discussion over dinner. "We'll also need to find a way to secure some kind of band on them. They can't fall off while they're running through the forest," Ty insisted. Their conversation continued for another hour. They were brainstorming now, each one expanding on the ideas of the other.

* * * *

Kylee finished her fried chicken and leaned back against the headboard. She was so tired. She'd had a close call today. She'd wrongly believed she was safe in the forest. When she saw Samantha and that man enter through the fort, she had to check it out. She had hoped to get close enough to hear what they were saying. She didn't know how that guy knew she was there, but somehow he had. She'd sat frozen behind that rock, praying she wouldn't be discovered. There was no way she could explain her presence in that forest.

Just when she thought it was safe to follow, Samantha and the guy took off running. Kylee sat in shock as she watched them run through the booby trapped pathway. If she had stumbled onto that trail, she would have gotten hurt for sure. She was glad she'd discovered it as an observer. She'd be sure to stay away from that area from now on. She'd also have to be careful every time she entered new terrain. She couldn't afford to get injured, not until she learned what was going on here. She wasn't going to figure anything out tonight. She was so tired she couldn't think straight but her mind was still racing. Kylee stood, undressed and slipped into bed. She'd need to get an early start again tomorrow.

She laid in bed thinking about Samantha and the mystery man. She had come to one conclusion today. This guy was not hurting Sam. She almost blew it when she saw the guy rush towards Samantha. Then, the trapdoor flew out from under Sam's feet and just when she thought Samantha was going to tumble to the ground, the guy leapt forward and saved her. They both careened over the edge and Kylee heard the loud crack as the man collided with a rock. She'd jumped up and started to run towards them then stopped herself. It was the hardest thing she'd ever done, but she slid back behind the bush and observed. She'd been sure the guy had at least one broken rib, most likely more. When he propped himself up and didn't wince or show any sign of the pain he should be in, Kylee was transfixed. She couldn't leave until she saw him walk back to the house himself. He did. He seemed fine. That was impossible. She'd heard the crack. Nobody could have taken that fall and walked away unscathed. She laid awake for hours, trying to reason it out in her mind before she finally drifted off to sleep.

* * * *

Lilith was tired of being cooped up in this small cave. She needed to get out. She couldn't wait to track down that menace of a human and torture her. Death wasn't enough, she needed to get revenge for the pain that woman had inflicted; twice. Lilith considered, her unrestrained hatred fueling the need for revenge. She wanted to start the hunt now, but she was still too weak. The large open wound was beginning to heal, but it was going so slow. She'd be vulnerable if she ran into one of the warriors or that fae queen and her fire throwing sidekick. No, she couldn't start the hunt, but others could. She smiled. She knew just the ones to do it. Lilith slipped out of bed and slowly wound her way through the cave. She needed to hurry. Night was about to fall and she wanted them to get started immediately. She rounded a corner and found the four vampires she was looking for. They always stayed together. She knew if she found one, she'd find them all. She walked towards them giving the group her most seductive smile. They all grinned back. This was going to be easy. Lilith began to explain her plan, confident these four would accept her challenge.

* * * *

Samantha stood and began to clean up. "I'll wash if you dry. I want to get started on the goggles while the ideas are fresh." She glanced back and saw Ty frowning at her. "What?" she asked.

"Do you ever relax?" he asked, annoyed.

"Sometimes," she said defensively.

"Prove it. Go into the study, turn on the TV and find a movie or something to watch tonight. The goggles can wait until morning," he challenged.

Now Samantha was frowning. She couldn't wait until morning. She was too excited to get started. "Let's just get this mess cleaned up and then we'll see," she said refusing to commit to the challenge.

"I'll do the dishes. You take off. You're not going to relax. Go ahead, get to work. I guess I was wrong about you. I should never second guess myself." He walked to the kitchen and started rinsing the plates.

"Wrong about what? What are you talking about?" she asked.

"For a minute today, in the forest, I thought you were having fun. I thought maybe I was wrong, that you could relax and have a good time. You almost changed my mind, but tonight your true colors returned. You are a workaholic, Samantha. You can't change who you are so go on, really. I'll take care of the dishes and I'll see you in the morning."

Sam wondered why Ty was always so formal with her. He knew Alex called her Sam, but Ty hadn't called her anything but Samantha since they'd been here. It was beginning to get on her nerves. Ty was getting on her nerves. "Just because I enjoy my work doesn't mean I don't know how to have fun. You can't make me feel guilty for doing something I love." She was glaring at him now. "What are you going to do tonight?" Sam challenged.

"I'm not working on the Sims or the goggles. I've spent enough time on that today. Don't worry, I won't bother you. Once I finish up here, I'll be in my room." Ty turned his back and began washing the dishes, signaling the conversation was over.

Samantha left the room angry with Ty, again. She was getting so tired of him brushing her off and treating her like she wasn't there, or that he was somehow better than she was. So she wanted to work tonight. Wasn't that what she was here for? She was being paid to do a job, being responsible didn't mean she didn't know how to have fun. She plopped down on the couch and tried to focus on the project. The nerve of that guy. She had fun. She angrily grabbed a piece of paper, a pencil and began drawing. After a few minutes she crumbled the page into a ball and threw it towards the trash can.

Hours later Sam was still frustrated. She'd tried to put Ty out of her mind, but couldn't forget his accusation. For the first time in her life, she couldn't lose herself in work. The floor was covered in discarded drawings. Sam laid her head against the back of the couch and closed her eyes. When was the last time she did something just for fun? She'd stopped visiting clubs. She never accepted invitations from co-workers to social events or even lunch. She'd become a loner. All she did was work and hunt. Hunting used to be fun, but lately even that felt like another responsibility.

Sam stood. She wasn't getting anywhere tonight. Ty had depressed her. She thought back over the day. The obstacle course had been fun, but the appeal was the company and the competition not really the course. No, that wasn't true, the course was amazing. Then she thought her and Ty had finally connected over dinner. Ty's idea was brilliant. Bouncing ideas off each other had felt good. Then she'd gone and blown it by insisting they get back to work. Sam reached the top of the stairs and was about to turn towards her bedroom when she noticed Ty's light was still on. His door was open slightly and she could hear keystrokes on a computer. She froze. Should she talk to him or just go to bed?

Dawn

After debating with herself for a few seconds, Sam quietly walked to the open door. Ty was sitting on his bed, laptop resting on his legs. He was concentrating on the computer screen. Was he working! Sam was furious. Here she was feeling guilty about focusing too much on work and Ty was in his room, working. She stomped to the bed and swung the computer around to face her. "You are such a hypocrite!" she accused.

Ty was surprised. He'd been concentrating so hard on the game he hadn't even heard her come in. Samantha was studying the screen intently. Ty reached for his computer to turn it back around but Samantha grabbed it off the bed and took a few steps backwards. "This is a game," she accused. "I thought you said you weren't working on the Sims tonight."

"I'm not," Ty said casually. "That's confidential," he added. "Do you mind giving me back my computer?"

Samantha narrowed her eyes at him. "This is clearly a game." She wasn't about to back down. "Don't lie to me, Ty. You're working on the Sim. You have the nerve to give me a lecture about all work and no play then you come up here and work all night? How dare you criticize me when you're worse than I am?" she demanded.

Ty smiled. "Samantha, it's not possible to be a bigger workaholic than you are." His smile widened when he saw her neck redden in anger. "I'm sorry if the truth hurts, but all you care about is impressing your boss and avenging your past. I stand by my assessment that you are incapable of having fun. Don't blame me for your shortfalls."

"My shortfalls!" she yelled. "Who gets up with the sun to work on the fort? Who retires to his room and works all night? Someone who lives in a glass house shouldn't throw stones. This..."

Samantha turned the computer around so Ty could clearly see the screen, "is work! And you're a liar."

Ty swung his legs off the bed and stood. "I already told you, I'm not working on the simulator. Now, give me back my computer." He was no longer amused. "I let it go the first time, but don't call me a liar again."

Samantha looked at the intricate code. She scrolled up and realized Ty wasn't lying. This was a video game. She studied the specific codes and realized it was an extremely complex program. "What is this?" she asked.

"I told you it's confidential," Ty held out his hand. "Give me my computer, Samantha."

"You're a gaming expert," she demanded. "That's why Alex sent you here to work with me on the simulator."

"I guess you could say that," Ty grinned. "My computer?" he pressed.

Samantha looked at the code again. She used the mouse to scroll down further. She was studying the codes more closely now. All of a sudden her head shot up and she looked at Ty wide eyed. "Ty as in Tyson Electronics?" she said amazed.

Ty sighed. He knew she'd figure it out eventually but he didn't have time for this.

"Is this Renegade II?" she looked back at the computer then to Ty. "It is!" she said, positive she was right. "I thought this game was supposed to be in production already. Game shops have been hyping it for weeks now."

Dawn

Ty reached out and grabbed his computer. "I'm well aware of the fact that I'm behind schedule." He set the computer on the edge of the bed. "Why do you think I'm working into the wee hours of the night trying to find the glitch? It's not because I enjoy working every hour of every day," he said grumpily.

"Oh," Sam heard the exasperation in his voice. Obviously the pressure was getting to him. She studied him more carefully and realized he looked worn out. Not just tired, but completely wiped out. "Well, since I've already seen it, do you mind if I take a look?" she asked. Maybe she could help him find the glitch. She knew nothing about gaming, but she knew plenty about computer codes.

"I told you it's confidential," Ty ran his fingers through his hair. "Anyway, I thought you said you didn't know anything about gaming," he said suspiciously.

"I don't but I do understand computer codes. Maybe I can see something you've missed," she offered. "Tell me about the glitch," she pressed.

"If I knew where the glitch was, I would have fixed it already." He was too tired for this. All he wanted to do was go to bed.

Samantha studied Ty. She felt bad for him. The hype about this game was out of control. She understood missing a deadline and the pressure that came with it. On top of that, he was tasked with coordinating setup at the fort. The guy needed a break. She walked over and sat on the bed next to the computer.

Ty watched her. Was she really trying to help or did she just want a sneak peek at his game. He'd trusted someone before and regretted it. Was it possible Samantha knew more about gaming than she was letting on?

"If this is about trust, I'll sign a confidentiality agreement. I'm not trying to steal your secrets Ty," Samantha assured him. "You're extremely grumpy when you're tired. If I have to live here with you, I'll do what I can to help you get some rest."

"You haven't been getting much sleep either. Who's the hypocrite now?" Ty countered.

"True, I've been going to bed just as late as you but I've also been sleeping in. You haven't. What's the harm in letting me look? Are you afraid I might find the problem and then you'd have to say thank you?" she teased. "Wouldn't that be awful?" she said widening her eyes at him.

Ty sat down in the large lounge chair. "Go ahead," he raised his arm to the computer. "At this point I'll take any help I can get," he sighed. "I'm getting desperate. You have no idea how many hours I've spent trying to figure out where the problem is."

Samantha picked up the computer and set it on her lap. "You say there's a glitch, but what does that mean? Give me an idea of what I'm looking for."

"The game works perfectly until you get to level four. Then the player can't gather the hidden treasures. The collection points stop working," Ty answered without emotion.

Samantha started at the beginning. She needed to familiarize herself with the pattern he was using. She didn't understand gaming codes, but she thought she might recognize a problem if she could find his style. She'd done this before with the law enforcement simulators. They had specialists that wrote code for the scenarios, but one of the guys had come to her frustrated because it wasn't working right. Once you got to the second level the cop cars would crash into the fire hydrant. She'd been able to scroll through the

Dawn

code and find something that didn't look right. She was using the same technique on Ty's game now.

Ty laid his head back and closed his eyes. He was so tired. It wasn't just the lack of sleep, he was extremely frustrated about his game. There was little to no chance that Samantha would find the problem. He'd gone through that code over and over again and still couldn't find it. How could someone inexperienced in gaming find what he kept missing? Oh well, he'd humor her. Maybe she wouldn't be so angry with him. She was right. He was being hypocritical. He felt a little guilty about giving her such a hard time when he had planned on heading to his room and working into the night.

"Ty?" Sam called interrupting his thoughts.

He opened his eyes and looked her way. "What?" he asked.

"Can you explain this to me?" she asked.

Ty stood and walked to the bed. "What?" he asked curiously.

"This code is different from the rest. I don't know enough to know if it's right, but it looks to me like it's missing something."

Ty took the computer and studied the code she was pointing to. Everything looked fine to him. He was so tired he couldn't think straight. He broke it down line by line. He wasn't sure what she was talking about.

"Look," Samantha said impatiently. "I can see a pattern here and here...and here." She was scrolling up the page. "Now, look at this code again. It's missing something. The patterns off."

Ty looked at the area again. All of a sudden it hit him. The code was missing part of the equation. Had Samantha just found his problem? Ty began typing, adding the missing elements then saved the program. He looked up in amazement. "Samantha, I think you may have just solved my crisis."

"Why do you always call me Samantha?" she asked, annoyed.

Ty was confused. "That's your name," he said not really understanding her. "What do you want me to call you? The computer genius?" he teased.

"The only person that ever called me Samantha was my grandmother. She refused to call me Sam because she said that was a boy's name. She didn't think it was proper. I don't think you're that stuffy so why are you always so formal with me?"

Ty couldn't answer that. Probably because he was trying to keep some distance between them. Calling her Sam made it feel like they were friends or something. He hadn't planned on getting to know her at all, he certainly didn't intend to be her friend. "I wasn't trying to be offensive. I guess I didn't feel like we knew each other well enough to be that informal. It seemed presumptuous for me to use your nickname," he confessed.

"I assume you're real name is Tyson. Tyson Electronics and all. How would you like it if I called you Tyson all the time?" Sam asked.

"I wouldn't," Ty admitted. "I guess I see your point."

"Will you please call me Sam from now on?" she asked. "We're going to have to work together for a long time and every time you call me Samantha it makes me cringe."

"Sure," he smiled at her. Would it be that bad if he let himself get to know her? She was attractive and smart. He'd grant her anything if she had just found his glitch. "I vaguely recall you claiming you've played video games before," he quizzed.

Sam smiled. "What's your point?" she asked.

"Well, we need to see if you just found the problem in my game. I was wondering if you wanted to be the first outsider to play the thing," he said casually.

"Really?" Samantha said excited. "I love Renegade. Will you really let me test Renegade II? Can I play it now?" she asked not trying to hide her excitement.

Ty smiled. When Sam was happy, she glowed. It made her even more beautiful. "You have a great smile. You should use it more often," he said trying to sound casual as he connected the computer to the large screen TV.

Sam's stomach did a little flip. She was shocked at the physical reaction Ty's compliment caused in her body. No man had ever made her feel so alive. In fact, she hadn't felt this alive since her family had been killed. The realization scared her. This man was infuriating and sexy. He seemed to bring out the best and the worst in her. How was she going to get through the next few weeks without falling for him? She had to be honest, she already had feelings for the man. Strong feelings that were getting more potent every day.

Ty turned and handed Sam a game controller. "Give it your best shot," he challenged.

Sam was having a blast. Renegade II was ten times more challenging than the first one. Once this hit the shelves it would be the hottest game on the market. She was finally on level four. It had taken her several hours to get there. Mostly because Ty kept distracting her with stories about his youth. He had then begun asking about hers. She found herself talking to him about her family. Something she never did with anyone, but it was easy to talk to Ty. He was so casual and unassuming. But once she reached the part about her families death, she'd shut down and refocused on the game. Now, here they were at level four. This was the moment of truth. Was the game really working the way it was supposed to? Samantha hoped so. She wanted the best for Ty. Plus, if he got this out of the way, they could work together on the Sim scenarios. She found herself looking forward to working with him. He challenged her she realized, professionally and personally. Once they were finished here it was going to be difficult to go back to her old boring life again.

Ty was alert. So far the game seemed to be working. Was it possible Samantha had really found the problem? "Do me a favor, head over to that rock and see if you can find anything."

"That's cheating," she teased as she moved the player to the rock. Jackpot. She'd found the emerald ring, the best treasure in the game. "Yes!" she exclaimed as she obliterated the monster coming towards her.

"You did it!" Ty said excited. "You found the glitch." He grabbed her and swung her into his arms. "You're amazing Sam," he said sincerely.

Sam was surprised. Her heart was pounding in her chest and all she could think about was Ty's strong body pressed against hers. She couldn't take her eyes off his. Was he affected the same way she was? Impossible. He was too aloof around her. He couldn't be attracted to her. He was just excited about his game. She held her breath and waited to see what he was going to do next.

Dawn

Ty was looking into Sam's large sapphire eyes. All he could think about was leaning in and kissing those small, tender lips. He was about to press his mouth to hers when he remembered she was human. What was he thinking? There was no way he was going to get involved with a human. He'd seen it too many times before. The devastation and heartbreak felt by the fae or the warriors when their human mate died was something he'd promised himself he would never experience. He quickly set Samantha back down and stepped away. "Thank you. I'm sorry I doubted you. Alex is right. You're the best," he said sincerely. "If there's ever anything I can do to repay you, all you have to do is ask."

Samantha inhaled. She'd been so sure Ty was going to kiss her. She stood frozen in anticipation, longing for his lips to press against hers. Maybe he was attracted to her, too. For just a second, she'd imagined them together. She wouldn't have to lie about where she was going at night. Ty was a hunter too. She was subconsciously fantasizing about them hunting together, at the same time anticipating his kiss. Then he released her. The disappointment caused her physical pain. She studied him. The closeness hadn't impacted him at all.

"Don't worry about it," she managed. "I was happy to help. Maybe you'll get some rest tonight." The room was closing in around her. She needed to escape. "I'm tired." She tried to sound casual but she couldn't breathe. "See you in the morning." She turned, forcing herself to walk casually out of the room. All she wanted to do was run.

"Good night, Sam," Ty whispered. He was fighting with himself. All he wanted to do was pull her back into his arms and forget she was human. He longed to lay her on the bed and kiss her until they both forgot all their troubles. How had this happened? He didn't even like humans. His stomach clenched as Samantha walked out of the room and silently pulled his door shut. Ty stood motionless, staring at the closed door. "Ugh," he said as he lowered himself to the bed. How was he going to resist her? They were living in the same house and for the next few weeks they'd be spending a lot of time together. He couldn't avoid her and complete the Sim project. He was doomed.

Samantha got to her room and quickly closed the door. Once she knew she was alone, the tears began to fall. She'd finally fallen for a guy and he was completely uninterested. How had this happened? She wasn't looking for a man. She was too busy. She slipped off her clothes and pulled the baggy t-shirt over her head. Her life was a disaster. Sometimes she thought Ty was perfect for her, but on the other hand he was so aggravating. She'd never felt so conflicted and uncertain in her life. The last couple days had been an emotional roller coaster ride. Well, it stopped now. Ty had made it clear he wasn't interested. From now on, their interaction would be completely professional. She needed to spend more time at D-tech anyway. Unfortunately they'd have to work together on the simulator and that was going to take a lot of time. But she'd also spend more time checking on production at the plant and focus more attention on the battle droids. She'd find a way to cope with the disappointment and do her best to be strictly professional while she was in Ty's presence. It was going to be difficult, but not impossible. Sam wondered if she was destined to be lonely forever.

She closed her eyes and cried herself to sleep.

Chapter Six

Two weeks later, the simulator was almost complete. They still needed the flooring, but Alex had promised it would be here by Friday. Remaining strictly professional with Ty had proved impossible. Now that his game crisis was over, Ty was a completely different person. He constantly teased her and didn't seem to worry about anything. Sam had never met a more easy going man in her life. Just more reason to love him. And she did love him. No matter how hard she tried to avoid it, she couldn't resist his magnetic pull. Over the past week Samantha had tried to spend more time at the plant. But after only a few hours, she found herself missing Ty's company. There was always a good excuse to head home. Once here, of course the two of them resumed work on the Sim. Three days ago she'd told Ty they were having problems with the droid line, hoping he would encourage her to spend more time away. That hadn't worked, mostly because it wasn't true. They weren't having problems with the robots. In fact, the employees at Romulus had already resolved D-Tech's biggest problem. Complaints had been coming in from customers about a breakdown when they gave the droids several commands at once. New York couldn't figure out the glitch, but Romulus had. The droids needed a larger memory chip. Samantha called Alex and they decided to do a recall. It was an easy fix. Technicians at all retail outlets could make the switch in less than five minutes. Customers were now completely satisfied.

Production had doubled, but so had demand. Romulus was now studying new ways to streamline manufacturing. These guys were good. She'd be sure to use them on major projects in the future. They were suspicious at first, but the employees eventually got used to seeing her drop by the plant at odd hours of the day and night. She worked by herself, knocking out as many battle droids as she could when she was there. They were going to need hundreds of them if each student was going to have their own practice droid. She had forced herself to spend the entire day at Romulus for once. That was quite an accomplishment. She missed Ty so much it scared her. Sam glanced at her watch, it was almost eleven o'clock at night. Time to head home.

Sam was beat. She slipped silently through the front door and hurried up to her room. She hadn't even seen Ty today. She wondered what he'd been doing but not enough to risk an encounter. Seeing him while she was this tired could prove disastrous.

Ty sat in the large study. He'd finished surveying the property today and sent Dimitri his suggestions for improvement. Security was now in Dimitri's hands. One more project complete. Dave, his production manager at Tyson Electronics, had called. Production on the game was being fast tracked. It was almost ready to release. He'd have to fly to New York as soon as he got a break to finalize the details, but it was such a relief to have his game completed and in his employee's hands. Everything was coming together nicely. He'd also finished the bunkers for the construction crew. They were supposed to arrive in the morning but something had come up again and they were delayed at least another week. Ty should be happy, but he wasn't.

Samantha kept finding excuses to go to the plant. The hours they spent together were amazing. He was more relaxed around her than he'd ever been around a woman in his life. Working on the Sims had been fun and educational but that project was almost complete. He worried things would change between them once that happened. He didn't want their friendship to change. Sam was smart and funny and full of attitude. He frequently found himself forgetting she was human, which was dangerous. That was something he could never forget. A relationship between them would never work, but more and more often he found himself wishing for exactly that. Sam was sexy, there was no doubt about that. He still couldn't believe he hadn't noticed her beauty from the beginning. Had he really been that preoccupied with his game that he completely missed that hot little body of hers? But that was only part of the attraction. She was down to earth and real. So different from the pompous models or corporate women he frequently found himself stuck with. When she wasn't around, he missed her company. And lately, even when she was there working on the simulator, she seemed distant and unreachable. Something had changed that night in his room, for both of them it seemed. For about the hundredth time, Ty wondered what the future held. Would it be possible to remain friends? Probably not with the chemistry they were both clearly fighting. Then what? How were things going to end? The idea of never seeing Sam again when the project was over actually caused him physical pain. Ty sat in the dark study, contemplating his dilemma until well after dark. He took another sip of his coffee and looked at the clock. It was almost eleven. He was beginning to worry about Sam. So far he hadn't seen any vampires, but that didn't mean they weren't out there. Dimitri had warned him Radek would eventually realize they were here. He'd be curious and suspicious. Eventually he'd send his vamps to the area to find out what they were doing. Until the security system was up and running they needed to be careful.

He was just about to walk over to the plant when the door opened and Samantha silently slipped through the door and walked upstairs. She hadn't even looked for him. His stomach clenched. He hadn't seen her all day. He missed her laugh and her sarcasm. Was he nuts? How had he let himself care this much about a human? Ty slowly rose and headed for bed.

Samantha woke early the next morning. She needed some fresh air. She walked to the dresser and pulled on a pair of sweats and a t-shirt. She wanted to run the obstacle course. At the last minute, she grabbed a video camera then headed for the door. She'd run the course and get video at the same time. They could use the footage as a baseline for the scenario. Once they perfected the course, they'd just need to add the vamps and other characters into the program. Ty insisted they throw in a few good guys to make the kids think before they struck. He wanted it to be as challenging as possible.

Samantha knew Ty would be up. He always woke with the sun, she just hoped he was gone already. Avoiding him hadn't dampened her feelings. She had such a hard time being in the same room as him. He wasn't only hot, but he was hilarious. She hadn't known that before. He had been so serious those first few days. Once his game was complete his whole demeanor had changed. His mood was lighter and he constantly made her laugh. Sam slipped into the kitchen and poured herself a mug of coffee. No sign of Ty so far. She silently slipped out the back door and headed for the forest.

Dawn

* * * *

Kylee sat quietly watching Samantha run. She didn't dare move, Sam had a video camera. If she drew attention to herself, she might get caught on film. She'd been following Sam for the past week, but hadn't discovered anything new. She was beginning to think she was wasting her time. Obviously the guy that had been hurting Sam was nowhere to be seen. Maybe she'd left him in New York. As curious as she'd been initially about what was going on at the fort, she was starting to lose interest. It was strange for Sam to be running through the forest with a video camera but even that didn't peak Kylee's interest that much. She'd stay a couple more days, but then she needed to get back to work.

* * * *

Samantha entered the farm house. It was after six and she was starving. When she finished the course this morning, she'd gone straight to the plant. She'd showered in their weight room and immediately went to work. Once she got started, she'd had a new idea for the training droids. She was feeling pretty good as she walked through the door. The smell hit her instantly and her stomach growled loudly. Ty appeared in the hallway. "Hungry?" he asked.

Samantha smiled. "Starving," she admitted. "Whatever you're cooking smells great."

Ty turned and headed back to the kitchen. "It's nothing fancy, just spaghetti," he admitted.

"Really?" she asked. "I love spaghetti."

"Me too," Ty admitted. "I know, when you live on a ranch you're supposed to be a meat and potato man, but I have a weakness for spaghetti. I had a craving and couldn't resist." He looked at Sam, that wasn't the only craving he was having a hard time resisting. "It's ready, have a seat." He waved her to the table.

Dinner was nice. Sam watched Ty attack his spaghetti and almost laughed. He strategically wrapped the pasta around his fork until it was a symmetrical ball. The first time he did it, she was sure the whole thing wouldn't fit in his mouth. She was wrong. He continued to eat fork full after fork full until his plate was clean. Then he got up and dished himself another heaping plate.

"How do you do it?" she asked.

"Do what?" he wondered, looking up at her.

"How do you eat that much and still stay so fit?" she questioned then blushed a little. She didn't want him to know she'd been checking him out.

Ty smiled. "Great metabolism I guess." Warriors couldn't get fat, their blood wouldn't allow it. He wasn't sure how the whole thing worked, but he thought the blood attacked the extra fat like it was an injury or something. Bastian could explain it, Ty was sure of it. Bastian had spent his entire life studying warrior blood. He sobered, Bastian wanted to find an antidote for being a warrior. Ty thought it was a waste of time, he didn't know any warrior that would take the antidote even if it did exist.

"Where'd you go?" Samantha asked.

"Huh?" Ty's attention snapped back to Samantha.

Dawn

"You were sitting there enjoying your meal and then all of a sudden you got so serious. I was just wondering where you went."

"Nowhere," Ty slid back from the table and took his plate to the sink. "You finished?" he asked as he walked back to stand next to Sam.

"Yeah," Samantha told him then quickly moved her arm as Ty took her plate. He placed the rest of the dishes in the sink and turned for the door. I'll be in my room. Don't mess with the dishes, I'll come back and do them later.

Before Sam could answer Ty was gone. What had upset him? They'd been having such a nice dinner. Sam was confused. She went to the sink and took care of the dishes. Ty had cooked, she wasn't going to leave the mess for him too. Once the dishes were done, she headed upstairs. She wasn't going to let him shut her out tonight. She got to his door and knocked loudly.

Ty opened the door and glared at her. "What?" he growled.

"Spill it," she demanded. He was going to talk to her. She needed to know what had upset him. She stood her ground and tried to ignore the fact that he was only wearing his jeans. Seeing him shirtless always took her breath away.

"Spill what?" he said casually.

Sam pushed the door wide open and slid past him. She walked to the bed and sat down. "I'm not leaving until you explain what went on down there."

"There's nothing to explain," Ty told her. How could he describe what was going on? He knew he'd fallen for her, but he was still resisting. She was human. Thinking about Bastian had brought everything back to him so clearly. Bastian's father had fallen for a human. She'd gotten pregnant and gave birth to Bastian, but then insisted on being turned. His father had put her off for eight years but then finally gave in. Something went horribly wrong. Bastian's mother didn't make it. His father was devastated and Bastian now devoted his life to finding an antidote. Bastian wanted to give warriors the option of becoming human. He hoped the process wouldn't be as dangerous as turning a human into a warrior. Ty wasn't sure that was possible, but it didn't matter. He couldn't risk Samantha's life that way and he couldn't bear to have her and lose her after such a short amount of time. If his feelings were this strong now, he couldn't imagine what they would be if they spent years together.

"You're acting strange Ty," she pressed. "Why are you keeping secrets from me? You know I already know all about the vampires. You don't need to hide things."

Ty felt a little guilty. He wasn't human, but he didn't know how to explain what he was. He wondered how she would feel if she knew. Probably betrayed. He studied her closely. He was going to have to tell her the truth eventually, but he found himself wanting one night with her before he lost her. He was sure he would lose her if she knew. What should he do? He wanted her, but he knew he couldn't have her.

Samantha stood up, walked to Ty and took his hand. She led him back to the bed and pushed him into a sitting position. Once she sat back down she took a deep breath. She didn't know what was bothering him, but she didn't like it. He seemed so conflicted and a little sad. It tugged at her heart and she had this uncontrollable urge to comfort him. Before she realized what she was doing, she had taken his hand in hers. "I'd like to think we've become friends over the past few weeks," she began. "I can tell there's something bothering you and I'd like to help. Please let me help," she urged.

Ty looked down at their joined hands. Her hand was so small and soft. He was losing his mind from such a simple touch. He couldn't think straight, he couldn't be rational. He closed his eyes and tried to do the right thing. He needed to resist her but he couldn't. He knew he couldn't resist her any longer. He sighed and looked into her eyes.

Samantha froze. Once their eyes locked, she couldn't look away. Ty's eyes were blazing. Was that desire she saw? She held her breath. She didn't want to get her hopes up again just to have them dashed. She didn't think she could take the disappointment. Unfortunately, she lost that battle, she wanted him to kiss her more than she'd ever wanted anything. Neither one of them moved for several seconds. Then slowly, Ty leaned forward and pressed his mouth to hers. At first it was soft and gentle, then he deepened the kiss. Samantha's heart was pounding. Could this be real? Could Ty really want her too? She closed her eyes and enjoyed the moment.

Ty ran his fingers through Sam's hair. It was so soft and smelled of strawberries. It was intoxicating. He pulled back and studied her. "You're beautiful," he murmured. He traced the outline of her lips with his finger.

Sam's heart was still pounding. She couldn't take her eyes off Ty. He gently guided her backwards until she was lying on the bed, her legs hanging over the side. Ty kneeled and pulled off her shoes. Then he walked to the other side of the bed and gently climbed on. "Come up here by me," he requested.

Sam pushed herself backwards until she was lying next to his half naked body. Ty brushed a strand of hair away from her face.

"I can't resist you any longer Sam," he confessed. "I know I shouldn't, but I want you. I want to make love to you all night long."

"Don't resist," Sam whispered. "I want you, too. Why have we been fighting our feelings all this time?" she asked.

"Because we're too different," he closed his eyes.

Samantha pushed herself up onto one elbow and watched him. "I don't think we're so different," she admitted. "In fact, I think we have a lot in common."

"Maybe," Ty admitted. She just didn't know how different they really were. He should tell her before he was with her, but he couldn't. He had to have this one night. If he explained what he was and she rejected him, he didn't think he could bare it. He leaned down and kissed her gently.

Samantha was in heaven. How many times had she fantasized about this over the past several weeks? Could this really be happening? She reached up and ran her fingers through the light hair on his gorgeous chest. He was so hot! She felt a shudder go through Ty's body. Sam smiled inwardly. So, she did have an impact on him too. She wanted to hope for a future with him, but for tonight she was just going to enjoy the moment. They'd deal with the consequences in the morning.

* * * *

Ty woke with a start. Someone was outside. He slowly moved Sam's head off his chest and slid from the bed. He pulled on his jeans and walked to the window. It was still dark outside so he couldn't see a thing, even with his night vision. He wished they had a security system. He looked back at Sam and groaned. She looked so peaceful and innocent. He smiled, she hadn't been so innocent last night. He was worried one night wasn't going to be enough. He still felt guilty. He should have been honest with her. It wasn't fair to seduce her before she knew what he was. He was sure once she knew, things would change between them. He wouldn't argue. How could things last when he was going to stay young all her life and she was going to age? When he got back, he'd break the news to her. Somehow he'd get over whatever this was and let her move on.

He tiptoed across the room and silently closed the door. He needed to find out what was out there in the darkness. Had the vampires finally found them? He didn't like venturing out alone, but he didn't have a choice. He wouldn't risk Sam and he couldn't let it go. He needed to know if they were in danger.

Ty slipped out the front door and into the darkness. He stood in the shadows and listened. There it was again. He'd walk the perimeter then check the forest. Ty pulled the knife from his belt and mentally prepared himself for battle. He just hoped there weren't too many for him to handle on his own.

* * * *

Samantha woke to pounding. What was that noise? She sat up and realized she was still in Ty's room. She smiled as she remembered the night before. She rolled over and immediately realized Ty was gone. There was that pounding again. Was that the door? She quickly dressed and ran to open it. Ariel stood there with a man, what was his name? Vince? No, Victor. That was it. "Hello," she said as she swung the door wider to let them enter.

Ariel and Victor stepped into the foyer. "Where's Ty?" Ariel asked looking around the empty house.

"Uh..." Samantha hesitated. "I don't know. I was still asleep. He normally gets up with the sun though." She looked outside and realized it was still dark. Her brow furrowed. Where was Ty?

Victor looked at Ariel concerned. "Is he still in the house?" he asked.

Sam looked around. "I don't think so," she admitted.

"Go check his room," Ariel encouraged Victor.

"He's not in there," Sam told them. "If he's not in the kitchen, he's left the house."

They all looked down the hall and realized the kitchen was still dark.

"Stay here," Victor ordered as he turned to leave the house.

"I'm coming with you," Ariel said, following Victor out the door.

Sam started after them.

"Stay in the house," Ariel ordered. "You don't have a weapon. If the vampires have found you, it's not safe for a human out there. Let us handle it."

Sam wanted to argue, but she knew Ariel was right. She'd be a liability without a weapon. By the time she went to her room and grabbed her bow and arrow the two of them would be long gone. She went back into the house and locked the door behind her. Where had Ty gone? She walked into the kitchen and out on the coffee. That's strange, Ty usually makes the coffee before he leaves. Something was definitely wrong here. Sam entered the study and sat on the couch. She was worried about Ty. She didn't even know how long he'd been gone. She couldn't bare it if anything happened to him. Last night had felt like the beginning of something wonderful. And what had Ariel meant by it's not safe for a human?

* * * *

Ty slipped into the forest and listened for movement. The rest of the fort was clear, they had to be in here somewhere. His senses were on alert and he was trying to catch a scent. He moved further into the trees and stopped. He could smell them, but he still didn't know how many he'd be dealing with or where they were. The scent seemed to come from all directions. Not a good sign. They came out of nowhere. Four of them attacked at once. One of them hit him in the head with something; a log or a rock. It almost knocked him out. Ty tried to fight them off, but these guys were good and he was a little dazed from that blow to the head. They must be seasoned vamps. Ty groaned as one of them shoved a knife through his thigh. He swung around and plunged his dagger through its heart. One down, three to go. Two of them flew at him at once. He swung his weapon forward again but missed his mark, the vampire turned just in time. At least he'd wounded him. The second one kicked Ty in the ribs so hard he felt them crack. Ty was dizzy. He needed to regain his composure or he was going to lose this fight.

All three vampires came at him from different directions. He was in trouble. One of them struck him from behind and he fell to his knees. Think Ty, he told himself. You're in trouble. How are you going to get out of this? He fell to the ground and acted like he was injured worse than he was. If the vampires swarmed him, maybe he could still take them out. He was shocked when a woman came running out of the woods swinging a large branch and yelling. She struck one of the vampires and was clearly surprised when he turned on her. The vampire flew forward, knocking her to the ground. Another human, just his luck. He stumbled to his feet planning to come to her rescue when he was once again struck from behind. A knife sliced through his side and Ty instantly fell to the ground. He couldn't breathe. The vampire must have struck a lung.

Kylee was shocked. What was this thing? It was strong and his eyes were green like an alley cat. He knocked her to the ground and then climbed on top of her. She screamed when she saw his teeth coming towards her neck. Vampires, she thought in disbelief. This thing was a vampire and she was going to die. She widened her eyes in amazement at what looked like a teenage boy. He was running towards them through the trees. Just before he reached her, he turned into a Bengal tiger. What kind of world had she entered? This was impossible. These things didn't exist outside Hollywood. The tiger lunged at the monster on top of her and ripped off its head. Kylee closed her eyes. She was living a nightmare. None of this was possible. The vampire evaporated into a cloud of dust. Kylee didn't move. She was in shock. She glanced over at Sam's friend again. He was in trouble and there was nothing she could do to help.

Suddenly a ball of fire flew through the trees. It was followed by a woman and a large man charging towards them. They were immediately by the injured man's side. The woman created fire from her fingertips and threw it at one of the vampires. He too dissipated into thin air. There was only one vampire left. The second man leapt forward and plunged a knife into the last vampire's chest. Kylee passed out. This was all too surreal for her to process.

Dawn

Ariel was at Ty's side in an instant. "Victor," she called. "He's in bad shape. We need to get him to the house."

Victor looked back at Ariel and Ty. "You," he said glaring at the shifter. "Shift back and bring her to the house. Then I'll need an explanation from you. You better have a good reason for being in the forest." He was now by Ariel's side. He cradled Ty in his arms and rushed toward the house.

The door swung open with a loud thud. Sam jumped to her feet. Victor strolled in without a word. He was carrying Ty. He took the stairs two at a time and disappeared into Ty's room. Ariel was at his heels. "Ty!" Samantha exclaimed as she ran toward the stairs. Ariel stopped her. "We'll look after Ty," she assured her. "I need you to take care of her." Ariel pointed to the door.

Samantha hadn't noticed the guy standing there with a woman in his arms. "But..."

"We've got this," Ariel pointed upstairs. "I need you to handle things down here."

Samantha understood Ariel wasn't giving her a request. Once she took care of the woman, she could check on Ty. She turned to the guy standing in the doorway. "Get her into the study."

Once Ariel knew she wouldn't be followed by Sam, she quickly ascended the stairs and disappeared into Ty's room.

"Put her down on the couch," Sam instructed. "What happened to her? Is she injured?"

"I don't think so," Dusty said unsure if he was right. "I think maybe the scene in the forest was too much for her."

Samantha had pulled a blanket from the closet. She returned to the couch and paused. Dr. Quintana? What was she doing out here? "Who are you?" Samantha turned on the guy. She thought he was a teenager, but he was large enough to be around twenty, she just couldn't tell.

"Dusty," he answered.

"Well Dusty, I need you to go to the kitchen and get me a glass of water. We need to see if we can wake the good doctor up." Samantha was pulling the large blanket around her patient.

"Uh..." Dusty paused. "Ma'am, I think that only works in the movies."

"Go!" she demanded. "Get me the water."

Dusty turned toward the door. "Where's the kitchen?" he asked.

"Straight down the hall, you can't miss it. Hurry, I need to know if she has any injuries," Sam added.

Dusty rushed to the kitchen and returned immediately balancing a glass of water in his hand. Samantha took it, removed the blanket and threw the contents into Kylee's face. Kylee sputtered and coughed then tried to sit up.

"Oh, no you don't." Samantha pushed her back down on the couch and pulled the blanket around her. She smiled. "Looks like the roles have been reversed. Today you're the patient and I'm in charge."

Kylee blinked in confusion. Where was she? "How did I get here?" she asked.

Dawn

Dusty stepped forward. "I carried you to the house, ma'am. I think the excitement was too much for you and you passed out in the woods."

That's right, Kylee thought. The forest. Those monsters. She jumped to her feet but felt dizzy and had to sit back down. "The man?" she asked. "Where is that man you've been hanging out with the past few weeks? He needs medical attention. I need you to take me to him at once," she demanded.

Samantha narrowed her eyes at the doctor. "How do you know we've been hanging out together for weeks?" she asked. "Have you been spying on us?"

Kylee was not going to get into this right now. The man needed help. She tried to stand again, but she was still too weak.

"Fine," Sam conceded. "We'll talk about that later. You just sit here and try to recover from the shock. I'm going to check on Ty." She turned and left the room.

Kylee knew she had to get to the man. He was in serious danger. She couldn't help until she settled down though. She began to take slow, methodical breaths. She just needed a minute, then she'd head upstairs and see what she could do to save him.

Dusty studied the woman. She was still pale, but she seemed to be coming around okay. "Are you hurt?" he asked.

"Huh?" Kylee looked up.

"Did he injure you? Before I got to you," Dusty asked again.

"Oh," Kylee understood. This was the kid that had turned into a tiger. She laughed. How was she so calm about all this after what she had seen in that forest?

"What's funny?" Dusty asked confused.

"You're the tiger," she said simply.

"Oh, yeah. About that..." Dusty was trying to think of something to say.

"It's okay," Kylee assured him. "You don't have to explain." She settled back and closed her eyes. She was already starting to feel better. A little more time and she could tackle that flight of steps.

Samantha ran up the stairs, then slowed as she reached the top. She was afraid of what she might find when she entered Ty's room. Was he okay? How serious were his injuries. What if he didn't survive? Samantha couldn't bear the thought. She slowly pushed open the door and took one step inside. She froze, shocked at the scene before her. Ariel was hooking Ty up to some kind of IV, but the bag contained bright red liquid. It looked like blood! Her gaze shifted to Victor who was cradling Ty's head in one hand and pouring blood down Ty's throat. What was going on here? People didn't drink blood. Nobody drank blood...but vampires. Samantha was horrified. They were vampires? She wanted to scream. How had she been living under one roof with a vampire all this time and not known it.

Her stomach clenched. She'd made love to a vampire. The very monster she'd vowed to hunt to extinction and she'd slept with one. "Vampires," she said out loud. Victor and Ariel looked up in surprise. "You're all vampires!" Samantha screamed.

"Samantha," Ariel began. She dropped the IV line and took a step towards Sam.

Dawn

"Don't come near me," Samantha warned. "You're all monsters!" she said with disdain. "Now I get it," she continued. "That night at the ballroom. I could have killed Lilith but you and Alex stopped me. What? Is she your leader or something? You pretended to be my friend to shield your disgusting vampire queen?" She was on the verge of hysterics now. The air was closing in around her and she couldn't breathe.

Ariel's face hardened. How could this human be such a moron? Vampires? Get real. She'd been with them in that alleyway. She'd seen her and Victor battle the newborns. She'd watched Alex attack Lilith over and over again. How could she believe they were vampires protecting that evil woman? "You can call me a monster if you like, but don't ever call me a vampire!" she said angrily. She took another step towards Sam. "If you'd just calm down I can explain everything," Ariel told her, trying to hide her anger and the hurt she was feeling. She'd begun to think of Samantha as a friend. Clearly the feeling wasn't mutual.

"Don't come near me!" Samantha warned. "If any of you come near me, I'll kill you!" She turned and ran from the room.

Ariel looked at Victor. "What now?" she asked.

Victor was still working on Ty. His side hadn't stopped bleeding. He was worried. Ty's injuries were pretty severe. "Let her go," he answered. "Give her some time. I think eventually she'll come around. I'm sure walking in and seeing me dumping blood into Ty was a shock. Alex has confidence in Sam. Let's give her a little space and see if she reasons it out on her own."

Ariel walked back over to the bed. She could hear the concern in Victor's voice. "What's wrong? Isn't he healing?"

Victor was about to answer when he heard a voice from the door. "I'd like to help," Kylee said hesitantly. She didn't understand the blood IV, but right now it didn't matter. This man had risked his own life to try to help her. She wasn't going to stand by and let him die. She walked to the bedside and took the gauze from Victor's hand. "Let me see. I'm a doctor. I've been working in the ER for the last couple years, but before that I was a surgeon. Let me see what's going on here," she pled.

Victor studied her for a moment then conceded. She looked okay. How was it that this human was taking everything so well when Samantha had freaked out over it. Sam had been around them for months. She already knew about vampires, yet she couldn't handle learning about warriors. This woman seemed perfectly calm about the whole situation. A situation she'd been exposed to less than an hour ago. Victor was impressed. It wouldn't do any harm to allow her to work on Ty. Maybe she could speed the healing along somehow. Victor slowly rose from the bed to make room for the woman. "What's your name?" he asked as she slid closer to Ty.

"Oh, sorry. I'm Doctor Quintana but you can just call me Kylee." She had removed the gauze from Ty's side and frowned. "I had a bag. Do you know what happened to it?" she asked no one in particular.

"Yes," Ariel answered. "I set it on the small table in the entry way."

"I need it," Kylee requested.

Ariel ran to the entry and back up the stairs. She noticed Dusty was still sitting in the study, alone. "Don't go anywhere," she called out. "We need to talk to you when we're finished up here." She darted into the room and shoved the bag towards the doctor.

Dawn

Kylee pulled a medical kit from her bag. She'd seen the knife go into the man and knew she'd need to perform surgery to repair that large of a wound. Could she do this here? He needed oxygen and a breathing tube. She didn't have anything like that in her bag. She pulled out an asthma inhaler and a needle to administer the antibiotic.

"No drugs," Victor insisted as he held out a hand to stop her.

"He needs the inhaler to open his airway and I can't perform surgery without giving him an antibiotic. We wouldn't even do that in the hospital under sterile conditions, but here...no way." She protested.

Victor shook his head. "No drugs. Trust me. They'll do more harm than good on him."

Kylee studied the man for a couple seconds. She trusted him for some reason. She didn't like it, but this was going to have to be done without medication. She took a deep breath and moved to the side of the bed. As she evaluated the damage she knew his breathing wouldn't improve without her help. And if she didn't get him oxygen he may not survive. "Do you have something I can make a breathing tube out of?" she asked.

Victor considered the request and strolled to the closet. He pulled out a roll of tubing and handed it to the doctor. She quickly inserted the chest tube. Blood and liquid immediately began to drain from the injured cavity. Victor was relieved. Ty sounded better already. He'd be fully recovered in no time. He watched as the doctor removed her scalpel from a small container. She doused it with alcohol, slid on a pair of gloves and moved towards Ty.

Victor watched closely not saying a word. She didn't need the alcohol. Warriors couldn't get an infection but since it wouldn't hurt Ty he didn't mention it. She obviously knew what she was doing but once she cut into him, she was going to get a shock. If she was experienced like she claimed, she'd immediately realize Ty had already started to heal. Victor didn't know what to expect. He just hoped her reaction wouldn't be anything like Samantha's. Really, the woman should have known better. How many times had they all been out and about during the daytime? And would they really have been battling those vamps in the alleyway if they were vampires themselves. Clearly something else was going on to cause such an emotional outburst. He watched Kylee as she cut into Ty and went to work on repairing his lung.

* * * *

Samantha bolted to her room and slammed the door, locking it behind her. She was horrified. What had she done? She felt nauseous and immediately lunged for the bathroom. She barely made it before her coffee came up. Moments later she laid sprawled on the bathroom floor, her head resting on the cold tile. She had sex with a vampire! No. She'd made love to a vampire, she corrected herself. Somehow, she'd fallen hopelessly in love with a vampire! The realization made her sick again. This time she didn't have anything left to come up so she dry heaved. What was she going to do? She couldn't stay here. Now that she knew what they all were, she couldn't continue to help them. Another thought hit her like a punch to the gut. Her job. Her life was over, destroyed. Everything she'd worked so hard for was gone in an instant.

If Ty, Ariel and Victor were vampires, Alex and Thomas must be vampires too. Had Luke been one? She began to question everything now. A quick image of Luke's battered body lying near a cabin bleeding shot through her mind. Had Luke been one of the good guys? But that would mean all the injured men standing over him were trying to kill him, not trying to save him. Thomas wasn't there, but did he know? Would a vampire be that greedy and callous to kill his own father? Thomas and Alex had inherited an empire. Samantha closed her eyes in agony. What was she going to do now? She couldn't continue to work for D-Tech if the owners were evil monsters.

But that didn't make sense to her. It didn't feel right. She'd seen Luke and Thomas together. She'd envied the bond and the love they shared. She often wondered if her parents had lived if they would have been that close and shared that kind of bond. No, Thomas hadn't killed his father. So did they know about their friends? Was Thomas and Alex victims in all of this? No, Alex knew. She'd been there on the roof as Ariel shot fire from her fingertips. Alex and Ariel had stopped her from killing Lilith that night at the ballroom. Alex was clearly involved in this but was Thomas? Samantha pulled herself up, rinsed her mouth and climbed into bed. Ty was a monster. Just the thought of it ripped at her heart. How had she not seen it? Why hadn't he killed her? They'd been alone in this house for days. He could have snuck into her bedroom at any time and drained her body. They were obviously up to something, she just couldn't fathom what it could be. She let the tears overcome her. Her world had been shattered and once again, she was all alone.

* * * *

Ty woke with a start and then realized he was in his own bedroom. He had no idea how he'd gotten here or what had happened to the rest of the vampires. He began to climb out of bed and got hung up on the IV. Ty carefully unhooked the line and headed for the door. Once outside his room, he heard voices downstairs. He felt much better, but was still a little weak. Just to be safe, he gripped the hand rail as he descended the staircase. He stepped into the study and paused. Ariel and Victor were here. When had they arrived? And there were two strangers with them.

Ariel looked up and spotted Ty. "Look who has joined the living?" she teased. All eyes turned to the doorway.

He slowly walked to an empty chair and sat down. "Aren't you the woman from the forest?" he asked a little surprised.

"Yes," Kylee affirmed. "How are you feeling?" she was always a doctor first.

"I'm fine," he told her. "But I'm a little confused. The last thing I remember is you attacking the va...uh...that guy with a tree branch. He threw you to the ground but I couldn't get to you, the other two were on me too fast." He looked in Dusty's direction. "Who are you?" he asked.

"Let me explain," Kylee requested. "I saw you get attacked by what I believed were four men. They ambushed you. They hit you in the head so hard, I was sure they'd knock you out. Somehow you stumbled, but remained conscious. When they came at you again I knew I had to help. I immediately started looking around for something I could use to fight them off. I found a large tree branch and headed your way. I realized there were only three attackers now. I briefly wondered what happened to the fourth, but brushed that aside because you were still outnumbered and needed assistance. That's when I charged in, swinging the branch with everything I had. I thought I got a good hit in on one of them, but he turned and effortlessly threw me across the clearing. Then he was on me, I knew I was going to die. He began to lower his mouth and his sharp teeth seemed to gleam in the moonlight. That's when I knew, these weren't men. They were vampires."

Ty watched this human explain the situation so calmly. Maybe he'd misjudged the species. He was beginning to think they were stronger than he'd given them credit for.

"That's when Dusty charged in from the other direction," Kylee continued. "I was grateful for the help, but then I realized he was just a kid."

"Hey!" Dusty objected. "I'm seventeen and this kid saved your bacon."

Kylee smiled. Teenagers were so predictably arrogant. Once they hit sixteen, they wanted to think they were adults. "You did," she admitted. "Dusty began running towards me and I hoped for a miracle. That's when he turned into a tiger. I wasn't sure if he was going to help me or eat me."

Ty's eyes shot back to Dusty. He hadn't noticed the kid was a shifter. What was he thinking shifting in front of a human, and into a tiger? Someone needed to have a chat with that boy.

Victor was watching Ty's expressions. "We've already discussed the hazards of shifting before he had a clear understanding of the situation. I've also suggested he picks another form in the future. Something indigenous to the area."

"Good," Ty mumbled.

"Anyway," Kylee continued. "So this tiger comes flying towards us and attacks the vampire. Well, the whole thing was a little shocking. He ripped its head off. Instead of blood, the vampire turned to dust. I was trying to take it all in when I realized the other two vampires were still attacking you." She looked at Ty. "I knew you were injured severely and was just about to crawl your way when a ball of fire flew through the forest. The first one hit a tree, but the second one struck one of the remaining vampires. Victor then stormed the area and killed the last vampire with a dagger I think. That's when we all returned to the house and took care of you," she concluded.

"Where's Sam?" Ty asked.

"She left about an hour ago," Ariel told him. The discomfort that had settled in the room was almost visible.

"I see," Ty sighed. "Should I assume she didn't take the news well when she found out what we are?"

"Well," Ariel began. "She didn't take it well, but she doesn't exactly know what we are either."

"What does that mean?" Ty asked.

Victor explained what had happened to Ty. "She's pretty upset and she's convinced we're all vampires. We thought it would be best to give her some time. I wouldn't go near her in your condition. She promised to kill us if we got too close."

Ty closed his eyes. So, he'd been right. Sam thought he was a monster. He'd known he'd only have that one night with her, but the reality of it was tearing him apart. His stomach clenched and he felt ill.

"You don't look so good," Kylee observed. "I think we should get you back to bed."

"I'm fine," Ty argued.

"Look, Victor explained the healing. I know all about you guys now," she began.

"Don't you think that was a little reckless?" Ty asked. "How many humans are we going to include in this?"

"She operated on you," Ariel cut in. "She saw the healing to your lung while she worked. We had to explain. It was better for her to know than to let her speculate like Samantha is."

"So now what?" he asked Victor. "We can't just set her lose and hope she keeps the secret."

"Kylee has agreed to remain here for a few days. She's not going to be missed for several weeks. That will give Alex and Dimitri time to come down and decide how to handle this."

"There's nothing to handle," Kylee insisted. "I already told you, your secret's safe with me."

"What about the kid?" Ty asked. "Why is he here?"

"Your people talked to my pack about the academy. I couldn't wait to check it out. I was hoping I could join you now. I'm a good worker and I thought I could help set things up. It looks like you could use another set of hands out there," he observed.

"That's up to Alex and Dimitri too," Victor told him. "Once they get here we'll figure this all out. In the meantime, you've been living with Sam. Is she going to do something rash or can we give her space and let her figure things out?"

"She loves her job. I think she'll struggle with what she thinks she knows, but she won't want to rush off until she's sure about Alex and Thomas." Ty considered the situation. "I'm going to leave in the morning. I've been planning a trip to New York anyway. I need to finalize the paperwork so we can release the game. With me gone, Sam might stick it out here, especially if you tell her Alex and Dimitri are coming." He turned his attention to Kylee. "It would probably be best coming from you. Right now, you're the only one here that's not the enemy."

"I don't think traveling in your condition is advisable," Kylee argued.

Ty smiled. "My condition will be vastly improved in the morning," he stood. "Now, if you'll excuse me, I need to pack and I want to get plenty of rest tonight. I still feel a little off. My injuries must have been pretty severe this time."

"They were," Victor confirmed. He silently watched Ty leave the room. He was worried about him. There was something going on here that Ty wasn't sharing. How close had Sam and Ty become? Victor hoped he was wrong, but he was beginning to think there was more to the relationship than work.

Chapter Seven

Samantha woke late the following morning. It was after ten. She hadn't slept in that late since she was a teenager. She slowly climbed out of bed and headed for the shower. She was sure she looked awful. Last night had been rough. She couldn't stop thinking about Ty. He had been so gentle and loving that night they were together. Spending an entire day at the plant yesterday had helped her calm down. The more she thought about the situation, the more convinced she'd been that Ty and the others couldn't be vampires. She'd been hunting them for years. She knew their habits, but more importantly she knew their limitations. Going outside during the day was one of them. Ty had worked from sun up to sun down almost every day from the beginning. If he was a vampire, he couldn't have done that. So what was he?

Nothing made sense to her now. Victor and Ariel killed countless vampires that night in the alley. They wouldn't have done that if they were vampires themselves. Alex had risked her own life to save Sam's. Sam had tried to convince herself that Alex was protecting Lilith. That she was intervening to make sure Sam didn't kill her, but she knew better. In her heart she knew Alex was trying to kill Lilith that night. She'd been wrong about them all. She'd been unfair to Ariel. A twinge of pain twisted her stomach at the loss of her new friend. Sam had seen the look on Ariel's face when she accused her of being a vampire. Clearly Ariel hated those monsters as much as she did. What had Ariel told her? "You can call me a monster if you want but never call me a vampire?" Ariel had shown such disdain for the creatures there was no way she was one of them. Sam doubted Ariel would ever forgive her for being so rash and cruel. She'd actually threatened to kill them all. How could any of them forgive that? Did she want them to? She still had no idea what they were and why Ty was drinking blood. If he wasn't a vampire, what was he?

Samantha climbed out of the shower and wrapped herself in a towel. She had decided one thing last night; she wasn't leaving. Not yet. She wouldn't walk away from her job and her friends until she knew the truth. She doubted any of them would trust her with it now, but she needed to try. She dressed quickly and headed for the kitchen. She was starving. She'd been too upset to eat yesterday. Her stomach growled as she walked through the door. She hesitated when she saw the doctor. Why was Kylee still here? Why was she here in the first place?

"Good morning," Kylee said cheerfully. "Did you sleep well?"

"Morning," Sam said hesitantly. "I slept fine. You never did explain why you are here," she said cutting straight to the chase.

Kylee sighed. "Initially I wanted to protect you," she admitted.

"What?" Sam asked surprised. "From what?"

Dawn

Kylee looked at her impatiently. "You know I was worried about you. I didn't believe you were having accidents. That last time you visited the ER I decided to take an extended vacation and keep tabs on you. I wanted to find out who was beating you. I was so sure it was a domestic violence situation. Boy was I wrong," Kylee grinned. "I had no idea I'd be entering the Twilight Zone."

"You can't tell anyone!" Sam blurted. "You can't expose this. It's got to be kept a secret." She was a little panicked. She didn't know this woman well enough to trust her and it was her fault the secret was now exposed.

"I thought you believed they were monsters. Why are you so protective of them?" she asked casually.

"I'm not," Sam said defiantly. Why was she protecting them? Because she wasn't so sure they were bad anymore.

"If I went around telling people there are vampires and warriors among us, nobody would believe me anyway. I'm not going to expose them. I'm fascinated by them. They think they're forcing me to stay here until they can decide what to do about me. They have no idea it's what I want. If they try to make me leave, I'll fight them on it."

"They won't let you leave?" Sam asked, a little annoyed. They couldn't just hold people hostage forever.

"For now. They said someone named Alex and Dimitri would be arriving on Friday. They need me to stay here until then. My fate will be decided this weekend," Kylee said casually.

"You don't seem too upset about that," Sam observed. "Aren't you angry about your loss of freedom?"

"No," Kylee answered. "I told you, I want to stay. These people fascinate me. I would never expose them, but they don't know me well enough to trust that."

"They're not people," Sam countered.

"No. They're not," Kylee studied Sam. "But they are the good guys. What they do is dangerous. If I can convince them I'm on their side, maybe they'll let me assist them. I was able to help Ty with his injuries. I could be a valuable addition to their cause," Kylee stood. "I need to head over to the cottage and collect my things. If I don't show up, the staff might get suspicious. I'll catch you later Sam," Kylee finished cheerfully then left the room.

Sam sat there stunned. This doctor had worked on Ty. His injuries must have been severe for Victor and Ariel to allow that. Was he okay? She shouldn't care. He hadn't been honest with her, but she did care. No matter how hard she tried to fight it, she couldn't stop loving him. What a mess. How had things gone from being so perfect to this? She still didn't understand. What was Ty? The possibilities were endless. Clearly the rest of the men in those photos were the same thing. Luke probably was, too. As well as Thomas. Kylee said they were the good guys. Was that true? She wanted to believe it, but she was afraid to hope. Then it struck her, what had Kylee called them? Warriors and vampires. What was a warrior? She couldn't face Ty just yet, so she'd try to track down Victor. She considered Ariel for about half a second, but ruled that out immediately. She needed time and a few answers before she could face Ariel.

Samantha found Victor and Ariel in the old apartment building. She hesitantly entered the room and took a deep breath. "Victor?" she called softly.

Dawn

Ariel and Victor spun around together and studied Sam. She looked tired and weary, but otherwise okay. Ariel was scowling. Was Sam here to kill them? She positioned herself for defense just in case. If Sam thought Victor was the weaker target because Ariel could throw fire, she was mistaken.

Samantha watched Ariel. She was clearly preparing for battle. "I'm not here to fight you. I come in peace," she smiled hoping to lighten the mood. It didn't work so she continued. "Look Victor, I have some questions and wondered if you'd be willing to talk to me," she said. No reason to beat around the bush. It was pretty clear where she stood with Ariel. That friendship was over. Sam's stomach clenched. She didn't have many friends and it hurt to lose one of the few she had begun to develop. She deserved it, but it still made her sad. She really liked Ariel.

Victor watched Samantha. Ariel obviously thought she was here to harm them. Victor wasn't getting that vibe. "We're almost finished here. Why don't I meet you in the study in about an hour? We can talk then," he offered.

"Thank you," Samantha answered sincerely. She glanced once more at Ariel and hoped this wouldn't cause any problems in their relationship. Ariel didn't trust Sam but Victor was giving her a chance. She turned and hurried out the door. She had an hour to waste. Maybe she'd take a walk. Try as she might, she couldn't get Ty out of her mind. Where was he? Probably still in bed. He might be down for days. That's good, Sam told herself. He needed the rest and she needed the space. She wasn't sure she could handle an encounter with him right now. She was still so confused.

An hour later Samantha sat in the study waiting for Victor. She was nervous. Where was he? She wondered if Ariel was going to join them. She knew Ariel didn't trust her anymore, so probably.

That would make this more difficult, but she was determined to get through it. The front door opened and Victor and Ariel strolled into the study.

"Sorry we're late. I found another problem that was pressing. It took longer than I anticipated," Victor said casually as he settled into a recliner. Ariel took the seat next to him but didn't say a word.

"I haven't been here long myself," Samantha lied. She'd started to walk the fort, but everywhere she went reminded her of Ty. Finally she'd just returned to the house to wait for Victor alone. The realization hit her again. She was all alone. It was almost more than she could bear.

"So, what did you want to talk about?" Victor asked getting right to the point.

"I was wondering if you could tell me what a warrior is," she asked. If he was going to be direct, so would she.

Victor's eyebrows raised. "I thought you believed we were vampires," he reminded her. "Where did you hear the term warrior?"

"Kylee said something about it this morning. She said the warriors are the good guys. I'd like to know what a warrior is so I can decide for myself if they are good or bad," Sam admitted.

Victor studied Samantha. He wasn't sure how much he should tell her. Could they trust her? Humans wouldn't believe the story, but just mentioning it could be a problem. If the right person became suspicious their whole world would be turned upside down.

"I only want to know for myself," Samantha assured him, reading the distrust in his eyes. "I've kept the secret about vampires for twenty three years and I despise those creatures. What would be the point in exposing your people?" she asked.

That was true. He looked to Ariel for guidance. "Go ahead and explain it," Ariel told him. "She already knows were monsters," Ariel paused for effect. "She might as well know the rest."

Sam closed her eyes. Things were worse than she'd originally thought between them. Why had her outburst upset Ariel so much? Sure, she'd been insulting and out of line, but she didn't understand why Ariel was still angry. "I give you my word. I'm not going to tell anyone anything. Who would I tell? I don't have any family. I don't have any friends. My entire life is my work and vampire hunting." Why had she just admitted to them she was alone? She never admitted that to anyone. She rarely admitted it to herself.

Victor took a deep breath and began to explain the history of the warriors. He had to explain about the fae as well. He really hoped he was doing the right thing. They were trusting this human with a lot of information.

Samantha sat back. "So," she looked at Ariel. "I assume you are fae."

"I am," Ariel said shortly. "But don't think that makes me any less lethal than the warriors," she added.

"And you are a warrior?" she asked Victor.

"I am," he agreed. He was still watching her for some reaction.

Samantha didn't know what to think. She no longer thought of Ariel as a monster. She was one of the good guys. But what about the warriors. They were part vampire. They had to drink blood to heal themselves. Did that make them monsters, having that genetic makeup? Samantha filled the silence with another question. "Other than drinking blood, do you have any other vampire qualities?" She tried to sound casual about it, but the answer was essential.

Victor studied her. She still thought they were monsters. He could tell she was uncomfortable with his explanation. "Not really. And we don't typically drink blood," he added.

"I saw you," she reminded him. "If we're going to talk about this, at least be honest."

Ariel was angry. Sam was treating Victor like he was some kind of rabid animal or something. "We forced Ty to drink blood because his injuries were so severe. Haven't you ever gagged down some kind of human medicine because it was essential for your recovery?" Ariel demanded. "I can't do this any longer." She turned to Victor, "I can't sit in a room with someone this callous and self-righteous." She turned back to Sam, "you haven't even asked if Ty is okay. You've spent all this time with him, working with him, getting to know him and you don't even care if he survived. We might be monsters, but I'd rather be a monster that can love and care about others than whatever you are Sam. You're pathetic." She stomped out of the room and never looked back.

Sam's insides clenched. She hadn't asked about Ty. She'd just assumed he was okay. What if he wasn't? What if he was gone forever? She'd been so angry, she hadn't even said goodbye. She looked up at Victor, tears were forming in her eyes but she quickly blinked them back. "Is he..." she paused. "Is Ty okay?" she asked not sure she wanted to hear the answer. Was he in his room recovering or was he dead too? Gone forever?

"Ty is fine," Victor assured her.

Dawn

Sam stood, she couldn't take his word for it. She had to go see for herself. No matter what he was, she didn't want him to be dead.

"Where are you going?" Victor asked.

"I need to see for myself that he's okay," she answered truthfully.

"He left," Victor announced. "You're not going to find him up there."

"What?" Samantha spun around to face him. "When? How? Where did he go? I thought he was seriously injured. Why would he travel so soon after that?"

"He left a couple hours ago. I'd guess the plane's taking off right about now. How? He flew. He went back to New York. He had some business to take care of and once he understood the situation with you, he thought it would be best if he wasn't around for a while. He's giving you space to deal with your discovery."

Ty was gone. Her heart sank. What if he never came back? What if she never saw him again? She didn't know how she felt about the things she'd just learned, but the thought of never seeing Ty again shattered her heart to pieces. She settled back into her chair, speechless.

"Why do you care?" Victor asked truly curious. He was watching the emotions run across her face. "If you think we are all monsters why do you care if Ty left. I would think you'd be relieved. One less warrior you have to watch out for. One less person around that you despise. One less monster to avoid."

Sam couldn't help feeling guilty. He was right, she still considered them monsters. She wasn't comfortable around him. She wouldn't be comfortable with Ty. Why was she so upset? "I'm sorry if that offends you, but you are part vampire," Sam pointed out the obvious. "How can I trust something that has that kind of evil inside?" she asked. "How do I know what your limitations are? What would you do to get blood if you needed it? Would you kill? Would you attack an innocent human to satisfy your own need? If so, what makes you any different than they are?" she accused.

Now Victor was angry. He needed to calm down and make a civil exit. He understood Ariel's anger. They had let Samantha into their circle. They had accepted her as one of their own and this was how she repaid them? With insults and accusations? With mistrust and disgust? "If you don't know the answer to that by now, I can't explain it to you," he said softly. "Now if you'll excuse me, I need to go check on Ariel." He stood and strolled out of the room.

* * * *

Ty entered the hanger hesitantly. Frank had been busy and couldn't make the trip today himself so Ty had arranged for another pilot to charter him to New York. He was mapping out a schedule when he saw the girl. She was clearly upset about something. A guy that looked like the mechanic was trying to console her. Ty stepped into the small turbo prop. He wouldn't be flying in luxury today. The Beech Craft King was old. It was obvious someone had taken good care of it, but Ty was still apprehensive about his flight. He glanced out the window and saw the woman headed his way. No way. If that was his pilot, he'd find another outfit to fly with. He was not putting his life in the hands of some emotional, possibly suicidal human!

Dawn

Ty exited the plane just as the woman reached it. "Where are you going?" she demanded. "We have a schedule we need to keep. I've already cleared us for take-off."

Ty studied her. Clearly she was distraught about something. "Are you the pilot?" he queried.

"I am," she said confidently.

"Then I'm not going," he informed her.

"What? Why not?" she demanded. "We have a strict cancellation policy. You can't back out now. You'll still owe us the price of the trip."

Ty pulled out his wallet. "Fine," he handed her a credit card. "Settle my bill on that. I'm finding another pilot."

The woman narrowed her eyes at him. "What's wrong with me?"

"That's just the problem lady. I don't know. I'm not putting my life in the hands of an emotionally distraught woman."

Lillie laughed. "What? You think I'm going to fly us into the side of a mountain or something?"

"Maybe," Ty confessed.

"Not a chance. I love this plane. I'd never do anything to harm it on purpose," Lillie sighed. "Look, this is my last flight. My cold hearted, cheating soon to be ex-husband has informed me he's filed a claim for my plane with the court. I could fight him for it, but I'd lose and to be honest, I can't afford the court costs. So, the plane I love more than anything in this world is going to be turned over to a man that will fly it into the ground in less than a year.

You'll just have to forgive me for being a little upset about that. I've devoted the last five years of my life to taking care of my baby and because that low life decided he wants to run off with some bimbo I lose everything." She inhaled in an effort to calm down. "But that doesn't mean I'm suicidal or that I would deliberately crash the plane. It's just hard to let something I love go so easily. If I thought I could win I'd fight, even though I can't afford it, but I can't. The business belongs to my ex. So, I'm giving in. I guess I feel a little guilty about that and it hurts to lose something I've devoted my life to loving. The plane not the man," she paused. "Let's try this again. Hi, I'm Lillie. I'll be your pilot today. If there is anything I can do to make your flight more enjoyable don't hesitate to ask."

Ty smiled. He felt for this woman. What was with him, two human women had touched his heart, in different ways of course, in a matter of weeks. "Well, I think I'd enjoy my flight more if my pilot's tears didn't flood the cockpit during our trip."

"No more tears," Lillie promised. "I swear."

"Once you finish this flight, what's next for you?" he asked. An idea had hit him. He didn't know why, but he liked this woman. She had grit. She wouldn't crash the plane. She'd see that as weak. No, she'd make her flight and return to this awful hanger to let go of the one possession that meant the world to her.

"I don't know. I used to fly for a large conglomerate stationed in New York. I thought I'd check them out. See if they need a good pilot. Jets are fun, I could get into that again. They don't have the character of a prop but you can't beat the luxury. I'll manage somehow," she assured him. "Now, you ready for takeoff? The tower's going to wonder where we are."

"My life is in your hands Miss Lillie." Ty smiled at her and climbed back into the plane. He was going to pay close attention to her flying. If she was decent, he'd offer her a job once they reached New York. He needed to replace Frank and they could use a pilot familiar with the area to shuttle the warriors back and forth between New York and Seneca. Ty was usually a good judge of character and he was sure this woman would be discrete. She might be curious, but she wouldn't ask too many questions and Ty thought eventually she might even be loyal. He relaxed a little and tried to enjoy the trip.

They flew into Dutchess County Airport a few hours later. Lillie's style was smooth and Ty thought she had potential. Now he just needed to convince her to accept the job. He gathered up his bag and headed for the door.

Lillie greeted him with a friendly smile. "I hope you had a pleasant flight Mr. Brody. And I apologize for any discomfort my previous outburst caused you. Unfortunately, I must recommend you find a different airline for future needs as my ex-husband is sloppy and reckless and not the type of person I can recommend to a gentleman such as yourself." She grinned wider and turned to leave.

"Lillie," Ty called after her. "I was wondering if you had a moment."

Lillie was surprised. She'd been such a shmuck. First she broke down in front of a client, then she dumped her dirty laundry at his feet. It was a miracle he agreed to fly with her today. She was grateful to him for that. She was broke. She needed this fare to start her search for an apartment. She had a little money hidden away to get her by until she found a new job but not enough if she had to use it for rent. "Yes," she said casually, "of course."

"Stop acting so formal," he growled. "I think we surpassed that once you shared the details of your personal crisis with me."

158

Lillie was even more embarrassed. What had she been thinking? Was this man going to proposition her? She didn't care if she was broke. She would not be used by some rich playboy who thought she was desperate. "Well, I'm sorry about that. I never should have spilled my personal problems that way."

Ty brushed that aside. "I'm looking for a pilot," he decided to be direct. He sensed he was making her uncomfortable. "You said you used to fly for some corporation. I assume that means you have experience flying jets?"

Was this man really offering her a job? Could she really be this lucky? "Why?" she asked.

"Why what?" Ty said confused.

"Why are you asking about my experience?" she pressed.

"I told you, I'm looking for a pilot. I don't own any props though. I only have jets. I'm specifically looking for someone to fly my Bombardier LearJet. Before we discuss it, I need to know if you've flown jets before," he said casually.

"Yes, but why would you hire me? You don't even know me," Lillie questioned.

"I like you," he laughed at the frown that immediately covered her face. "Not that way," he assured her. "I think you have spunk. And you obviously care about your plane. I'm hoping if you accept, you'll take just as much care with mine. I need a good pilot that is responsible and loyal. I think you could be both," he admitted.

Lillie studied him. "When would I start?" she quizzed. Could this really be happening? He seemed like a nice guy and she thought she would enjoy working for him, but had she really fallen into such a great arrangement so quickly? Wait, he hadn't discussed salary. Maybe he thought she was desperate and he'd get her for cheap.

"First you'd have to go through a training course. You said you'd been flying this prop for five years. A lot has changed in that time. Once you pass the course, you would need to spend some time with Frank."

"Who's Frank?" Lillie asked. So far, she wasn't happy about the training course. That could be a deal breaker. She could barely afford an apartment. She didn't have the funds to pay for training she didn't feel she needed.

"Frank is my current pilot. He's getting ready to retire. He's been with me a long time and knows how I like things," Ty explained.

"Is he going to show me how you like things or tell me how to fly?" she challenged.

"Oh, he might try to do both knowing Frank. He has his own way of doing things. I don't expect you to change yours," he assured her. "If you're game, I'll meet you at the office tomorrow and we'll negotiate a salary. Once you sign the contract your salary will start immediately. I want my trainees to have the ability to focus completely on their courses. That means no part time jobs while you're there. There is one more stipulation," he said hesitantly. This one sometimes threw a wrench into things.

"What's that?" she asked wearily.

"I have an apartment complex. It's strictly for my employees that are in training. All new employees live at the complex while they train. No exceptions, it's included in the package. Once you pass the course, you can move anywhere you like." Even though this was a sticking point in every negotiation, once the employee moved in and saw all the amenities, they were happy he'd forced them to live there.

"Why?" she asked.

"Is that the only word you know?" Ty questioned rolling his eyes in exasperation. "Lots of reasons. First, New York is expensive. I told you, I want my employees to devote all their time to their studies. It's important to me that I have the best. If you have to rent your own apartment people tend to look for work, that's not acceptable to me. Also, I've found that living around others who are in the same boat as you, so to speak, gives most people the social interaction they need. If you go out bar hopping all night, you're not going to be alert in the morning. However, if you spend the night with others who know they have to not only pass the course, but pass it with flying colors, people tend to be more responsible. I realize there are a few exceptions that would be responsible anyway, but this is my buffer. If you want to work for me, you have to spend a month or so living in my apartment complex refreshing your knowledge on LearJet's." Ty hoped she'd accept but the ball was in her court now.

Lillie considered. Living in his apartment wasn't a drawback. It would save her from making a hasty decision before she was homeless. She still didn't like having to take a refresher course, but she could live with it. "I'm not making any promises, but give me the address and I'll be in your office tomorrow morning."

"Good," Ty gave her his card. "Be there at nine. I have a few things to take care of first thing."

"Deal," Lillie agreed.

Dawn

Ty strolled towards the familiar pickup truck waiting at the end of the lot. He couldn't wait to get to his ranch. He'd missed it and his dogs. He was seriously thinking about taking the two rascals with him when he returned to the fort. They'd be good company and the barn was secure enough to house them overnight. If he was alone, he'd let them inside the house but he wasn't going to force them on the other guests. Bo and Ace could be a handful and he wasn't going to push their exuberance onto others. He slid into the passenger seat and relaxed. "Everything going okay at home?" he asked Pete, his lead ranch hand.

"Fine," Pete grunted. Ty liked that about Pete. A man of few words. They rode in silence all the way to the ranch. Ty's mind drifted to Samantha. He hadn't wanted to get involved with her in the first place. How had this happened? She was human. The pain he felt at the loss was surprising. He couldn't imagine what it would be like to spend fifty or sixty years with someone and then lose them. Ty thought it would be unbearable. No, this was better. He'd enjoyed one night with her, now he had to let her go. It wasn't like he had a choice in the matter anyway. Samantha thought he was some kind of monster. He'd be lucky if she even talked to him once he returned. The simulator was almost finished. There was really no reason for them to spend time together anymore. When he got back he'd just focus on the fort and his dogs. He'd need his dogs there with him. The guys here at the ranch would miss them, but they'd get along. It was Ty's turn. He smiled and pulled the cowboy hat hanging on the window hook over his eyes. He was tired, maybe he'd doze awhile.

* * * *

Victor was beginning to worry. His father had been visiting New York regularly for the last several weeks. Now, all of a sudden he had excuses. This was the third week in a row his father begged off. Something was wrong, Victor knew it. He just didn't know what to do about it. Being sent out here to work at the fort had taken him even further away from the problem. Who could he ask to go out and check on his father? He was sure Jake would do it, but he didn't want to impose so soon after his wedding. Jake needed time alone with Marta. Then it hit him, Ty. He'd ask Ty to fly out before returning to the fort. Ty wouldn't mind. He didn't seem all that anxious to get back anyway. Victor thought Ty was escaping something, he just didn't know what. He rushed into the house and dialed Ty's cell.

Ty hung up the phone and looked out the window of the large high rise. He knew this office was essential, he'd just rather be at the farm right now. He'd rather be lazily riding his horse across his property enjoying the scenery and the peace and quiet of the outdoors. He'd rather be riding fences and doing repairs. He loved developing games, but he hated all the rest. He checked his watch. Lillie should be here any minute. Hopefully, she'd be available for the unexpected addition to their itinerary he just agreed to. Victor was really worried about his father. Ty happily agreed to swing by and make sure everything was okay. He just hoped Lillie would be game. The phone buzzed and his receptionist's voice came over the speaker. "A Miss Lillie Shepherd to see you, sir."

"Send her in," Ty said. "Thank you, Selena. Why don't you take a free day today? I'm sure there's nothing pressing that can't wait until tomorrow. We've all been working a little too hard on the new project lately. You deserve a fun day."

"Oh…I'm fine," Selena insisted. "I'll stick around in case you need something."

"I'm leaving as soon as my meeting is over. Go ahead and go. I'll be fine," Ty insisted.

"Oh alright," she agreed. "I have been wanting to get out to that new shopping mall. They're supposed to have great deals on shoes."

Ty laughed. Women and shoes. He didn't get it.

The door opened and Lillie glided in. "That was nice of you," she told him. "She was so excited about her shopping spree. Do you treat all your employees that well?" she quizzed. She was still a little apprehensive about accepting this job. The deciding factor was going to be her salary.

"I try," he said, amused.

"Nice digs if you like this sort of thing," she commented absently.

"You don't?" he asked. Good, she wouldn't be demanding some fancy office anytime soon.

"Naw," she turned to him. "I'm more down to earth than this. Give me a little hole in the hanger and a coffee pot and I'm in heaven."

"I tend to agree with that," Ty admitted.

"Then why the fancy digs?" she asked.

"Image," Ty said soberly. "If I'm going to sell myself as the best electronics company around, I have to look the part."

"Yeah, I noticed. Tyson Electronics. I never would have pegged you for the stuffy corporate type. I guess you never know," she stated casually.

"Actually, I'm the love to design games type. The rest is a necessary evil." Ty's opinion of Lillie was improving with every minute.

"Can't you hire someone to do this for you?" she asked.

"I could, but I haven't found anyone yet that is capable of having this much power over the company and not letting it go to their head. Egos tend to grow once you reach this level. So far, there's no one I can trust to do things my way." Ty motioned for her to sit. "Anyway, I have this contract for you to look over. Once you read it we'll talk about any clauses you disagree with. Fair?"

Lillie took the contract and began to read. Her head shot up. Was he really willing to pay her that much? She'd be making more than the top guy at her last corporate job. She carefully read the entire contract, then skimmed it again for a trap. There had to be a catch. Her apartment was free while she lived there and the company was going to pay for her training.

Ty sat back in his chair, watching Lillie. She was obviously surprised when she saw the salary. He'd done that on purpose. He wanted her and it was only money. No big deal to him but if she couldn't afford to fight for her plane, she must be struggling. He wanted her to live comfortably. He enjoyed taking care of his employees. He continued to watch as she became skeptical and carefully read the contract thoroughly. Good. He'd guessed that about her, but it was nice to be sure. She wasn't easily fooled and she paid attention to detail. This might be a perfect arrangement after all.

"So what's the catch?" she finally asked.

"No catch," he assured her. "Everything is right there in the contract," he paused. "Do we need to negotiate any of the terms?"

"Is this charity?" she finally asked. She hadn't planned on being so direct, but she wasn't going to accept a job because some rich guy felt sorry for her.

"Nope. I expect you to work hard and earn every penny," Ty assured her. "You need to understand something, Lillie." He waited for her to look at him. "I'm hiring a pilot for my company, but I intend to use you on other more personal business as well. Some acquaintances and I will need to fly to Romulus pretty regularly. I need someone familiar with the area, which you are, but I also need someone willing to drop everything and head out at a moment's notice. The job is going to be demanding. Your salary is more than most because of the sacrifices you will be expected to make. If you're not up to it, I understand. Just let me know now. I'll continue searching for the right pilot for the job."

Lillie studied him. She trusted him for some reason. She was surprised at that. She didn't trust easily. The one time she'd convinced herself to believe in a man had been a disaster. "Okay," she finally said. "I'm in. As you know, I don't have a life anyway. When does training start?"

Ty went over the details with her and handed her the key to her apartment. He also handed her what looked like a business card. One side had an address engraved in gold, the other side a five digit code. "That's the address to the apartment and the number on the back is your assigned alarm code. Don't lose it. I run a successful business, but it's competitive. You may be approached by more than one person trying to get you to spy for them. You need to be aware of that. I've also had people talk unsuspecting students into giving them access to the building. Don't let anyone in, not even if they claim to live there. If they belong, they'll have their own code. Any questions?"

"Not right now," Lillie admitted. "What if I have some later?"

"Do you still have the business card I gave you yesterday?" he asked.

"I do," she assured him.

"My numbers on that card. Call me anytime, but I won't give you the answers to a quiz," he teased.

"So, will I be working directly for you?" she asked hesitantly.

"Yes. Once you pass the course and get started with Frank you will only answer to me," Ty assured her. "Now, I have a favor to ask."

Lillie narrowed her eyes. Was this the catch she'd been waiting for?

"You're so cynical," he laughed. "I need to check on a friend before we go back to Romulus. It's a little out of the way. Will there be a problem changing the flight schedule?"

"Uh..." Lillie paused. "How much out of the way are we talking?" she was worried. The court order said she had to turn the plane over by noon tomorrow. An extra stop might make her late and she knew her sleazy ex wouldn't play nice.

Dawn

"I need to go to Pennsylvania," Ty told her. "It's extremely important. I'm sensing there may be a problem. Does this have to do with your ex?" he guessed.

"Well, to be honest it does. You see I have this court order to turn over the plane. If I don't have it secured in the hanger by noon tomorrow I'm in trouble," she hated this. Why couldn't Brad be more understanding? He was the one that left. Why was he making this all so contentious?

"I assume your ex won't understand if you're a little late?" he asked.

"Not at all. He'll try to have me thrown in jail I'm sure," she confessed.

"What if I try? Do you think he'd be open to an extension if he knew it was an emergency?" Ty asked.

"No," she told him. "And he's such a cheat that he'll probably assume you're my new boyfriend or something. He'll think it's a con," she was thinking about her options. "Maybe..." she trailed off.

"What?" Ty asked hopefully.

"He might be willing if I agreed to a compromise," she thought out loud.

"What kind of compromise?" Ty didn't want her to give up anything else just to make a flight deviation.

"I'll tell him if he agrees to let me have the plane an extra day, I won't fight him for it in court," she suggested.

"I thought you weren't going to fight him anyway," he said confused.

"I'm not, but he doesn't know that," she confessed. "He'll think he won and I can take you to Pennsylvania to check on your friend. We all win. Of course it's gonna cost you extra for the added stop," she said sheepishly.

"I'll pay you double if you can swing it. I really need to get to Pennsylvania," Ty agreed.

Lillie called her ex and a heated conversation ensued. Finally, he agreed to give her an extra day but wanted something in writing immediately confirming she was going to drop the battle for title on the plane. "Just a minute," she told him turning to Ty. "I need to fax him something in writing promising I won't fight him over title. Can I do that from here?"

"Sure, I'll have my attorney write something up." Ty left before she could remark. She hadn't planned on something that official. She finalized the arrangements and got a number where she could send the agreement.

Ty returned with an official looking document in hand. "You just need to sign here then give me the number. I'll have it faxed over immediately," he explained.

Lillie read the wording then looked up at Ty. "You've covered us pretty well in this. He's not going to be happy about it, but he won't change his mind. He wants that plane. Not because he cares about it, but because I do. He's determined to cause me as much pain as he possibly can before we go our separate ways."

Dawn

They touched down at the Lancaster Airport early the next morning. Bo and Ace were used to flying so once they were off the ground, they settled in for a nap. Ty exited the plane and approached Lillie. "I hate to ask, but would you mind keeping the dogs?"

Lillie smiled. Ty's dogs were adorable. They were both so friendly and each of them had their own charming personality. "I'd love to," she told him. "Do they have leashes? I'd like to get them off the plane for a while."

"They're in the chair. Thanks, I owe you one," he said sincerely.

Lillie was surprised. Her new boss wasn't anything like the men she'd worked for six years ago. He was easy going and down to earth. You'd never guess he owned a multimillion dollar enterprise. He didn't even dress the part. He'd been in a suit yesterday, but today he was in jeans, cowboy boots and a t-shirt. It was something you'd expect to see on a Texas range, not from a rich New Yorker. She watched him walk toward the waiting rental truck and wondered why he wasn't married. Well, she assumed he wasn't. No ring. Some guys didn't wear wedding bands, but Lillie was sure if that guy was married, his wife would want everyone to know he was taken. She climbed back onto the plane to collect the dogs.

Ty pulled onto the gravel road that led to Atticus's farm. Something was wrong. He could feel it. He floored the truck. He needed to find Atticus quickly. Just as he came around the last bend, he heard it. A loud explosion near the back of the barn. Ty jumped from the truck and ran through the front door. He had to find

Atticus. He knew a bomb when he heard one. If Atticus was under attack, there could be more. The house was empty. He flew out the door towards the barn. The back side was on fire. Ty ran through the smoke calling for Atticus. Just as he reached the last stall, he saw him. He was lying on the ground face down, blood streaming from his head. "No!" He screamed.

Ty dropped to the ground and felt for a pulse. Relief washed over him as soon as he found it. Atticus was in bad shape, but he was alive. Ty gently picked him up and carried him to the truck. He needed to get those horses out of the barn before it came crashing down. He laid Atticus across the seat and ran to the burning structure.

Ty cautiously slid into the large building and approached the first stall. The horse was nervous but let Ty lead him to the outer corral. He rushed back, intending to free the next horse when he saw the man lying face down near an empty stall. Ty rushed forward and dropped to his knees. He turned the body over and knew instantly the man was dead. He felt for a pulse just in case, but there was nothing there. The man was definitely dead. He was a human and Ty didn't know him, but Atticus probably did. What had gone on here? A beam crashed to the ground, reminding Ty there was a raging fire and horses that needed his help. He'd come back for the body if there was time, but right now the living needed his attention.

He was escorting the last horse out of the barn when he saw it, another bomb. He secured the stallion in the corral and quickly returned to the barn to defuse the device. This one was made by the same person that had made all the others. This didn't make sense. Why would someone target Victor's father? He wasn't involved in the war. He rarely went to New York and he never fought against the vampires. Once the bomb was defused Ty rushed back to the truck. He was going to take Atticus back to Romulus, to Victor.

Dawn

The horses would have to go with him, too. He couldn't leave them here unprotected, they could be in danger.

He checked again for a pulse then pressed a towel against Atticus's head. If they could get the bleeding to stop Atticus would be okay. Ty swung around when he heard a second explosion at the rear of the house. How many more bombs were there, he wondered. He spotted a tractor a short distance away, it had a wire hanging from beneath the frame. Another device. Someone had been sloppy. Obviously the person that planted these bombs wasn't a farmer. Anyone familiar with farm equipment would know that wire was out of place as soon as they saw it. There's not a farmer around that wouldn't spot it immediately. Ty quickly defused that bomb and cautiously entered the house. He just hoped he could find any additional devices before they exploded. Each one was on a timer. They seemed to be going off in intervals so if they remained consistent, he had time.

Ty rushed to the main bedroom. That was the most likely place for another bomb. It took him a minute, but he found it. It was secured inside the night stand drawer. Pretty clever, Ty conceded, but not clever enough. He defused that bomb and returned to the truck. As long as there weren't any explosives near the corral, the horses should be fine. He glanced at the barn, it was completely engulfed now. There was no way he could get to the body, it would just have to wait for the firemen to find it. Ty did one last sweep then took off. He'd get Atticus to the plane and then head back to the ranch. He'd need to extend the lease on the truck and then he'd trailer the horses to Romulus. They had the barn and a large pasture there. The horses would be safe and so would Atticus. Once Lillie was in the air, he'd call Victor and break the news.

Lillie was surprised when she saw Ty speeding across the pavement. He looked angry. She called to the dogs and rushed back to the plane.

Ty jumped out of the truck and ran to the passenger side. He reached in and pulled out a man. Lillie gasp. He was covered in blood. "Ty," she exclaimed. "That man needs to go to the hospital."

"No," Ty corrected her. "This man needs to be flown to Romulus. I need you to get him there as fast as you can. Bo, Ace...truck," Ty ordered. The two dogs took off and leapt into the back of the truck.

"Ty," Lillie pressed. "Look at all that blood. He needs a doctor."

"Lillie, I don't have time to argue. You're just going to have to trust me on this. Get Atticus to Romulus. I'm calling his son. Victor will be at the airport when you arrive. Once he collects his father you can return the plane to your ex and begin your new life. I'll send Frank out to pick you up when you're ready to move. You need to hurry. Atticus does need medical attention, but Victor is the only one that can help him."

Ty turned and walked to the truck.

"What about you?" Lillie called out.

"I'm going back to the farm to gather up his horses. It's no longer safe there. I'll drive them to Romulus myself. Now go," he ordered and climbed behind the wheel. Within seconds he was speeding out of the airport.

Lillie hesitated only a second. Should she call the police and an ambulance? The man was losing a lot of blood. She sighed, ran her hand through her hair and made her decision. She was going to trust Ty. He was her boss now and if she couldn't trust him, how could she work for him. She'd just have to believe he knew what he was doing. Maybe this man's son was a doctor. She rushed to the cockpit and radioed the tower.

Hours later, Ty pulled into the ranch and surveyed the damage. The barn was a complete loss. It was a soggy mess now and police tape was surrounding the entire area. They had also sectioned off the small workers cabin nearby. Ty had been able to saved most of the house, but the door and window had been blown off the back. The police obviously weren't interested in the house anyway, just the barn and the cabin. Had that man been living there? Did they know the body they'd found didn't belong to Atticus yet? Would they be looking for him as a suspect? Ty hoped not, he'd need to get Dimitri on this right away. But first he was going to protect the rest of Atticus's belongings.

He looked around for something to board up the place and found a small pile of two by eights. That would have to do. He went to the shed and found a bucket of nails. Twenty minutes later he was loading the horses. He was glad Atticus had a trailer large enough for all of them. He'd called Victor once he got back to the farm. Atticus would be in his son's hands soon enough. He hadn't told him about the bomb's maker. He needed to talk to Dimitri about that first. He still couldn't understand why someone would bomb Atticus. It just didn't make sense. Ty took one last look around then jumped inside the cab of the truck. The horses were secure, the house was boarded up, he'd done all he could do for now. Bo and Ace were lounging on the hay Ty had loaded in the bed. They'd enjoy their journey. They both loved to ride in the back of a truck, any truck. It was like an adventure for them. Dogs were so easy to please.

He pulled onto the highway and called his father. The panic he'd felt when he found Atticus unconscious made him want to hear his dad's voice.

"What's wrong, son?" his father asked after only a couple seconds. He always could read Ty like an open book.

Ty proceeded to explain the situation. He was surprised at his father's anger. He knew all the old timers were protective of Atticus, but he hadn't expected this kind of reaction. "Did you secure his house?" Ken Brody finally asked. He was livid. Who had attacked Atticus? He had a pretty good idea. If Dannica's brothers had anything to do with this, they'd be answering to him.

"I boarded it up, but I'm worried about his stuff. I grabbed his photo albums and a few things I thought would be important to him, but I don't know him well enough to know what items inside the house he would treasure. If the culprit comes back, they may be angry he survived and burn the whole place down. Do you know anyone that could load everything up and secure it?"

"I'll do it myself," Ty's father assured him. "I'm done working for the day. Me and your mother will gather up a few friends and take care of cleaning out the property tonight. Call me when you get back to the fort. I'm worried about you. You don't sound like yourself," he paused. "Is something else bothering you?"

Ty wished he could talk to his father about Samantha, but not today. He'd explain everything in person the next time he visited. They'd understand his disappointment and it might help to talk about it with someone. Until then, he'd just need to cowboy up. "I'm fine, dad. Just a little tired. Jet lag I guess. It's been a long trip so far and I'm worried about the police. I hope they don't blame Atticus for this. It's going to be difficult to explain. Maybe you should call them before you come out," he suggested.

Dawn

"I know someone," Ken said after a short pause. "Don't worry about the police. I'll take care of things on this end. One of my workers has a brother. He's a shifter and a cop. I'll explain everything and he'll know how to handle it."

"Sounds good. Thanks dad. I'll call you in a couple days. I should be back at the fort by then," Ty said soberly.

"Be careful," Ken warned. "I love you, son."

"I love you too, dad. Talk to you soon," Ty hung up. He was glad he'd decided to call his father, just talking to him made him feel better. He picked up the phone and dialed Dimitri.

Dimitri sat on the large couch staring out the window. This didn't make sense. The only people that had a grudge against Atticus were the Dillinger's. But if the bombs were all made by the same person that complicated things. Foster Dillinger was almost killed in the ballroom. He wouldn't have stayed if he knew bombs were going to explode. The only reason he was alive today was because Victor had saved his life. What about Lawson, Dimitri wondered. Would Lawson risk his own brother's life for revenge? Maybe, he conceded. Lawson was a little crazy. He'd left the family business years ago because he didn't think he should have to work for a living. He wanted everything handed to him. That's why he was so obsessed with losing the monarchy. If Lawson was in charge, the entire fae community would be paying him taxes to support his life of luxury. Lawson would blow up Atticus's property in an instant and he was capable of the ballroom explosions, but why would he attack the shifters? That still felt like revenge for killing Hector and rescuing the women. And Sam said she saw Lilith plant those bombs at the ball. He needed to call Oberon. Maybe the council leader would have some answers. At least they didn't have to worry about the police. Ken Brody was confident that was handled.

* * * *

Lilith paced the room. She was finally feeling better. She wasn't completely healed, but she wasn't weak any longer. It had been days since she'd heard from the vampires she'd sent to track down that human. Radek had been furious with her when he found out she'd risked four of his best fighters on a human female. But when word came back that one of the warriors was at that old military base, he'd changed his tune. Now he was strategizing, determined to discover their purpose. He was talking crazy. He wanted to blow up the military base. He'd lost it. Lilith shook her head. Did he want every human in the nation snooping around? That's what would happen if a military base was bombed. The human's wouldn't back down until they found the culprits.

She paused at the door. She needed to convince Radek her plan was the right way to go. She needed to get to that base and take the human. She couldn't wait. She flung the door open with anticipation. She was going to the base with or without Radek's blessing. It was just easier with it.

* * * *

Victor sat next to Ariel impatiently waiting for the plane. He should have been there. He knew something was wrong. He should have gone to his father instead of flying to the fort.

"Stop it," Ariel chastised.

"What?" Victor asked surprised.

"You couldn't have known your father was in danger. Stop second guessing yourself. Ty said he was injured, but the bleeding had stopped. Have a little faith," she said gentler now. "Anyway, if we hadn't gotten here when we did, Ty might be dead. Then you'd be condemning yourself for going to your father. No matter what you did, someone was going to get hurt. You can't be everywhere Victor. You can't protect everyone." She slid in closer to him and took his face in her hands. "Stop fretting. Atticus will be here any minute and we'll take care of him. I promise," she leaned in and gave him a gentle kiss.

Victor relaxed a little. Ariel always knew how to calm him down. She was right. If he hadn't flown to the fort and Ty had died, he'd never forgive himself. But if his father died... he couldn't even finish that thought.

"There they are," Ariel pointed in the air to a small plane coming in for a landing. "It's going to be okay. You go to your father. I'll handle the pilot." They climbed out of the car and waited for the plane to come to a stop.

* * * *

Samantha sat in her room thinking about her situation. Well, if she was honest, she was also avoiding everyone. She'd shut herself off completely. She wouldn't even talk to Kylee and she knew Kylee was human. She didn't get it though. Kylee was loving it here. She'd discovered a world of monsters and the truly bazaar, but she soared with excitement. Couldn't she see the danger? Sam laid her head back against the headboard. Or was Samantha the one that was wrong? She'd heard something on her way up about a man being injured. Victor and Ariel had gone to the airport to retrieve whoever it was. Sam shuddered. Did that mean more blood? How could Kylee watch them drink a glass of blood like it was a Coke and not worry about her safety? No, she wasn't wrong. These people, no these things, were not the good guys. A picture of Luke flashed into her mind. He was one of them. But he wasn't a monster. He was good and kind and generous. None of this made sense. She was so conflicted about everything. She wouldn't allow herself to think about Ty. He was the worst of all. He'd lied to her. He'd let her believe he was something he wasn't. He seduced her.

Well, that wasn't true either. That night had been mutual. She couldn't blame Ty for what happened. She was the one that stormed into his room and refused to leave. He tried to escape her. What did that mean? She couldn't think about that right now, she missed him too much. Everywhere she went she was surrounded by memories and her heart broke all over again. She tried to throw herself into work, but even that hadn't blocked out the memories of him. Tears formed in her eyes. For the first time in her life she longed for her mother. She needed advice. Oh, she'd longed for her family numerous times in the past, but it was always when she felt lonely, when she'd longed for their company. Tonight she longed for a mother. Someone she could share her burden with. She curled into a ball and let the tears flow.

Kylee waited patiently for the man to arrive. She'd offered her services again, but hoped they wouldn't need them. The door flew open and Victor walked in. He had his arm around a man's waist, supporting his weight. This was supposed to be Victor's father? She was astonished. They could be brothers. The man didn't look old enough to be Victor's dad. If their bodies could heal themselves, did it also slow down the aging process? That was something to ponder later. The man looked like he was in pain. She saw a gash on the back of his head and stepped in to get a better look.

Victor studied the doctor, but didn't say anything. He was curious what she would say.

"Someone hit this man over the head with a blunt object," she declared.

Everyone looked at her skeptically.

"I know he was in a fire, but did Ty say the barn had started to fall apart? Were beams crashing to the floor?" she asked.

"No," Victor answered slowly. "He didn't say one way or the other. Not specifically, but I doubt it. Ty said he carried dad to the truck and then went back into the barn and evacuated the horses. If the barn was that far gone, some of the horses would have been injured or killed and Ty wouldn't have been able to get them all out. He also said there was an additional bomb that he defused. That takes time. I don't think the barn could have been falling apart the way you described."

"Then someone hit him over the head with something," Kylee said with confidence. She turned to Atticus. "Did you see your attacker?" she asked.

"No," Atticus admitted. "I didn't see anything. The horses were acting up, so I went to the barn to check it out. That's the last thing I remember," he glanced toward Victor. "Things have uh...gotten a little worse than dead snakes on the porch," he admitted.

"Dad!" Victor said exasperated.

"Don't start. I knew you'd worry and if it got too bad I planned on asking for help. This attack came out of the blue. I didn't expect it," he confessed. "It went from snakes to someone killing a few of the wild cats. Last week I think I scared someone off. I heard a noise and went outside to see what it was. My tires were slashed and I saw movement, I thought it was a man running into the trees. I tried to follow, but he was long gone by the time I got there. That was the last of it. I planned to come out for a visit this weekend, but when nothing happened all week, I got worried. Then when the horses got so riled up, I was worried the violence had escalated to one of my stallions. I never imagined it would jump to trying to kill me," he said soberly then his face turned to shock. "Did you find Peter?"

"Who's Peter?" Victor asked, worried it was the man Ty had found dead in the barn.

"Peter Babcock," Atticus said glancing from Victor to Ariel. "He's dead isn't he?"

"Why do you say that?" Ariel asked.

"Because of the way the two of you are acting. The horses were acting up but I saw Pete's truck outside. I figured that must be why they were making such a ruckus. Pete moved in a while back but his barn needed work. He was housing his mare at my place while he shored things up. He spoiled them horses, brought carrots or apples every time he came. They always riled when he stopped by for Molly. I let my guard down, figuring it was just old Pete again. I entered the barn, looking for him and the last thing I remember is seeing him lying there, on the ground all lifeless and still. I headed that way to check on him, then nothing. I don't remember anything after that."

Dawn

"Yes dad," Victor said placing a hand on his father's shoulder. "Ty found Pete's body in the barn. He had to leave it there. The barn was on fire and he needed to rescue the horses."

"Come and sit on the couch," Kylee directed. "You still look a little pale."

Atticus looked at Victor, he was frowning. "Who is she?" he asked curiously. "Since when do we enlist humans to help with the healing?"

"It's a long story. I'll fill you in later." Victor took his father's elbow and led him to the sofa. "Do you want something to eat?"

"Not yet," Atticus looked at Kylee. He was hesitant to ask, but he really needed blood.

Ariel breezed in and handed him a glass. He was shocked. Was he supposed to drink blood with a human in the room?

"Go ahead," Kylee urged. "It's not going to bother me." She moved away from him to sit in a chair across the room. Maybe he'd be more comfortable if she wasn't so close.

Atticus paused then began to drink. It was strange at first, but Kylee did her best to put him at ease. The group discussed the developments of the day and tried to come up with an answer. Atticus explained that Pete was a widow and didn't have any other family. There was no one to notify and anyway the police would take care of things on that end. They brain stormed late into the evening but finally decided they weren't going to solve the puzzle tonight, so they all retired to bed.

* * * *

Alex and Dimitri pulled into the drive of the farm house. They'd realized the construction crew was heading out today and offered them a ride. Why pay for two planes when one was enough? They had dropped the men off at the bunkers and made sure they settled in before heading to the house. Alex opened the door and immediately stopped in the foyer. It was quiet. Where was everyone? She heard movement and looked up. Samantha was standing at the top of the stairs. Alex sighed. She looked terrible. Clearly she still wasn't taking things well. Alex wished she could help, but this was something Samantha would have to work out on her own. If Alex pressured her, Sam would retreat within herself even more. She'd learned that lesson with the vampire hunting.

Samantha saw Alex and Dimitri walk in and froze. She didn't want to talk to Alex. She didn't want to hear her explanations. She just wanted to be left alone. She was about to retreat when Alex's eyes locked on hers. She hesitated only a moment, then turned and went back to her room. Once inside she locked the door and sat back on her bed. She could wait it out. Everyone else was on the back patio. Soon Alex would join them and the coast would be clear for escape.

Alex sighed and turned to Dimitri. "I've ruined her life," she whispered.

"No, you haven't," Dimitri argued. "You can't take this on yourself."

"I'm the one that sent Sam here," Alex said soberly. "I'm the one that decided not to explain things months ago when she brought us those pictures. She knew the warriors hunted vampires, but she didn't know they weren't human. She mistakenly believed they were just like her. I allowed that. Her suffering is my fault. I could have prevented it."

Samantha heard Alex and Dimitri talking and overheard her name. She was curious. She slipped silently out the door and hid behind the wall next to the stairs. She felt a little guilty about eavesdropping, but she was too curious. She couldn't stop herself.

Dimitri pulled Alex into his arms, gently rubbing her back for comfort. "This is not your fault baby," he consoled. "Samantha's not stupid. She saw you and Ariel fighting the vampires. She saw Ariel throwing fire. She saw you healing people at the ball. She couldn't have witnessed that and believed you were human. Sam chose to remain in the dark. If she assumed we were just human vampire hunters like her, it's because she didn't want to explore the truth." Dimitri lifted Alex's chin with one finger until she had to look him in the eyes. "Sending her here was not a mistake."

"But..." Alex interrupted.

"No. Let me finish," he pressed. "Sam's job is to manage D-Tech. She accepted the promotion and everything that goes with that. Using the plant at Romulus was essential for production. You told me how amazed you were that they found the problem with the droids so fast. A problem New York had been working on for weeks. You know as well as I do that with higher pay comes increased responsibility. If Sam can't handle it, maybe she shouldn't have accepted the promotion."

"That has nothing to do with the rest. I forced her to come here and work on personal projects. Okay, so sending her to deal with production wasn't a mistake, but what about the rest? Accepting the promotion didn't mean she willingly joined the war. Fae business is separate from D-Tech business. I drug her into a battle she had no idea she was entering. Radek sent those vampires here after us, you know that. He's going to send more. Samantha is already struggling with the fact that her family was murdered by vampires. None of my research has produced an explanation for that. There's no reason Radek would target her family. It's not the way they do things. But still..."

"We'll figure it out," Dimitri assured her. "I've been researching a little on my own. I have a couple feelers out. Give it time, we'll determine the reason for all this." He pressed his hands over her face and brushed back her hair. Then he leaned down and gently kissed her forehead. "Part of the reason I fell in love with you was your caring nature, but you have to stop taking everything on yourself. We'll work this out. I promise. Somehow we'll find a way to help Sam deal with this and move on," he paused to kiss her lips. "You know Samantha made her own choices in this. You didn't force her to join the battle. You hired her for a side job, just like you've done before. Just like Luke did countless times before. Samantha understood the reason for the project. She knew what she was getting into. You hired her to do a job and provided a means for her to accomplish it. Do you know anyone else that could have come up with the phenomenal simulators that Sam and Ty developed? Were there two other people we could have put on this that would have been as successful?" he asked.

"No," Alex admitted. "I just hate to see Sam so upset. She's shut herself off and won't listen to anyone. Her imagination has taken over. She's convinced herself that we, the warriors and the fae, are somehow evil and dangerous. For the life of me I can't imagine how she got there. How can you sit in a room with Ty for five seconds and not see his goodness. He's such a fun loving, easy going guy. How can you spend any time around Victor and not see how totally selfless and compassionate he is. She's grasping at straws and holding on to her belief that we must be bad. It just

Dawn

doesn't make any sense. Sam is smarter than that. I can't help feeling responsible for how she found out. If I had just explained it to her earlier..." Alex drifted off.

Dimitri pressed his forehead against hers. "I'll agree with you that we should have explained things to Sam. If we had, this whole mess could have been avoided. But, you've heard the saying hindsight is twenty twenty. That applies here Alex. There is no way we could have known that Sam would walk in on that scene. Sure, it's always a possibility, but with her knowledge about our world, I never would have guessed she would handle it this way. You will never convince me that you had any indication she would either. This is not your fault. So we made a mistake, I admit that. Instead of blaming yourself let's try to think of a way to fix it. I know you don't want to hear this, but maybe you should send her back to New York. Maybe if she got away from us and went back to work she'd be able to handle it better."

"I've thought of that. I just can't get past the feeling that if I send her home right now, she'll immediately start hunting again. I'm worried she'll be even more reckless because of this and get herself killed. I couldn't live with myself if that happened. I just don't know what to do," Alex admitted.

Dimitri gently brushed a tear from Alex's cheek. "We'll figure it out. I promise," he assured her. "Now, let's go find the others. They have to be around here somewhere. I think the company will do you good." He took her hand and led her towards the kitchen.

Samantha slumped against the wall and slowly let herself slide to a sitting position. She didn't know what to think. Alex and Dimitri were looking into her family's death. Why? Why would they care? Were they really doing it just for her? For her wellbeing and her safety? If that was true, how could they be the monsters

186

she'd decided they were? Was she holding on to some made up conclusion that didn't fit? Was Ty good? Was Victor compassionate? And was her ignorance her own fault? Her own doing? Dimitri was right. She'd seen Ariel throw fire. She'd been surprised, but not worried about it. She'd just decided there were other creatures in the world like vampires that humans didn't know about. So, what's different now? Victor had explained Ariel's gift to her. Alex was wrong, she didn't think the fae were monsters. She just had her doubts about the warriors.

But did that make sense? A few minutes ago it had made perfect sense. But now she just didn't know what to think Seeing Dimitri with Alex shook her. How could a monster be that loving? How could a monster care so much about the wellbeing of someone else? She slid her legs up and rested her head against her knees. She didn't want to think about this anymore. She wished she could just escape it all. No, that's not what she wanted either. Her stomach had clenched when Dimitri told Alex to send her away. As hard as things were here, she didn't want to go back yet. She didn't want to return to that lonely, pathetic apartment. Samantha waited for a signal the coast was clear. Once she heard Alex and Dimitri out on the porch she'd make her escape. She needed time to think. Time away from the farm, the fort and even the plant. Once she was sure she wouldn't run into anyone she was going to head to the lake. Maybe she'd be able to think there. Maybe she could work some of this out. She went to her room and changed, grabbed a large towel and waited.

Dimitri and Alex entered the kitchen and heard voices. "They must be outside," she told Dimitri.

"Yeah," Dimitri agreed. "Let's grab a cup of coffee and join them." He reached for two cups and pulled out the coffee pot.

Dawn

Alex took her cup, doctored her coffee and headed for the door. Dimitri was at her heels. They opened the screen and stepped onto the porch.

"What a bunch of slackers," Dimitri said jokingly. He was determined to lighten the mood. He hated seeing Alex like this. Hopefully the company would cheer her up a bit.

Victor laughed. "Slackers? You're one to talk. I thought you were supposed to be here yesterday. I don't see any fancy security system up and running yet. We're all waiting on you my friend." Victor smiled, but he wasn't fooled. Alex was upset about something. She looked stressed and he was pretty sure she'd been crying. If he had to guess, he'd say this had to do with Samantha. Ariel hadn't been herself for days. He'd tried to get her to talk about it, but she was shutting him out. She refused to talk about Sam. In fact, she'd ordered him not to bring up Sam's name around her again. He wasn't stupid, he'd dropped the subject permanently.

"Pull up a chair," Ariel told them. "Oh, you need to meet these two. This is Dusty, he's a busy body that has decided he wants to help with setup at the fort." She grinned a little then motioned to Kylee. "And this is Doctor Kylee Quintana. I believe Victor has filled you in on her situation. They are both anxiously awaiting your verdict."

That wasn't exactly the way Kylee had hoped to be introduced. She had no idea what Victor had told them. Should she try to convince them to let her stay, or wait and see what they said before she argued her case? She was at a loss. She didn't know these people. After a couple seconds of debate, she decided to wait. She stood and held out her hand. "It's very nice to meet both of you," she said politely.

Alex was studying the woman carefully. She'd been curious about a human that had discovered and accepted their world so quickly. Why was she so different than Sam? "It's very nice to meet you," Alex finally told her. She was going to spend some time with the good doctor before she decided what to do about her. Alex and Dimitri pulled out chairs and joined the group.

"Dimitri?" Victor called.

"What?" he asked.

"I have another request," Victor looked over at his father. "Uh, dad is sort of displaced right now. Ty should be here today with his horses and we thought we could house them in the barn now that we've cleaned it out. But I don't believe it's safe for dad to return to his house until we figure out how everything is connected."

"I agree," Dimitri assured him. "What did you have in mind?"

"Well, I was wondering if he could stay here. The horses are going to need a break after such a long trip anyway. This house has plenty of room and I think he could be a lot of help with setup."

Dimitri looked towards Atticus. "How do you feel about this?" he asked.

"I don't like leaving my farm unattended. I think it's vulnerable to attack," he paused. "But I'm no longer comfortable living out there on my own either. If Ty hadn't stopped by when he did, I'm sure I'd be just a memory right now." He patted Victor's leg. He knew his son was worried about him. "I think I'd like to stay awhile if you can use me that is. It's been a long time since I've been involved in the community. Helping out here might make up for my absence a little."

Dawn

"You don't need to make up for anything," Dimitri assured him. "But I think keeping you on here is a great idea. Ken Brody and his family already cleaned out your house. They were worried a vacant house would be vulnerable. He stored all your stuff in a large container on his business property. He assures me it has good security and will be safe there. I can't make any promises regarding your home while you're gone though. I wish I could. If anything happens we'll rebuild later. Right now your safety is more important than anything. I plan to hire an investigator to look into this. It's going to take time because I haven't found anyone I trust to do the job. Are you willing to stay here until we can get to the bottom of this?" he asked.

Atticus hesitated. Was he willing to live here until they found out who was after him? That could take months. "Do I have to give you a commitment for that long right now?" he inquired.

"Dad!" Victor objected. "We talked about this."

Dimitri smiled. "How about a commitment for a couple months. Then we'll reevaluate the situation and decide then."

Could he commit to a couple months? For Victor he could do anything. He studied his son's face then turned to Dimitri. "It's a deal," he held out his hand.

"Great!" Dimitri took his hand and shook it firmly. He was pleased that Atticus was going to help out here. He had a lot to offer.

"Well," Victor stood. "Ariel and I need to get over to the apartment complex. I'd like to take care of the plumbing issues today. There's a lot to do, but if I get an early start I may be able to finish before dark. You sold me a lemon Dimitri," he laughed. "But

I'm up for the challenge. Just don't expect miracles overnight." He took Ariel's hand and pulled her to her feet.

"See ya later," she called as they walked around the house headed for the fort.

Dimitri looked at Dusty. "Do your parents know where you are?" he asked sternly.

"Yes sir," he said enthusiastically. "I called them once I arrived," he frowned. "They are a little worried about me, but they understand my desire to help. I have their support if that's what you're asking."

"Let's go into the study and have a little chat. I have some questions for you and then you can explain how you are qualified to assist."

"I'm coming too," Alex added. "I have some questions of my own." The three of them stood and entered the kitchen letting the door close behind them.

"I guess that leaves you and me," Kylee smiled at Atticus. "I was wondering if you could tell me about Alex and Dimitri. I'd like some idea of what I'm up against when I try to convince them to let me stay and help," she smiled shyly at Atticus.

"Well, I don't know a lot about Alex. She's new to our community. I know Dimitri a little, I was good friends with his father. I guess I could share some of what I know. Don't you worry, they're fair people. They'll listen to your argument if you decide to make one."

Atticus settled in for a morning of storytelling.

Chapter Eight

Ty pulled into the driveway of the large farm and stopped. He jumped out of the truck and walked to the car that had been following him since New York. "I need to take the horses around back and unload them. They've been cooped up for hours. I'm headed to the pasture so they can stretch their legs and run. You two pull around the front, up that drive over there." Ty pointed in the other direction. "You can't miss the other cars. Go ahead and go inside. The guest rooms are upstairs, just snag one of the empty ones and get settled."

"Thanks," Orin smiled. "Victor and Ariel are going to be in for a surprise."

"Maybe, but it's a good surprise. I know Ariel will be thrilled to have a friend here full time." Ty turned and strolled back to the truck. He backed in the trailer and began unloading the horses. Bo and Ace were just as happy to romp and play. Once the horses were settled he'd take a few minutes to play ball with them. They both loved playing catch. Ty turned the last horse loose and secured the sturdy latch, confident the horses would be safe in the pasture. Now he just needed to unload the hay then he could track down a tennis ball. He thought he'd seen one in the old shed around front. Half an hour later he still hadn't found a ball, but he did find some rope. That would have to do for now. He tied a large knot then threw it across the back yard. The dogs took off, anxious to play. He watched as Breena and Orin exited the house then headed towards the fort. No need to check on them, clearly they had settled in just fine without him. Maybe he'd walk to the small store up the road and buy a couple tennis balls. The dogs needed to stay busy or they'd get into trouble.

Ty decided he shouldn't leave without telling someone where he was going. He called the dogs and headed for the fort. Victor and Ariel would be working on the apartment for sure. He was also certain Breena and Orin had joined them.

He sauntered into the apartment and listened for noise. Upstairs, he decided and quickly ascended the steps. He found them in the large apartment at the top of the complex. They were all excitedly catching up on each other's lives.

Ariel spotted Ty first. "You!" she narrowed her eyes at him trying to sound angry. "All this time you've had Bree and Orin in tow and never said a word. If I wasn't so thrilled to see them, you'd be in trouble mister." She walked over and gave him a huge hug. "How was the trip?" she asked casually.

"Very productive actually," he admitted. "I found myself a pilot on the way out, she's in training right now but I've informed her she'll be flying back and forth from here and New York on a regular basis. She's fine with it, so I think I've solved part of our transportation problem. Thomas can't pull his company jet away every time we need to go somewhere."

"Can we trust her?" Victor asked. "I'm not sure having another human around is the best idea at the moment," he cringed at Ty's expression.

"I take it Samantha is still struggling," Ty said soberly.

"We're not talking about that woman," Ariel insisted. "I'm in too good a mood to discuss her right now." She linked her arm through Ty's and escorted him to a chair. Ace and Bo followed, promptly lying down at his feet. "I see you brought friends." She smiled as she reached down and stroked each one behind the ears. "I love your dogs, Ty. I'm glad you brought them with you."

She returned to Victor's side and picked up a pipe. "Okay hon, I'm back. Let's get this room finished so we can move on to the outside problem. Didn't you say that was the big one?"

Victor leaned in and gave Ariel a quick kiss. "I think I'm the luckiest man alive."

"How so?" Orin asked. "Look at me. How could you be any more lucky than I am?" he reached out and took Breena's hand.

"I have news," Breena finally said glowing. She looked around the room at the curious faces. "We're going to have a baby!" she exclaimed.

Ariel jumped up and pulled Breena into a huge bear hug. "That's wonderful!" she said happily. "Wait, should you be traveling in your condition?" she asked concerned.

"Well..." Orin began. "That's kind of why we're here. We plan to stay until after the baby's born."

"Really?" Ariel said enthusiastically. "That's wonderful," she turned to Victor. "Isn't that wonderful, Victor."

Victor smiled at her. It was nice to see her happy again. The last few days had been difficult. "Yes, it is." He walked to Orin and held out a hand. "Congratulations man," he said sincerely. Orin took his hand and Victor pulled him in for a quick hug. "I know this is what you've wanted for a long time. I hope everything works out for you."

Ariel studied Breena. She looked good, but a little tired. "Is the pregnancy going okay?" she asked concerned.

"Oh it's fine," Breena assured her. "I get tired a lot quicker, but other than that I feel fine. Tianna told me what to expect and what to watch out for. She was a little concerned about me coming out here where there's no medical help but I really think everything is going to be okay."

Ariel and Victor looked at each other and immediately knew they had the same idea. "Well, that's not exactly true," Ariel told her. "We have a doctor in the house."

"She's still here?" Ty asked. "Has Alex and Dimitri decided to keep her on for a while?"

"They're discussing it now." Victor answered. "I'm not sure if they've come to a decision, but last time I talked to Dimitri he was leaning towards letting her stay. She wants to be here and this way we can keep an eye on her. We'll have more time to determine if she'll keep our secrets."

"That makes sense," Ty admitted. "What about the boy? The shifter? Have they decided anything about him?"

Dawn

"I don't think they've decided on that yet. I have mixed feelings about having him here. He's young. So he's still a little reckless," Victor mused.

"You do realize once we're finished there are going to be a lot of young, reckless kids running around. Maybe it's a good idea for us to get used to this one so we know what we're in for with the rest," Ty suggested.

"Maybe," Victor answered not quite convinced. He turned to Ariel. "Okay, we're done with this one." He stood and held out his hand to pull her up. "Ready to head downstairs and tackle the main valve coming into the building?"

"Ready as I'll ever be," she said hesitantly.

Victor laughed. "Don't worry babe, I'll do all the work. Just hold on tight and don't let go. It won't take long, I'm fast and smooth. It's big and might get a little slippery but I'll have things flowing before you know it."

"And on that note, I'm outta here." Ty laughed as he left the room, dogs at his heels.

Orin and Breena were trying to hold back a laugh, but failed. After a couple seconds they burst out laughing. Victor and Ariel both glared at them, but then they too joined in the laughter.

"I guess I'm going to have to watch how I phrase things from now on. I'm surrounded by perverts. Since you two have your mind in the gutter, I guess that did sound a little bad," Victor admitted.

"A little?" Breena questioned wiping tears from her eyes. "Gutter or not, that sounded down right dirty!"

They all exited the apartment and headed for the north side of the building. Orin and Breena sat on the lawn while Victor and Ariel worked on the outside water system. They were saving the main water valve for last.

A few hours later, Breena yawned. "I'm beat. You guys mind if I head in for a nap?"

Orin immediately stood and helped Breena to her feet. "I'm not any help when it comes to plumbing. I'll come with you, Bree. I'm a little tired myself after that long ride."

"See you guys," Ariel called out as they walked toward the house. She turned to Victor. "I'm so happy for them. They've wanted a child for so long and now, thanks to Alex it is finally going to be a reality for them."

Victor glanced at Ariel cautiously. She seemed happy. Ever since Breena announced the news he'd been watching her carefully. He knew she wanted children herself, but she still didn't know if she was capable of conceiving. Being with her was such a miracle in his life. He wanted all her dreams to come true. When she was ready, he'd make sure they did everything in his power to get pregnant. Before Ariel, he hadn't wanted children. Now, he thought it would be a blessing to create a life with such a wonderful woman. But unlike Ariel, if they never had a child, he'd still be happy and content. She was everything a man could want. For him a child would just be a bonus.

"Where'd you go?" she asked.

"Nowhere," he lied avoiding her eyes.

"I really am happy for her," she told him. "Stop worrying about me. I'm fine with this. We're not ready to think about children. We're not even married yet. If I can't have a baby, I'll deal with it when it happens. For now, I just want to share in the joy of my best friend's dream coming true." She grabbed Victor's face and made him look at her. "If you analyze me every minute that Bree's here it's just going to piss me off. Let's be happy for them and enjoy our time together."

"Deal," Victor grabbed her around the waist and pulled her to him. Then he took her mouth in a long, hard kiss. When he sat her down, he looked at her seriously. "Are you having second thoughts about our plan to wait a year before we marry? Because if you are, we can talk about it again and come up with a new plan."

"No," Ariel assured him. "There's so much going on here and with Alex and Dimitri planning their big wedding this spring I don't think trying to push up the date is a good idea. I still think we should stick to the original plan and get married next summer sometime," she smiled at him. "With any luck maybe Radek will be dead by then and our world will settle down a bit."

He leaned in and kissed her again. "I love you," he whispered.

"I love you too," she whispered back.

Victor released her and turned back to the job at hand. "Now my dear, we need to do the hard part. I need you to hold this in place while I solder it. Please, whatever you do, don't let go until I'm finished."

"Got it," Ariel said cheerfully. She really was in a good mood.

A few minutes later Ariel looked up as she heard a car drive down the gravel road. That was strange, they all parked at the house and walked to the fort. Who would be driving onto the property?

She continued to watch as the car approached. When it got to the barricade blocking the drive, it came to a stop. Ariel could see two people inside. She blinked in disbelief when the door opened and a man stepped out. "Tank?" she said quietly.

Victor looked up. Did she say Tank? Was her old boyfriend here? Before he knew what was happening Ariel dropped the pipe and took off. Victor scrambled to secure the pipe, the soldering gun and the spool. Once he had everything under control, he stood. He was pissed. She promised him she wouldn't let go for anything. Then her old boyfriend shows up and she's off like a horse at the Kentucky Derby. He turned around and saw Ariel in a tight embrace with a man. He couldn't see his face, but obviously it was this Tank character. His scowl deepened as he headed toward them.

"I can't believe you came to visit," Ariel exclaimed. "Who do you have in the car?" she quizzed.

Tank turned and motioned for his passenger to join him. He was happy to see Ariel again. When his father called to tell him the rumors of what was going on out here, he had to come check on things for himself. A gorgeous woman stepped out of the car and walked gracefully around the vehicle.

Victor strolled purposefully towards the couple. He was surprised when a woman exited the car and headed towards Ariel and Tank. Maybe the guy had a new girlfriend. That would be nice. He was worried about Ariel's reaction. She said they were just friends, but she'd completely forgotten Victor was there when the guy climbed out of his car. What if she still had feelings for him?

Victor was just a few feet away when Tank stepped to the side and Victor finally saw him clearly. His face lit up in a huge smile. He reached the group just as the other woman did.

Dawn

Ariel felt Victor slide in next to her. He immediately wrapped his arm around her waist. Was he protecting her or claiming her? She felt a little guilty. As soon as she saw Tank climb out of the car, she'd forgotten what she was doing and left Victor hanging. She looked up at him and froze. Victor was smiling and clearly amused at something. Well, at least she wasn't in trouble. "What's funny?" she asked.

Victor ignored her. His eyes were locked with Tanks. "So, Tank is it?" he said sarcastically. Then he burst out laughing. "I thought you hated that name." He reached out and pulled Tank into a big bear hug. "What are you doing here?" he asked. "Aren't you supposed to be hanging out at the castle getting a manicure or some shit like that?"

Ariel was dumbfounded. Did these two know each other? She looked to the woman in confusion. Ariel didn't know who she was, but she didn't seem surprised.

Tank reached for the woman and put his arm around her shoulders. "I'd like the two of you to meet my wife, Megan Fitzgerald DeLacy," he said proudly. "Megan, this is Ariel and Victor."

Megan held out her hand to Victor. "It's a pleasure to finally meet you. You have no idea how often your name comes up in conversation," she turned to Ariel. "It's also a pleasure to meet you. I think I owe you for rejecting this wonderful man and sending him my way."

Ariel took her hand and smiled. "He is a wonderful man," she agreed. "I'm really happy for you. Now," she glared at Victor then at Tank. "Would one of you like to tell me how you know each other?" she turned back to Victor. "And what is so funny?" she demanded, glaring at him. He was still laughing every time he looked at Tank.

Victor pressed his lips together and tried to hide his grin. "I just think it's ironic that..." he laughed again. "That Tank here has finally decided to accept such a perfect nickname after all this time."

"Knock it off," Tank warned. "If you even think about calling me that stupid name I'll break your nose...again." They both burst out laughing.

Ariel cleared her throat loudly. "An explanation, please?" She emphasized the please to make sure they knew how annoyed she was. They were acting like children.

"Oh alright," Victor gave Ariel a quick peck on the lips. "Tank Master Tony here..."

"Victor," Tank warned. "Do you really want to spend the night drinking blood and trying to heal from the damage I plan to cause if you don't stop with that sarcastic moniker?"

Victor grinned at him, unmoved by the threat. "As I was saying my dear, the Tank Master...or is that Royal Tank Master, I forget?" He ducked and turned to miss the punch Tank threw his way.

"Consider yourself warned, man. The next one will connect and it's gonna hurt," Tank promised.

"I get it, you know Tank," Ariel said sharply. "How?"

Victor threw an arm around Tanks shoulders and turned him towards the house. He reached back and grabbed Ariel's hand. "Come on, this calls for a celebration. My best friend got married," he turned to Tank and scowled. "I would like to know why I wasn't invited to the wedding though. It can't be about class, you were there?" he joked. He leaned forward until he could see Megan. "Or was that your doing?"

"Not exactly," Megan began. "Only my mother and Tony's parents were able to attend the wedding. It all happened pretty fast. Plus, Tony didn't know where you were at the time."

"Yeah well, that's no excuse. Tony here has a lot of explaining to do. When I dropped him at the airport he was supposed to be headed back to Clontarf Castle. I think that's pretty far from New York my friend. How exactly did you end up here hitting on my future wife instead of Dublin, Ireland?"

Tony looked at Victor, then to Ariel, then back to Victor. "Really? You two are getting married?"

Ariel glowed. "We are," she told him, watching for a reaction.

"Whoa-hoo!" Tony grabbed Victor and swung him around in a circle. "Mom and dad are going to be thrilled! I have to call them tonight and give them the news!" Tony released Victor. "Am I invited to the wedding?" he asked sheepishly.

"I haven't decided yet," Victor teased. "But Charles and Elizabeth are welcome," he added as a challenge. He knew if Tony's parents were there Tony would come too, whether he was invited or not. Which he definitely would be, Tony was the closest thing Victor had to a brother. "Don't think you can crash the party without an invitation. I plan to have security at the door," he added.

"Look, our marriage was a bit controversial. Richard didn't even make it," Tony confessed.

"Controversial how? I can't imagine anything that would keep Richard from attending your wedding," Victor said, concerned.

They had reached the front door of the farm house. "Let's go have a drink and celebrate our women," Tony smiled at Megan. "Yours is pretty wonderful, but I have to tell you I'm the luckiest man in the world." He took Megan's hand as they walked into the study.

"Tony," Dimitri greeted as they stepped into the room. "I didn't know you were coming. How have you been?" He walked across the room and shook Tony's hand.

"Hello Dimitri," he grinned. "It's been awhile. How are things?" he asked. Dimitri had been out of town on business the last time he'd been to New York. Tony had been grateful for that. If Dimitri had seen him, his cover would have been blown immediately.

"All things considered I guess I can't complain," Dimitri said honestly.

"Yeah, I heard. In fact, that's why we're here. Dad called once Ariel's Aunt Dorothy told him what's been going on. He was concerned about you." He looked over at Victor. "Sometimes I think you are dad's favorite son," he smiled. He didn't mind. He was glad his family had accepted Victor so completely. "Anyway, he was concerned about the recent events and ordered me to come out and make sure that weakling over there was okay."

Victor rolled his eyes. "I think we know who has saved whose butt about a million times over the years. You were just scared and wanted me to protect you, again." Victor laughed at Tony's expression. "Oh, come on. You know it's true."

Dawn

"I know no such thing. In fact, I think we're about even on the saving your butt scale." He sat on the couch and pulled Megan down next to him. "Hey, Atticus. It's good to see you again. How are things on the farm?"

Everyone sobered. "Before I tell you that story, I think there are some introductions to be made," Atticus smiled at Megan.

"Oh sorry," Tony turned to Megan. "This is my wife, Megan," he introduced. Then he turned to Victor, "and this is the prodigal son my father never had."

"And this is Master Tony," Victor grinned. "Heavy on the Master part. He kind of has an ego problem."

Tony scowled. "Will you stop already? You know how much I hate that."

"It's your own fault. Why did you tell this whole community your name is Tank if you didn't want to be reminded of yet another instance when I saved your pathetic behind? I think deep down you love that name. You just know it's pretentious so you object out of principle."

Alex was watching Victor. She'd never seen him so happy and playful. Tony was good for him. Ariel looked a little off. Alex thought she was seeing the same thing and probably didn't know what to think of it.

Victor walked to the small bar and poured himself a drink. "What's your pleasure?" he asked Megan.

"Do you have any white wine?" she asked.

"Absolutely," he poured her a glass. "How 'bout you babe?" he asked Ariel.

"I think I'll have the same," she told him.

"Alex?" he asked.

"I'm fine," she assured him. "I still have plenty. Dimitri and I were just winding down for the day."

"I'm good too," Dimitri offered.

Victor started back across the room towards the chair next to Ariel then stopped when he noticed Ty standing in the doorway. "Hey come on in," he called. "We were just about to celebrate Tony and Megan's marriage. What will you have?"

Ty entered the room hesitantly. He was tired. He really wanted to go up to bed. "You got any beer over there?" he asked.

"You can't have beer," Victor protested. "How about a screwdriver?"

"Just give me a beer," Ty argued. "I can drink to forever with a beer. I've seen you do it a million times at the club."

"Fine," Victor grabbed a beer and tossed it to Ty.

Ty pulled up a chair and joined the group.

Tony turned to Atticus. "Now, what's the story about your farm?"

Atticus proceeded to explain the situation. Every once in a while he asked Ty to explain a few details.

"Wow," Tony sighed. "Things here really have gotten out of hand. It seems you may be battling two fronts. Do you think it's the Dillinger's?"

Dawn

"Maybe," Dimitri admitted. "The problem I have is that Ty said all the bombs were built by the same hand. All of them, including the ones at the shifter camps. That still feels like revenge to me. There's just no common thread that ties everything together. I can believe Lawson was hassling Atticus. It's also plausible he was responsible for the ballroom explosions. I think we all agree Foster's clear on that one."

"Absolutely," Victor agreed. "Foster's lucky he survived." He linked his hand with Ariel's when he saw her scowl. That was still a touchy subject. Victor noticed his father was also scowling. "Anyway. Foster's clear, but I think you might be right about Lawson. In fact, I just remembered something. Foster seemed to be wondering if Lawson was responsible that night. Dinner at the Dillinger's may not be so pleasant right about now."

"But that still leaves the shifters," Alex added. "The Dillinger's have no beef with the shifters. What's the motive?"

Everyone was silent for a long time. Megan was the first to speak. "I don't think you're going to solve that mystery tonight," she paused. "I hate to change the subject, but would the rest of you guys mind introducing yourselves? I've met Ariel and Victor and Tony's talked about Atticus, Victor's father, but I'm a little lost on the rest of you guys."

"Sorry," Tony apologized.

"Let me," Victor offered. "That's Ty," he pointed to the corner. "He's one of the warriors and he's been working day and night around here to get this place running."

Ty nodded in Megan's direction. "Nice to meet you ma'am," he added.

"He's our gentleman. Anyway, this over here is Dimitri. He's the leader of the warriors and next to him is Alex, our illustrious queen and my strip poker buddy." He laughed when Ariel swatted him in the stomach. "Okay, so we've never actually played strip poker. But everyone has to have a goal."

"Move on," Dimitri warned.

"We have a couple others staying here," Victor continued. "Orin and Bree arrived today. Breena's expecting, so they went to bed early I think. We also have a teenage shifter somewhere around here named Dusty and a human doctor named Kylee."

Tony looked at him surprised and curious.

"Long story. We'll save that for later," Victor continued. "There's also another human, but I doubt you'll see much of her. She works for Alex in electronics. Her name is Samantha, but she's just discovered our secret and is having a hard time coping." He glanced at Ty and noticed he was expressionless so he continued. "Try to avoid her. Until she works things out, she may be dangerous."

Ty closed his eyes. He hated this. Samantha should be part of the group, not on the outside avoiding everyone.

"Dangerous how?" Megan asked.

"She threatened to kill us all," Ariel said flatly. "She's an experienced vampire hunter, so she's got a few skills."

"I really don't think she'll attack anyone," Alex cut in. "She's just struggling right now. So far, she's avoiding us all."

Dawn

"Okay, now that we've drunk to your union and have the intro's out of the way, I want an explanation for not being invited to the wedding," Victor insisted.

Tony and Megan glanced at each other, they seemed to be communicating somehow. "Uh," Tony finally said. "There are some people that aren't comfortable around Megan," he looked around the room. He hoped they took this okay. "Don't get me wrong, my parents love her and Richard didn't miss the wedding because he didn't approve. He really couldn't get away at the time."

Victor was studying Tony. He was stalling. "Megan's not going to make any of us uncomfortable. Spill it. You're among friends."

"I'm a shadow," Megan answered before Tony could continue.

"Really?" Ariel said excited. "That is so cool. I've never met a shadow before."

Victor raised one eyebrow. "I can see how this could be complicated. So when you say some people aren't comfortable does that mean word got out in Dublin?"

"It did," Tony admitted. "We're not sure how they found out. We think maybe someone knew her mother, but it doesn't really matter. There was a faction that tried to get mom and dad ousted as rulers. Another group introduced a new law forbidding any union between shadows and royalty. We didn't want to wait and see what happened. We had to expedite our marriage before they could vote. Once we were married they could pass any law they wanted, it couldn't be retroactive so we were safe. Mom and dad flew out immediately and Richard planned on coming to Denver the following day. A storm came in and nobody would fly. We couldn't wait so we had to go ahead without him."

Alex was confused. What was a shadow? Why would the people take such a strong stand against the marriage of two people who obviously loved each other? She hated it when she got lost because she was so new to this world.

Dimitri noticed Alex's confusion and gave her hand a gentle squeeze. "Megan, Alex is new to our world. Would you mind explaining to her what a shadow is? I think you can probably describe things better than anyone."

Megan didn't understand how a Fae Queen could be new to the world, but she didn't mind explaining her genetic makeup. "Sure," she agreed. "A shadow is a type of fae that can read people's thoughts."

"Oh," Alex said even more interested.

"Don't worry. I don't sit around reading people's minds. In fact, I never read the minds of fae," she glanced around the room, "Or warriors," Megan assured them.

"Why not?" Alex asked. "I would think that would be helpful especially when meeting new people."

"Well, that's why we're called shadows. Supernatural beings are more difficult to read. Sometimes when they are stressed or concerned about something I can't help it. It's like they're screaming their thoughts at me. But typically, it's difficult to push into the minds of members of our world. If a shadow does it too often, it can cause damage. That's one reason we're called shadows. If I damage someone's mind, it creates a type of shadow in their brain. A dark spot where they can no longer access those memories and sometimes it can impact brain functions," she paused. "Anyway, I think it's rude to invade people's privacy that way, so I avoid it."

"So it's easy to control?" Alex asked. "It's something that you have to concentrate to do?"

"With our people, yes," she looked to Tony. "Not really with humans. Most humans are like an open book. They tend to throw their thoughts at you whether you want them or not. It's a little hard to explain."

"So can you just read their thoughts or can you manipulate them?" Alex asked.

"Both," she admitted. "That's why a lot of people are uncomfortable around us. They worry we'll plant something in their mind and they'll do something they didn't intend to do. Or, they're hiding something and they don't want us to read their thoughts and know about it. Everyone has secrets," she answered.

Alex thought for a moment. "Do the shadows use their powers against humans often?"

"Sometimes," Megan admitted. "For instance, my mother is a private investigator. She obviously has a lot of success in the human world solving crimes and mysteries. It's a lot harder when she works on a supernatural case, but she's been doing this for so long, she also has a lot of success in our world."

Megan paused and looked at Tony. He was shooting a thought her way. She mentally heard his request to talk to her mother about Atticus and his case. She gave him a subtle nod.

"Did you two just have a conversation?" Alex asked, still amazed and intrigued.

Megan smiled. "We did."

"Cool!" Alex exclaimed. "I can think of so many instances when that would be useful." She turned to Dimitri. "Wouldn't it be cool if you and I could talk without actually talking?"

Dimitri smiled at her. Of course Alex wasn't uncomfortable with the news. She was so open and accepting of everyone. "I think sometimes we do," he smiled at her.

"True," Alex admitted. "But that's not the same. Those two can really communicate. They can actually have a conversation without anyone else knowing what they said."

Victor was pretty sure Tony was thinking the same thing he was. Maybe Megan's mother could investigate his father's situation. He wasn't going to ask in this setting, but he'd find a chance to talk to them about it later. "So you didn't say how long you can stay," Victor changed the subject.

"Well, we were hoping we could stay awhile," Tony said reluctantly. "Things are still a bit contentious in Dublin. You know how old school those people are," he smiled at Ariel. "I guess they're a lot like some of your clan over here."

"Speaking of that," Ariel put in. "How did you find us?"

"Easy. I just sauntered into town and waited for a busy body to accost us," Tony began.

"They didn't!" Ariel gasped.

Dawn

"MaryAnn Sanders was not thrilled to see me," he grinned. "She promptly told me my hussy was out here at the depot. Now that I see who you're dating I understand the new rep." He shot a glance at Victor. "You really should raise your standards. Do you know what a scoundrel Mr. Keisser really is?"

"That may be true, but she's not dating my father," Victor announced. The whole room laughed.

The group continued to visit well into the night.

* * * *

Samantha sat in her room trying to ignore the voices and regular bursts of laughter, hoping they would disburse soon. Obviously they were all having a good time. She had no idea who the new arrivals were. She recognized the first couple from New York. She'd watched them with Ariel and Victor this afternoon. They were obviously very good friends. Ariel was glowing since they got here. The arrival of the second couple was a little strange. Initially she thought Victor was upset by it but once he reached the car, he was obviously delighted to have them here. By the time they headed to the house, the two men reminded her of young boys; maybe brothers. Now they all sat in the study joking and laughing without a care.

She thought back over her day. She'd gone to the lake that morning hoping it would help her figure things out. It hadn't, not really. She couldn't get Alex and Dimitri's conversation out of her mind. Dimitri was so loving and gentle with Alex. The longer she stayed at the lake, the more conflicted she was. After a few hours she decided to return to the farm. That's when she saw Ty. Her heart had ached at the sight. She wanted to hate him. She wanted to be afraid of him. All this time she'd been telling herself he was a monster, something to despise. One look and she remembered all the reasons she loved him. She sat, hidden in the trees watching him play with his dogs. He obviously loved those animals. Again she questioned her assessment of the warriors. Weren't dogs supposed to have some kind of instinct? She'd always heard a dog can discern good from evil. If that was true, how could they be so happy and loyal to a warrior? Unless warriors really were good.

It wasn't long before she forced herself to leave. She couldn't stand watching Ty from a distance. If she didn't move on, she knew she'd go to him. But what could she say? She wandered over to the fort and witnessed the interaction between Ariel and the new arrivals. She'd even observed a private, intimate moment between Ariel and Victor. She was beginning to feel like a voyeur. First Alex and Dimitri this morning, then Ariel and Victor this afternoon. Watching them together had confused her even more. Alex's words echoed in her head. "How can you spend any time around Victor and not see how totally selfless and compassionate he is?" As Sam continued to watch Ariel and Victor and then Victor and the new guy she couldn't think of him as a monster any longer. He was compassionate.

She was beginning to believe in her heart that she'd been wrong. It was obvious how much Dimitri loved Alex. You could see the love in his eyes. The same was true about Victor and Ariel. She didn't know if Ariel's friend was a fae or a warrior, but the love between those two was evident as well. Her mind drifted back to the night of the ball. The explosions went off and the warriors swarmed the area. Every one of them risked their own lives to save the innocent. Ty and Thomas scoured the area for bombs and worked right on top of them trying to defuse the threat and prevent another explosion. The rest of the warriors entered the unstable building and carried the wounded to safety. Monsters wouldn't risk their own lives for others. Monsters wouldn't love their partner more than themselves.

With each passing moment it was getting harder to hate them. Why was she fighting her instincts? She had realized one thing today at the lake. Her heart was telling her the warriors were good, but her mind was fighting it. She had to constantly remind herself of all the reasons she shouldn't trust them. All the reasons she should be afraid of them. What had Victor said the other day before he walked out of the room? "If she didn't know already, explaining it would be useless," something like that. She was beginning to think she did know. Not one of these guys would harm the innocent. Not one of them would take a life to get blood. Not one of them would harm the human race. She closed her eyes. Somehow, she knew she was right. So, she might as well take that last step; the warriors were the good guys. She'd been wrong. She'd been unfair. Her outburst was unforgivable. How could she ever face them again? She was embarrassed. She was ashamed. She had acted so horribly. Maybe Ariel was right and she was the monster. Otherwise, how could she have been so cruel?

Now she was depressed. After so many years of being alone she'd finally started to make friends and she'd blown it. There was no doubt in her mind, Ariel would never forgive her. What about Ty? She hadn't called him names or threatened to kill him, but she had abandoned him. She'd turned her back on him. She'd found the man of her dreams and she'd thrown it all away. She climbed into bed and tried to block out the laughter rising from below. Everyone but her was downstairs socializing, once again she didn't belong.

* * * *

The instant they were secure in their room Megan turned to Tony. "You want to be personally involved in helping Victor's father, don't you?"

"Yes," he admitted. "He's like a second father to me. I can't stand the idea that someone is trying to kill him. Do you think your mom would be willing to help?"

Megan studied her husband, he was really worried about this. "I'll call her tonight."

"Should we ask them if they want her help first?" he wondered.

"Let me call mom first and if she's game, then we can offer her services. I don't want them to get their hopes up if mom is busy and can't help," she smiled. "Victor is just as great as you said he was. I like him. I hope we can become good friends. I'll do my best to get mom." She turned and picked up her cell phone.

A few minutes later Megan hung up. "She said she's just finishing one of her cases. That's going to take a few days. Once I explained the situation, she insisted on tracking down Cornelia."

"Who's Cornelia?" Tony asked.

"She's fae. Mom's worked with her in the past and from what mom says, she's good at investigating the supernatural. Mom is going to have to try to track her down though. Last time she heard from her, Cornelia was spending time with her mother in Utah. Be prepared, that could add to the delay. Mom promised to get here as soon as she can. We'll have to find her a place to stay. She won't be comfortable here in the house. She needs her privacy to work. Do you think Victor could have an apartment ready that soon?"

"No problem," Tony assured her. "Victor's a miracle worker and I'll help." He was going to enjoy spending some time with Vic. The last time they were together Victor was depressed. He'd just been sent packing on his yearlong suspension over that panther. Tony had tried to make it a vacation, an adventure, but no matter how hard he tried he couldn't cheer Victor up. It was good to see him so happy now. "Maybe he can set one up for us, too. I'd like our own place. We might be here awhile. Are you okay with that?" he asked reluctantly. They really hadn't discussed how long their visit would be, but Tony wanted to stay as long as he could. It was going to take time for things to settle in Dublin and he knew Megan's mom was ready to move on. She'd spent too much time in Denver already. They really didn't have anywhere to go right now.

"We can stay as long as you like," she snuggled in for a hug. "I know how much these guys mean to you. We don't have anywhere to be and I'd like to stay as long as mom is here anyway. She doesn't know anyone. I think it will make things easier for her if we stay too. Let's talk to Victor in the morning about the apartments."

"Deal," he leaned down and kissed her gently. "I knew I was the luckiest man alive."

Megan laughed as they climbed into bed.

* * * *

Lilith sat in the large chair trying to talk some sense into Radek. He wasn't budging. "You can't just blow up a human military base where there are still law enforcement, coast guard and military personnel coming and going. The entire human race will be up in arms," she argued. "Radek, the humans will know it was bombed. They won't give up until they track down the person responsible. You're going to expose us all. Please, don't go through with this plan," she begged. "Let me try it my way. I can take them out one at a time. They'll never know what hit them. My sources tell me that several warriors are coming and going all the time. They've even seen the queen," she offered hoping that news would change his mind.

"That's even more reason to blow the place off the face of the earth. I want a bomb big enough to eliminate the fort all together. Nobody will survive," he relished in his new plan. He was sure if they struck at the right moment, Alex would soon be dead and he'd finally be in charge of his kingdom.

Three vampires strolled into the room. Sammael followed, chasing behind them. "I'm sorry sir," Sammael squeaked. "They wouldn't let me announce them."

"It's fine," he waved Sammael off in dismissal. "To what do I owe the honor of this visit?" Radek said sarcastically. A visit from three vampire kings was not a good sign. Something was up.

One of the vampires, a large man with chocolate skin and an intricate turban spoke first. "We've heard rumors about what's been going on here, Radek. We're not happy," Ammit warned.

"I'm not sure what you're talking about," Radek lied. He knew exactly what they were upset about. He hadn't even tried to hide his efforts. He didn't really care if the humans discovered their existence. "I trust your trip was pleasant," he was trying to sound casual. "You're a long way from Egypt, Ammit. Can I get you a human to snack on?"

Dawn

The second man narrowed his eyes. "That," Typhon accused. "That is the reason for our visit. You are entirely too callous about attacking humans." The enormous black man made the cave look small. His body decorations somehow made him more threatening. He had large earrings dangling from his ears. They were bones of some kind. There was a large gold ring looped through his nose. He was dressed as an amazon, of course. He lived in the Amazon rainforests. His waist was wrapped in an ivory cloth, he had no shirt and his large feet were laced in sandals. His arms were covered in what looked like ancient symbols.

Radek was trying to control his temper, but he was livid. How dare they try to tell him what to do? This was his kingdom. He didn't show up uninvited in Egypt, Ireland or the Amazon and try to give them orders. Who did they think they were anyway? "I'm not callous, Typhon. I was just trying to be accommodating. You don't offer visitors a drink in the Amazon?"

"Enough," Maedoc ordered. "Word has gotten all the way to Belfast about your activities."

Radek shrugged. "I hear rumors about your activities all the time."

"I'm not talking about vampire rumors Radek," Maedoc continued. "Word has hit the humans everywhere. People are panicked. I understand you are turning humans at an alarming rate. Too many people have disappeared in one area in such a short amount of time. That is inexcusable. Nobody cares if you want to rage a war. Fight the fae all you want. Just don't risk exposure for the rest of us by being reckless."

"I'm not reckless," Radek glowered. "Every action I take is carefully planned out. It's methodically executed. I have never been reckless."

"Oh really," Typhon interrupted. "Why don't you explain to us how creating vampiric animals isn't reckless. Your father tried that years ago. You somehow thought you could control them better than he did? Have you completely forgotten your history? Or do you just enjoy experimenting without regard for your own species? Then there was the bombing of two shifter communities in one night. The humans are aware of that as well, they're just confused as to why it happened."

What was he talking about? Radek didn't know anything about vampiric animals. He glanced at Lilith and knew. What had she done? He couldn't let them see he was in the dark. "I'm not going to explain my strategy to anyone. You'll just have to trust me when I tell you I know what I'm doing and this will all be over soon."

Ammit was watching Radek carefully. He didn't know about the animals. Had he completely lost control of his kingdom? "I'm afraid we don't trust you, Radek," Ammit said honestly. "We wouldn't have traveled thousands of miles if we did. We're here to help you understand the situation a little better. Let me explain what's going to happen. I want you to listen very carefully because I'm only going to warn you once."

"Wait a minute," Radek stopped him. "Do you honestly believe you can show up in my house, my kingdom and order me to do anything?" He was getting angrier by the minute. These three were talking to him like he was an idiot or something.

"Yes, we do," Maedoc informed him calmly. "To begin, you might want to listen to Lilith. If you go through with this asinine plan to bomb a military installation you're going to have to answer to us."

Dawn

Radek was breathing heavily now. So, they had overheard his earlier conversation. He was not going to tolerate this injustice, not even from another vampire king. "I'll rage my war the way I see fit. I don't answer to anyone!" Radek was almost screaming.

"That's where you're wrong," Typhon said calmly. "If word of your methodically planned activities reaches just one of us," Typhon paused for effect. "If even the slightest hint of trouble spreads through the human world and reaches our end of the earth, you're going to regret it," Typhon took a step closer to Radek. "We know your struggling with this war. That's why you've turned so many humans in such a short amount of time. New York is on alert. The disappearances are international news now. Humans in the Amazon Rainforest have even heard of the problem. That in itself is unheard of. This reckless disregard for secrecy will stop immediately!" He warned.

"And if I don't?" Radek challenged.

"If you don't," Ammit answered quietly. "You will not only be fighting a war with the fae, you will be fighting a war against us. Our soldiers have not been depleted. My army is strong, Typhon's army is unbeatable. Maedoc's army has more experience in warfare than all of us put together. You truly do not want us as your enemies. Back down Radek. If I hear you have bombed the military base off the face of the earth, the attack will be swift. You won't even see us coming."

"Swift and concise," Maedoc added. "You can't win. Back down now. Fight your war responsibly. We will not sit back and allow you to expose our presence to the world. We will not suffer because of your greed. This is not a negotiation, Radek. You need to understand that. It's all or nothing."

Lilith was holding her breath. She'd almost panicked and ran when Maedoc entered the room. She hadn't offended him personally, but his extended family wasn't too happy with her. And, numerous vampires in his region would kill her in an instant if they saw her. She'd had to flee for her life, literally, the last time she was in Ireland. Seeing him here was unnerving. She watched Radek carefully. He was so angry. She sat there, silently hoping he didn't blow this. One wrong move and they were all going to die.

Radek didn't like it, but he had to back down. His army was depleted. The warriors were too powerful to attack with two or three vampires. Every time he planned a mission hundreds of men were lost. He was being reckless, but it was only because he needed a larger army. He needed more vampires to conquer his kingdom. Radek was determined to have his whole kingdom. He would not settle for anything less. There was no way he could fight these men too. "I will admit I have taken a few too many humans within New York City. That is easily rectified," he agreed. Even that annoyed him. Who cared about the stupid human's anyway?

The three men studied Radek. They all knew he was angry, but was he unstable? Maedoc had heard rumors about Radek's relentless passion and greed for years. Many among their people believed he was actually crazy. Radek's father Balthazar had been sadistic and reckless as well. Maedoc believed Radek was just as mentally unstable as Balthazar had been. Clearly it was genetic. Some wire had been crossed in that bloodline. Balthazar had been feared by all. Every king in the land knew Balthazar would assassinate them in an instant if he wanted their kingdom. Radek was now being as reckless as his father. He had to be stopped, regardless of the price.

The four men continued the standoff until Radek appeared to relax. "For now I will appease your wishes," he conceded. "I will

Dawn

hold off on bombing the military base. I will also hunt and recruit somewhere other than New York. Does that satisfy you? The humans will remain blissfully ignorant," he said with contempt. He really didn't care about the humans. His war was bigger than that. Once he created his heir, once he had a son that could shift, these three kings would change their tune. His boy was going to rule the world! Radek would not forget this inexcusable offense. He began to think about ways to get revenge against these arrogant kings. All three of them would suffer for their intrusion and interference. In time, Radek's son would make them pay dearly. That knowledge calmed Radek's anger, slightly.

Typhon was not satisfied with Radek's words, but he knew that was all they would get for now. Radek was on edge. The slightest push could lead to disaster. They had taken their stand. They had made their position clear. Now it was time to go home and wait. He planned to keep a closer eye on Radek from now on. He knew his two friends would do the same.

It was Ammit that answered. "For now," he agreed. "For now we will accept your word that your tactics will change," he paused and glanced at his comrades. "But I hope you have taken us seriously, Radek. This is not an idol threat. We've told you what will happen if you expose us again. Break your word and we go to war." He turned and strolled out the door, his long black cloak billowing behind him. Maedoc and Typhon exited as well.

Lilith let out the breath she was holding. She was relieved, but she could see Radek was beyond pissed. She slowly rose and walked towards him. Once she was standing in front of him she rubbed her body seductively against his. "Don't fret my love," she cooed. "Nobody will know about their visit. Let me go to the fort and proceed with my plan. I know I can pick them off one at a time. I'll start with the two humans and the young shifter. That will give me time to heal. Then, I'll work on the fae and the warriors. Our dream will be a reality soon. The kingdom will be yours. Your minions will never know about any of this. Besides you and me, the only one that knows about their visit is Sammael. He won't tell anyone. He's too loyal."

"Yes. Sammael is loyal," Radek said still wondering if Lilith was. He didn't really have a choice now. He had to let Lilith execute her plan. He supposed it could work. If not, Lilith would be dead. He mused, would that be so bad? If she'd been with Hector, she had to die anyway. This way, he wouldn't have to admit to his followers that his partner had betrayed him. He began to fantasize about his future. Soon he would be bedding a shifter. Then, he'd have a son. He'd miss Lilith, but betrayal could not be tolerated. He would enjoy the time he had with her, then move on. He may never know if she had betrayed him for sure, but a king could not doubt his partner's loyalty.

Lilith gently pushed Radek's robe over his shoulders and watched as it tumbled to the ground. "Give Sammael a job," she suggested as she gently kissed his neck. "We need to recruit outside of New York. We have several strong men and women to choose from." She pressed her body harder against his and took his mouth in hers. "Choose a few and let Sammael organize the distribution. If you make him part of the plan, he will be even more devoted to you and your cause." Lilith slid her hands over Radek's naked body. Maybe if she seduced him tonight, he wouldn't work himself up over the unpleasant visit he'd just endured. As unsettling as it was to be in a room with three powerful, angry vampire kings. She was kind of grateful for their surprise visit. Radek's hands were tied now. He had to let her go to the military base. Soon, she would have that pesky human just where she wanted her. Somehow she needed to convince Radek to let her leave tonight.

Dawn

Radek gave in to Lilith. He always enjoyed being with her. She was wild and uninhibited. He wondered if he would ever find another mate that would satisfy him as she did. He couldn't resist her. He didn't try. Slowly they made their way to the bed. Radek sat down and gently pushed Lilith away. "Once we are finished here, I need you to put your plan in motion. If I can't bomb that base, I want the killing to begin at once. Your plan will take longer than mine. We must begin tonight."

Lilith pretended to pout. "If you wish, my Lord," she whispered. "I was hoping for an entire night with you, but I understand the need to begin immediately." She climbed on top of him, pressing her body to his. She smiled seductively, "I'm going to miss you. Let's make this a night to remember." She grinned when Radek laid back on the bed. Sex with Radek tonight was going to be satisfying for a change. She was going to celebrate. She was going to the fort.

Chapter Nine

The large group sat in the study, relaxing after a long busy day. Kylee and Samantha had retired to their rooms. Dusty was organizing his bunker. Dimitri had agreed to let him stay on. The more he thought about it, the more he liked the idea. "Once Dusty gets a few more bunkers organized, I think I'm going to recruit more kids to come out and help," Dimitri announced.

Ty was surprised. They weren't ready for students yet. "Don't you think we should wait on that?" he asked. "There's still so much to be done. I don't have time to supervise kids. We don't even have the professors lined up yet."

"We're not opening the academy," Dimitri assured him. "I just think it might be a good idea to recruit future attendees to help with the setup. Most of the droids are ready. We can set up oh...maybe a dozen bunkers and bring the kids out. You only have five bunkers ready, Ty. At this rate it will be years before the academy can open. If we have the kids to help, they can paint the bunkers, cut the carpet, lay the mats and furnish the rooms. They'll work most of the day, but each of them will be assigned their own droid. That way they get a jump start on training as well."

It wasn't a bad idea, Ty thought. It just meant more people to contend with. Kids could be reckless and a lot of work. "Who's going to supervise?" he asked.

Dimitri turned to Atticus. "I was wondering if you would do that for us Atticus," he began.

"Me?" Atticus said surprised.

"Yeah," Dimitri confirmed. "You're good with kids. You're experienced as a warrior, they can learn a lot from you."

"I suppose I could try," Atticus said reluctantly. He was beginning to feel useless around here. At home he had things to do, a farm to run. Here, he was lost and was beginning to get bored. "I've been wondering what I could do while I'm here to help. Maybe this will give me a purpose."

"Dimitri?" Megan began.

"Yeah?" he turned towards her.

"I was wondering if you would mind if my mother joined us," she requested.

"Of course not," he assured her. "We might get a little tight on space though."

Megan glanced at Victor. He wasn't saying a word. "Well, there would be more to her visit than just socializing."

"Oh?" Dimitri was curious.

"I don't know if Victor told you, but mom's a private investigator. I've asked her to come out and look into Atticus's case. We're all worried about his safety and mom can poke around without raising too much suspicion. Nobody knows her here. She blends in well," Megan assured them. "It's time to move on from Denver anyway. She's been there too long. She needs to assume a new identity."

"That's a great idea!" Alex exclaimed.

"Mom has already agreed to come. She didn't say what she wanted to be called though. Right now she goes by Tala, but when she arrives we'll find out what she wants you to call her. It's usually some sort of deviation of her given name," Megan grinned.

"What's her given name?" Atticus asked. "I've been around a while, I wonder if we've met."

"I doubt it," Megan continued. "She doesn't usually go this far east. Her parents were a little eccentric. They named her KyraTala Dylana Fitzgerald."

"That's certainly a mouthful," Victor teased.

Megan smiled at him. "Now you know why mom hates it." Megan loved her grandparents, but they were a little nuts. "Anyway, mom usually sticks with some form of that monstrosity for her first name, but changes the last one around. It makes it a lot easier to remember who you are. She prefers Tala, but she's used Kyra or Lana or even Dylan in the past."

Alex turned to Victor. "Are you okay with this?"

"I am," he assured her. "Tony already asked me to work on getting one of the apartment's ready. It sounds like Megan's mother is a few days out so that should give me enough time. Megan and Tony also wanted to move over to the apartment complex. That way Megan can be closer to her mother. I thought that was a great idea. But I wanted to double check with you," he addressed Dimitri. "We'll be taking two of the rooms intended for instructors."

"I agree. The apartment complex is the perfect arrangement for our new arrivals." He turned to Tony and Megan, "does that mean you'll be staying with us for a while?"

"We'd like to," Tony confessed. "I'm looking forward to spending time with an old friend and getting to know new ones," he added looking towards Alex. "I don't know if you are aware of this, but my father and Luke were very good friends. They fought together in many wars. Our people haven't always been at peace," he added.

"No, I didn't know that," Alex confessed. "I'd love to hear about it sometime."

Tony hesitated. He wasn't sure what Alex knew about her mother's past. "There's another closer connection as well," he finally said.

"What's that?" Alex asked. She was curious now. Tony seemed a little hesitant to share what he knew about their family history.

"My mother owes your mother a great debt," he finally told her. "It's one she will never be able to repay. I want you to know that you have the full support of my family. If there is ever anything myself or my parents can do for you please don't hesitate to ask. My older brother Richard is on board as well. Mom ordered me to tell you the debt has been passed onto you now that Marlena is gone."

Victor was studying Tony. He knew when the man was uncomfortable. What was the connection between Marlena and Elizabeth? Victor didn't realize they even knew each other. What debt could Elizabeth and her family owe Alex? He knew Tony. His friend would be humble about his family and downplay their importance. Victor decided it was up to him to explain the situation. "Alex," Victor said getting the attention of everyone in the room. "Tony's parents are very powerful in our world," he smiled as Tony shifted uncomfortably. "I guess the best way to demonstrate their position is to compare them to the British Monarchy in the human world. Not as they are now, but as they were before Great Britain shifted to a democratic form of government.

Charles and Elizabeth are highly regarded among our people. If we were to have some kind of global situation, their opinions and desires would be honored above all others. They are very powerful allies. Sorry Tony," Victor glanced at his friend, "I know discussing this makes you uncomfortable. I just think Alex needs to know what a powerful ally she has in your family. If they feel indebted to her for some reason, she needs to know what that means. She needs to know how monumental that is."

Tony nodded. He knew his family was powerful and very well respected. He just didn't like to flaunt that power.

"Were our mothers friends as well?" Alex asked. She was surprised someone that powerful would blindly offer their support so easily.

"Eventually," Tony confirmed. "They eventually became very close," Tony paused. "There is something I need to tell you, Alex. It might be difficult to hear." Megan slid closer to Tony. She was getting his vibes of anxiety, but she didn't know why. He hadn't told her anything about a connection involving his mother. She was sure whatever it was, it was horrible.

Alex studied Tony. She'd come to like him a lot over the past couple days. She loved the joy he brought into Victor's life just by being here. Nothing he could tell her would make her change her mind about him. "What is it you're worried about Tony? I know my mother had a difficult past. If you can shed some light on any of it, I would be grateful. You see, she never talked to me about this life. She sheltered me from it. What little I know I've gotten from old friends like Atticus and a book she left. It would be nice to learn more about her life, the life I wasn't a part of," she pressed.

"This story isn't a happy one," he warned.

"Please tell it anyway," Alex requested.

Everyone in the room was curious now. No one said a word. They just waited for Tony to share his story.

"Well, you probably don't know this, but the monarchy in Dublin flows through my mother's lineage, not my father's."

Victor knew that. It was a common joke in the family. But what did that have to do with Tony's mother and Alex?

"I'm ashamed to say I don't know much about other fae governments or their royalty," Alex admitted. "As I said, mother kept this world from me. I still have so much to learn. I would love to meet other monarchies, but unfortunately that is going to have to wait until things calm down a bit. I can't leave my people while they are at war."

Tony took a deep breath and began his explanation. "The year 1340, was a turbulent year in Ireland. For many years there had been a struggle between the Irish and the English. During this particular time, the Irish were trying to regain control of their government, their lands, everything from what I hear. It was the beginning of several hundred years of conflict which culminated in the Cromwellian Conquest of Ireland in 1649," he glanced at Victor. They both had a lot of memories of that war. It's where they first met. He hated that war, but wouldn't change a thing about his experience. Otherwise, he and Victor wouldn't have such a strong, unbreakable bond. He wouldn't give up their friendship for anything.

"Anyway, they were still recovering from Edward Bruce's invasion in 1318. Then there was the Burke Civil War in 1338 and numerous battles in between. Land was changing hands by force. According to my father there was a new battle almost every year," he paused to take a sip of his coffee. "None of the battles were really related. It was just a hard time in that region," he paused. "The fae tried to stay out of it. They would only get involved if the fight directly impacted them or their family. Well, to be honest that hasn't changed. It's the reason the fae and vampires of Ireland can still coexist. They mind their own business for the most part."

Victor laughed. "Aren't you forgetting that incident with your father?"

Tony knew exactly what incident Victor was talking about but if he explained, they would be getting way off subject. "Why don't we leave that for another day?"

"I'll tell the story, then you can get back to your saga," Victor offered. Clearly Tony's story was going to be serious and probably depressing from the way he was acting. Victor wanted to lighten the mood a little. "Don't forget where you are. We'll get back to you in a minute," he winked at Megan. "So, one day Charles is taking a leisurely evening walk, minding his own business. Oh, Charles is Tony's father and the Fae King in Ireland. Anyway he's out walking, minding his own business when he hears his neighbor scream for help. He tries to ignore it, but the man is carrying on to the point Charles can't just walk away. He had noticed some new vampires in the area lately and is worried the neighbor, who also happens to be human, is going to expose them all if he doesn't shut up. The man was screaming loud enough to wake the dead.

So, Charles silently sneaks around the castle to take a look. He's not surprised to see a vampire attacking his neighbor. Charles is hesitant to get involved. He doesn't want the vampire world to think the fae are going to interrupt in their feeding habits, but Mr. Stoker won't shut up. He's making such a racket that Charles decides he has to intervene, there are too many humans in the area. He quickly moves in and a battle ensues. Charles eventually disposes of the vampire and is extremely relieved to discover Stoker is unconscious. After carrying him to his bed chamber, Charles heads for home. Imagine his surprise when a few years later, his neighbor writes a book about Dracula the Vampire!" Victor laughed at the look on everyone's face. "You got it, Charles saved Bram Stoker from a vampire attack and the result was that ridiculous book. To this day, Charles hasn't forgiven himself for saving that man's life. He's just grateful Stoker was unconscious when he arrived or the fae would be featured just as prominently in that farce of a story as well," Victor laughed. "Don't get Charles started on the ridiculous idea that vampires can shift into bats."

Tony couldn't help but join Victor, he grinned uncontrollably. "To this day dad won't walk past old Stoker's castle. The whole incident still pisses him off."

The room erupted in laughter. Ariel had wondered how Bram Stoker came up with his story. She'd always assumed he'd had some kind of encounter with a vampire. He couldn't have known much, most of it was hogwash.

"Anyway, back to my original story before I was so rudely interrupted." Tony flashed a grin at Victor. "The fae mostly kept to themselves. It's a lot easier for vampires to wreak havoc when the humans are fighting each other since any deaths are credited to the war. During this time the population of vamps in Ireland increased substantially. Which meant there were occasional attacks on the fae. We all understand the bloodlust vampires have for our kind. Needless to say, the double threat of the human battles and the vampires made everyone afraid. Parents kept their children at home. Nobody wandered around after dark," he said soberly.

"My mother was very sheltered," he continued. "Her parents literally hid her away from everyone. In addition to the complex dangers of war, there had also been rumors within the community that Keehan Donahue wanted to overthrow the monarchy and take over as king. The easiest way to do that would be to get rid of the Gallagher's daughter, Elizabeth, who happens to be my mother." Tony glanced at Alex. She looked like she was getting impatient. He needed to hurry. "One night when mom was about sixty two years old, she snuck out of the compound. They never let her leave so she was elated to be free. She wandered around the countryside all day. She had no idea where she was when she stumbled onto a little village of humans. They were having some kind of festival so mom joined in. She loved the food and the music and she loved being able to socialize. Mom was having so much fun, she lost track of time. She panicked and ran for home when it began to get dark. Unfortunately, she'd gotten lost. She had no idea where she was or which direction would lead her back home.

Eventually she stumbled onto a road and decided to follow it. It vaguely looked familiar. She walked the road for miles before she was sure about her surroundings. Her hopes soared, she was going to make it home again. That's when Balthazar jumped out of the dark and attacked."

"No!" Ariel exclaimed. The room was in shock. Radek was bad, but his father was sadistic and ruthless.

Tony glanced at Ariel then continued. "Mom was obviously terrified. She'd heard about vampires, but had never actually seen one. She'd been so sheltered she didn't even know how to fight back. She was lying on the ground, curled up in a ball. The vampire was on top of her. She assumed he was trying to find a good bite. Mom kept twisting and turning to avoid the sharp teeth. Then, suddenly the vampire's weight was gone. Next she heard a big thud. She hesitantly looked up to find out how she'd been saved when she saw Marlena valiantly fighting the monster.

Mom didn't know Marlena at the time, it was just a woman not much older than she was battling the vampire that had attacked her. Mom didn't know what to do. She was looking around, desperate to find something she could use to help her savior when Balthazar struck Marlena in the head and knocked her out cold. Mom froze, she felt terrified and helpless. She didn't know what to do. Balthazar quickly gathered up Marlena and fled into the nearby forest. Mom ran home and tried to enlist her parents help. They needed to go after them. They needed to rescue the brave woman that had saved her life. My grandparents were horrified that their only daughter had almost been killed. They refused to help and proceeded to lock mom in the cellar to ensure her safety." Tony looked at Alex. He wanted to see how she was taking it. She seemed okay.

"That's how mom became pregnant with Radek," Alex finally said. She looked at Dimitri. "Did you know about this?"

"No," he shook his head. "We all knew Radek was Marlena's child, but nobody seemed to know how it happened."

"Not even in my day," Atticus added. "Things were different back then. I think maybe it was easier to keep secrets," he looked at Victor. They had a few family secrets of their own.

"Nobody knew what had become of Marlena," Tony continued. "Mom and her parents assumed she'd been drained by Balthazar. One day, fifty three years later, mom was again traveling home from the village when she spotted what looked like a body. It was in the middle of the day, so she wasn't concerned. She was mostly curious. As she got closer, she heard the lump moan. Mom rushed over and turned the body over. It was Marlena. She was almost in the exact same spot she had been when she disappeared. Marlena was a mess. She was so small and weak. She was also covered in bruises and had a few scrapes on her arms that were bleeding. Mom took her back to her home and insisted her parents take care of her. They did.

Marlena stayed with my mother's family for several years after that. She refused to go home for a long time. That's how the two women became very good friends. Mom always felt guilty that Marlena had been taken instead of her. Marlena insisted it was for the best," he gave Alex an apologetic look. "Your mother had endured unspeakable conditions the fifty three years she was imprisoned. Balthazar had raped her regularly in his desperation to create an heir," Tony paused. Alex was crying now. He hated relaying this story but he knew it was important for her to know.

"Do you want me to stop?" he asked her gently.

"No," she sniffed.

Dawn

Dimitri had gone to her. He pulled her into his arms and cradled her gently. After a few moments, Dimitri sat in the large chair and pulled Alex onto his lap. "Finish your story Tony. She can take it."

"Mom and Marlena became very close," he reluctantly continued. "Eventually, Marlena was able to open up to mom and explain to her what had happened. By this time Marlena was a very different person than the woman mom saw battling the vampire to save her life. She'd become subdued. She was quiet and very introverted. One day Marlena confessed to mom that she had a child. She explained that Radek was only three when she escaped. At first, she thought maybe she could take him with her. She hoped that if she raised him with the fae instead of as a vampire, Radek could be a good person. Marlena was good and Radek was half hers. One night, she awoke to find Radek torturing a small boy. He was clearly enjoying it. She was horrified at the sight, but realized there was no hope. Radek was already his father's son. He would never be anything but a vampire. She had a plan to escape in place already and without the added risk of stealing Radek, her escape would be much easier.

Once Marlena could see light coming from the cave opening, she put her plan into action. She was weak and injured, but she got herself out. Once in the sunlight she knew she was free. Nobody could follow her now. She pushed herself to continue and eventually got to the clearing near the road where she had been taken, but she was too weak to go any further. Balthazar rarely provided food or any type of nutrients. He wanted Marlena weak. He couldn't control her otherwise. After fifty years in captivity the fierce fighter mom admired was gone. Marlena was broken.

One hundred and fourteen years of war between the vampires and the fae, followed Marlena's escape. By this time Radek was 117

236

years old. He was just like his father. One night, a large group of fae fighters and warriors snuck into Balthazar's cave. When the raid was over, Balthazar was dead as were most of his best fighters. Radek was insecure and immediately signed the peace treaty. That treaty has lasted for over five hundred years," Tony said regretfully. "Marlena stayed in Ireland for a while, but eventually she couldn't take it anymore. In 1607, she heard about a group of settlers moving to a new region. Marlena and her parents boarded the ship and settled in Jamestown with the rest of the humans. Radek remained in Ireland for years after that."

"So I don't get it," Alex said. "When did mom's family become rulers over their people?"

Atticus answered that. "They actually already were. Marlena's grandfather Titan was one of the brothers that had experimented until the warriors were created. They took the monarchy away from Darren Dillinger. Darren's father, Joseph, was a great man. The people loved him. Their community thrived under Joseph, but eventually vampires also discovered the island where they lived. The human occupants traveled frequently by ship to trade. On one of the trips back, the humans brought a shipload of vampires with them. Shortly after that, Joseph was attacked and killed by a large group of vampires. Naturally, his son Darren took over. He was weak and afraid. He had witnessed the attack on his father and was horrified at the carnage. Darren refused to fight or even go near the vampires. The community was falling apart. That's when Titan and his brothers decided to create their protectors. Once the warriors were developed it was easy to overtake the monarchy. Titan was the obvious choice. He was a born leader. Years later when he died, his son Oedipus took over as king.

Oedipus and his wife Athena moved their people to what is now England when their island was destroyed. They weren't happy there and traveled to Ireland to consider their options. They were only visiting when their daughter Marlena was captured by Balthazar. Of course they were devastated. They had heard about the Gallagher's and rumor had it their community was a peaceful place to live. Eventually Marlena returned to her family. Oedipus was instrumental in rallying the fae to fight back in retaliation for the trauma his daughter had suffered, which is what began the long war that Tony talked about. Once Balthazar was killed, the area was relatively peaceful. Athena loved Ireland, which is why they decided to stay. The entire community relocated to the region. When Marlena and her family left for America, many of their followers joined them. Gradually, over the next several years the rest of them followed as well. A few stayed in Ireland and joined the Gallagher clan, but not many. They were so used to being together they found it difficult to be separated. All of them had lived through so much," Atticus added.

"I didn't go over with the original group, but after my uh...trouble, I knew it was time to start a new life in a new land. Victor and I relocated. Jamestown was dwindling by then. Oedipus decided to relocate again. They all thought it would be suspicious if only their families survived. At that point we kind of scattered. I went to Lancaster, of course it wasn't Lancaster at the time. I settled on the farm and made a life for myself. I can't tell you much about the rest of the community. Oberon would have more information than me regarding that. Oedipus and Athena were killed in 1892. The events leading up to their death are still a mystery. Most of us believe Radek was responsible, but there was no way to prove it. Also if we accused him of breaking the treaty we would be at war again. Nobody wanted that, especially without proof of wrongdoing, so no action was taken. Marlena accepted her position as queen and actively ruled our people for the next 83 years. She was a very private, introverted person back then. We all knew her time with

Balthazar had taken a toll. Even so, she was still compassionate and a very good leader. Her people loved her.

In 1974, she met James," Atticus turned to Alex. "Your father. He was human of course, but I was told that Marlena was finally happy for the first time since her childhood. I think you know the rest," Atticus finished abruptly.

Atticus had caught Ty's attention. He'd never heard Marlena's human husband's name before. His mind was reeling. Was this a coincidence? He didn't think so. "Atticus, do you remember what year James was killed?" He was trying to sound casual but he thought he was onto something.

"Uh...that would have been in 1985 I believe, why?" Atticus asked.

"No reason, I was just curious. I've been trying to keep a time line of events in my head. A lot of the history you and Tony have described here, I've never heard before," he said honestly.

"I think most of it is new to all of us," Ariel added. "Orin, have you heard any of this from the council?"

"No," he admitted. "We don't really talk about history though. We only get together to discuss problems."

"I'm beat," Breena told Orin hesitantly. "Are you ready to go to bed?"

"I am," Alex chimed in. "Dimitri and I need to get an early start."

"Are you going back to New York already?" Megan asked.

Dawn

"We have to," Alex told her. "Dimitri has finished installing the alarm and Jack has an emergency back in New York that can't wait. The construction crew will be meeting us at the hanger early tomorrow morning. I hope they can come back soon and finish the project but who knows. Anyway, Dimitri and I plan to come back as soon as we can."

The group scattered and headed for bed.

* * * *

Ty was staring at the ceiling, wide awake. He couldn't sleep. Ideas were running through his head. He couldn't stop thinking about that night in his room with Samantha. The night she fixed his gaming program. She'd sat for hours trying to conquer that game, or at least get to level four so they could know for sure it was fixed. In the beginning Ty had sat quietly watching her play. He enjoyed seeing her have fun. It reminded him why he loved to create games so much. Knowing his work brought others joy made all the junk that came with it worth the aggravation.

Eventually, Ty had started a conversation with her. He wanted to know about Sam's past. He knew her family had been killed by vampires, but nobody could figure out why. He hoped if she opened up to him, they might have a clue to follow. He started off by talking about his family. He told her how he'd gotten his start in explosives capping wells in his family's oil fields. That was the only part of the oil industry that was tolerable. Working the fields was dusty and dirty. The heat was unbearable. He still didn't know how his Aunt Pearl could love it so much. His father couldn't take it either. Eventually his dad and his Uncle Steve went back to construction. Ty jumped at the chance to join them.

Ty immediately began to research explosive demolition. He didn't tell Sam, but he was using it before it really became popular. He was careful not to let on how much time had gone by between each career change. Ty eventually moved away from construction and started his gaming business. He was happy now and couldn't imagine changing careers again. He still helped his father and his uncle occasionally when they needed a building demolished. These days his explosive knowledge had more to do with his personal life than his business.

Samantha had eventually opened up a little. But not until she chastised him for distracting her while she was trying to play. She'd told him about her childhood. About the country home her parents had owned and then about her Uncle James and Aunt Lana. They were obviously very close. She described her cousin Lexie as full of energy and adorable. Sam said Lexie had followed her everywhere. Anything Samantha did, Lexie wanted to try. Sam had only briefly mentioned her brother Michael. She said Lexie worshiped him and followed him everywhere. That's when she started to shut down. She quickly added that when she was twelve her uncle and his family were murdered by vampires. Then three years later, her family was murdered. That's when she went to live with her paternal grandparents. They hoped the vampires had been after her mother's family for some reason. It seemed logical since Uncle James was killed first and then her mother. Her maternal grandparents were also killed a short time later. Sam didn't seem to know them very well. They must have been right because the vampires never bothered her paternal grandparents. After college, Sam moved to New York and immediately got a job with D-Tech

Ty continued to think about Sam's family. Could it really be that simple? He ran it through his mind, connecting the dots. The puzzle pieces just seemed to snap together. He had a few things to clarify before he took this to Dimitri, but he was beginning to think he had solved the mystery. He closed his eyes but his mind was still racing. Over an hour later he finally drifted off to sleep.

The following morning, Dimitri and Alex stood at the front door. They needed to get on the road. Alex pulled Breena into a big hug. "I am just so happy for you," she said enthusiastically. "Keep me posted. I'm so excited. This will be my first baby as queen. Do I have to dub the child a member of the community or something?"

Breena laughed. She pressed her palms to her stomach. "I can't believe it's real," she was glowing. "We owe it all to you, Alex. I can never repay you for the miracle you've given us. Thank you."

"Don't mention it," Alex brushed her off. She was glad she'd decided to heal Breena completely while she was taking care of the other injuries. At the time she'd worried she was being presumptuous. But Breena's joy made her glad she was a healer. She was proud of her gift. It was something that could actually help people. "We've gotta go," she hugged Victor and Ariel. "See you soon," she called as Dimitri ushered her out the door.

Dimitri pulled the car onto the highway. He glanced at Alex. "I guess it's good you're rich," he teased. "You would never make it on time to take a commercial flight like normal people."

"In case you've forgotten, I used to live in Paris. I had to get there somehow. It wasn't on one of Luke's private jets, either. I also took a commercial flight back on that awful day Luke died. Now, I get to leave when I want and know my private plane will be waiting whenever I arrive," she said lightly.

They drove in silence for about a mile before Dimitri decided to broach the subject he'd been struggling with. "Alex?" he said, glancing her way.

"Yeah?" she answered still watching out the window.

"I need to talk to you about something serious," he told her.

Alex swung her head around and studied Dimitri. His expression was sober. "What?" she asked.

"It's about Ariel," he said hesitantly.

"What about her?" she asked. "Is something wrong?"

"No. Not exactly," he paused. "Nothing new, anyway," he answered secretively.

"What do you mean by that?" Alex asked him.

"I don't really know how to ask this. I want you to do me a favor. A favor that is actually for Ariel, but she would never ask it of you," he paused. "When Ariel had her...situation. You know what I'm talking about, right?"

"When she was kidnapped and shot," Alex supplied.

"Right," Dimitri agreed. "Well, the injury was pretty serious. I think if she was human she would have died. She healed, but nobody knows if that bullet damaged her too severely. Ariel has always wanted children, but we just don't know if she's going to be able to have them. You know the fae have difficult pregnancies anyway. If Ariel is already damaged going in, she may never be able to carry a child."

Dawn

Alex sobered. "I had no idea there could be permanent damage," she told him softly. "Why didn't Ariel say anything? Why didn't she just ask me to check her out and fix any problems she might have?"

"Like I said, Ariel would never ask for that. I'm sure she's considered it. I know she would be grateful to you if you did it. But she'd never ask. She'd see it as a betrayal of your friendship. She'd feel like she was using you for your powers. Do you understand?" Dimitri asked.

"I understand what you are saying, I don't understand why she would feel that way," Alex told him. "What good is my gift if I can't help the people I love? If my gift can give Ariel the ability to have a child with Victor, I'd never hesitate to use it for that purpose."

"I know that. Ariel does, too. I'm just telling you she will never ask. She might secretly wish for it. In fact, I would be surprised if she hasn't seriously considered it. But she'll never ask. I know her. Her sense of right and wrong will not allow her to use your gift to gain personally."

"So, you want me to just take care of it?" She realized what Dimitri was asking. "You want me to go in and heal her if necessary without her permission. Like I did with Breena."

Dimitri looked at her. "I do," he admitted. "The difference is that with Breena you didn't know if she would want it. I'm telling you, there's no doubt that Ariel would want this. She'd be thrilled if you took care of her. You don't need to stress about it. You don't need to worry if you're doing the right thing. You will be," he assured her.

"I don't know. First of all, I can't do anything unless she's already injured. She's good. The chances of that are pretty slim. Now that she's with Victor it's even less likely," Alex considered. Should she heal Ariel if she had the chance? What if she was angry with her? She couldn't bare losing her friendship.

"Alex I know you're over analyzing this," Dimitri chastised. "I've known Ariel longer than anyone. We're close. I'm telling you it's something she longs for but could never ask. That's why I'm asking for her. I'm not saying seek her out and try to create an opportunity. I am just asking you to take care of it if she's ever injured and needs your help."

Alex was silent for a long time. Was this the right thing to do? She'd seen how excited Ariel was for Breena. She'd been protective of Bree since she arrived at the fort. It wasn't like she had to do it right away. Ariel wouldn't even try to get pregnant until her and Victor were married. That gave Alex time. Would it be so bad to go in and take care of any problems without Ariel's knowledge? According to Dimitri she didn't know one way or the other. Maybe she could heal Ariel's problems and keep it a secret. No. If Ariel had a problem and Alex fixed it, she'd have to tell her. For Alex, the not knowing would be worse than anything. She was still conflicted, but she could see it was important to Dimitri. She knew she'd give him anything. "Okay," she finally agreed. "If I have the chance, I'll do what I can."

"Thank you," he said sincerely. "I know you're not sure I'm right, but this will mean so much to Ariel," he assured her. "You will tell her, right?"

"Yes," she answered. "I thought about doing it on the sly, but I know I could never keep something like that from Ariel. It doesn't seem honest somehow. Plus, if it were me, I'd want to know that everything was fine if I could. It seems cruel to do it and then make her worry about it. If I do it, I'm going to have to tell her."

Dimitri pulled into the private drive of the airport and stopped. He walked to the passenger side of the car and pulled Alex into his arms. "Thank you," he said again as he leaned down and gave her a gentle kiss. "This really is the right thing. I wouldn't ask you to do it if I believed it was something she didn't want. Just think about Breena and how happy she is that you took care of her," he suggested.

"I agree. I think Ariel will be grateful. I just don't like doing it without her permission. It's not a deal breaker though. I'll take care of it if I can." She leaned in and kissed him this time. "I promise."

* * * *

Samantha was still avoiding everyone, but not because she was afraid or conflicted. She just didn't know how to face them. She'd behaved so badly and she was embarrassed. She was sure they would never forgive her. Samantha walked into the house and froze when she heard someone walking towards her.

"You left early this morning," Kylee said as she entered the foyer. "Working at the plant again?" she asked.

"Uh yeah," Samantha stammered. "I had some things I needed to look into. It was kind of important so I wanted to get an early start."

"Liar," Kylee accused. "You wanted to escape before anyone got up."

"Uh," Sam began. What was she supposed to say to that?

"Don't deny it. I know what you're doing. You missed Alex and Dimitri. They had to leave this morning. Something pressing in New York. Everyone else is still over at the fort I think. I know Victor and Ariel are working on the apartments and Dusty's busy on the bunkers. I got hungry," Kylee confessed. "I had to come back and find me a snack before dinner. I don't know how they do it. They can work themselves to death and then sit up socializing all night, then get up and start fresh the next day."

Sam smiled. "They do seem to have extraordinary stamina," she agreed. She was sorry Alex had left before she'd had a chance to talk to her. Maybe that was better though. It would give her time to figure out what to say.

"Well, I've gotta get back to the lab," Kylee informed her. "I still have an hour or so before it starts to get dark. I want to get the work space finished today. If I don't leave now, I'll never achieve my goal."

"You seem to be settling in here nicely," Samantha observed. "Do you miss the hospital? I mean, don't you have to get back soon or something."

"I love it here," Kylee confessed. "If they'd let me. I'd quit the hospital and work for these guys full time. I really don't want to leave. Especially once I heard they were going to build a lab. They told me some guy named Bastian was supposed to be here already to get it started, but something about a problem at his pharmaceutical company delayed him. Sounds like it was an emergency. Anyway, his delay was my gain. Working on the lab has given me a purpose. I was getting tired of sitting around all day while everyone else worked. They said they want to teach the kids survival skills. You know, have them work in the lab and study the different plants and their healing powers and all that. It sounds interesting. I think I could help them with the scientific stuff and the research but I doubt they'll let me. I don't feel like they've accepted me yet. They still aren't sure if they can trust me," Kylee paused. "Sorry, but I really do have to go." She rushed out the front door.

Samantha walked to the study and looked around. What was she going to do now? She spotted the VR goggles and had an idea. Ty was still working on the games for the Sims. He hadn't even started the program for the obstacle course. Sam thought she could use the video footage she'd taken on her run a week ago. Or was it longer than that? She really didn't know. How long had she been here anyway? It seemed like a lifetime. So much had happened since that run in the forest. For one thing, she had no idea Kylee was hiding in the bushes watching her. She didn't even know Kylee was in the area at the time. Then there was that night with Ty. She couldn't think about that right now. She grabbed the goggles and rushed to her room. Once inside, she flipped on her computer and searched for the video. When she found the footage she immediately scrolled through each entry hoping she had the other file. She was looking for a program they'd developed for law enforcement. If she could find it, she thought she could overlay the program onto the video of the obstacle course and test out the goggles. There it was. It didn't take very long to create the overlay. It didn't fit perfectly. The old file was a murder scenario. It began with a man murdering a woman in a shop. A nearby policeman heard the shots and rushed to the scene. He spotted the suspect just as he darted behind the building. The transition from the city, where the original program took place to the forest where the obstacle course was located was rough. It would have to do for now. It's not like they were going to use this scenario anyway. She just needed it to test out the system.

Sam saved the program onto the SD card and slid it into the slot. She changed her clothes and started for the front door then stopped. She couldn't just take the goggles without letting Ty know. She didn't know what he had planned for this evening and she knew he was using them while he wrote the program. She shut the door and silently listened for any noise inside the house. She didn't hear anything inside, but she thought she heard banging out by the barn.

Samantha exited the kitchen door. She walked across the back patio and headed for the barn. She was just about to walk around the side to where the shed was located when she saw movement inside. Sam slowly moved to the door and stopped. Ty was shoeing one of the horses. She was a little surprised to see Ty instead of Atticus. He was usually the one to care for the animals since they were his. Samantha hesitantly stepped forward. "Uh...Ty," she called.

"Ty's head popped up in surprise." Sam hadn't talked to anyone in days.

"I just wanted to let you know I'm taking the VR goggles. I need to use them to work on something for a while," she paused. "I hope you didn't plan on using them tonight."

"No. Go ahead," he said, studying her closely. She was still beautiful, but she didn't look well. He was sure she hadn't been eating like she should. She also looked tired.

"Okay thanks," Sam said as she turned to leave.

"Sam?" Ty called.

Samantha heard him, but she couldn't return. She wanted things to go back to the way they were before the attack. She wanted him to hold her, whisper to her, kiss her. Being in the same space as him was painful. She had no one to blame but herself. She'd overreacted to the blood and she'd been cruel. There was no way Ty would forgive her. Her behavior was inexcusable. She walked briskly to the course and slipped on the goggles. She had to wait for the fake beginning. Once the suspect took off running, so did Sam. She ran through the course until she reached the trap. She pulled off the goggles and found she was a little late. The trap was up ahead. She returned to the beginning and started again. This time she almost fell on her face when she tripped on a rock.

She pulled off the goggles and pulled the memo pad from her waistband, jotting down several notes. She returned to the beginning and tried to remember where the rock was. Sam stubbed her toe, but continued. For the most part, the goggles were working the way they had hoped. Samantha ran the course several times. She'd have to do something about the limited view, she had tripped on that same rock almost every time. She didn't noticed when dusk fell silently over the course. In the goggles, it was still sunny and bright.

* * * *

Lilith eagerly watched as the woman ran through the forest. How had she got so lucky? Was the human really going to fall into her hands so easily? Lilith wasn't sure what the glasses were for but she didn't care. She watched the girl run the path, then turn around and run through it again. She practically laughed out loud when the human tripped over a rock. Was it possible the girl couldn't see? How was she running then? Lilith slipped from the trees and blocked the path. The anticipation of what was coming was almost unbearable.

Samantha was delighted with the goggles. For the most part, they were working just as they had hoped. She was going to have to run the course again with the video. The first time she hadn't captured obstacles on the ground. That's why she kept tripping on that stupid rock. She turned and ran back to the beginning of the course. One more time through and she would have what she needed. She was so used to the goggles now, she didn't even take them off before she began again. She reached up and reset the program then began to run. This time she was going to test the wand Ty had her develop. It was similar to a Wii remote, but they shaped it more like a dagger. It was made from hard plastic. The tip was just for show, all the controls were in the handle. Samantha swung the wand as she ran. They were going to have to test it again once Ty finished the real game. It was difficult to know how well it worked when she was watching a cop program. The cop had a gun, not a dagger.

Lilith hid in the shadows eagerly watching her prey. The human was almost directly in front of her, but abruptly turned and ran away. Had she seen her? Lilith wasn't worried. A human could never outrun a vampire. She slowly walked the path in the direction the girl had gone. As she came around the bend she stopped. No, the human hadn't seen her. She was just starting the course again. Lilith was excited and overflowing with anticipation. She'd let the girl run the course again. Once she stopped this time, Lilith would grab her. It was better this way anyway. Humans got tired so easily. She stood on the side of the path and watched as the unsuspecting human ran past swinging a strange object. Then, Lilith slowly stepped back onto the trail and followed.

Samantha reached the area with the trap again and stopped. She was starting to get tired and she wasn't sure how long she'd been out here anyway. It was impossible to tell with the goggles on. She pulled them off and froze. It was completely dark already. She was too vulnerable. She didn't even have a weapon. She glanced at the game wand and rolled her eyes. Brilliant Sam, she scolded herself. You're out in the woods after dark with a plastic toy. She needed to get back to the house and quick. As she turned around, she saw Lilith. Her heart sank. Too late, she was doomed.

Lilith was on her in an instant. The girl was going to pay for every injury she'd caused. She wasn't so clever without her water was she? Lilith didn't stop when she reached the human. She wanted the momentum. She simply reached out and gave the girl a powerful shove. The redhead flew across the clearing and slammed into a tree. Lilith laughed as the human let out a scream then fell to the ground.

Sam knew she was in trouble. This vampire was old and seasoned. There was no way Sam could hold her own in a fight against her. She couldn't even win this one with all her gadgets and tricks. She certainly wasn't going to win out in the woods without a weapon. She groaned as her body slammed into a tree. Crrrack. Sam gritted her teeth as her ribs broke into pieces, then she fell to the ground. She knew she should get up, she needed to get away, but deep in her heart she also knew it was useless. She couldn't outrun a vampire. They were too fast and too strong. Her only weapon was the stupid plastic dagger. That wouldn't kill Lilith, but maybe it could hurt her. Sam remained on the ground, not moving as Lilith approached her laughing.

Think Sam, she commanded. You have to think! Could she find the spot she had shot the arrow through the last time? It had struck Lilith in the stomach, but to the right. She had no idea if vampires healed the same as warriors, but with any luck Lilith would still be hurting.

Lilith stood over the crumpled body in anger. The woman couldn't be dead. Had she used too much force? She wanted the girl to suffer more than this. "Get up," she demanded. The girl didn't move. "I said get up!" Lilith screamed. She reached down to pull the girl to her feet when the human struck. She still had that object in her hand and she jabbed it into Lilith's stomach. She got a second hit in before Lilith slapped it away and heard a bone break. She glared at the girl angrily. Somehow this human had injured her again. Her wound was throbbing and she could feel liquid forming on her skin. The human had reopened her gash. She was going to pay for that.

"What is your name?" Lilith demanded.

Sam didn't take her eyes off the vampire. She wasn't going to answer any questions. The monster didn't need to know what her name was. She was sure she'd injured Lilith. She could see it in her cold green eyes. Lilith was trying to ignore the pain, but she couldn't. Good, I might die before this is over but at least Lilith is going to walk away in pain again. She thought.

"Your name!" Lilith demanded again. "I want to know the name of the human that has caused me so much aggravation. I want to relish in it when I deliver that final death blow," she laughed.

Samantha remained quiet.

Lilith lost her temper and tossed the girl across the clearing again. For the second time, she struck a tree.

Sam flew through the air like a rocket. Before she could right herself her head struck a large tree trunk. Samantha immediately saw white spots. No, no, no...she urged. I can't pass out or I'm doomed. As the blackness settled in, Samantha admitted to herself she was doomed anyway.

Dawn

Lilith walked to the tree. She shouldn't have lost her temper. If she kept this up she would kill the girl too soon. She wasn't going to be fooled again. She stopped in front of the human and kicked her in the shin. Nothing. Nobody could fake it with a kick that forceful. She grabbed the girl's leg and drug her into the open. Had she already killed her? Lilith hoped not. She needed this girl to suffer excruciating pain before she died.

Lilith looked down and saw the glasses the girl had been wearing. She was curious about them, but couldn't leave the girl unattended. The human was too clever. Lilith looked around and spotted a large trunk hanging from sturdy ropes. She wasn't sure what this place was yet, but that looked like a trap someone had built. It would be perfect for her needs. She quickly tied the girl up and directed her attention back to the glasses. She only hesitated a moment then slipped them on.

Lilith saw the path in the forest and two men. They were human. One was dressed as a cop, the other must be the bad guy. Lilith took a step forward and the two men began to run down the path. She pulled off the glasses and sat on a nearby rock. The girl wasn't dead. She'd been able to feel her pulse as she tied her to the log. Had she just discovered the reason they were here? Radek had been so sure this had something to do with him. This made more sense. The Deveraux's were creating some kind of police academy for humans. The location would be perfect, there was already a police station at the other end of the base. The academy would fit in perfectly here. That would also explain the presence of two human's.

Oh, this one could be included if it was about vampires. She obviously knew all about them. But the other one? The other woman was human, too. The fae were just as protective of their secret as the vampire community was. They wouldn't continue to involve humans in their war. She was sure she was right. The fae wouldn't include two humans in a supernatural project. She smiled broadly. This was good news. She couldn't wait to report back to Radek. He'd be relieved to hear the battle hadn't shifted. He was still in control and eventually would win this war and have his kingdom.

The girl groaned. Good, she was going to wake up soon. Lilith had time. Nobody had come for her yet. That meant they either didn't know she was missing or didn't care. Lilith decided they didn't know.

Sam slowly came to and realized she was hanging from something. How long had she been out? There was no way to know. What now? She opened her eyes and realized she was still in the forest. Maybe someone would save her? No, there was no hope for that. She had insulted them and avoided them for days. Everyone would just assume she was at the plant or in her room staying clear of the others. She'd been so stupid. She'd never get the chance to make things right. She'd been a coward. She'd procrastinated facing everyone because she didn't know how to apologize. Now she'd never get the chance.

"I see you finally woke up," Lilith drawled. "I've been waiting patiently to continue our talk." Lilith approached the elevated girl. "First I want your name," she growled. "Then we're going to have a little talk about what's going on at the fort over there." She jerked her head toward the warehouse.

Samantha remained quiet.

"I'm not going to ask you again," Lilith warned. "You're only making this worse on yourself. Once you tell me everything I want to know, I'll kill you quickly. If you refuse to talk, you leave me no choice. I'll have to torture it out of you." Lilith began circling the extended body. The human was going to be tortured regardless, but she didn't need to know that.

Samantha was not going to talk. She had been cruel and insulting to the only friends she had in the world. She'd shut them out and avoided them. But she would never betray them. She didn't care what Lilith did, she could torture her to death. Samantha was not going to tell her what they were doing at the fort. Sam looked up to see what she was dangling from. It was the log Luke had rigged as an obstacle. Lilith had unwound the rope, then secured it again wrapping the thick strands around Sam's arms and the trunk. There was no way she could get free from this contraption. Her wrists ached from the weight, but Sam thought this would be over soon. Her head was throbbing and her ribs were killing her. She was pretty sure her shin bone was broken as well. How had that happened?

Lilith was pissed. Did this human really think she could outlast a vampire as ruthless as she was? The girl was going to tell her everything. After watching that game in the goggles, Lilith already knew. But it would be even better if she could hear it from the human. There would be no doubt she'd discovered what they were up to. Lilith reached out and took one of the human's bare feet in her hand. She effortlessly slit a long gash down the length of it with her sharp knife.

Sam screamed, but she still didn't talk.

Lilith waited. Nothing. She took a deep breath and slit the other foot as well. Blood trickled to the ground and pooled in the dirt. Lilith smiled, this was going to be fun.

* * * *

Ty rode the large mare into the barn. After his encounter with Samantha he had needed an outlet. He'd saddled the horse and took a quick run on the beach at the lake. He knew he couldn't be out long, it was going to be dark soon. Once he put away the saddle and tack, he headed for the house. Maybe the ride had helped a little, but not much. It wasn't the same as riding the open range at his ranch. He missed being at home. He missed his horses and the freedom from all his troubles. He missed the tranquility he always felt when he was there. Maybe he could find an excuse to take a break and escape soon. He called for the dogs and opened the back door. "Stay," he told them. Both dogs immediately plopped down on the throw rugs near the door looking bored.

Ty was headed for the study, but when he entered the foyer he saw Victor and Ariel headed out the door. "Where are you two going?" he asked. "You know we shouldn't be going out at night. There's no telling how many vampires Radek has sent here."

Victor took a deep breath and turned to Ty. "We're going to look for Sam," he confessed.

"What?" Ty said alarmed. "She's not here? She knows better than that. Are you sure she's not just holed up in her room again?"

"Kylee checked. The last anyone saw of her was almost two hours ago. Kylee stopped by to grab something to eat just as Samantha returned from the plant. We don't know where she went from there. All we know is she's not here," Victor softened. Ty was obviously upset about the news. "We've all been a little busy today. First thing this morning Alex and Dimitri took off. Then, Tony and Megan decided to head to town to do research into dad's problem.

Dawn

I haven't exactly been myself all day. Ariel's been worried about Breena and the baby. Bree hasn't felt well, so she and Orin have stayed in their room most of the afternoon. With everything going on, Kylee was the last one to see her."

"I think I probably saw her last," Ty told them. "I was in the barn. She wanted to know if I needed the VR goggles because she wanted to work on them."

"Then she's probably at the plant," Ariel assured him. "I'm sure that's where she took them to work on the system. Kylee's in the study. We'll hurry back." She closed the door softly behind her.

Ty walked to the study. He barely noticed Kylee sitting on the couch. He went straight to the table and opened the black case. The goggles were still gone. He closed his eyes and hoped he was wrong. Then he turned and quickly headed for the door.

Kylee was on her feet in an instant. "Where are you going?" she demanded.

"To look for Sam," he said not missing a beat.

"You don't think she's at the plant?" she pressed.

"I hope she's at the plant. But no, I don't think that's where she's at." He gave Kylee a quick glance, then pulled open the door.

"So where is she?" Kylee asked, following him outside onto the porch.

Ty hesitated. "I think she might be on the obstacle course," he admitted. "I have to go check. Stay in the house. Lock the door and set the alarm. Go upstairs and get Orin. He needs to know what's going on."

"You can't go out there alone," Kylee argued. "Wait for Victor to get back. You know what happened the last time you went into the forest alone."

"That's exactly why I can't wait. Get back in the house and lock the door." He took off running towards the forest.

Kylee didn't know what to do. She only hesitated a minute then she darted toward the bunkers. Ty wasn't willing to wait for Victor, but she thought maybe Dusty could help.

* * * *

Sam was losing too much blood. She felt dizzy. She was going to pass out again. Lilith was losing it. She was becoming reckless at Sam's defiance. Good. Sam thought. She knew she was going to die tonight, but at least she had injured Lilith and she had outlasted her. Nothing Lilith could do would make her say a word. Samantha couldn't hold her head up any longer. She let it fall forward then slowly gave into the blackness.

As soon as Ty entered the forest he could smell it. Vampire. He was starting to panic, but he had to stay calm. He jogged through the course looking for signs of Sam. He knew she was here. Somehow he could feel it. He wanted to sprint, but he was afraid he might miss her. Out of nowhere he heard a loud scream. Not Sam. It sounded more like a scream of frustration.

Lilith was beyond angry. That stupid human hadn't told her anything. No matter what Lilith did, she just stared at her in defiance. It reminded her of that annoying councilman. Lilith inhaled sharply. Her stomach felt like it was on fire. That stupid, menacing woman had done more damage than Lilith had originally thought. She couldn't deal with the wound now. She had to decide what to do with the human. She was just so mad. She let out a yell in frustration as she kicked a large rock across the clearing. She wanted the girl to cry and beg for her to stop. The human's spirit should have been broken already. She should have told Lilith everything she wanted to know. Instead, she passed out. Lilith watched as the blood began to clot around the wounds on her feet. They were no longer bleeding profusely. Now what? She struggled with her options. She could wait and see if the girl woke up again or she could just kill her now and get it out of the way.

Ty rounded the bend and saw Samantha. She was strung up on a log, her body just dangling in the air. She wasn't moving. Her head was bobbing in sync with the log as it swayed back and forth. Was she already dead? No, he couldn't think about that. Lilith had her back to him but that wouldn't last long. She was going to die. For Sam, this vampire was going to die. Ty charged.

He came out of nowhere. Lilith barely had time to react. She felt the air shift and twisted around just as he was about to plunge his dagger through her back. She wasn't wearing that armor tonight. She was sure the knife would have hit its mark. Unfortunately for her, he had unknowingly hit another mark. He slashed her through the stomach, hitting the burning wound she already had. Lilith cried out in pain. She was in trouble. In her condition she couldn't fight a warrior. He was coming at her again. She pushed herself up by a rock and flung forward towards the angry man. Her feet hit their mark and the warrior flew backwards. She was pretty sure she had broken a couple ribs. He stumbled a little when he stood up. She was just about to take advantage of his weakened state when a tiger flew out of the trees. She ducked and twisted, but he caught her shoulder in his teeth. Lilith screamed as a large chunk of flesh was ripped from her arm. She stumbled, got up and ran with all she had.

* * * *

Ty was standing at Samantha's feet, trying to figure out how to get her down without hurting her. She was in bad shape. He wasn't even sure she was still alive. Dusty approached him. "What if you stand on my shoulders? That should get you high enough to reach the ropes. You can cut her lose and I'll catch her when she falls."

Ty continued to study the log and the ropes, then Sam. "No, you cut the ropes. I'll catch her." He flipped the knife around in one swift movement and was holding his dagger out, handle first to Dusty. Then he linked his hands together to give Dusty a boost.

Dusty hesitated only a moment, then he secured his foot in Ty's hands and was boosted into the air. Within seconds Samantha was free. Ty cradled her in his arms as he searched for a pulse. Dusty had wrapped his arm around the thick rope above the log to support his weight before he cut the last line. He wanted Ty to be free to catch Sam when she fell. He was just grateful the log was secured so well. He was sure it would remain stable even after cutting two of the cords. He held onto the rope, dangling in the air for only a second before he released his arm and jumped to the ground. "Is she..." he paused, worried he didn't really want the answer. "Is she still alive?" he asked.

"Barely," Ty said soberly. He turned quickly and headed for the house. Dusty began to follow then saw the dark glasses. He quickly grabbed them, then caught up to Ty. He felt helpless and depressed. He liked Sam. He hadn't really been able to get to know her, but he had been watching her from a distance. He really didn't want her to die.

Chapter Ten

Victor opened the door and frowned at the loud screeching sound of the alarm. "What the..." he began but was cut off.

"You have to go help Ty!" Kylee yelled.

Ariel quickly went to the alarm and punched in her code. The alarm quieted immediately. "Where is Ty?" she asked.

"He went to the forest," she told them. "He said he thought that's where Sam was. I tried to talk him out of going alone, but he wouldn't listen. He ordered me to lock the doors and set the alarm." She glanced at the box then back to Victor. "Sorry about that," she apologized.

"No, Ty was right. The alarm would alert you if any vampires tried to storm the house. You guys alright?" he asked glancing at Orin and Breena standing in the doorway to the study.

"We're fine," Orin assured him. "I was about to go after Ty myself. I'm glad you returned. I was struggling with leaving Bree and a helpless woman here in the house alone, but I couldn't neglect Ty either."

"I sent Dusty after him," Kylee said quickly. "I didn't know what else to do. I know he's just a kid, but I couldn't let Ty go out there alone."

"You did the right thing," Victor assured her then quickly left the house.

"I'm coming with you," Ariel said following Victor down the front stairs. "Kylee, lock the door again and set the alarm. We'll be back as soon as we can." Ariel reached out and grabbed Victor's arm. "I'm coming," she insisted. "We do this together."

Maybe it was selfish, but Victor wasn't going to argue. He felt better having Ariel at his side. If the house was attacked while he was gone and she got hurt, he'd never forgive himself. Orin would just have to handle the other women. If there were vamps out here, hopefully they could keep them a safe distance from the house. The couple hurried across the long expanse of the fort headed for the obstacle course. As they reached the last bunker, they stopped. Ty was walking so fast he was almost jogging. Dusty was following close behind. Ty had Samantha cradled in his arms.

"She's bad," Ty said as he approached them. "I'm not sure she's going to make it," he said soberly. His stomach churned and he wanted to be sick. He didn't know how he was going to live if she died.

"Vampires?" Victor asked.

Dawn

"It was only Lilith as far as I know," he looked at Dusty. "Did you see any others?"

"No," Dusty answered quickly. "Just the female and once I bit her she didn't want any part of the fight," he paused. "Coward," he finally added.

Ariel smiled at him. She really liked this kid.

"You injured?" Victor asked Ty.

"Don't worry about me. I'm fine. We need to get help for Samantha." Ty took a few more steps then asked, "Is Kylee still up? We're going to need her help."

"She is, so are Breena and Orin," Ariel assured him. "Bree might be able to help, too."

The group entered the house together. Kylee shot up when she saw Samantha. Ty didn't break stride. He continued up the stairs and into his room. He gently set Sam on the bed and turned to Kylee. "She needs your help, doc." He motioned for her to come to the bed. Then stepped back to give her room.

Kylee was astonished at the sight of Sam. Her feet were bloody and her head was a mess. She needed to undress Sam to see the extent of her injuries. "I need everyone to leave," she ordered.

"Not a chance," Ty refused.

Kylee looked over her shoulder as Breena entered the room. "I need to get her undressed and see exactly what I'm dealing with." She looked Ty straight in the eyes. "You can come back in when I've finished my assessment, I promise."

Breena stepped forward. "I'm not a doctor, but I might be able to help."

"Good, you stay, everyone else out!" Kylee said sternly.

Victor took Ty by the arm and guided him into the hallway. Ariel followed shutting the door behind her. Orin was leaning against the outside wall. "How bad?" he asked.

"Bad," Ty told him as he let his body slide down the wall. He sat with his head in his hands, letting the wall support his weight.

Victor put his arm around Ariel. He knew she had been angry with Samantha, but he also knew she was struggling with the seriousness of the situation. If Sam didn't make it, Ariel was going to feel guilty.

Kylee gently pulled Samantha's shirt over her head. She inhaled sharply when she saw the bruising. She pulled off her jeans and gently slid her beneath the sheets. Samantha's feet had stopped bleeding so they were going to have to wait. She looked up and saw Breena standing behind her. Neither woman said a word. Kylee gently ran her fingers over Sam's ribs. Two of them were broken. She continued her examination for several minutes. Finally, she turned Sam's head to examine the wound that was still bleeding. This was the worst injury by far.

"I'm going to need some water and my medical bag. It has alcohol to clean the wounds." She paused and looked at Breena. "I don't think she's going to make it," she confessed. "Her head is bad. I'd say she was thrown against a tree." She pulled a piece of trunk out of Sam's hair. "The skull is cracked. That means her brain is going to swell. If there's any hemorrhaging, which I believe there is, I can't save her."

Dawn

Breena closed her eyes trying to hold back the tears. She'd heard so much about this crazy human that hunted vampires, she felt like she knew her. Ariel was going to be devastated. So would Alex and probably Ty. How was she going to break the news to the rest of them? "Where's the bag?" she finally asked.

"It's in my room," Kylee stood and faced Breena. "Let the rest of them in. I'll break the news while you get the bag."

The entire group stepped into the room as Breena hurried past headed for Kylee's room. "I need to grab the medical bag," she called as she hurried down the hall. "I'll be right back," she said glancing at Orin as she disappeared down the long corridor.

Victor, Ariel and Orin walked into the room and stood by the bed. Ty hung back, he had a decision to make.

"I'm not going to beat around the bush with you," Kylee told them. "I don't think Sam is going to make it."

Victor put an arm around Ariel and held her tight. "How can we help?" he asked.

"You can't," Kylee said in a matter of fact tone. "Her head wound is severe. Her skull is cracked and you can see here..." she moved so the group could see where she was pointing. "It's already started to swell. It's very rare to have a head wound this severe without hemorrhaging." She looked towards Ty still standing in the doorway. "I'm not a brain surgeon, but I know a few. They would tell you the same thing. Her wounds are fatal. There's nothing I can do for her." Kylee closed her eyes and wiped away the tears that were running down her cheeks.

"How long?" Ariel asked.

"It's hard to say," Kylee admitted. "Maybe an hour or so. I'll give you some space to say your goodbyes," she turned to rush out the door.

Ty reached out and stopped her. "You can't save her, but I can," he paused. "Please don't leave, I'm going to need your help."

"Ty," Victor called sternly. "This is not a good idea."

"It's the only way to save her," Ty persisted. He walked over to the bed and sat on the edge. Then he calmly reached down and began to remove his boots.

Ariel realized what Ty was planning. "You can't," she burst out. "She hates us. She fears and despises the warriors. You can't just turn her into one. She'll never forgive you."

"She doesn't have to," Ty answered. He had already made up his mind. He wasn't going to change it now.

"You don't know what you're saying," Victor argued "You'll feel the hatred. For the rest of your life you'll have to live with that every day. Nobody could deal with that. It's going to drive you insane."

Ty dropped his second boot to the floor and laid back on the bed. "Will someone get me my cell phone, I need to call my father. It's in the kitchen."

Victor turned and left the room. He was so frustrated with Ty right now he wanted to strangle him. Ariel followed him out. "Go ahead and get him the phone," he growled. "Nothing we say is going to change his mind."

Ariel reluctantly headed for the kitchen.

Dawn

Victor walked downstairs into the study and slammed the door. He kicked a pillow across the room and ignored the crash as the lamp tumbled to the floor. He couldn't stand this. Ty could die. And for what? Samantha was in such bad shape, the chance of her surviving this was almost zero. He turned and punched a hole in the study door. The girl hated them all. Ty had no idea what he was getting himself into. He crossed the room and dropped into the recliner. Then he pulled out his phone and called Dimitri.

"What's wrong?" Dimitri asked as soon as Victor identified himself. Victor's tone was angry and concerned.

Victor explained the situation to Dimitri. "He won't listen to reason. The stubborn, bullheaded..."

"Unlike you," Dimitri interrupted. "You are the epitome of rational thinking, I suppose?"

"This isn't about me," Victor growled. He couldn't stand losing Ty. He was one of his best friends. Next to Tony and Dimitri, Victor was closest to Ty and the moron was risking his life for a woman that wouldn't care if he lived or died. A woman that was so seriously injured she was probably going to die anyway.

"No. It's not," Dimitri said calmly. He was worried, but he could also feel Ty's emotions. Ty was in love with Sam. Nothing anybody could say would change his mind now. "Victor, what would you do if Ariel was lying up there about to die from injuries that only you could save her from?"

"That's different," Victor argued. "Ariel and I are in love."

"Ty's in love with Samantha," Dimitri confessed. "I don't think it's any different for him."

"Shit!" Victor grumbled. "I was afraid of that," he paused. "It's still not the same. Sam's not in love with Ty."

"I don't think any of us knows how Sam feels. But I don't see the difference anyway. Can you tell me a while back when you and Ariel returned from rescuing Abby that you wouldn't have done anything in your power to save Ariel? Even though she wasn't speaking to you at the time?"

Victor didn't answer. He couldn't because he knew he would have done anything to save her. He would have given his own life to save Ariel's. It didn't matter how she felt about him.

"That's what I thought. You and I can understand because we know what we would do for the women we love," he paused. "Neither of us would do anything less than Ty is doing now. Instead of fighting him on this, I need you to support him. He needs to know you're going to be there for him."

"I'm not sure I can do that," Victor admitted. "I know what it's going to be like for him when this is over. If by some miracle both of them survive. That in itself is a big if. I know what it's like to live with someone hating you. Feeling that hatred every day of your life. As bad as it was for me, it's going to be worse for Ty. There's nothing he'll be able to do to escape it."

"That's why Ty needs you," Dimitri said gently. "You are the only one that can help him now. You are the only one of us that can understand. He's going to need you even more once this is over."

"I'll do what I can," Victor finally conceded.

"How bad was he injured?" Dimitri asked.

"He said he wasn't," Victor said surprised.

Dawn

"He lied," Dimitri said flatly. "I think he broke a rib or two. Try to get him to drink a little blood before he goes through with this. It's going to be difficult enough without the added injury."

"That son of a..." Victor exploded.

"Victor," Dimitri interrupted. "Support. Do what you can for them tonight. Alex and I will be there as soon as we can."

"You do know Alex isn't going to be any help in this, don't you?" Victor asked.

"I have no idea what Alex can do. But I agree, I doubt she'll be able to do anything about this particular situation. Has Ty told his family what he's planning?" Dimitri finished.

"He asked for his phone to call his father, so I assume they know," Victor confirmed.

"Go take care of Ty, I'll see you soon." Dimitri hung up and hesitantly went to give Alex the bad news.

Victor walked back into the bedroom and saw Ty snuggled up to Samantha. He was gently washing the blood from her head. Ty glanced up when he heard Victor enter the room.

"Good. You're back," Ty said casually. "I need to talk to you alone. Can you shut the door so nobody will interrupt?"

"Did you talk to your father?" Victor asked.

Ty sobered. "No," he admitted. "I just got his voicemail. We both know this could be a disaster," he began. "Don't argue with me, Victor. One thing we've always had was honesty between us."

"Okay. It could end in disaster," Victor agreed.

"If I die, I need you to tell my parents how much I love them. I need them to know what great parents they have always been to me. You know what it's like to have a bad parent. I think you are the best person to explain how wonderful it is to have two parents that are good, kind people."

"Okay," Victor said silently. "I'll tell them."

"I know you're angry with me for doing this," he paused and stared out the window. "I guess I understand, I'd be angry with you too," Ty admitted. "You probably don't think it makes any sense." Ty paused as Victor handed him a glass of blood. He hadn't even noticed Victor walk to the small fridge in the closet. "What's this for?" he asked.

"Your broken ribs," Victor said calmly.

Ty closed his eyes. "Good, you've already told Dimitri about this then. That was going to be another request. I don't want him blindsided when he begins to feel my pain." He was watching Victor. His friend was calmer now, maybe he'd accepted it. "How did Dimitri feel about this anyway?" he asked curiously.

"He understands," Victor admitted. "I guess I do, too. As much as I hate it, I know I would do the same for the woman I love " Victor watched Ty for a reaction.

"So he knows that too," Ty said softly. "I can't explain it. I never meant for it to happen, but I do love Samantha. I tried to fight it. I've tried to accept her hatred of us. I believe I have accepted that. I understand we're never going to be together, but I can't just sit back and let her die knowing I could have done something to save her life. Please help my parents understand that too," Ty asked concerned how this was going to impact them.

Dawn

Victor sat down on the bed. "I'll try. I know you couldn't just let her die," he said softly. "I do understand. I'm just not sure you understand how hard it is going to be to love someone and know how deeply and passionately that person hates you. Ty, you're going to feel that hatred, literally every day for the rest of your life. I don't think she's going to thank you for this if she lives through it," he warned.

"I don't expect her to and I do understand. I'd rather live with her hatred every day than live with her dying today," Ty said soberly. He sat up and drank a second glass of blood in one gulp.

"Better yet?" Victor asked.

Ty held the glass out to Victor. Instead of taking it Victor pulled Ty into a hug. "Don't you die on me," he ordered.

Ty pulled back. He was filled with a lot of emotion right now. He wished he'd had the chance to talk to his parents. He started to choke up then cleared his throat. "There is one more thing I need you to talk to Dimitri about if I don't come out of this," he finally said.

"What's that?" Victor asked.

"I think I know why Samantha's family has been targeted. I think I've solved the mystery," he confessed.

"What?" Victor asked. "Why?" He was curious now.

"I'm pretty sure Samantha and Alex are cousins." He knew they needed to get started and he didn't have much time. "I'm running out of time here. Can you get Kylee so she can hook up the blood lines and I'll tell you all about it? Don't let anyone else in though. I don't want this to get out yet."

Victor was dumbfounded. Alex and Sam were cousins? If it were true, that would be an excellent explanation for the killings. He walked to the door and opened it slightly. "Kylee, I'm going to need your help in here." He waited as she slowly, hesitantly walked to the door. Ariel was right behind her.

"I'm coming in," she declared. "Don't try to stop me. I'll break down the door if I have to."

Victor sighed and opened the door, letting the two women into the room.

Kylee was the first one to speak. "What exactly is Ty planning?" She was a little nervous about the whole situation. No, she was terrified.

"I need you to hook up a line to my femoral artery. You will then run it to the axillary artery on Sam's arm. Then, I need another line reversed. That one runs from Sam's femoral artery to my axillary. Do you follow?" Ty asked.

"Why?" Kylee inquired.

Ty ignored her question. "Victor, do we have everything we need here? Do you have the line?"

"I can just use the line you've been using for the IV," Kylee interrupted.

"I have it," Victor answered Ty. He turned to Kylee. "You can't use the IV line because it needs a valve."

"I don't understand," Kylee said confused. "What exactly are we doing here?"

Victor handed her the line. "We're running out of time. Please hook up the line the way Ty asked you to. This end has to hook to his leg, this end to her arm."

Kylee continued to hesitate.

Ariel stepped forward. "Either you do it or I will," she said calmly. "It has to be done and it's going to be better if you handle it. You're a medical professional."

Kylee reached for her bag and began to run the line the way she had been instructed. She was extremely confused and was not going to rest until she got an explanation from these two. Once the lines were connected she stepped back and observed. It was like a blood transfusion, only the blood was flowing directly from Ty into Sam and then from Sam into Ty. What exactly were they doing here? She turned to Victor, a million questions running through her mind.

Victor spoke before Kylee could regain her composure. He knew she had a lot of questions. "I need you to go downstairs and wait for us in the study." He hurried on when she tried to protest, "Ty needs to talk to me about something and it's confidential and important. As soon as we're finished, I'll explain everything. Then I'm going to need you to monitor these two and make sure everything goes as well as it possibly can. Do you understand?" he asked.

Kylee heard concern in his voice. Whatever they were doing was dangerous. "Okay," she finally said, turning and heading for the door. "But if you don't show in the study, I'm going to come looking for you."

Victor smiled. "We'll show," he promised.

Kylee hesitantly left the room and directed Breena and Orin to join her in the study. Instead of continuing into the room with the women, Orin slipped out the front door and headed to the apartments.

Ariel wondered what these two were going to talk about. Did she need to leave? She needed to talk to Ty before he was too out of it to understand.

"She insisted on coming in. Do I need to physically remove her? Keep in mind, it might cause me substantial injury when I do," Victor asked Ty.

"No. She's fine." Ty watched his blood flowing into Samantha. He really hoped this would work. He hoped her body could take the change. She had so many injuries already.

"Okay. Now tell me why you think Alex is Samantha's cousin," Victor asked.

"What?" Ariel exclaimed. "Is that possible?"

Ty began to explain his theory. "It all started to come together when Megan was talking about her mother changing names, then Tony told us the story about Marlena, and Atticus picked up and finished the time line. One night, just after Sam and I arrived here, she told me about her Uncle James. She said his wife was Lana and their daughter was Lexie," he paused. "Mar...Lana?" he emphasized Lana. "Alexandria...Lexie." It fits. I also didn't know until the other night that the human Marlena was married to was named James. Another fit. Then there's the timing. I've charted it all out. There's a diagram in that drawer. He pointed to the dresser.

Ariel rushed to the drawer and studied the diagram. Ty was right, it all fit perfectly. Samantha was born in 1973. Two years

Dawn

later Samantha's uncle and his new wife Lana moved in next to them. The same year James and Marlena were married, 1975. One year later Sam's brother Michael is born. Then in 1980 Lexie is born. The same year Alex was born. Sam's Uncle James was murdered in 1985, so was Alex's father. That's when Alex and Marlena go into hiding, but Sam believes they were killed with James. Two years later, Alex and Marlena are captured by Radek. Alex is now seven. They are held for five months until the warriors rescue them. A few months later in early 1988, Marlena marries Luke. Later that same year Samantha's family is murdered.

"Radek would have been beyond pissed," Ariel said looking up. "If you're right, and I don't see how this can be wrong it fits too perfectly, Radek would have been out for blood. Not only had Marlena escaped, but she was now married to a warrior. He had to know it was going to be almost impossible to get to her with Luke around," Ariel paused. "Does anyone know why Radek wanted to imprison Marlena in the first place? Nobody's ever been able to explain that to me."

"What if he was really after Alex?" Victor mused.

Ty and Ariel sat motionless, interested in Victor's train of thought.

"Radek wants the fae kingdom," Victor began. "We already know that. He is sticking to the ridiculous notion that he should be ruler because it's his birthright. He's the first born child and all that crap. But he had to know the fae community would turn to Alex as their queen. So take out Alex and there's no competition," Victor said solemnly.

"Samantha said her mother was very close to her Uncle James. Once he married Lana, she became like a sister to Sam's mom. What if Marlena and Sam's mother stayed in contact after they went into hiding?" Ty wondered.

"It's possible," Ariel admitted. "But even if they didn't, what if Radek believed they did? That would explain the execution of Sam's family. Radek could have been looking for information. He still could have been trying to get to Alex. He may have hoped Sam's mom could identify when Alex was vulnerable," she concluded.

"Did Sam say anything about the night her family was killed?" Victor asked Ty.

"Not much. At that point she pretty much shut down. I don't even know how she escaped when everyone else was killed," Ty admitted.

"Maybe she wasn't home," Ariel suggested.

"Maybe but I think she was," Ty said. "I think she was traumatized by it. I think she knows who killed her family. She did tell me she isn't going to stop hunting until she finds the vampire with the violet eyes," Ty jerked in pain. The process was already starting.

"Ariel, change of plans. Go get Kylee. We're going to have to explain everything to her up here," Victor ordered. He couldn't think about Radek personally killing Sam's family now. He had to think about Ty.

Ariel rushed out of the room.

"Stop worrying about me," Ty chastised Victor. "You know this is going to get a lot worse before it's over. If you can't handle it now, I'm going to have you removed from my room." He smiled at Victor's scowl.

"I really hope you know what you're doing." Victor growled as Kylee and Ariel entered the room. Atticus was standing in the doorway. "Who got you out of bed?" Victor asked.

"Orin. I'm kind of wondering why it wasn't you, though," Atticus scolded.

Victor closed his eyes. He'd been so concerned about Ty he'd forgotten about his father. "Sorry," he said walking to his dad. "I didn't mean to leave you out of this."

"Tony and Megan are downstairs. They just got back from town. Why don't you come down for a minute, then you can come back and check on Ty. This process is going to take a very long time. You look like you could use a break already." Atticus put a hand on Victor's shoulder and guided him towards the stairs.

"You are not going anywhere!" Kylee ordered Ariel. "If you want me to help, I need to know what is going on here. I can't take care of these two while I'm in the dark." She cringed when she saw Ty's face fill with pain. "What's happening to him?" she demanded.

Ariel took a deep breath and approached the bed. "Here Ty," she held out her hand. "It's going to be a long night. I'd like to be here for you as long as I can."

Ty took her hand then jerked in pain. Was this normal, or was something already going wrong?

Kylee sat on the bed next to Ariel. "Spill it," she demanded. She was concerned. Now she not only had one patient, but two. Ty was clearly in pain and Samantha hadn't moved an inch.

"Okay," Ariel said defensively. "First, do you understand the healing process of the warriors? You saw Ty heal the other day, but did you get what was going on?"

"Well, nobody explained it to me in detail. You just said a warrior's body can heal itself and it needs extra blood to do it," Kylee told her.

"It's in the blood," Ariel supplied. "I don't understand it all, so you're not going to get a very scientific explanation from me. If you need more detail, you're going to have to talk to Bastian."

"The guy that was supposed to set up the lab?" Kylee asked.

"The warrior that was supposed to set up the lab. Yes," she paused. "For now, you're just going to have to accept my explanation." Ariel took a deep breath and began, "There is something in the warrior's blood that makes them heal. When a warrior is injured, the blood rushes to the wound and attacks the injury. It somehow regenerates the cells needed to heal the wound. The problem with this, is that now the warrior is short on blood. Eventually it would replenish itself, but the healing is quicker if they have new blood right away. It doesn't matter what kind because the antibodies in their own blood will convert it to usable blood. The new, usable blood replaces the lost blood and is now the same as all the other warrior blood in their system."

"That's not possible," Kylee argued.

"It's not possible for a human, it is possible for a warrior. I told you, don't ask me to explain the details. I don't understand it myself," Ariel scolded.

"So, Ty is trying to use his blood to heal Samantha's wounds?" Kylee asked.

"No," Ariel admitted. "Ty is turning Samantha into a warrior. He's sharing his blood with her, but her blood is also entering Ty. As Samantha's blood enters Ty's body, his blood is going to attack it. I've heard about human's having organ transplants, but they have to take special medication so their body won't attack the foreign object in their system."

"Right," Kylee said reeling from what Ariel was telling her. Could a human really be turned into a warrior?

"Well, I guess Ty's blood is doing the same thing right now. That's why he's in pain. First, we are taking a lot of his blood and pushing it into Sam. So, he's low on blood and his body is reacting to that. Then at the same time, we're pushing Sam's blood into Ty to replace it. Just like when he drinks blood or we introduce it through an IV, his blood is going to consume the new blood and turn it into warrior blood." Ariel paused to see if Kylee was understanding.

"How long does this process take?" Kylee asked.

"Days," Ariel told her. "There's not a set time. Everyone is different. With these two there's an added problem. Samantha is seriously injured. Once Ty's blood enters her system it will frantically try to consume her blood and turn it into usable blood. But, it's also going to rush to Sam's wounds and heal them. In the beginning, until Sam is healed, Ty's blood is going to be wasted. It's going to be used up to heal Sam."

"So won't they be low on blood? How is Ty going to survive if he's lost so much blood to the process and to Sam?" Kylee said concerned now.

"He might not," Ariel answered honestly.

"What?" Kylee screamed.

Ty was in a lot of pain, but he wasn't completely out of it. "Kylee," he said as gently as he could. "Don't write me off yet." He grasped the bed post and waited for the cramping to stop.

Kylee studied him. He was in so much pain. She reached for her bag, but was stopped by Ariel.

"No pain killers," she warned. "We told you last time, human medication could kill him. Something in them damages a warrior's blood. He's having a hard enough time as it is. He doesn't need another handicap."

"I can't just sit here and watch him suffer," she argued.

"You're going to have to." They both turned when they saw Samantha stir, then moan.

Kylee jumped to her feet.

"No. Wait," Ariel said. "This is a good sign. It means Ty's blood is working. Her wounds are beginning to heal."

Kylee sat back down. "So you're telling me that once this process is complete, Ty and Samantha will have the same exact blood. If I draw blood from one and blood from the other, then study it under a microscope I won't be able to tell the difference?"

"That's correct," Ariel said hesitantly.

"What else are you not telling me?" she demanded.

"The connection is stronger than that," Ariel finally confessed. "We don't know how or why but once a warrior turns a human they are bonded together forever. If one is in trouble, the other can feel it. If one gets injured the other knows. I've never known of a warrior attempting this with anyone other than their mate. The bond is too intimate."

"You guys are worried about Samantha's reaction, aren't you?" Kylee asked. "She's been so upset about what they are, you think she's going to be angry that she is now one of them?"

"That's one worry. If she continues to hate and despise the warriors, Ty's going to feel that hatred for the rest of his life," she paused. "I'm not going to lie to you Kylee, this procedure is dangerous. Either one of them, or both, could die from it. We're concerned about her reaction but it might be a moot point in the end."

Kylee looked back towards Ty. "He knew he could die, but he did it anyway to save her life? He's a better person than I am," she admitted. "I'm not sure I could have done that. Knowing Sam might hate him. Knowing he was going to live with that hatred forever and on top of it, knowing he might die from it. How could Samantha ever believe someone like Ty was a monster or something to be afraid of?"

"I don't know," Ariel sighed. "Are we good?" she asked. "I need to go check on Victor. He's pretty close to Ty, I know he's going to be worried every minute until this is over."

"We're good, but what am I supposed to do?" Kylee asked. "You said I can't give them pain killers, so why am I here?"

"Mostly to keep them from pulling the lines out. Ty is managing his pain pretty well right now, but don't expect that to last. Keep them together no matter what. They can't lose any of the blood. You know if the line is yanked out, blood is going to spew everywhere. They need every drop if they're going to survive this," then she turned and headed out the door leaving Kylee to care for her patients.

* * * *

Ariel stood in the doorway and watched Victor. He was sitting on the couch, his father next to him and Tony was in a chair on the other side. At least he had plenty of support. Ariel knew Victor wasn't close to many people. The ones he was close to, he was very protective of. You wouldn't think the cowboy and the motorcycle riding bad boy would be close, but they were. She smiled, pretty much anyone that knew Ty was close to him. He was just that kind of guy. You couldn't know him and not love him. Other than his grumpy patches when he was frustrated over a game, a deadline or some other business crisis, he was the life of the party. Lately he hadn't been himself. Ariel knew exactly who to blame for that…Samantha.

She wondered how Alex was going to take the news that Sam was her cousin. Of course, there wasn't any proof. Human DNA tests couldn't resolve the mystery either, especially now. But the evidence was too compelling. There were too many coincidences. It was also interesting that Radek had done the killing himself. He rarely killed these days, he thought it was beneath him. And how had he missed Sam? There were still a lot of questions to be answered. Some of them may never be solved, especially if Samantha died from the transition.

Ariel slowly entered the room and approached Victor. Atticus moved to the left to make a spot for her beside his son. She sat down on the couch and laid her head against the backrest. What a night, she thought. And it was only going to get worse.

Dawn

Victor put his arm around her shoulders and pulled her in close. He kissed her forehead and finally asked, "How are they?"

"As well as can be expected," she answered. The room was so quiet. It was too depressing, Ariel thought. She needed to lighten the mood somehow. "So, Tony?" she asked.

"Yeah," he answered immediately.

"Are you going to tell us the story of how you chose your nickname?" She smiled when Tony cringed.

"I didn't plan on it," he admitted.

"Awe come on," Breena encouraged. She knew what Ariel was doing and thought it was a good idea.

Ariel turned to Victor. "If he's not going to tell it, you have to. Tank is an unusual nickname. There has to be a story behind it."

"It was just a stupid name Victor gave me a long time ago when we got involved in a war. I tried to drive a tank, but I had some trouble and things went a little bad. Now he thinks it's funny to call me Tank Master, or Tank Man Extraordinaire," he glared at Victor. He was not going to forgive him for this any time soon.

Megan was amused at Tony's discomfort. She had asked him the same question and gotten pretty much the same response. She was just as curious as everyone else to hear the real story. She turned to Victor, "I guess it's up to you then. Tony's being a bad sport." She took Tony's hand in hers and smiled at him.

Tony groaned. This was going to be bad.

Victor smiled, "What's it going to be?" he asked Tony. "You gonna tell these guys about your little bit of trouble or am I?"

"Before you start, which war were you in together?" Megan asked.

"We've actually fought together more than once," Tony told her. "The first time was around 1650 I believe. It was in Ireland during the Cromwellian Conquest," he glanced at Victor and smiled. "I had to save his butt and he's kind of followed me around like a puppy dog ever since. It's actually pretty pathetic."

Victor laughed. "Actually, I think we ended up even by the end of that war," he sobered. "We were lucky. There were a couple times I wasn't sure we'd make it out alive. It was a brutal time. We only joined because Cromwell was confiscating land left and right. The fae were worried they would lose their property. So they all agreed to have their able bodied men join in the fight."

"Richard was livid when my parents refused to let him go. We were planning on joining up together," Tony reminisced. "Richard is the oldest, so he had to stay home. He's expected to take over the monarchy when my parents are gone. Thank goodness for that!" He grinned. "I'd be terrible at it."

"I doubt that," Megan objected.

"No. He would," Victor agreed with Tony. "Your boy there can't stay in one place for any amount of time. He's pretty much a wanderer. That makes it difficult to live in Ireland and lead an entire community. Some of them have this unreasonable expectation that they can find their King when they need him."

"Very funny," Tony objected. "I'm just spending my youth seeing the world."

Dawn

Victor burst out laughing. "You're five hundred and fifty two years old. I think you're past your youth pal. You're a wanderer."

"Anyway, I first met Victor in the Cromwellian Conquest," Tony said ignoring his friend's outburst. "We hooked up with the same regiment purely by accident. Neither one of us knew anyone there. We just tried to blend in with the humans. Our first battle was ugly. I had no idea what I was getting into. Victor and I realized we would be better off as partners."

"I think that's probably the only thing that saved us," Victor added. "Once the war was over, we were friends for life." The two men shared a long, knowing look. They both knew nothing would ever ruin their friendship. Victor was glad he liked Tony's wife and they both liked Ariel. It would be difficult if there were hard feelings between any of them.

"But they didn't have tanks in 1650," Orin pointed out. "What war were you in when you got the nickname?"

"Well, first off..." Tony began. "That's not my nickname."

"I would have to disagree," Breena told him. "Our community knows you as Tank, and that was all your doing."

"Why did you decide to do that anyway?" Victor asked. "I know you hate the nickname and nobody but me has ever gotten away with calling you that."

"Well, you dropped me at the airport and I was supposed to be headed home. Dad called and said the council was going to make a ruling on something important and he wanted the entire family there to support mom's position. I had every intention of going home. I even bought the ticket. But I was sitting in the chair thinking about your situation and the more I thought about it, the more pissed off I became. I finally just got up and walked out the door. I had to come to New York and look into the situation myself," Tony admitted.

"Moron," Victor said shaking his head. "I told you nobody here knew anything. You should have gone home. I bet your parents were livid. They do know it wasn't my fault don't they? I don't think I should have to apologize for your bad decisions, but I will if they're going to hold it against me."

"Naw," Tony grinned. "I called dad and told him what I had to do. He agreed. We both thought it would be best if I could get some answers. You don't believe me but you're still dad's favorite son," Tony shrugged. "Anyway, I was hoping I could help clear your name. I guess that didn't work out that well," he grinned at Ariel.

"If that was your intention, why did you insist on using a fake name and acting like a vagabond? Why didn't you just let everyone know who you were?" Ariel inquired. "I remember asking you what you were hiding back then but you wouldn't tell me."

"I knew I wouldn't get answers if your community knew I was a DeLacy. I'd have to spend all my time at fancy dinners and social events. That's not the way I wanted to conduct my investigation. Plus, I knew none of those social climbers would have been Victor's friends. They wouldn't be able to help me get to the bottom of things. So, I had a plan. I just didn't think of a name. When I got into town I immediately found a hotel I knew was owned by a fae, it was one of the Dillinger's. That's when I realized I hadn't thought things through. It took me off guard when the clerk asked me who I was. I had Victor on my mind and the only thing I could think of was Tank."

Dawn

"I guess that makes sense," Ariel admitted. "Sorry it didn't work out for you."

He smiled at her mournfully. "I'm sorry I couldn't fix Victor's problems but I'm not sorry I came. I got to meet a great girl who broke my heart and sent me packing to Denver." He turned to look at Megan. "That's where I found the most wonderful woman in the world."

"You still didn't say what war you were in," Orin pressed.

"He got his nickname in June of 1944 near the battle of Normandy," Victor told them. "World War II."

"You two were in the battle of Normandy?" Ariel asked. "Do you want to explain how that happened? The fae didn't get involved in that war," she was sure of that. She was living in France at the time.

Victor's mouth quirked into a slight grin. "Well, Tony and I were kind of bored I guess."

"Are you seriously telling us the two of you joined World War II out of boredom?" Megan exclaimed. "What have I gotten myself into?" she moaned.

"It's too late for you, but I can still back out," Ariel teased.

"Not a chance," Victor pulled her close and kissed her hard.

"Okay, you're right. I'm hooked," Ariel grinned at him. "Please, break it to me gently, just how crazy are you two?" she looked at Megan. "We may need to keep them apart from now on."

"Well, we can get a little crazy when left on our own," Tony admitted. "But now that we have you two, I'm sure our wayward habits are behind us. Right?" he asked Victor.

"Of course," Victor tried to sound innocent.

"Whatever," Ariel said unconvinced. "Finish the story."

"Alright," Victor agreed. "So we were in France hanging out, enjoying our youth."

Ariel rolled her eyes.

Victor laughed. "Okay, we were looking for trouble. Tony and I tend to be more adventurous when we're together too long. We get bored and our imagination gets the best of us. Anyway, we somehow found ourselves in the middle of the Battle of Normandy. We hung back and just watched for a while, curious how things were going to turn out. We'd both seen war before so we knew we didn't really want to get involved. It wasn't our fight," he explained.

"So we come around this bend and see an empty Sherman Tank," Victor continued. "We were both partial to the Americans and I was feeling a little guilty about not helping my fellow countrymen. That's when we decided it must be fate. Tony said something about always wanting to drive a tank and I commented about how cool it would be to shoot down a Nazi plane. No more discussion was needed. We darted toward the tank and closed the hatch. It took Tony here awhile to figure out how to start the thing. Eventually we got it going and headed out across the battlefield. To say the least, that was the most eventful ride I've had in my life." Victor burst out laughing.

Tony couldn't help it, he joined Victor. They both sat their laughing hysterically remembering their adventure. "A German

Dawn

Messerschmitt 109 spotted us and decided it was his duty to take us out," Tony finally continued. "I pushed that tank with all it had, but we were still vulnerable."

"We were hauling ass across that field when the German fired its first shot. It barely missed us," Victor admitted. "I knew we were doomed if we didn't try something so I jumped into the turret and began to fire my first 75 mm weapon. I was having a blast and actually scared the plane off when I suddenly found myself hanging upside down."

"What?" Megan asked. "What happened?"

"Well, your ace driver over there..." he pointed to Tony. "Who I now refer to as Tony the Tank Master wasn't paying attention to the terrain and drove over the bank of a river. The tank took a tumble and we finally settled upside down in the water." He was barely able to explain it, he was laughing so hard.

"Obviously you got out okay, what happened to the plane?" Orin asked.

Victor sobered. "I climbed out of the tank coughing and sputtering and swam to shore. I assumed Tony was right behind me. I could hear the plane circling above us and began frantically looking for Tony. I realized he was still inside the tank."

"When we rolled, it completely took me by surprise," Tony admitted. "I really hadn't been paying attention to where I was going. I was too engrossed in the gun battle Victor was fighting against the German. When the tank rolled, I hit my head on the hard metal wall and knocked myself out," he looked at Victor. "Thank goodness Vic came back for me. I was covered in water and completely unconscious."

"Once again, I had to save the man's butt. I barely got him out and was swimming to safety when the Messerschmitt dropped the bomb. The tank exploded instantly," Victor laughed. "That woke him up."

"You idiot," Megan smacked Tony across the chest. "You could have been killed."

Tony smiled, "I almost was," he laughed when she hit him again.

"Needless to say, Tony and I decided participating in that particular war wasn't such a good idea." He winked at Ariel who was sitting there shocked. They were lucky to be alive. Warriors and fae both healed, but they wouldn't survive something as destructive as a bomb.

"Hey, don't get the wrong idea. I've saved Victor plenty over the years. He just likes to rub that one in. Maybe after another hundred years or so he'll find a new joke," Tony hoped.

"Maybe, I just won't get into a car with you when you're the one behind the wheel." He looked over at Megan. "If I were you, I'd drive from now on."

"Very funny," Tony retorted. "I happen to be a very good driver. Too bad you can't say the same. I've ridden with you pal. As soon as the engine roars to life you seem to think you're Jimmy Johnson."

Everyone laughed. They all knew Victor liked to drive fast.

Victor glanced at his father. He hadn't told him about that close call. He wondered how he was taking it.

Dawn

Atticus smiled at his son. He knew Victor had been reckless in his youth. It scared him to hear how close he'd come to ending it, but Atticus had taken more than a few chances in his younger days as well. Although not as many as those two boys had. He was just grateful everything had turned out alright. He sometimes wondered if he should try to keep Victor away from Tony, but he couldn't do it. He loved Tony like he was his own son. Plus, Victor was always so happy when Tony was around.

Victor thought of Ty and sobered. His friend needed him, starting now. He immediately stood and glanced around the room. "It's getting late, you guys should go to bed. I'm going to sit with Ty for a while." He hated to bring the topic up again, but he was anxious to check on his friend.

Hours later, Victor and Ariel sat in the dark room watching Samantha and Ty. Samantha wasn't exactly awake, but she wasn't really unconscious anymore either. Kylee had eventually strapped them to the bed. They were both jerking and moving around too much. She was afraid the lines were going to be dislodged. Victor and Ariel were each lost in their own thoughts, neither one wanting to speak. They both knew it was going to be a very long night.

Ariel shifted her weight in the lounge chair and stretched. She let out a loud yawn as she glanced out the window. It was finally morning. Hopefully Alex and Dimitri would arrive soon. She knew Victor wouldn't budge until Dimitri ordered him to, but the stress and lack of sleep were taking a toll.

"You should go in and get some rest," Victor said frowning at Ariel. She'd been up all night, forcing herself to stay awake every time her eyes started to drift shut. He wished she would take a nap.

"I'll go when you do," she challenged.

"Ariel, we don't both need to be in here. Kylee tied them down as well as possible. They're not going to get loose," Victor argued. "Go to bed."

"Well in that case, you go to bed. I'll sit with them," she countered.

Victor sighed. He was never going to win this argument. He stood and walked to the recliner. "Scoot," he told her. When she slid over Victor climbed into the chair with her. He pulled her close and held her tight. He had to admit he was glad she'd sat up with him. Watching Ty suffer was difficult. Having the woman he loved with him made it more bearable somehow.

The two of them looked up when the door slid open. Dimitri walked in. He frowned at Ty then spotted Victor and Ariel in the chair. "You two go to bed," he ordered.

"I'm fine," Victor argued.

"No, you're not. Go to bed," Dimitri demanded. He turned back and pushed the door open wider. Ty's parents walked in.

Victor stood. "Sir," he held out his hand to Ken Brody.

Ty's father took Victor's hand and didn't let go. "Thank you for staying with my son through this ordeal. You should get some rest now, Lizza and I will take over."

Victor nodded slightly and turned to Ariel. She was also standing. "Hi, I'm Ariel." She held her hand out to Ty's mother. "I'm so happy to meet you."

Ty's mother took the small extended hand. "Lizza Brody," she said. "This is my husband Ken."

Dawn

Ariel shook Ken's hand. "It's a pleasure to meet you, too," she smiled then yawned.

Lizza smiled. "You two are beat. We'll take care of Ty for a while. Please go get some rest."

* * * *

Ariel and Victor walked downstairs and entered the study. They were surprised to see all the warriors scattered around the room.

"How is he?" Dante asked immediately.

"He's in a lot of pain," Victor admitted. "Samantha's in pain too but it doesn't seem as bad as Ty."

"Figures," Dante grumbled.

Alex shot him a dirty look. "We want both of them to be okay," she snapped.

"Uh...sorry," Dante mumbled.

"Thanks for coming," Victor addressed the room. "I feel better about hitting the sack knowing you guys are here for him."

Victor and Ariel headed to bed.

Ariel woke abruptly. She was starving. She hesitated a few seconds then tried to slide out of bed without disturbing Victor. He needed all the rest he could get. She slowly slid from beneath Victor's arm and moved inch by inch toward the side of the bed. She was just slipping off the edge when he wrapped his arms around her and pulled her back against him. "Where are you going?" he said groggily.

"I'm starving," she admitted turning around to face him.

Victor brushed the hair away from her face. "Me too," he told her. "What time is it anyway?"

Ariel pushed herself up on her elbow and glanced at the clock. "It's almost dinner time. No wonder I'm starved."

Victor couldn't resist. He pulled her to him and kissed her passionately. Before he was finished his stomach growled. They both laughed. "Okay, so we both need food." He climbed off the bed and pulled Ariel with him. "Let's eat." The first thing they noticed when they entered the kitchen was the absence of Ty's dogs. Only Dimitri's puppy lounged on the floor in front of the back door.

"Where's Bo and Ace?" Ariel asked. She walked to the door and looked outside. They weren't on the porch either. That was strange. Ariel opened the fridge and rummaged inside. "Chicken or pie?"

"What kind of pie?" he asked.

"Cherry," Ariel answered absently. She was looking for something to go with the chicken.

"Both," Victor told her. He was starving.

Ariel brought the fried chicken to the table. "Here's some kind of salad to go with it." She set the bowl on the table and returned for the pie.

Dawn

Victor grabbed a couple plates and the silverware and set them on the table. He returned for two glasses and turned to Ariel. "What would you like to drink?"

"Milk," she said, not looking up. She was already dishing her food. They sat at the table eating in silence. They were both so hungry. Ariel jumped when she heard a loud high pitched noise. "What was that?" she asked.

"I don't know," Victor admitted, rising to investigate. It wasn't the alarm. When he reached the foyer he could tell it was coming from the second floor. He took the stairs two at a time. It was coming from Ty's room. Victor opened the door and froze. Ty's mother was sitting next to Ty holding his hand and crying. His father was standing behind her. Kylee was frantically pulling an IV from Ty's arm. Bastian was performing CPR. Victor's attention went to the machine hooked to Ty, wires were running from the display to Ty's chest.

Ariel shoved past him and ran to the bed. She pushed Kylee out of the way. "I can do that, help him!" Ariel quickly unhooked the IV and pushed the metal stand out of the way.

Kylee was watching the electronic display. Ty's heart still wasn't beating, but every once in a while they'd get a blurb. "Move out of the way," she ordered Bastian.

Bastian glared at her, but didn't move.

"Move it!" She said loudly. She pushed past Bastian and took over. Finally Ty's vitals were normal again. Kylee stepped back and sighed in relief.

Lizza looked at the machine. It wasn't screaming anymore. "Does that mean he's okay?" She asked.

"For now," Kylee assured her. She walked across the room and slumped into a chair. Throughout this whole thing Samantha didn't move. She seemed to be sleeping. Kylee turned to Bastian. "How long do they have to be connected?" she asked.

Bastian looked at Samantha then back at Ty. "Why?"

"Samantha doesn't seem to be in pain anymore. It's more like she's sleeping. As soon as I can, I'd like to move her into the other room. I think we can make Ty more comfortable if the lines are gone. I just don't know how you can tell when the process is complete."

Ken was the one to answer her question. "I think Samantha's transformation is finished. She's now suffering from the after effects. Once the change takes place it wipes you out. She's going to sleep for at least twenty four hours. Don't worry if she seems comatose. As long as her vitals are normal, she's okay."

Bastian walked to Samantha and withdrew a vile of blood.

"What's that for?" Kylee asked him.

"I want to check it and make sure it's complete," he told her strolling out of the room.

Kylee followed. "Can I come?" she called after him.

"Do you think that's wise? What if he crashes again?" Bastian asked.

Kylee turned and called into the room. "If I go with Bastian can you guys handle things here? If you need me I think we'll just be downstairs." She turned back to Bastian, "are you leaving the house?"

Dawn

"No," he said shortly. He didn't need some human busy body looking over his shoulder. He didn't know why Dimitri kept her here in the first place. So she was a doctor. That didn't mean she knew anything about treating warriors. He had humored her when she insisted on getting that machine from the local hospital. He thought it was a waste of time, but he had to admit it did come in handy. They immediately knew when Ty had a problem. But if the woman didn't stop looking over his shoulder and treating him like he was an idiot, he was going to explode. This wasn't a warrior biology program and he didn't have time for a hundred questions. Bastian continued to scowl as he left the room and headed downstairs.

Victor stood quietly watching Ty's parents. He was hoping they would offer an explanation of what just happened on their own. After a few minutes he lost patience and had to ask. "Ken, can you fill us in on what went wrong?"

"Oh sorry," he apologized. Ken paused when the whining and scratching started on the attached bathroom door. He walked over, opened it slowly then watched as Bo and Ace ran out and leapt onto the bed. Both dogs immediately laid down. Ace with his chin resting on Ty's chest, Bo on the other side resting his chin on Ty's thigh.

"Is that a good idea?" Ariel asked. "They could pull the lines out if they jump around too much."

Lizza was the one that answered. "We worried about it at first, but as you can see, the dogs seem to relax Ty somehow. They are extremely careful with him. I'm willing to do anything that helps."

"How did you discover that?" Ariel asked surprised.

"The dogs were locked in the kitchen, but a few hours ago Ty began screaming in pain. The dogs heard him and began howling. We couldn't get them to stop," Lizza explained. "I'm surprised all the racket didn't wake you two up."

"Me too," Victor admitted. "But we were both pretty beat after all the work on the apartment and then being up all night."

"Anyway, we finally thought if we brought them up here and let them see Ty maybe they'd realize nobody was hurting him and they'd calm down. They immediately jumped into that exact position and didn't move for hours," she told them. "Ty also stopped screaming."

"What changed?" Victor asked, anxious to hear what was going on with Ty.

"Kylee was worried about his blood level," Ken told him. "She took his blood pressure and said it was extremely hazardous. She didn't know what impact that would have on a warrior, but she said if Ty were human it would be fatal. Bastian was concerned as well. We decided to try to increase his blood level by hooking up an IV." He paused, clearly upset about what came next. "Things went bad immediately. As soon as the blood began to flow into Ty, his heart stopped. We were trying to unhook the bag and get his heart going when the two of you came in."

"I see," Victor said pondering the situation. He was studying Ty. He looked bad. His color was almost gray. If they didn't do something he might not make it. He shifted his attention to Samantha. She looked fine. She was still unconscious, but other than that she seemed okay. "Are Samantha's wounds completely healed?" he asked no one in particular.

Dawn

"She's fine," Lizza said with obvious resentment. "That girl is the one that's taken all the blood. She's the reason Ty doesn't have enough right now. She's the one putting him at risk."

Ariel was studying Ty's mother. Of course she would be concerned about her son, but she wasn't being fair. Samantha hadn't done this on purpose. Samantha hadn't had a say in this at all. They may not be friends any longer, but she was getting tired of everyone's attitude towards Sam. "Ma'am," Ariel said as gently as she could. "I understand your concern for your son, but I don't understand your resentment towards Samantha."

"Ariel," Victor warned.

Ariel ignored him. "Sam didn't choose this. In fact, Sam didn't even have a say in it. Ty made the decision for both of them. Samantha isn't putting Ty at risk or selfishly taking all the blood for herself with careless disregard for Ty's life. The blood is in control, Ty's blood."

"I'm sorry," Lizza said tears filling her eyes. "That's not like me. I'm not that cruel and uncaring. I'm just so worried about my son and I'm still having a hard time understanding why he would do this. Everyone here believes she is going to be upset about the change. Why would he risk his life this way?"

"Because he loves her," Victor answered. "It doesn't matter how she feels. Ty loves Samantha and he had to do everything in his power to save her. You're his parents. You know him better than any of us. You know he couldn't have done anything less."

Lizza studied Ty. Victor was right. If Ty loved this girl, he wouldn't hesitate to risk his life to save hers. She had always been so proud of her son's compassion and selflessness. Now, it could actually kill him. "She must be a special woman. I'll try to remember that, no matter what happens," she said quietly.

Ken was watching Victor. He had something on his mind. "Victor, what is it? What are you debating?"

Victor looked up at him. "Ty needs more blood," he began.

"We're not hooking that IV back up. I will not risk my son's life that way again," Ken said immediately.

"I don't want to hook it to Ty. I think we should hook it to Sam." He looked to Ariel for support.

Ariel was studying Samantha now. She looked fine. Before she was going to agree, she needed to see for herself that Sam's injuries were healed. She gave Victor a supportive smile. "Let me check her injuries first," she headed for the bed.

"Why are you giving her more blood?" Lizza asked confused. "She's fine."

Ken finally understood. "That's why we should do it," he told his wife. "Ty's system is already tapped beyond what it should be. Then, we introduced more blood. Just another drain on his system. That's what pushed him into cardiac arrest. The girl's system is repaired. She can handle the added strain to turn the blood."

"But how will that help Ty?" she asked.

Victor answered this time. "Because Sam's body doesn't need the blood. It's keeping as much as it needs and leaving Ty short. Once it has extra, her system will allow more blood to flow into Ty."

Dawn

"Her head is completely healed," Ariel announced. She checked under the sheet and studied Sam's ribs. They also appeared to be healed. The last thing she checked was Sam's feet. They were completely healed as well. "I think we should try it," she studied Ty. "He needs help fast. Victor's suggestion will only risk Sam but I don't think it's much of a risk. I believe this could help Ty. Let me go get Kylee. We're going to need her here in case something goes wrong." She quickly left the room.

"Do you really think this will work?" Lizza asked her husband.

"I do," Ken assured her. "It makes sense," he studied Samantha. "She seems fine. I think she's just suffering the after effects of the change. That's the only reason she isn't already awake. Her body has shut down to conserve energy. It might delay her recovery a little, but I don't think it's going to harm her."

"Ty would never forgive us if we risked her life to save him," Lizza admitted hesitantly.

Kylee walked in and went directly to the bed. She spent a few minutes checking Samantha's vitals and finally looked at Victor. "Let's try it," she agreed. "Everything seems normal," she said as she turned to Ariel. "I need you to stay close in case I need your help," she smiled. "You seem to be good with IV's."

They hooked up the IV and watched for some kind of reaction. Sam's system handled the extra strain just fine. It wasn't drastic, but Ty also appeared a little better. When the IV bottle was empty, Lizza wanted to add another bag.

"I'll agree to one more, but then we'll need to wait awhile. I don't want to overload Sam's system all at once," Kylee told them.

302

"I agree," Victor put in. "She's doing fine with it but I can see her body's struggling to make the change. One more bag and then we wait a few hours."

* * * *

Samantha woke slowly. She wasn't sure where she was at first. She pushed herself up and looked around. She was in her room at the farmhouse. How had she gotten home? The last thing she remembered was hanging from that log in the forest. She was sure Lilith was going to kill her. Who had come to her rescue? Samantha slowly stood expecting to be in pain. Nothing. She felt fine. No, she felt better than fine. She had never felt this good in her life. How long had she been out? She looked down and realized she was only wearing a large t-shirt. She pulled it up and studied her ribs. It wasn't possible. She was sure they had been broken. Then suddenly she remembered her feet. She plopped back down on the bed and studied the bottom of one foot then the other. Nothing. No cut, no scars, nothing. Her hand flew to the back of her head. Nothing there either. It was fine, but it did feel a little gross. She needed a shower.

Samantha grabbed some clothes and headed for the bathroom. She stood in front of the mirror looking at her reflection in amazement. She looked great. Her skin was vibrant, in fact it almost glowed. Her hand flew to her face. Her skin was so soft. She'd never had skin this perfect in her life. She studied her arms, they looked bigger, more muscular somehow. But they couldn't be, that was impossible. She climbed into the shower and enjoyed the feel of hot water running over her body. She thought she should be tired. She'd just woken up from serious injuries, but she felt like dancing. She had so much energy.

Dawn

Once dressed, Samantha ventured downstairs. Voices were coming from the study. She hesitantly stepped into the doorway. Clearly one of these guys had saved her life. She had no idea why, after she had behaved so badly. How could she ever repay them? It seemed that everyone in the room noticed her at once. "Uh...hi," she said not knowing what else to say. She slowly took in the large group sitting around the room. Alex was next to Dimitri with a puppy on her lap. The tiny animal was chewing a squeak toy in the shape of a bone. The small dog looked like a miniature version of one of Ty's dogs. Sam looked around at the group. Other than Alex, she also knew Thomas, Ariel and Victor but that was it. The rest of the group looked familiar, but she had never actually met them. She stood there for several seconds, the silence was uncomfortable and she didn't know what to say or do next.

Ariel was waiting for something more. Some kind of acknowledgment for Ty's sacrifice. An inquiry about Ty's condition. Some reaction to the transformation. Nothing followed. So, nothing had changed. Samantha was still angry. Ariel wasn't going to sit here and pretend this was all okay. "I need to go check on Bree," she stood and headed for the door. Once she reached Samantha she paused and added. "It takes a lot out of her, carrying the devil's spawn and all. Don't worry, you won't have to interact with her. Kylee has her on bed rest for the next couple weeks," then she continued out the door.

Well, nothing had changed there, Samantha thought. "Sorry to interrupt," she said quietly. "Uh...is Breena okay?" She didn't know Breena, but obviously she was important to Ariel.

"We think she'll be fine. Kylee's worried about the baby and ordered her to stay in bed as a precaution," Alex supplied.

"Well, I hope everything works out okay for her. Sorry again for the interruption," Sam mumbled as she turned to leave.

Alex stood, "Sam, I need to talk to you before you take off." She turned to the crowded room. "Will you excuse me. we need some privacy." She handed Cane to Dimitri then followed Samantha into the foyer. "Do you mind joining me on the back porch? It will only take a minute," she promised.

Well, at least Alex was still talking to her. Her boss could be painfully honest at times though. Was this going to be a good talk, or a lecture? Sam wasn't sure, but she knew she deserved anything she got. "Okay," she finally answered.

The two women slid out the door and settled into the comfortable patio chairs. "How do you feel?" Alex asked.

"Actually I feel better than I ever have," she confessed. "How is that possible? How long was I out?"

"A few days," Alex told her, waiting for a reaction.

Samantha looked at Alex in shock. "That's impossible. I know how seriously I was injured by Lilith. My ribs were broken I'm sure. And my shin. What about those cuts on my feet? I couldn't have healed in a few days."

"You were in pretty bad shape, I agree," Alex said softly. She was trying to decide the best approach to give Samantha the news.

"What are you afraid to tell me, Alex?" Samantha asked. She'd never seen Alex like this before. She was usually so confident and direct. The change was unnerving.

Maybe it was best to just get it over with, Alex decided. "Once Ty got you back to the house, Kylee tried to work on your wounds. It didn't take her long to realize your head wound was going to be fatal," Alex paused to let that sink in.

"Fatal?" Samantha asked. "Then why am I still alive?" She didn't understand what Alex was trying to tell her.

"Ty insisted on saving your life," Alex told Sam.

"How? If my wounds were fatal?" She was studying Alex and her stomach sank. Where was Ty anyway? He hadn't been in the study with everyone else. Alex was sober now, something wasn't right.

"It's a little difficult to explain, but he used his blood to save you," Alex began.

"His blood? What do you mean by that?" Sam was beginning to panic. Ty's absence was even more concerning now. "Where is Ty?" she demanded.

"Ty is still in bed. He's having a hard time recovering from the procedure," Alex confessed.

"What procedure, exactly?" Samantha demanded.

"I really don't know how to break this to you Sam. I'm worried about how you're going to take it, so I'm just going to say it. Ty used his blood to turn you into a warrior. It was the only way to save your life," Alex waited for a reaction. "I'm so sorry, Sam. I know this is a shock and probably the last thing you would have wanted. I know you think the warriors are unnatural and evil. I'd like to help you come to grips with this if you'll let me."

She was a warrior? How was that possible? She didn't feel any different. Well, except for the physical changes she'd been trying to figure out. That would explain the perfect skin, the phenomenal energy and the extra strength. "A warrior?" she mumbled in disbelief. "I'm a warrior?" she didn't know what to say.

"Yes," Alex affirmed.

"What do you mean Ty's not recovering? Did he give me too much blood or something? He's going to be okay, right?" she said in a panic.

"We hope so," Alex said vaguely.

"You hope so?" Samantha stood. "What does that mean? Are you telling me he could die because he saved me?"

"Unfortunately, yes. He might. His body isn't recovering as well as we had hoped. We're not sure why. He had a few broken ribs himself before he started the process. That obviously gave him a handicap to start with," Alex explained.

"Does this process usually work? I assume it's been tried before, is it typically successful?" she asked.

"I'm a little new at this myself. From what I'm told it fails as often as it works," Alex told her.

Sam interrupted. "There was only a fifty percent chance that Ty would survive this and you guys let him do it anyway? What is wrong with you?" She was angry. She was beyond angry. How could they risk Ty for her?

"The risk is the same for the human as it is for the warrior. Just as many humans die from the process as warriors," Alex corrected. "In your case, it was even more risky because you had so many injuries. Like I said, I'm new to this but I'm told that has never been tried before."

Dawn

"I need to see Ty. Where is he?" She was still standing and turned to enter the kitchen.

"Uh, I'm not sure that's a good idea." Alex ran to catch up with Sam.

"Why not?" Sam demanded.

"To be honest I still don't know how you feel about the change. I can see you're worried about Ty but you did threaten to kill all the warriors if they came near you," Alex continued. "Plus Ty's parents are with him. Emotions are high for all of you right now. Maybe you should wait."

"I assume he's in his room." Sam continued through the house and headed for the stairs.

"At least let me warn them you're coming," Alex urged.

Samantha didn't answer. She marched up the stairs and into Ty's room. She'd only taken one step inside when she saw him. He looked terrible. He was ghostly white, no he was worse than that. Kylee was hovering. Wires were stretched from a machine to Ty's chest, rows of squiggly lines ran across the screen. She was shocked. Why was she feeling so good and Ty was in such terrible condition? It wasn't fair. She had to do something.

"So, it's the girl my brother risked his life for." A stranger stood and walked towards Sam. "I'm Gavin, Ty's younger brother." He held out a hand.

Samantha absently took the man's hand and shook it. Her eyes never left Ty's face.

"You look good, how are you feeling?" he asked.

"Uh...alright," Samantha answered absently. She finally turned her attention to the man standing next to her. "I'm sorry," she glanced back at Ty. "Uh...I feel good. Really good, thanks."

Lizza was watching the woman. As soon as she'd stepped into the room her reaction said it all. Samantha was in love with her son. She continued to watch silently as Gavin tried to start a conversation.

Samantha cautiously moved forward until she was standing right next to the bed. She closed her eyes to hold back the tears. Ty was so weak, he looked like he could be dead already. Standing there, so close to him, she realized she could feel the weakness. It was unlike anything she'd experienced before. It wasn't just sympathy, she could actually feel how tired and weak he was. Her head shot around and she addressed Alex. "You said Ty gave me his blood to save me. Why can't I give some back to help him? He's too weak, he needs more blood."

"You have been," Lizza finally spoke softly. For the first time she understood why her son had risked his life to save this woman.

"What?" Samantha asked, noticing the woman for the first time. She was beautiful and she had many of Ty's facial features. Obviously this was his mother.

"We've been transferring your blood to Ty once a day to help replenish his system," she paused. "Now that you're awake, it will obviously be up to you if you want to continue."

Samantha spotted a wooden chair in the corner of the room. She walked over, drug it to the side of the bed and sat down. She held out her arm. "Kylee, take some of my blood and give it to Ty now."

Dawn

"No way," Kylee protested. "I already took some this morning."

"Do it again," Samantha demanded.

"I can't," Kylee objected. "I can't take too much at once or it will harm your system."

Samantha was furious. She stood and walked to Kylee. "You have two choices, either you do it, or I will," she warned.

"You don't know how," Kylee hoped she was right.

"I have the internet. In about two minutes I will know how," she countered.

Lizza was watching the exchange. No wonder Ty fell for this woman. She was perfect for him. "Samantha?" Lizza interrupted. She smiled inwardly when the whole room looked at her in surprise. Okay, so she hadn't called the girl by her name before. She was just a girl then. Now she had personality, she had spunk. Lizza was sure they were going to get along wonderfully. She waited until Samantha turned to face her. "Ty needs regular infusions. If we take too much from you in one day, you may have a relapse. It might harm you too much to take blood the next day. We don't want to risk the strain on your system."

Samantha blinked in disbelief. "Are you serious?" she asked incredulously. "Ty is lying there fighting for his life because he saved mine and you won't give him what he needs because it might cause me a little discomfort? Have you people completely lost your minds? If you haven't noticed, I feel fine. No, I feel better than fine. Kylee," Samantha swung back around to face the doctor. "I'm serious. Either you do it or I will."

"I won't..." Kylee began.

Alex cut her off. She'd been watching Sam. She really was fine. They wouldn't take too much blood and clearly Samantha's body could take the loss. Maybe they had been too cautious. "Kylee, do what Sam asked."

"What?" Kylee exclaimed. "But..."

"No," Alex interrupted again. "Samantha is right. Ty made a huge sacrifice for Sam. She's willing to repay him by offering her blood. We all know he can use whatever he can get. If Sam says she's up for it, we're going to trust her. Sam you're going to need to lie on the bed. The chair won't be close enough."

Sam studied Alex. She wasn't giving anything away. Okay, she'd lay on the bed. She walked over and gently sat down. One of Ty's dogs lifted its head and studied her for the slightest second then jumped off the bed and laid at the foot. The second dog followed. That was strange, Sam thought. She realized they must be used to this. Ty's mom said they'd already been using her blood to help Ty. Maybe the dogs had become accustomed to the routine. She slowly laid down and waited for Kylee.

"This might hurt a little," Kylee warned. She hooked the line to Sam's axillary artery this time. Under the circumstances she didn't think it was necessary to use the femoral.

Sam watched as Kylee ran the line and connected it to Ty's arm. Once she was done, Sam watched the blood flow from her to Ty. She didn't see any change. She laid on her side watching Ty, then the blood running from her arm to his, then back to Ty. It was very slight, but she began to feel a little relief. Was she somehow feeling what Ty felt? How was that possible?

Dawn

Kylee stepped forward to remove the line. As soon as she reached for it Samantha knocked her hand away. "Samantha, that's too much."

"No it's not," Sam argued, still watching Ty. She could feel the blood rejuvenating Ty's system. There was no way she was going to let them stop now.

Lizza was watching Sam. They were taking twice the amount of blood they had before. She couldn't let this continue. "Kylee, stop the flow. Now," she ordered.

Samantha looked up at Ty's mother's worried face. "I'm fine ma'am. He needs this, let me help him."

"You have helped him more than you know," Lizza answered. "Now it's time to step back and let Ty do the rest for today."

Samantha realized she was starting to feel a little dizzy. "Okay," she agreed. "Kylee go ahead." Samantha took Ty's hand for the slightest instant. It was electric. Tears formed in her eyes, she had to get out of here.

"Once you're finish with that Kylee I wonder if you, and everyone else, could give me a moment alone with Samantha," Lizza asked.

Ken was watching his wife. What was she up to? She must have felt his gaze because she quickly looked into his eyes. She was asking him to trust her, to go along with her wishes. He knew his wife, she needed this. He would accommodate her. He turned to Gavin and motioned for him to leave the room. Gavin proceeded to the door, his father following close behind. Alex followed and then Kylee.

Samantha sat up on the edge of the bed. She was going to stand, but she felt a little off. No way was she going to let Ty's mom know she'd given too much blood.

Lizza walked to a tray and poured a glass of water. "Here this might help," she said as she handed Sam the liquid.

"Thanks," Sam said as she took the water and slowly began to sip.

"I was told you hated the warriors," she said bluntly. "I think maybe you did at one time, but I don't believe you still feel that way. Am I right?"

"You are," Samantha answered honestly.

"I see," Lizza studied her. "I'm grateful for what you just did for my son. I know it's hard to believe, but your blood is helping him. I don't think he would have made it this long without it. I can see the difference even if you cannot."

"I think it was the least I could do considering what he did for me," Samantha answered. She was nervous around this woman. It was Ty's mother. Why had she wanted a private talk?

"You look a little peaked," Lizza observed. "I think if you drank some blood, it might bring your strength back."

Samantha cringed. The thought of drinking blood was repulsive. She didn't think she could do it.

Lizza smiled knowingly. "I know, the very idea seems unbearable and disgusting to you. All the warriors hate it. I've never met one that didn't have to gag it down, but sometimes it's necessary. It's up to you of course, but I think a little blood would help steady you," she paused. "Samantha you're a warrior now. At some point you're going to have to accept that, all of it."

"Are you a warrior too," Sam asked.

"Me?" Lizza laughed. "No, I'm fae. We got off easy. When we're injured we have to drink a special tea to help us heal. It's still pretty bad, but there are ways we can mask it. Warriors are stuck with blood. We could hook up an IV, but drinking it is so much quicker."

Samantha didn't think she could do this. The idea was just too horrible.

"I remember the first time I made Ty drink a glass of blood. He fought me for twenty minutes. Ultimately, he realized it was part of who he is. He held his nose and gulped it down as quickly as he could. He was only five at the time. Once he finished he ran to the fridge and drank at least a quart of milk straight from the jug. Well to be honest it wasn't a fridge, it was an icebox. Refrigerators hadn't been invented yet. In home refrigerators weren't readily available until the late 1920's."

Samantha blinked. She'd forgotten the part about living for hundreds, maybe thousands of years. Did that apply to her now? She really did have a lot of questions.

"I've startled you," Lizza observed. "I'm sorry. I assumed you knew about the benefits of being a warrior."

"I think I do. Most of them anyway. I had just forgotten about the living forever part. Does that apply to me now, too?" Sam asked.

"It does. However, warriors don't actually live forever. But with luck, it can seem that way," Lizza smiled. "You really are taking this better than everyone seemed to believe you would. They were all convinced you were going to panic and freak out once you knew about the transition. It seems they were wrong."

"Uh…I guess I was kind of behaving badly before all this happened," Sam confessed. She didn't know why, but it was easy to talk to this woman. "At first I was freaked and I jumped to a lot of wrong conclusions. I was pretty cruel. It took me a couple days, but I finally came around to the realization that the warriors were the good guys. They risk their lives constantly for others. Anyone that selfless couldn't be a monster," she said shyly. What must this woman think of her?

"Sensible," Lizza agreed. "So you don't hate my son?"

"Of course not!" Samantha exclaimed. "I could never hate Ty," then she stopped. She didn't want anyone to know how she really felt about him.

Lizza smiled. "That's what I thought." Now she was positive. This woman loved her boy as much as he loved her. "I assume by now you have realized that the two of you have a special connection. Can you tell me what you felt when you walked to the bed? Yes, I saw it in your face. Plus we all know about the connection the two of you are going to feel."

"I felt weak," Sam confessed. "Tired and weak. I thought it was strange, are you telling me that's normal?"

"It is," Lizza assured her. "How does he feel now?" she asked.

Dawn

Samantha hesitated. "When I first went to the bed I felt tired and weak like I said. It took a while, but once the blood was flowing I began to feel refreshed or rejuvenated. It's hard to explain. That's why I didn't want Kylee to stop. I thought I could feel how the blood felt to Ty. It felt so energizing and essential I guess. I know I'm not making any sense. While it was happening, I thought I was crazy."

"You look a little better, but you're still pale. I really think we should try the blood. Just take a little, for me?" she pressed.

"Uh...is there blood in this room?" Sam asked. She hoped the answer was no.

Lizza walked to the closet and opened a small fridge. She pulled out a tiny container and walked back over to the bed. Once she was standing in front of Sam, she pulled out a stopper then held out the container. "Just close your eyes and gulp it down. The first time is the worst I promise."

Samantha slowly took the container from Ty's mother. She knew she was going to have to do this sometime, but the thought still gave her the creeps.

"That's it," Lizza cooed. She took Samantha's hand in hers. "Now, bottoms up." She pushed the container towards Sam's face. "You can do this," she assured her. "I have some Oreo's right here, and a glass of milk. That seemed to help Ty when he was young. One gulp then the cookie."

Sam took a deep breath and then gulped down the blood. It was worse than she'd thought it was going to be. In addition to the metallic taste, the texture made her want to throw up. "Yuck," Sam choked.

"Here," Lizza shoved an Oreo and a glass of milk towards Sam. "Oreo first. It will get rid of the taste, then wash it down with the milk."

Sam did as she was told and was surprised at how well the cookie and then the milk worked to get rid of that awful taste in her mouth. She waited, wondering what was going to happen. Should she feel better immediately? Would she feel the transformation of the blood?

"It happens pretty quickly, but you won't feel it. Give it a couple more seconds, then stand up. I think you'll feel more stable," Lizza said.

Sam was surprised. It was like the woman could read her mind. She looked down and noticed Lizza was holding her hand. Is this what it was like to have a mother? Sam's insides twisted. She had missed out on so much. She'd always blocked out the memories of her own mom. Now, sitting here with Lizza they all came rushing back. "Uh, thank you. I really appreciate you helping me through that." Sam was desperate to escape. She stood, pulling her hand away. "I think Alex still needed to talk to me though." She quickly rushed out of the room.

The poor dear, Lizza thought. She still has a lot of things to deal with. She glanced back at Ty. He now had a little color to his face. Samantha had given that to her son. For the first time in days, Lizza had hope.

* * * *

Radek sat in the executive chair behind his large desk. He needed to change tactics. Lilith had failed at the fort. She hadn't killed any of the warriors. It wasn't a complete loss, she had brought him some valuable information. Unfortunately the information she'd obtained told Radek one thing, the Deveraux's were continuing with business as usual. He'd been sure they were at the fort planning something for the war. Instead, they were working on another money making project with the humans. That was the problem and what was putting Radek at a disadvantage. They had plenty of money. He did not.

If the Deveraux's were comfortable enough to spend so much time and resources on a human project, Radek was failing. They should be worried. They should be focusing on him. He needed to do something to occupy their time and simultaneously isolate the warriors so he could pick them off one by one. He had to admit, Lilith had been right about that. At least she'd taken care of the human. Lilith had been too obsessed with revenge to do him any good lately. Now that the human was dead, Lilith could get back to focusing on what he wanted. With Hector gone, he was counting on her to execute his plans.

An idea was beginning to form. They were all expecting him to target Alex. If he came at them from another direction maybe he could catch them off guard and keep them preoccupied. They used the humans, maybe he should too. He didn't care what those other busybody kings thought. Using bombs against the shifters had been a brilliant idea. Lilith had found the right man for that job. Now she could be put to use on another project, he considered. He needed to work out the details, but this time his plan would work. Once he was finished, the fae community was going to be begging him to be their king.

Chapter Eleven

Samantha rushed out the door. She needed air. She thought she was just walking aimlessly, but she suddenly found herself standing in the middle of the forest. She was in the exact spot she'd encountered Lilith. The log was still hanging above her, but she could see where someone had cut her wrists free. She wondered if the log was safe. Maybe she should cut it down. Later, she thought as she sat on the edge of the platform and just stared at her surroundings. She wasn't really seeing them. Her mind had gone back to the countryside, to her childhood. She could actually see the little farm where she lived with her family. Her mother and Aunt Lana loved to sit on that porch and visit. They could talk for hours about nothing. Her thoughts shifted to Michael. They had both loved to ride horses more than anything. That was one thing they made sure they did every day. Sometimes Lexie would join them, but Lana was always so worried about her getting injured. James encouraged her though, he wanted Lexie to experience life. The good and the bad. He always said the bad is what gave you character. If that was true, Samantha had all the character she could handle.

Once again Sam realized she was crying. What was it about this place? She felt like such a baby. She hadn't even let herself get this emotional after her family was murdered. She'd told herself she had to be strong, crying wouldn't bring her family back. Maybe it was time to face the truth. For twenty years she had only allowed herself to think about Michael. She thought about him frequently, but she always avoided thinking about her mother and father. Remembering what it was like to have parents who loved and protected her was just too hard. She was beginning to wonder if that had been unhealthy. Maybe locking those memories and feelings away all this time had made them fester, which was now making her too emotional. Watching Lizza with Ty had touched her heart and made her long for her own mother. When Lizza held her hand and guided her through the unpleasant business of drinking blood, Sam had lost it. All Samantha could think about was that one time when she was ten and she had the flu. Her mother had sat with her all night long, holding her hand the same way Lizza just had. Maybe being around so many people was the problem. But she wanted to be able to socialize. She wanted to be normal like everyone else. Sam sighed, she'd never be normal.

How was she going to live for hundreds, maybe thousands of years all alone? She had no one. Now because of her, the only man she'd ever loved might die. It should have been her. She should have died right here. It wasn't fair, Ty had so many people that loved him. So many people that would be devastated if he didn't make it. Nobody loved her. Nobody would care if she was gone. She sat there, staring into space when it hit her. She could make this right. She'd watched Kylee set up the line. If she could get Ty alone, she could transfer enough blood to his body to save him. She could give him life. It didn't matter if she lost hers in the process. Ty would be okay.

Sam stood and walked slowly to the house. She needed to get to her room and clean herself up. Nobody could know what she was planning. Nobody could know she was upset. She'd have to be very convincing. Otherwise Ty's family would never leave the room. Samantha silently walked up the stairs and slipped into her bedroom. Once inside, she quietly closed the door behind her. It was time to develop a plan.

* * * *

Alex sat in the study with Thomas. "I have to tell her. She needs to know she's lost everything because of me. I wish I could find some other explanation, but nothing else makes sense. Ty's conclusions all fit too perfectly." She laid her head on the back of the couch. "Why can't I remember anything before I was seven, Thomas?" she asked sincerely.

Thomas walked over and sat next to Alex. "Maybe it was too traumatic," he suggested. "You said Marlena wrote in that book that her husband, James, was a wonderful man. Someone she loved very much. I'm sure his death was a huge blow to your mother. So much so, that she couldn't even talk to you about him years later. I can only imagine what that must have been like for a five year old. Then, you were uprooted from the only home you'd ever known and the two of you went into hiding. Another trauma. Two years later you were captured and imprisoned by Radek. I remember how long it took after the wedding for you to stop having those nightmares. I suspect your brain shut everything out. It was just too much for a small child to handle." Thomas put an arm around Alex and pulled her head onto his shoulder.

Dawn

"I'm not a child now and I still don't have any memories of that time. The only thing I can remember are those nightmares. Running through that dark cave, terrified, holding onto mom with everything I had because I was so afraid we'd get separated. I can remember the horror, but not the joy? What does that say about me?" she worried.

"You're assuming you will never remember the joy as you put it. What makes you so sure? The last couple years have been unbelievably difficult. I know it's been harder on you than me and sometimes I can barely get through the day without breaking down. We lost both our parents and we've been thrown into a war we don't want. On top of that you've had to cope with the shock of learning who and what you really are. I know having Dimitri has helped, but this has all been hard on both of us. I think you should cut yourself a little slack, sis. So you can't remember your childhood right now. Don't you think you have enough to deal with? When the time is right, the memories will come back. I'm sure of it," Thomas promised.

"Maybe," Alex said not really convinced. "But enough about that. Samantha is dealing with the change better than any of us thought she would. Now I have to tell her she's lost everything because my evil brother wants me dead. I don't know how she's going to take that. I'd like to give her an out. I know you don't care for technology, but if she's more comfortable reporting directly to you will you let her? I don't want her to feel she has to quit her job to get away from me."

"We'll cross that bridge when we get there," Thomas began.

"But..." Alex started to argue.

"No," Thomas cut her off. "My first instinct is to say no. Not because I don't like electronics but because I think you and Sam need to deal with this, not run from it. If that's not possible I'll consider it. I really think we need to put that off until later. We'll decide what to do once we talk to Sam."

"We?" Alex asked.

"Yes we," Thomas assured her. "This is personal family business. We're family. I want to be there when Sam finds out the truth. As far as I'm concerned she's my family too."

"Are you sure?" Alex asked.

"Positive. I think we should leave it for morning though. Sam's had enough shock for one day. Let's put it off and let her get a good night's rest. We'll talk to her after breakfast." Thomas stood and took Alex by the hand. He pulled her to her feet and gave her a big, brotherly hug. "Go find your man little sister. I'll check on Ty and then I'm going to bed too."

"Thanks," Alex said, grateful she had such a wonderful brother.

* * * *

Sam casually walked into Ty's room. Well, she hoped she looked casual. Ty's family was sitting in various chairs around the small space. "How's he doing?" she asked no one in particular.

"He seems better," Gavin told her. "We owe it all to you," he added. "Thanks for sacrificing the blood today."

"I was happy to help," she said honestly. She turned her attention to Lizza. "Have you gotten any sleep since you arrived?"

Dawn

"No," Ken answered for his wife. "I keep trying to get her to take a little nap, but she won't leave his side."

"It's a mother's right," Lizza said defensively. "I'm worried about my son."

"Maybe you guys should take a break tonight and get some rest. I'll sit with him. I promise if there's any change, I'll let you know." Sam hoped she sounded normal. She had to get them to leave.

"That's a great idea," Gavin agreed. "Mom, you need rest. Ty's doing better. You and dad go get some sleep. If it'll make you feel better, I'll stay here with Samantha."

No! She had to get rid of the brother, too. He'd never let her go through with this. "You look tired too," she told him. He actually did. "I promise I'll tell you if anything changes. Ty's going to be upset if he wakes up and sees his family looking so haggard. Go rest for a while. I've got this." She smiled, trying to assure them everything would be fine.

"I think Samantha's right," Ken told Lizza. "We're all tired. Let's try to get a couple hours and then we'll come back."

Lizza hesitated then gave in to him. She was so tired and Ty was doing better. His face had held its color since the last blood infusion. If Sam was up to it, another burst of blood in the morning might improve his condition significantly. "Okay, but just a couple hours," she agreed.

"I promise," Ken told his wife as he took her hand. "Thank you Samantha, for everything." He turned and quietly headed for the door. "Are you coming?" he paused to ask Gavin.

"I slept last night. I think I'll just stay here." He didn't know why, but he thought something was off.

Now what? Samantha thought. "You're loss," she said casually. "I just thought you'd want to hang out with Ty once he's better instead of crashing."

"Come on," Ken told his son. "You could use a couple hours, too."

Gavin hesitated, but didn't have a good argument. Sam seemed okay. Why was he so reluctant to leave? Maybe he was overreacting. He could use a few hours' sleep and she was right, once Ty was up Gavin wanted to spend some time with him before he headed back to Texas. "Alright," he agreed as he stood to join his parents. They walked out the door and quietly pulled it shut.

Sam breathed a sigh of relief. Once the house was quiet she could get started. She'd already checked, the only ones still up were Thomas and Alex. When she peeked into the study they seemed to be having a serious, personal conversation. She wasn't going to eavesdrop. She'd done enough of that over the last few days. Samantha sat next to Ty and studied him. She wondered if she'd feel his condition again. She jumped a little when she heard voices outside the door. Now what?

Thomas walked in and was surprised to see Samantha alone. "Don't tell me you talked Ty's parents into getting some rest," he said casually. He wanted to keep things light.

"Actually, I did," she grinned. "They both looked so tired, I assume they haven't slept for days. I promised them I'd let them know if there was any change."

Dawn

"He looks better tonight," Thomas told her as he double checked Ty's monitor. "He owes that to you."

"If I remember correctly, he also owes his present condition to me. It was the least I could do. I wish Kylee would have let me give him more," she said soberly. She really wasn't up for small talk. She just wanted Thomas to leave so she could get started.

Thomas studied Samantha. Had she meant something by that? "You want me to sit with him for a while?" he asked.

"No, everyone here has been up for days. You all look beat. I've had plenty of rest. Let me take this tonight. I'll let you guys take over again tomorrow." She hoped he would go because she didn't have the energy to argue.

Thomas studied Ty one last time. He really did look better. He reached down and gave each dog a quick ruffle behind the ears and then headed for the door. "Just call if you need anything. I'm right down the hall."

Finally alone, Samantha thought as Thomas slid the door closed. She'd give it ten minutes just to make sure, then she'd get started.

Exactly twelve minutes later Samantha went to the dresser and studied the tube. It was obvious which end she needed to attach to her arm and which went on Ty's. The one with the extra thing on the end went on hers. She secured it to her arm just like Kylee had then turned to the wonderful man sprawled on the bed. She couldn't mess this up. Once the line was securely in place, she laid down next to Ty and opened the valve. She might not make it through this, but she was confident Ty would. He was the one that should survive. He had too much to live for. He had his family, the warriors and a successful business to run. D-Tech would be fine without her. Alex had plenty of capable technicians to choose from. She snuggled in closer until she could rest her head on Ty's shoulder. Perfect.

Samantha closed her eyes and remembered that wonderful night they had together. She knew that no matter how long she lived, nothing would be as perfect as that night had been. She couldn't ask for anything more. She could give her life now to save his. She groaned a little, she was starting to get dizzy. Samantha tried to concentrate. Was it working? Was Ty getting stronger? Yes, she felt it. She could feel the energy pulsing through him. It was like she could feel his system recovering. She sighed. Good, Ty should be awake by tomorrow morning. She closed her eyes and let the sadness and despair overtake her. At least she wouldn't die alone. She felt weak, but she wasn't in any pain. That was a relief. This was going to be easier than she'd thought. It suddenly felt like the bed was moving, like she was riding a wave on a boat. She used to go out on the boat with her grandfather years ago. That had been fun. It always took her mind off her troubles. Out on the boat she could sometimes forget she was so alone. Samantha sighed, it was finally over. No more hunting vampires, no more loneliness, no more heartache. Soon, she would be with her family again. That alone gave her peace.

Thomas jerked awake. What was that noise? Barking? It was Ty's dogs. He jumped out of bed and ran to the room. "Samantha!" he yelled. "No! What are you doing?" He was frantically trying to remove the line when Gavin ran in.

"What's going on?" he asked as he sprinted to Thomas' side. He shoved the dogs off the bed and studied Samantha in shock. "What was she thinking? This could have killed her. Good boys," he said patting the dogs on the head.

Dawn

"Get that line out of Ty. I'll take care of Samantha," Thomas ordered. He was worried, she was unconscious and not responding.

Alex and Dimitri rushed in, "What's going on?" Dimitri demanded.

"Sam convinced everyone to leave her alone with Ty then hooked up the line and let her blood transfer to him. She's unconscious and I can't get this stupid line off her," Thomas growled frustrated.

Kylee walked in and gently pushed Thomas aside. "Let me take care of it," she ordered.

The room was getting crowded. Ty's parents joined them followed by Victor and Ariel. They all stood in shock as Kylee calmly removed the tube and stopped the bleeding. Sam was so pale. Lizza buried her head in her husband's chest. "We never should have left her alone," she cried.

"We didn't know what she had planned," Ken argued. "There was no way to know she was in danger."

"I should have known," Gavin objected.

"I never knew you were a mind reader son," Ken said clearly annoyed.

Gavin ignored it. "I thought something was off, but I just told myself I didn't know her well enough. Then the next minute she acted normal, so I brushed it off. I should have followed my instincts and stayed."

"It's not your fault," Ariel said solemnly. "It's mine."

Victor's head shot around to look at Ariel. She was upset. "This isn't anybody's fault. Nobody knew what Samantha was planning. Instead of standing around beating ourselves up we need to concentrate on helping Sam." He pulled Ariel into his arms and tried to comfort her.

Ariel felt guilty. Why had she been so mean to Samantha this morning? Because she hurt me, Ariel admitted. I immediately went on the offensive before she could say something that would hurt me again. I hurt her before she could hurt me. That's not like me. Ariel wondered why she was behaving so badly. She'd been trying to avoid it, but she had to admit she was jealous of Breena. Bree was healed and pregnant and getting everything she'd ever dreamed of. But what if she lost the baby? Ariel reminded herself that Breena was on bed rest and the baby was in danger. Losing the child would crush her friend. Ariel felt selfish. But she was still jealous. She didn't know if having a baby was even possible for her. At least Breena had that answer now. Ariel loved Victor more than anything, which is why she wanted to have a child with him. She wanted to create something wonderful that was part of them both. What if she never could? Would she be satisfied with a life without children? Could she be satisfied if it was just her and Victor forever? She held onto him, pulling him closer. She hoped so but only time would tell. In the meantime, she needed to stop taking her frustrations out on others.

* * * *

Samantha slowly opened her eyes and realized she was back in her room. Somehow she'd survived. She wasn't sure if that was good or bad. She sat up and felt a tug on her arm. Oh, she was hooked to an IV. How had she gotten caught, she wondered. She was pulling at the IV when she felt him. Ty was in the room and he was pissed.

Ty stood impatiently and walked to the side of the bed. He quickly unhooked the IV and scowled at Samantha. "How could you?" he said glaring down at her.

Samantha closed her eyes. She wasn't ready for this. Maybe she could avoid him somehow. She pushed to her feet and moved past him. "I need a shower." She had only taken one step when Ty's arms encircled her. He spun her around and threw her back on the bed.

"I think you've been avoiding me long enough. Now we're going to talk," he growled.

Sam was furious. "Nobody, and I mean nobody, throws me around," she managed through gritted teeth.

"Good, I've pissed you off. Maybe you'll finally start acting like the woman I used to know instead of a coward," he challenged.

She was a coward and she knew it. But she couldn't face Ty right now. She hated that he knew how cowardly she really was. There were too many emotions going through her head, she had to get away. She stood up and tried to push past him again.

Ty wasn't going to let her avoid him. She could have killed herself, she had wanted to. He reached out and grabbed her again. This time he pushed her up against the wall and pressed his body against hers, holding her in place. He could feel her anger for just a second as she struggled to get away, then it dissipated and she was engulfed in sorrow and despair. Sam surrendered and stopped fighting. She felt so alone. It broke Ty's heart. He immediately gentled his grip. "Oh baby," he pulled her against him, "You're not alone." He cradled her in his arms as she wept. "You never have to be alone again." He lifted her into his arms and walked to the bed. Once he reached the edge he sat, settling Sam onto his lap. He continued to hold her, gently rocking while she cried uncontrollably.

Samantha sat in Ty's arms marveling at the love she felt from him. How could he love her? She'd been so cruel. She'd abandoned him when he was injured. She hid from him when she should have been by his side. "Why don't you hate me?" she sniffled. "I behaved so badly." She felt a twinge of guilt.

"I could never hate you," he assured her. "I love you," he whispered close to her ear. He knew she could already feel his love. The same as he felt hers. If he'd only known how she felt days ago all this might have been avoided.

Sam was surprised at the depth of love she was feeling. Ty's love and her love combined was so intense it was a little overwhelming. He did love her. She couldn't deny that, she could feel it deep in her soul. So why hadn't he trusted her? She was still hurt by that.

"I'm sorry," he told her pushing her forward so he could look into her eyes. "I'm so sorry, Sam. I didn't mean to hurt you. I planned to tell you about the warriors, I really did. But then I heard the vampires outside and I ended up injured. It must have been so shocking for you to walk in and see them feeding me blood like that. I wish things had worked out differently. I wish I had a chance to talk to you myself, to explain what I am, so you didn't have to find out that way. I know you would have hated us anyway, but maybe it wouldn't have been such a surprise. You wouldn't have been so traumatized over it," he said softly.

"Why didn't you trust me?" she asked. "Why did you just assume I was going to hate you?"

Dawn

"I don't know," he said honestly. "I just knew I was falling for you. I guess I really didn't know what your reaction was going to be, so I was preparing myself for the worst. I didn't want to fall in love with you," he smiled when she scowled.

"Why not?" Samantha demanded.

"Because you were human. I couldn't imagine loving you for such a short amount of time and then losing you," he paused thinking about their night together. "I was selfish. I needed one night with you, then I was going to tell you everything and let you go," he confessed.

"But you could have turned me just like you did," she said confused.

"I never even considered it." He wanted to be completely honest with her. "The process is dangerous. I'm actually shocked we both made it through. I only did it to save your life."

"Speaking of that," Samantha stood up and placed her hands on her hips. "You have a lot of nerve waltzing in here chastising me for risking my life to save you, when you did the same thing for me. You could have died," Samantha choked out.

Ty reached out and pulled her back onto his lap. "I could have," he admitted. "But I didn't want to. You did," he accused.

Samantha looked at him in shock. How did he know that?

Ty laughed. "You thought it only went one way? That only you could feel what I'm feeling? Sorry babe. The line flows both ways," he sobered. "It killed me to lie there and feel how sad and desperate you were. How alone you felt when I couldn't do anything about it. I couldn't move. I couldn't wake up. I just had to lay there helpless, while the woman I loved more than anything tried to end her life. The very life I'd risked mine to save." He gave her a forced smile. "I'd say that was pretty ungrateful."

Samantha was horrified. She didn't want anyone to know what was going on in her mind. She was hoping she could just pretend she was trying to help Ty and it got out of control. She jerked her head up to look at Ty. He could feel everything she felt. He knew what she was feeling right now. This connection wasn't as neat as she originally thought.

Ty smirked. "It might be a little inconvenient at times, but I kind of like it." He pressed his lips to hers and kissed her passionately.

Samantha gasped for air. The intimacy of that kiss was unreal. Feeling her emotions and his wrapped up together was intoxicating. She wondered what it would be like to make love. Then she realized Ty was serious again.

"Don't ever do anything like that to me again," he ordered. "I need you, Sam. I know I can't make up for the loss of your family, but I love you. You will never be alone again," he pulled her close and held her tight.

"I'm sorry," she said emotionally. Feeling his love and his need for her was unnerving. "I was hoping nobody would know about that," she sighed. "I thought I could just play the incompetent hero. You know, pretend like the dangerous part was an accident. I guess I have to come clean now."

"Why?" he asked. "Nobody else needs to know."

She looked at him in surprise. "But..."

Dawn

Ty laid back and pulled her onto the bed with him. "But what? I don't see the point in telling anyone else about your moment of weakness." He pushed himself up on one elbow and towered over her. "That can be our little secret. I like your idea about the incompetent hero. Let's go with that. You thought you could give me blood and unhook the line at just the right moment, but things got out of hand, you got dizzy and passed out."

"But that would be a lie," she objected. "I think I've lied to everyone enough."

"It's not exactly a lie. You did pass out. Anyway, what have you lied about?" he asked curiously.

"I guess it was a lie of omission," she confessed. "You were right. I'm a coward. I was horrified when I saw that scene in your room. I was so sure all of you were vampires and I had somehow been tricked. I couldn't figure out what the purpose was though. Mostly all I could think of was the fact that I had made love to a vampire. That thought consumed me. I wasn't being logical. I was so cruel and I know I hurt Ariel," she paused. "She hates me. I don't think she's ever going to forgive me. For the first time in my life I was starting to make friends and I blew it."

Ty studied her for a minute. "From what I heard you were pretty cruel. Ariel will come around eventually, but it's going to take work. She's..." Ty pondered. "Selective about her friends. But once she lets someone in, she's completely loyal. Passionately so. I don't think she's angry, I think she feels hurt and betrayed. You're going to have to work at it if you want her friendship back," he warned. "And I doubt Ariel is going to make it easy for you. You'll have to rebuild that trust and that's going to take time. But I still don't get it. What was the lie?"

"After the initial shock, I think in my heart I knew I was wrong. It took a while for me to admit that to myself. I realized right away you couldn't be vampires. You go out in the daytime too often. I got Victor to tell me about the warriors. Instead of being open about his explanation, I clung to the vampire DNA and drinking blood part. I knew I was wrong, I was fighting with myself constantly. I guess it all hit me at once. One day I just couldn't deny it anymore. I watched Alex and Dimitri together. Dimitri loves her, that's obvious. He is always so gentle and caring. Victor's the same with Ariel. Then I sat for a long time watching you play with your dogs. The evidence was too overwhelming to deny. I had to admit the warriors are the good guys. Then came the lie. I was ashamed of my behavior and didn't know how to face everyone. I knew I'd ruined my friendship with Alex and Ariel. But what hurt the most was the knowledge that I had lost you. You were right, I was a coward. I couldn't face you, so I continued to avoid everyone. It was easier that way. It was easier to let everyone think I still believed you were bad.

The night I encountered Lilith was the worst. I stood there in the doorway to the barn and wanted so badly to run to you. I wanted you to hold me again the way you had before. I wanted to beg for your forgiveness, but instead I escaped. I couldn't stand to be in the same room with you. I didn't trust myself and I was so sure you'd push me away."

Ty leaned down and kissed her again. They'd all been so wrong about everything. He pulled back and brushed her hair away from her forehead. "My beautiful Samantha," he closed his eyes. "You have no idea how horrible it was to come around the bend and see you dangling from that log, Lilith at your feet."

"Will you tell me what happened? Nobody told me how you found me or why," she added softly. "I was so sure nobody would even notice I was gone. That reminds me, those goggles have a flaw. I didn't even know Lilith was there until it was too late. I also didn't know it had gotten dark. I lost track of time again, but the goggles were deceitful because I filmed the course during the day. It's going to make the kids vulnerable. I panicked when I took them off, but that was nothing compared to the panic I felt when I saw Lilith standing there grinning. She had me right where she wanted me."

Ty wasn't interested in the goggles or Lilith right now. He ran his hand down her arm then linked his fingers with hers. "We'll talk about that later," he told her. "Right now I just want to think about you," he took her mouth with his. Neither one of them gave another thought to work or vampires or the war. They were immediately lost in each other and the powerful emotions they were experiencing for the first time. The explosion of love was more intense than either one could have imagined.

A while later Samantha and Ty were cuddled together on the bed. Ty was gently rubbing Sam's back. Making love to her was an experience he would never be able to explain. Their new shared emotions definitely had amazing benefits. He was pretty sure she had drifted off to sleep. Maybe he should have waited a little longer before they were together like this. She had lost a lot of blood. It had taken three full bags before she'd shown signs of improvement. He'd awoken in a panic. He knew she was in trouble. Sitting there waiting for her to wake up had been the worst five hours and twenty three minutes of his life.

"I can feel your anxiety. What are you thinking about?" she asked groggily.

"Sorry," he leaned down and kissed the top of her head. "I was worried I rushed things," he paused. "Then I was remembering how terrible it felt not knowing if I'd lost you."

Samantha snuggled in closer. "We didn't rush things, I feel fine. Just a little tired, that's all. What time is it anyway?" She started to get up to find the clock.

Ty pushed her back down. "Sleep," he ordered. "It's still early, about six. No one will expect you to be awake for at least a couple more hours and you need the rest."

"Only if you do," she challenged. "You're not back to a hundred percent yet either." She tipped back her head and kissed him lightly. "You worried me too you know? I've never seen anyone look that chalky white, no actually you were gray. It was awful," she paused. "Saving me wasn't worth the risk," she scolded. "You could have died."

"Hey," he tipped her head backwards again so he could look her in the eyes. "Yes, it was," he said seriously. "I would risk anything for you," Ty hesitated just a moment then he forged ahead. Their eyes were still locked on each other. "I love you Sam," he smiled. "You know that. Just like I know you love me." He took a deep breath studying her. "Will you marry me? Will you be my partner forever?" he waited. No answer.

Samantha was shocked. Yes, they did love each other, but how did he know he'd feel like this forever. Would she? Absolutely. But she wasn't good enough for Ty. Could he really love her for centuries?

"Okay," he slipped from the bed and pulled Sam to the edge forcing her to sit up. Then he knelt down on one knee and asked her again. "Marry me, Sam. I want you to be my wife. Please let me love you and take care of you forever."

Sam was still stunned. She was consumed by Ty's love mixed with the anticipation he was feeling because she hadn't said a word. "Okay," she finally said still captivated by the look in his eyes. Then she began to laugh. "Okay, I'll marry you." She flung herself off the bed and into Ty's arms. He hadn't expected that and he wasn't prepared. The force of the impact flung him backwards into the wall.

Ty realized they were both naked and making a racket. He was happier than he'd ever been in his life. But, he wouldn't be so happy if someone walked in and saw them this way. He quickly picked Sam up off the floor and set her on the bed, then he climbed in next to her. He had just pulled the blankets back over them when the door flung open. Gavin stood in the doorway.

"Is everything okay in here?" he asked anxiously. "I heard a thud." It was about that time Gavin realized Ty was in bed with Samantha. "Oh, never mind." He quietly slipped back out the door and closed it tightly. He smiled as he walked away. "Way to go big bro. Way to go."

Samantha was horrified. Gavin might have walked in on them sprawled naked across the floor. "Ty!" she exclaimed. "What must he be thinking?"

"If I know Gav, he's silently congratulating me. Oh, and I'm sure he thinks I'm about to score." He laughed when she hit him square in the chest.

"That's not funny," she scolded. "It's embarrassing."

"So you're embarrassed to be seen with me? I'm hurt," Ty feigned.

"I know you're faking it. I can feel what you feel remember?" She tried to sound annoyed, but knew she couldn't fool Ty either. "You know, this is going to be really inconvenient."

"Why?" he asked. He gently rolled over her body and settled against the wall pulling her against him so they were spooned together. "I kind of like it. I'll have plenty of warning when I piss you off," he began. "I'll always know when to bring you flowers before we even have the fight. And I already like the fact that you can't pretend to be mad. No manipulative women tricks to get what you want. No, I don't see how it's going to be inconvenient at all." He kissed the back of her head. "I think it's going to be perfect," he told her honestly.

"You say that now, but just wait until you want to go hang out with Victor. You're going to have to tell me the truth. I'll know if you're lying. You can't pretend you need to work late to get out of honey do's either. And there's no way you can have a little bimbo on the side a few years from now when you get bored with me. You might want to reconsider that marriage proposal, pal. If we get married we're talking what? Two or three hundred years with the same woman. That's a long time." Samantha was joking, but she was actually really worried about that.

"Shush," Ty put his hand over her mouth. "Sleep," he whispered in her ear. "We're going to be together for thousands of years and you will never bore me. I love you my dear and I always will." Ty's eyes were getting heavy. He could use a couple hours of sleep before they faced the crowd downstairs. He held Sam close and surrendered to his exhaustion.

Dawn

Samantha pushed the worries out of her mind. She could feel Ty's love. It was as strong as hers. She'd just have to work on making sure he stayed happy forever. She wanted him to be as happy as she was. He seemed to be right now, so she would just have to make sure he stayed that way. She closed her eyes and drifted into a deep, dreamless sleep.

* * * *

Gavin walked into the kitchen and spotted his parents then Alex and Dimitri sitting at the table. He pulled up a chair and sat next to Lizza. "What's for breakfast?" he asked turning to face her. He knew his mother would cook, she always did. Lizza stood and walked to the counter.

"I was thinking about cooking up the ham in the fridge and some eggs. You hungry?" she asked as she slid a cup of coffee in front of her youngest son.

"Starved," he admitted.

"Just give me a minute to check on Ty and I'll get started." She walked back to the counter and returned with sugar and cream then set it gently on the table.

"Uh, I don't think that's a good idea," Gavin grinned. "I checked on them a couple hours ago. He and Samantha are getting to know each other a little better, if you know what I mean." He winked at his mother and grinned slyly. "I don't think they'd appreciate the interruption, especially from you." Gavin paused to sip his coffee. "Nothing would ruin the mood quicker than his mother walking in. I think it's only fair to let them finish what they've started. Not that I don't enjoy seeing my big brother frustrated, but the last few days have been a little rough on him. A little action might be just what the doctor ordered."

Lizza smacked her youngest son on the back of the head. "Mind your manners," she scolded. "I raised you better than that."

"Ouch," Gavin said in protest as he rubbed the back of his head. "I'm just saying," he ducked and barely missed her second swat.

"If this is how you're going to behave when you spend time with those dirty men out in the oil fields, I'm going to rethink my support of your chosen career. It seems to be having an adverse effect on your manners," Lizza scolded. "I saw that Ken," she turned on her husband. "Don't you encourage him. You were heading down the same road yourself before I met you. That's how you got hooked up with that hussy Valerie."

Ken tried to hide his smile, but failed. He was happy for Ty. And it was surprising how much he already liked Samantha. He barely knew the girl.

"Who's Valerie?" Gavin asked, curious now.

"Thanks a lot," Ken growled at his wife.

"Valerie is the woman your father was seeing when I met him," she said coldly. "That dreadful woman thought your father was young and naive. She was sure if she seduced her way into his heart, she'd also have control of his pocketbook." Lizza walked over to stand near her husband. "You need to be careful Gavin. There are a lot of women out there that won't see black oil, they'll see green money every time they look your way," she paused. "And hanging out with dirty old men who talk trash is not where you're going to find your mate."

Dawn

"You can imagine how upset Valerie was when she found out she hadn't touched my heart and I wasn't that innocent," Ken said casually. "I was just using her for sex." He reached up and pulled his wife onto his lap. "I was biding my time, waiting for the love of my life to come along." He leaned in and kissed her gently.

"You always do know how to get out of trouble." She giggled as they rubbed noses.

"Please stop!" Gavin begged. "You two can be so embarrassing."

His parents just laughed at him.

"Ugh," he sighed loudly and took another sip of his coffee. "I'm sorry you two have to be a witness to this. Please, I beg you, make them stop. Otherwise, they'll get so mushy you'll want to throw up."

"Gavin's just jealous," his father finally answered. He gave his wife another quick kiss and set her on the chair next to him. "One day he'll understand," he grinned at his wife. "Until then, we do enjoy making him squirm."

"Very funny," Gavin grunted. "I'd think you would have a little more respect for your favorite son."

Lizza stood and walked to the stove. "Oh we do," she assured him. "We never carry on that way when Ty's in the room."

"And cruel too," Gavin said holding his hand over his heart. "We all know you love me best," he pressed. "You just have to pretend otherwise so you don't hurt Ty's feelings. I don't mind. I understand."

Lizza set a container of butter on the table. Then she hugged Gavin from behind the chair. "I love both my sons equally. I don't know what started that ridiculous argument between you and Ty. How could a mother love one son more than the other?" she asked the room. "Impossible," she proceeded to place large pieces of ham in the frying pan. "Why don't you go round up everyone else? There's plenty of ham and eggs. I might as well cook for the whole clan."

Alex jumped to her feet. "No. You don't have to do that," she protested. "Let me cook."

Lizza shook her head. "I don't know how long we can stay, Ken's got to get back to the business. Let me do this small thing for you. It's the least I can do after you've all taken such good care of us and our children."

"Don't argue with her," Ken added. "She always wins. Just give in gracefully now and you won't go away wondering how the woman managed the victory," he winked at her.

"Now I agree with Gavin. You really aren't very funny, dear." She turned and continued to load the pan with ham.

"How long have you two been together?" Alex asked curiously.

"Five hundred and twenty three years," Lizza said proudly.

Alex was stunned. They acted like newlyweds. She hoped her and Dimitri were still like that after being married for over five hundred years. "That's wonderful," she told them. "You two are still so much in love. How do you manage it?"

Dawn

"It's easy to love my Lizza. I waited a long time to find her," Ken answered. "I'm grateful she was foolish enough to love me too, every day of my life. Oh we fight and disagree sometimes, but I know what it was like living alone for over 300 years before we met. It's impossible to take someone like her for granted. And I will never forget what it was like without her," Ken said soberly. "I'm sure Dimitri can understand what I'm talking about. It took him a very long time to find you, too."

"I do," Dimitri agreed smiling at Alex before he took her hand.

"I was younger," Lizza told them. "I was about a hundred and forty, forty one to be exact. Ken took my breath away the first time I saw him. Having a great marriage takes work. You have to be willing to compromise if you want things to last. Don't worry, the two of you will figure it out. It's impossible to be around you and not feel your love for each other. Our kind is lucky that way. Once you have that kind of love it never goes away," she glanced at the ceiling. "I hope my Ty has finally found it." She hurried on when she saw Ken about to protest. "Oh, I know. Ty's still young, but still. I don't want him to have to wait over three hundred years before he finds happiness. I hope that neither of my boys will have to wait that long." She turned back to the stove and continued her cooking.

"You waited a long time before you had kids. Was that on purpose?" Alex asked. She hoped she wasn't prying but she was curious.

"Yes and no," Ken admitted. "At first we just wanted to enjoy our lives together. We thought we had plenty of time to work in children later."

"Being fae, I always thought I would just have one," Lizza told them. "Most of us do. I'm so glad I was blessed with two wonderful boys. I had a hard time conceiving once Ken and I decided it was time. It took us seventy four years of trying before I got pregnant," she smiled at Ken. "So, once you two want kids, never give up. It's worth the wait."

"Gavin was a surprise," Ken picked up the story. "We were just so thrilled to have Ty and we never thought Lizza could get pregnant again. We were lucky. Most of us aren't. It was perfect for Ty, too. Gavin is only four years younger than him They're very close because of their age. They were inseparable as kids. Even now they get together as often as they can. I think Gav sees Ty more than we do. All of our schedules are so busy. But Ty and Gavin always make sure they find time for each other."

Lizza placed a large plate of food on the table. "Dig in," she ordered. "You get the first round. By the time Gavin gets back with everyone else, another round will be ready."

Everyone dug in. It had been a long time since any of them had a hot breakfast. Alex was enjoying her meal, but she was also stressing over her talk with Samantha. There was no way to know how she was going to take the news. She thought about the brothers. They did seem close. She was grateful she had Thomas here. They may not be blood, but she didn't think they could be any closer.

* * * *

Ty woke slowly and glanced at the clock. They had slept just over two hours. It felt good to wake up next to Samantha. He pushed her hair behind her ear with his finger as he watched her. She slept so peacefully. He thought she looked like an angel. He remembered Sam's ridiculous worries before he had drifted off to sleep. The idea that he could want anyone but her was complete nonsense. He thought of his parents, they were still so in love after all this time. He was sure it would be the same for him and Sam. He wanted to start his life with her as soon as possible. He needed a ring and he needed to convince Samantha to marry him now.

"You're staring," she told him groggily. "I can feel you staring at me. Stop it," she slowly opened her eyes and scowled. "I must look awful." She ran her fingers through her tangled hair and her frown deepened.

"You stop it," Ty took her hand. "You're beautiful." He leaned in and kissed her, gentle at first, but then he deepened the kiss.

Samantha relaxed and got lost in the kiss then pulled away when a thought hit her. She was horrified. She must have terrible morning breath. Wait, why didn't Ty have morning breath?

Ty grabbed the back of her head and kissed her again. He frowned when Samantha pulled away immediately. "What?" he asked.

Samantha covered her mouth with her hand. "I need to brush my teeth and use some mouthwash. How can you stand to kiss me like that?"

Ty smiled and pulled her hand away from her face. "Warriors don't have bad breath, ever," he assured her. "Our systems won't allow it. They fight it off I guess. We can't get sick, no colds, no flu, we can't get infections and we don't have bad breath. Now, come back over here I wasn't finished." He pulled her against him and began kissing her again.

"Really?" she asked a moment later. "I never thought about that, but it makes sense. I'll never have a runny nose again!" she said enthusiastically. "You have no idea how wonderful that news is."

Ty smiled. It was going to be fun teaching her about being a warrior. He sobered. Was she going to continue fighting vampires? If so she was going to have to get used to having a partner. No more fighting alone. Ty sat up and leaned against the headboard. They needed to join the others, but he wanted a few more minutes.

"Now what?" she asked. "Your emotions are making me sea sick. They're off the charts, winding in every direction. I can't keep up," she teased.

"I was just wondering if you plan to continue vampire hunting," he tried to sound casual.

"Yes," she said hesitantly. Was this going to be a problem?

"I don't mind you hunting, Sam. I just mind you doing it alone. It's reckless and dangerous. None of us go out after dark alone. If you still need to hunt, can we hunt together?" He asked.

Sam was watching him. He really didn't seem to mind the hunting. He was just worried about her. "Do you want to know a secret?" she asked casually. When he just stared at her she continued. "Before all this happened, when I was still getting to know you, I kept wondering what it would be like to have someone like you in my life. Someone that I didn't have to lie to or make up ridiculous stories about why I was sneaking out late at night. I kind of day dreamed about what it would be like to have you as a boyfriend. To have someone I could go to dinner with and fight vamps with. Back then, it sounded nice," she paused. "It still does."

Dawn

"I don't want to be your boyfriend, Sam. I want to be your husband," he reminded her.

"I haven't forgotten," she whispered. "I just can't believe it's true. I'm having a hard time wrapping my head around the idea that someone as wonderful as you could want me to be their wife."

"I happen to think you're the one that's wonderful," he corrected. "So, how soon are you willing to marry me? And remember, you already said yes."

"How soon?" she repeated. "Uh...I don't know. How soon do you want to get married?" She wasn't like Alex. She didn't need any time to plan. In fact, she'd be happy if they just ran to the courthouse and took care of it. Did warriors run to the courthouse or did they have their own people that had to perform the marriage? She still had a lot to learn about her new world.

"Today," Ty said casually. "But if that's too soon we can wait until tomorrow," he grinned at her.

"You're serious," she said a little flabbergasted. Ty really wanted to marry her right now? "I can't get married today. I don't even have a dress."

"Okay, then tomorrow it is," he said lightly. He stood and pulled her to her feet. "Let's shower and get dressed. I'm sure everyone is anxious to see us and I can't wait to tell them the news."

Sam followed Ty into the bathroom. She was still in shock. This was all happening so quickly.

Ty gently pushed the door shut then trapped Sam between it and his body. "I love you Samantha Reed. I want to marry you as soon as I can but if this is too fast for you, tell me when." He kissed her softly. "I'll wait as long as you want."

"You really are serious aren't you?" she asked. "If I say okay, we'll get married tomorrow."

"Uh-huh," Ty said as he gently kissed the side of her neck, then her ear, then her lips.

"Ty!" Samantha pushed him away. "How can you be so nonchalant about this?"

Ty sobered. "I'm not at all nonchalant," he disagreed. "I know what I want and I'm ready to start my life with you. I don't see any reason to wait," he studied her for a moment. "I know your family was killed, but is there anyone else you would want to be here? I'd like your friends to be involved too," he said gently. "I already have everyone I love here. Well, Uncle Steve and Aunt Pearl's not here but other than that," he finished gently. "Is there anyone I can bring here for you?"

Samantha was struggling to hold back tears. "No," she finally said. "I don't have anyone."

"That's not true," he told her as he wrapped his arms gently around her waist. "You will always have me," he grinned. "And although I think that should be enough, you also have Alex, Dimitri, Thomas, Victor and Ariel." He put his hand over her mouth. "No, don't argue. You do still have Ariel. She might be angry with you but that doesn't mean she stopped caring."

"You know," she said pushing his hand away. "If you keep doing that, I'm going to bite you."

"I'll heal," he laughed then continued as if she hadn't interrupted. "Plus, my family was really worried about you. Somehow you've already made an impression on them. I think they already love you too. You'll never get rid of me, but you have others in your life. You're only alone if you choose to be," he assured her. "And I know that's not what you want," he studied her. "So can we get married tomorrow?" he asked earnestly.

Samantha thought about it. He was right. His friends and family were already here. Why wait? She'd go into town, find a dress and they could get a preacher or whatever and be done. "Yes. We can get married tomorrow," she agreed. "But I'm going to need a car. I have to go find a dress before the wedding."

"I'm sure we'll figure something out," he was glowing. He picked her up and swung her around. "Thank you," he said softly. "You have no idea how happy this makes me, Sam."

Sam smiled, "Well, actually I do."

Chapter Twelve

Samantha and Ty walked into the kitchen hand in hand. Ty was anxious to tell his parents the good news. His mother was standing over the stove, the rest of the clan was sitting at the table except for Alex and Dimitri who were leaning against the counter. Dimitri's arms were around Alex's waist.

Gavin stood and slowly walked past Ty and Samantha. "I'm impressed bro," he whispered. "You took a lot longer than I expected." Ty reached out and shoved him. Gavin stumbled across the kitchen laughing.

Lizza looked over just in time to see Ty shove his brother. She shot Gavin an angry look. When she looked back at Samantha she was embarrassed but healthy. "You two hungry?" she asked casually. "I just pulled these off the stove. They're nice and hot." She looked at the table, it was full. "Ken, give Samantha your chair."

Dawn

Ken immediately stood and held out the chair for Sam. "Oh no," Samantha waved him off. "Don't get up on my account."

Dante was in the chair next to Ken's. He immediately stood. "Here Ty, I'm done too. Have a seat."

Ty walked to the chair and sat down pulling Samantha with him. She hesitantly took her seat, but felt extremely guilty about it. "Thanks mom," Ty turned to his mother. "Now, knowing you as I do I'm sure you haven't eaten yet either." He pointed to the chair Gavin had vacated. "Sit down and join us. I have something I want to talk to you about."

Lizza shot a look at Ken then sat down in the empty chair. Ty shoved the food her way so Lizza quickly dished herself a plate. "What did you want to talk about?" she asked hesitantly.

Ty looked at Sam then held her hand under the table for support. He could feel her anxiety and wished she would relax. "Well, a couple of you already know this." He focused his attention on Dimitri and Victor, "but I'm in love with Samantha."

"Actually, I think we all know that son," Ken announced. "You wouldn't have risked your life to save her if you didn't."

The entire room nodded in agreement.

"Well, I guess that's good." He gently rubbed his thumb across Sam's hand trying to comfort her.

Sam cleared her throat. "Uh…what you probably didn't know was that I'm in love with Ty, too."

"I knew," Gavin grinned. Everyone ignored him.

"So," Ty paused. "We've decided to get married," he announced with a smile.

Lizza jumped out of her chair and ran to her son. She wrapped her arms around him and gave him a huge hug. "I knew it," she kissed Ty's cheek.

To Sam's surprise Lizza released Ty and pulled her into a tight embrace. "I knew you were in love with my boy," she paused. "I knew it that day we were alone in his room. I am so happy to have you as a daughter!" she exclaimed.

Alex watched in silence. She was happy for Sam and Ty. Everyone was celebrating. She shot a look at Thomas and saw he was studying her. She could tell he was nervous, just like she was, but he was also urging her to pull Sam aside for their talk.

"I think it's time you had that discussion with Sam," Dimitri whispered in her ear. "Now that she has a wedding to plan, she needs to know she has family."

Alex swallowed hard and nodded. Dimitri was right, but that didn't make this any easier.

"Uh..." Ty said trying to get everyone's attention. "We were hoping we could do it tomorrow while everyone is still here." He turned to his father, "I know Uncle Steve and Aunt Pearl are busy, but would you ask them if they could fly out? I'd like to have them here if possible."

"Tomorrow!" Lizza exclaimed. "But that's not enough time to plan. Samantha needs a dress and we have to order flowers. What about her family and friends. That's just not possible," Lizza declared again shaking her head.

Samantha spoke up before Ty could. "I don't have any family," she paused. "The only friends I had are here, but I blew that too." She glanced at Ariel but the loss hurt too much, she had to look away. "Anyway, I thought I'd drive into town today and find a dress. I didn't think about flowers, but we really don't need them." She turned to Ty's father. "If you can arrange for the rest of Ty's relatives, the wedding will be perfect." She smiled at him warmly.

"I'll do my best," Ken promised.

"So it's set," Ty concluded. "Sam and I are going to start our lives together." He looked around the room at the warriors. "I'm so glad all of you are here," then he frowned. "Who's taking care of things in New York?" he asked Dimitri.

"Jake's got it covered," he assured him.

"So," Dante interrupted. "I guess that means no bachelor party for you either?" he scowled at Dimitri. "How's a guy supposed to have any fun when all his friends refuse to have a bachelor party before their big day." He turned to Ty with a huge smile. "We have tonight. I saw a bar up the road. Just say the word."

"Not a chance," Ty laughed.

"Fine," Dante grumbled. "But what have you been drinking?"

"Huh?" Ty asked confused.

"I'm making a list. Anything that you, Dimitri and Victor have consumed in the last month I'm staying away from. You guys are dropping like flies." He turned to the other warriors in the room.

"It's starting to feel like an epidemic." The room erupted in laughter.

Alex and Thomas waited for Sam to finish her breakfast. When she picked up her plate and walked to the sink, Alex followed. "Sam, I was wondering if I could talk to you for a minute alone."

Sam set the plate in the sink and turned on the water. "Sure," she turned to look at Alex and stopped. Something was wrong. "Um, give me a minute to let Ty know where I'm going."

"Thanks," Alex said quietly. "I'll meet you in the study," she glanced back at Dimitri then slowly walked out the door.

Thomas took the cue and followed Alex down the hall.

Samantha walked into the study and was surprised to see Thomas there, too. She hesitated, did this have to do with her job? Was she going to get fired? Well she probably deserved it, she told herself. Whatever it was she could handle it. Maybe she could help Ty with his gaming business. She wondered where Ty lived. She'd never asked him. She thought of her awful apartment. No, they definitely couldn't live there. Her gaze was shifting from Alex to Thomas. They looked nervous. So, she was about to get fired. The realization hurt more than she'd expected.

"Before you sit down, would you mind shutting the door?" Alex asked softly.

Samantha turned and quietly pushed the heavy door closed. Then she walked to the chair opposite the siblings and sat down. She could handle this. She wouldn't break down. She'd take it like an adult and move on with her life.

Dawn

"I have something I need to explain and I'm afraid it might upset you," Alex began. She was holding her hands in her lap, ringing them together.

"Look," Samantha decided to spare Alex the discomfort. "I understand if you feel I'm not the right person for the job anymore. I know I've behaved badly. Don't worry about it. I don't deserve your trust after the last few days," she paused. "I do have a few suggestions for my replacement. I'm not vain enough to think my opinion would matter but there are some very good people that I think deserve a chance at..."

Thomas interrupted her. "We're not firing you, Sam." He watched the emotions spread across her face.

"You're not?" she asked confused. "Why not? I mean..." she paused to change directions. "I know I didn't take the whole warrior discovery well. I know I've let you down. Why would you keep me? Not that I'm complaining," she added quickly.

"This is personal," Alex jumped in. "Once I finish what I have to tell you, then you can decide if you still want to work with us. Or more to the point...me," she corrected.

Now Sam was really confused. Why wouldn't she want to work with Alex?

"Before I begin I need to tell you that Ty already knows about this. Please don't get angry with him. He was ordered not to talk to you about it. We have laws and rules, actually you're going to have to abide by them now as well."

"Ty?" she asked. What did Ty know that he wasn't allowed to discuss with her.

"Maybe I should explain the order of our people to you first," Alex began. "Ty is a warrior, you know that. But I'm not sure if you know Dimitri is the warrior leader. Ty must do what Dimitri tells him to. If he defies an order, he will be punished severely."

"And Dimitri ordered Ty to keep something from me? Why?" Samantha asked.

"Because I felt it was important that you hear this from me," Alex answered. "I also ordered Ty to give me some time."

"And as Dimitri's..." Sam hesitated she didn't know what to call her. "Uh...future wife, Ty also has to obey you?" she asked. "Because that's a little inconvenient. I have to obey you at work and in my personal life?"

Thomas laughed. "You don't know the half of it," he said lightly.

Alex gave him a dirty look. "Not because I'm Dimitri's fiancé. Because I'm the Fae Queen."

Sam laughed. "I always knew you were a royal pair, I had no idea you were really royalty," she sobered. Was that out of line?

Thomas laughed again. "How many times have I told you what a royal pain in the butt you are? Now I have an ally."

Alex knew Thomas was trying to help. She smiled at him. "Right back at you," she turned back to Sam.

"I'm sorry. Was that disrespectful?" Sam apologized.

"Of course," Alex grinned. "Don't start treating me all formal or I will fire you," she sobered. "Anyway as I was saying, as a warrior it is going to be your duty to follow Dimitri's commands. Can you do that?"

"Sure," Samantha assured her. She knew Dimitri would be a decent leader. "But why are you the queen? Thomas is older than you. Why isn't Thomas the king?"

"I'm a warrior not fae," he told her.

"Oh yeah. I knew that," she paused. "So how does that work? I guess I'm a little confused," she admitted.

"Marlena was my mother, Luke was only my step-father," Alex admitted. "Thomas is actually my step brother. Luke was also a warrior. My mother was the Fae Queen before she was killed."

"Uh...Marlena died of a heart attack didn't she?" That's what Sam had been told.

"A heart attack caused by a poison arrow," Thomas corrected. "She was assassinated."

"Does that happen often?" Sam asked, concerned. "Does the queen have a lot of enemies?"

"Not a lot," Alex assured her.

"It is a risk," Thomas corrected. "That's one reason she has warriors to protect her."

"So it's the warrior's job to protect the queen?" Sam asked. "Kind of like the musketeers?" She smiled.

Alex smiled too. "I guess kind of like that, yes."

"So now it's my job to protect you?" Sam asked.

"Only if you want to," Alex assured her.

"We'll get into that later," Thomas cut in. "I think Dimitri wants to talk to you about that part."

"Okay," Sam agreed. "I never would have pegged Luke for a step-father." She looked at Thomas. "You either. Your family is so close. I always thought..." she trailed off.

"We are close," Alex agreed. "Not many people realize we're not blood relatives."

"So was your natural father fae as well?" she asked

"No," Alex hesitated. "I don't remember my natural father. He died when I was very young. I'm told he was human."

"So, your mother married a human knowing she would outlive him by about a million years? Is that common?" Samantha thought that would be difficult. She couldn't bare it if she basically lived forever, and Ty only had a few years.

Thomas answered this one. "It's not exactly common. If a warrior falls in love with a human he has the option of changing her. Like Ty did with you. But I assume Ty explained the risks of that already?" he asked.

"Yes," she answered.

"Because of that, warriors don't always change their spouses. My father was married to a human and he didn't change her," he paused.

"Really?" Sam said in surprise. "Why not?"

"Well, that's a little off the subject, but humans don't always love as deeply as warriors and fae do. Maybe we should just leave it at that." Samantha still looked confused. "My father loved my mother, but she struggled with our world. She wouldn't have wanted to become a part of it. Unfortunately, before she could sort out her feelings, she died in a car crash."

"I saw Luke with Marlena. They were truly in love. I guess everything happens for a reason." She was still wondering why they were here.

Alex took a deep breath. "I'm going to try to explain this to you the best that I can. Since I can't remember any of it, I am relying on accounts from others."

"Okay," Samantha said. She didn't get it, but she settled into the chair to listen to what Alex had to say.

"My father died when I was five," Alex began. "He was killed by a vampire. A vampire that is my half-brother." She was watching Sam for a reaction. Sam was more attentive, but Alex thought she was just empathizing, not that she knew the gravity of the situation. Suddenly Sam sat up.

"You mean Marlena had some kind of relationship with a vampire?" Sam demanded. "No, I don't believe it. She wouldn't have. I knew Marlena. Especially if she was the Fae Queen. No way. That's just not possible," Samantha said with finality.

"She did, but not like you think. I'm not going to go into detail, but..." Alex took a breath. It was still hard to talk about this part.

Thomas moved closer and took Alex's hand. "I'll tell it." He gave her hand a little squeeze. "When Marlena was young she was captured by the vampire king at the time and imprisoned. For many years she was tortured and raped. She finally became pregnant and gave birth to Radek, Alex's half-brother and the current vampire king."

Sam was horrified. She couldn't imagine what Marlena must have gone through. "I'm so sorry Alex," she said sympathetically. "Marlena was so strong and self-assured. How did she deal with it all so well?"

"At first she didn't. I know most of this from Tony. I'm not sure if you've met him yet. He's a good friend of Victors. He and his wife are visiting right now but they are staying in the apartments not here at the house. Anyway, mother escaped and was found by Tony's mother. They became very good friends and mom confided in Elizabeth. She was devastated that her son had turned out so horrible, that he was like his father not like her," Alex paused. "Mom left Ireland to escape the memories and moved to America." She shot a glance at Thomas who nodded, encouraging her to go on.

"Many, many year's later mom met a human and fell in love." Alex pulled her book from her bag and opened it to the first page. She handed it to Sam. "Read, starting right there."

Sam took the book and read the paragraph Alex had indicated. Marlena clearly loved her husband and was heartbroken that her own son had killed the man she loved. She handed the book back. Why was Alex sharing something that personal with her? "It sounds like she loved him very much." Sam didn't know what else to say.

"It does," Alex agreed. "After my father was killed. We went into hiding. Like she says she was devastated and we were vulnerable. Two years later Radek found us. Mom was once again imprisoned, but this time I was with her. We were held for five months until the warriors broke in and saved us."

Dawn

"I'm sorry," Sam said again. She didn't know what else to say.

"I don't really remember that either, other than a few snippets. I remember us leaving, that's all. I remember being terrified and holding mom's hand as tight as I could because I didn't want to get separated." Now came the difficult part, Alex thought. "I guess you're wondering why I'm telling you all of this."

"Well to be honest, yes. It all seems so personal. I'm not sure why you'd want me to know," Sam confessed.

"Ever since you told me about your family being targeted by vampires I've wondered why. That's not normal. Vampires don't target humans. They kill out of convenience. Are you following me?" Alex asked.

"Yes," Sam said hesitantly. Why had Alex shifted gears so abruptly? "I always thought that was strange, too."

"I don't think they randomly picked your family. I believe your family was targeted specifically."

"Why?" Sam asked.

"Because of me," Alex answered honestly.

"You?" Sam questioned. "What do you have to do with this?" Now she was really confused.

"My half-brother Radek is still the vampire king. He is the one that had my mother assassinated. Hector, his second in command, is the one that killed mom as well as Luke," Alex paused. "Well, Hector planned the attack on Luke, he didn't actually do it himself."

"Have you found Hector?" Sam asked. She knew these two would not sit back and let him get away with killing their parents any more than she was willing to let that monster with the violet eyes get away with the murder of her family.

"I killed him," Thomas said without emotion.

"Good," Sam told him.

"Since then, Radek has shown himself to my people. He captured and, with Lilith's help, killed one of our council members. He then brought Dahl's lifeless body to a council meeting and asked the other members to assist him in ousting me as queen, then accepting him as their true ruler. In short, Radek wants my kingdom. He is taking the position that he was mother's first born son and therefore is first in line to rule now that she has died."

"What?" Samantha exclaimed. "Is he nuts? He must be. That's the only way he would think your people would follow a vampire."

"I think maybe he is a little crazy," Alex admitted. "He seems unstable, although I have never actually met him."

"Uh, hello! He wants you dead. I don't think you should invite him to Thanksgiving dinner any time soon," Sam burst out. Then she threw her hand over her mouth. "Sorry," she said ashamed of her outburst.

Alex and Thomas both laughed.

"Sam, I don't want you to change the way you see me. I thought we were becoming friends. Don't worry about being yourself around me," Alex urged.

"Okay," Sam agreed. But she couldn't help it. If Alex was supposed to be her queen now, how could she treat her like a casual friend?

"I now believe that was the reason he killed my father and imprisoned myself and my mother when I was seven," Alex continued. "He must have known my people would not embrace him. He thought if he eliminated me, they would be more likely to accept him."

"I guess that makes sense in a twisted, crazy sort of way. But what does that have to do with my family?"

"I believe my family and your family are one and the same. My father, James, was your Uncle James." Alex waited for the blow to penetrate.

"Not possible," Sam said immediately. "You think that you are Lexie?" she asked.

"I do," Alex admitted.

"Nope. That really isn't possible," Sam insisted. "Lexie and James were inseparable. Lexie followed him everywhere. She worshiped her father. Okay, I get it. You were five when your dad was killed, she was five when she was killed. But that's one flaw in your theory. James and his whole family died."

"Are you sure?" Alex pushed. "Did you actually see their bodies or did you just assume they were killed in the attack?"

"No. Mom said the vampires had taken Lana and Lexie. They drained them for food," Sam gulped. It was difficult to talk about this.

"So, it's possible that instead of dying and being consumed, that Lana and Lexie went into hiding? Just like my mother and I went into hiding after my father's death," Alex insisted.

"Maybe," Sam paused. "Okay, maybe that part is possible. I'll give you that. But I still don't believe that you could be Lexie and not remember James. Lexie had a special bond with her father. James loved her so much. He was always so patient with her. If he was milking the cows, Lexie sat beside him and pretended to help at first, but then she really did help later on. She'd follow him around the farm all day helping him with the chores. We were all close," Samantha gulped and held back tears. "Me, Lexie, Michael, James. We all spent a lot of time together. After Lexie, Michael was with Uncle James the most. James was teaching Mike how to be a farmer," she paused. How was she going to get through this?

"Michael and dad didn't always get along. My father was hard on Mike. He didn't understand that pushing him that hard just made him shut down. James knew how to teach Michael. So, they spent hours every day together. Michael wanted to grow up to be just like James. At first dad didn't like it, but eventually mom convinced him it was for the best. Once dad and Michael stopped spending time together at the farm, they got along fine. Anyway, we were together a lot, especially Lex and Mike. I don't believe you could be Lexie and not remember any of us. Lexie and Michael were too close. Michael could get Lexie to do things nobody else could. There's no way you wouldn't remember any of that. There's no way you wouldn't remember Michael," Sam insisted. "Anyway, I was old enough to remember Lana. I would have known if she was your mother," Sam hesitated. Was it possible? No, Marlena couldn't have changed that much.

"What is it?" Alex asked. She'd sensed the hesitation in Sam when she talked about her mother.

"It's nothing," Sam objected. She didn't want to admit how much Marlena had looked like her Aunt Lana. It was shocking the first time she saw her. But then as she got to know Marlena, she realized just how different the two women were.

"There's something you're not telling me," Alex insisted.

"Okay, fine. Marlena did have a strong resemblance to Aunt Lana," she admitted.

"So why are you fighting this?" Alex asked. "If mom looked so much like your aunt, why can't you accept what I'm telling you?"

"Because it doesn't fit," Sam told her. "Marlena looked like my aunt, but she acted nothing like Aunt Lana. I'd worked for D-Tech awhile before Luke introduced us. When Marlena walked into the lab I almost fell off my chair. Then she introduced herself. She invited me to join them for lunch. By the time lunch was over, I knew. They looked like each other, but they had nothing in common."

"Are you willing to explain the differences?" Thomas asked.

Sam took a deep breath. There were so many. "Okay," she concentrated. "Aunt Lana was soft spoken and very introverted. Marlena was strong willed and confident." She forced herself to think about her aunt. "Lana was small town. I don't know how else to explain that, do you guys understand what I mean?" she asked.

"She was easy going?" Alex suggested.

"Yes, but it was more than that. She was perfectly happy to just sit on the front porch for hours and talk. She and mom did that almost every day. The rest of us would go out on the farm, or over with James, and mom and Lana would just sit in the shade of the porch and visit. They would shuck corn or clean peas, whatever needed to be done at the time," she paused. "Your mother on the other hand was always on the go. She was sophisticated and elegant. I couldn't imagine your mother sitting on the porch in an old dress shucking corn," Sam laughed.

"Mom had a lot of sides to her," Alex countered. "You may not have seen them, but I did. I don't have any trouble envisioning mom relaxing on a porch shucking corn."

Samantha was beginning to doubt her conviction. But she still couldn't buy it. She adamantly believed that if Alex were Lexie she would remember her father. "Why do you want to believe this so badly?" Sam argued. "It's like you're trying to make things fit even if they don't."

Alex handed Sam the diagram Ty had developed. "Tell me what doesn't fit," she challenged. "What am I trying to force?"

Sam took the diagram and studied it carefully. Looking at it in black and white was convincing. Everything did seem to fall into place perfectly. "This is pretty detailed. How long have you been considering this theory?"

"Actually, Ty drew that," Alex admitted. "He's much better at diagrams than I am. He said he came up with that in one night. For him it all fell together the night Tony told me about my mother's past. It started when Tony's wife Megan was talking about how her mother assumes a new identity, but still keeps a part of herself. She does it by manipulating her name. Then he found out my father's name was James. Apparently you had told him about your Uncle James at some point. You have to admit it fits. Marlena, Lana. Alexandria, Lexie. James. One or two things could be coincidental, but not that many. You know I'm right. Why are you fighting it so hard?"

Dawn

Well, that explains why Ty hadn't discussed this with her. He'd come up with it when they weren't talking. She continued to study the diagram. The way he put it together was tough to dismiss. "I guess because you don't remember anything about your father. I just don't see how that's possible. You don't remember me. You don't remember Michael. I just don't believe that's possible," she repeated.

"I disagree," Thomas told her. "If Alex was that close to her father, it makes sense that his death would have been so tragic for her that she would block it out. It would be too traumatic for a child of five to deal with. Especially when she lost you and Michael at the same time. She and her mother were forced into hiding. Two years later she was captured and imprisoned. Another traumatic event. A child can only take so much. She may have remembered her father until she was imprisoned. We don't know when she lost that memory," Thomas argued.

Samantha stood and walked to the window. "We were so close," Samantha said softly. "I remember a time, just before James died." She paused to compose herself. "We'd been working in the field but it was so hot that day. James insisted we stop early and go for a swim." She didn't turn around, she just continued to stare out the window. A tear slid down her cheek. It was so hard to talk about these memories. "We all went to the dock. Lexie was such a curious and energetic little girl but Lana had scared her away from the lake. She told her there were animals in the water that would bite her. James would get angry with Lana every time she told one of those stories because he was afraid it would have a long term impact on Lexie. He was determined to teach his little girl to swim. He thought that way if she fell in she could swim to the edge and get out safely.

Anyway, we all ran to the dock and jumped in. Lexie wouldn't even step onto the platform, she just huddled by the edge of the brush terrified an animal was going to bite one of us. James stayed in the water the entire time, trying to convince her there was nothing in there. Lexie was even more terrified. She just knew her father was going to be attacked. Michael and I took turns diving in. The only thing dampening the mood was Lexie's reluctance to join us. Finally, Michael couldn't take it any longer. He climbed out and walked over to Lexie. He was the only one that could have enticed her. He promised they would jump in together and then her father would be there to catch her. At first she refused, but Mike told her he was too old to hang out with babies. If she didn't do this, she couldn't spend time with him until she grew up and stopped acting so scared. I think she gave into him because she wasn't sure if he was serious. The thought of being shunned by Mike scared her more than the animals. Michael took her hand and together they slowly walked out onto the dock. Lexie was holding his hand so tight both of their knuckles were white. Michael stopped when they reached the edge. 'I promise, I won't let go. We'll jump in and come back up together,' he told her. 'Once we surface, Uncle James will be there to catch you. You trust us, don't you?' he asked her. Little Lexie cautiously bobbed her head. I was right there next to James treading water, holding my breath waiting to see if Lexie would really jump in. She did," Sam said quietly.

"Michael and Lexie stepped off the dock and fell feet first into the water. Uncle James was so proud of her. I could see him beaming. His little girl had overcome her fear. A fear her mother had instilled in her for years. He started whooping and yelling then lifted Lex into the air. They were both so happy. He swung her around and around. We ended up swimming for over an hour; Lexie was having so much fun jumping off the dock. James wouldn't leave until he was confident she knew how to swim. He even made Michael push her in when she wasn't expecting it. He needed to know if she fell, she would be able to save herself. Lexie was so mad at Michael at first, but she could never stay mad at him for long. She loved him too much." Tears were running down Sam's face, one after the other. She hadn't let herself think of those times since Uncle James had died. She turned back around and was shocked to see Alex was crying too. Thomas was holding her close.

Alex studied Sam for a long time before she picked up the story. "Dad realized we were going to be late for dinner and he rushed us all out of the water. He lifted me up on his shoulders and carried me all the way home. I remember he was singing that stupid song," she paused. "What was it? Something about magic in a young girl's heart."

"Do you believe in magic?" Sam said in awe. Nobody could have known that but her, Lexie, Michael and Uncle James.

"That's it," Alex said softly. "Dad insisted on walking you and Michael home, which made us even more late. We were already in trouble when we walked in the door and then when mom saw how wet we were she really freaked out. Dad was so excited about teaching me to swim, nothing mom said could phase him. She finally gave in and joined in the frivolity. She could never stay mad at dad, no matter what he did. His charm was contagious." Alex laid her head on Thomas' chest. "How could I have forgotten that time in my life?" she sniffed. "We were all so happy. Now, because of me, they're all dead." She was crying uncontrollably. Thomas was rubbing her back gently.

"Not because of you Alex," Sam corrected. "Because of an evil vampire."

There was a soft knock on the door. Thomas stood and opened it a crack, then he pushed it open and Ty walked in. He took one look at Sam and rushed to her side. He immediately pulled her into his arms. "Are you okay?" he looked grim.

"I think I'm better than Alex," Sam admitted. "I guess I'm still in shock," she told him.

Ty brushed the tears from Sam's face. "I'm so sorry you have to talk about this. I know how difficult that is for you."

"It's getting a little easier," she told him. She let him lead her to the small couch and sat down. "But I still don't understand. Why is it you think you're responsible for my families deaths, Alex?"

Thomas answered this question. "We believe Radek was trying to get information on Alex from your parents," he paused. "Radek killed James because he was Marlena's husband. He was threatened by him once Alex was born. We really don't know what happened that day or how Marlena escaped with Alex. The only thing I do know is that Marlena never would have left James unless he was already dead."

"I agree," Sam told him.

"They go into hiding but Marlena is devastated," Thomas continued. "According to her own writings she felt she was putting their lives at risk, that they were an easy target for Radek. I personally wonder if that was because she stayed in touch with your mother. She may have needed someone to talk to. She had to feel so alone at the time. Your mother is the one person that would have understood. Marlena wouldn't have realized she was putting your family at risk," Thomas continued.

Sam was thinking about that time after Uncle James died. They were all so devastated, especially her mother. She was so close to her only brother, but she had become close to Lana too.

Dawn

After about a month, mom seemed better somehow. It was all of a sudden. Had Marlena contacted her? Knowing Lana and Lexie were okay would have helped mom to cope with the loss of James. Plus, talking to Lana about James would have helped them both. "I think you might be right," she agreed. "About a month after the deaths, mom seemed better somehow."

"Marlena was able to hide from Radek for two years. None of us know where she was or how she managed to avoid him. She would check in periodically with one of the council members but it was sporadic. She refused to tell anyone where she was," Thomas continued. "Suddenly, after two years, they were captured by Radek. That's when dad organized a rescue."

"They were imprisoned for five months because it took us forever to find the hideaway," Ty put in. "Once we located it, the planning went quickly. We actually went in blind. Nobody knew how many vampires would be inside or exactly where they would have Marlena and her child. None of us knew anything about Alex at the time. We knew she existed, but that was about it. We rushed the cave and split up. Luke and Jake found Marlena. Alex was in a separate cell right next to her mother. Dimitri's father Dylan found her. The rest of us rushed to the dungeon to warn the others we were under attack. We had to fight a lot of vampires, but we finally got everyone out alive."

"You helped rescue me?" Alex asked surprised.

"Yeah, Dimitri wasn't here at the time, he was in France with Ariel I guess. Victor was there and so was Bastian. Dante and Nicholas were visiting Nick's parents in Italy. Obviously Thomas was too young to participate. Dad was there too, so was Uncle Steve. We also had a few of the retired guys that helped out. It was a huge operation. We probably over killed a little, but we had no idea what we were getting into."

"That still doesn't explain why you think any of this caused my families death," Sam pressed.

"Six months after Luke rescued mom, they were married," Alex admitted. "Radek would have been livid. Now we were under the protection of the warrior leader. Shortly after the wedding, your family was murdered."

"But what's the connection," Sam asked.

"We think Radek was trying to find a weakness," Ty said softly. "He wanted your mother to tell him when Alex would be vulnerable. She was still a threat to his plan to rule the whole world basically. As long as Alex was alive, the fae community would follow her. If he could find a weakness or a time Alex was vulnerable, he could sweep in and take her out without anyone knowing. Or they wouldn't know until it was too late."

"I see," Sam finally said. Was that possible? Had he tried to get information from her parents? For the first time since their death she tried to remember exactly what happened.

"Are you willing to tell us how you survived?" Thomas asked gently. "I understand if you don't want to, but it might help us figure this out."

"Mom knew what was happening before any of the rest of us. It was like she was expecting something." Sam looked up, she hadn't realized that before. "Is it possible she was still in contact with Marlena at the time?"

Dawn

"I don't see why not," Thomas answered. "Dad wouldn't have minded, in fact he probably would have encouraged it. It sounds like they were very good friends."

"Anyway, mom heard a noise and she rushed to my room. She told me I had to get away. She wanted me to take Michael and run. By the time we got downstairs she realized it was too late. The vampire had already discovered Michael. He was carrying him by the back of his shirt towards the living room. Mom shoved me into a small cupboard, closet type thing and locked the door. She wanted to make sure I couldn't get out and nobody could get in. She had just turned around when the vampire grabbed her and threw her across the room. She landed on the ground with Michael. Dad came at him with the fire poker, but the vampire was too fast," Sam paused. Had he asked them anything? Yes! She remembered, she hadn't understood it at the time. What had he said?

"What is it?" Alex asked. She had finally stopped crying and was studying Sam.

"I remember the vampire grabbing dad and holding him up by the throat. The vampire was yelling something at mom. I just can't remember exactly what it was. He was threatening dad's life if she didn't tell him what he wanted to know. He kept yelling something. What was it?" She paused. This was hard. She'd spent so much time trying to forget it, now she needed to remember. "At first I thought he was talking about me," Sam admitted. "I thought he wanted to know where I was but it didn't fit. It didn't really make sense. What did he say? How do I find the brat? No, how do I get to the brat? I think that was it. I'll kill him if you don't tell me how to get to the brat." Sam was staring into the distance, they all knew she'd gone back to that awful time.

"Mom just kept telling him, I don't know, I don't know. Why are you doing this? We don't know anything. Everyone's dead," Sam looked at Ty. "I thought she meant they were all going to die. Neither one of them were making any sense. Then the vampire twisted dad's neck and he was dead. Just like that, he was gone." Sam hesitated and closed her eyes. "He dropped dad to the ground like he was nothing and picked up Michael. He asked mom if she wanted him to kill her only child to protect the brat. I almost started banging on the door. I was so sure he was talking about me. Mom was so calm when she told him he was going to kill her whole family anyway. All three of them would die together no matter what she did. The vampire started laughing, an evil sadistic laugh. 'You're a smart woman,' he said. 'Now you can watch your only child die.' That's when he killed Michael. Mom was last. 'My family knows how much I love them,' she said just before she died. 'No matter what you do, my family will always know how much I loved them and there was nothing I could have done to save them.' I knew mom was talking to me, but I also realized the vampire couldn't know about me. He couldn't have been asking about me, he thought Michael was her only child."

"He wanted me," Alex said soberly. Tears running down her face again. "Sam I am so sorry!" She took a deep breath. "I am so sorry you lost your family over me."

"So that monster that killed my family is your half-brother, Radek?" Samantha asked her.

"From what I understand...yes," Alex said soberly. "Like I said, I've never met him, but I'm told by those who have that he's the only vampire they know with violet eyes. It must have something to do with being half fae."

"Do you know where he is?" Sam asked.

Dawn

"No," Alex answered honestly. "He hides out most of the time and sends others to do his dirty work. I have no idea where he is."

"I see," Sam said disappointed. "At least I know who he is now. That's more than I've been able to find out on my own."

"I understand if you don't want to have anything to do with me now. I've already talked to Thomas. He will be your contact at D-Tech if you're still willing to work for us."

Ty was watching Sam. She was emotional and this was taking a lot out of her, but she wasn't angry. She didn't have any animosity towards Alex. He could feel her sorrow, but he also felt her love for Alex and amazement that she was still alive.

Sam studied Alex. Was she serious? She'd just found out her cousin Lexie was alive after over twenty years and Alex thought she was going to turn her away. "I guess you really don't remember your childhood," she began.

"What?" Alex said confused.

"There were a lot of years between us, Alex. At first I wasn't thrilled about spending so much time with you," Sam said honestly. "Michael convinced me to let you come along though. Michael could talk me into anything. But by the time you were five, the three of us were inseparable. I miss the horseback riding the most I think. We had so many adventures on those rides."

"What are you saying?" Alex asked.

"I've spent too many years believing my entire family was dead. Alex, I thought you were dead. I didn't only suffer from the loss of my parents and my brother, I suffered almost as much at the loss of James, Lana and Lexie. Finding you again is something to celebrate," Sam smiled. "I'm not alone anymore," she glanced at Ty. He nodded in understanding. "I have my cousin back. I guess you can't understand what that means to me. Unless you felt the loss and the loneliness, you can't imagine the joy."

"So you don't hate me?" Alex said in surprise.

"Alex, you were five when your father was killed, seven when my family was killed. Exactly how is any of this your fault? Okay, so your crazy step brother is the psycho that murdered them all. Should I have hated Marlena for that, too? It was her child. Do you hate your mother because your brother killed your father?" She turned to Thomas, "Do you hate Alex and Marlena because this Radek maniac killed Luke?"

"Of course not," he said quietly.

"Exactly, why would you? It has nothing whatsoever to do with Alex," she said confidently. "Well, other than the fact that this monster is out to kill her too," Sam sobered. "You guys are protecting her aren't you? You're taking precautions to ensure her safety?" she said in alarm.

"We are," Thomas assured her. "Plus, she's almost always with Dimitri so it would be very difficult to get to her."

Samantha considered that. "But Marlena was always with Luke and they got to her," she was worried now. She was thinking about Luke and Marlena when a thought hit her. She turned to Thomas, "Did you know about me?" The question was more accusation than inquiry.

"No," he assured her. "Well you, yes. Your connection to Alex, no. In addition to our interaction at the lab, you were the only employee dad ever invited to family dinners after Marlena died and Alex moved away. So I knew of your talent and how happy dad was to have you on his team, but that's it."

Samantha studied Thomas, he seemed to be telling the truth. "I think your parents knew." She considered her past and was sure of it. "I think Marlena must have kept tabs on me."

"You could be right, I don't know," Thomas answered. "I do know they discussed you a lot. Like I said dad was thrilled with your talent. He and Marlena discussed your projects and progress frequently. Now that you mention it, that was a little strange. I remember walking in on a discussion they were having about your living arrangements."

Ty was curious now.

"Dad was livid that he paid you so well but you continued to live in that dive in the Bronx." Thomas paused, "Marlena wanted dad to force you to move, but dad didn't feel that was his place. He knew you wouldn't take it well if he suggested you find a more appropriate area to live in."

"You lived in the Bronx?" Ty asked, annoyed.

"I still do," Sam said absently. "But why would Luke and Marlena care about that unless Marlena knew who I was?" she mused. "Then there was the mysterious scholarship," she paused.

"What do you mean you still do?" Ty interrupted.

"Huh?" Sam said confused. "Oh, I still live in that same apartment, but I hate it. It was a bad idea from the beginning. I was thinking about moving when Alex sent me here," she looked back towards Thomas. "Does Deveraux Industries have an association of some kind with a scholarship organization? What was the name? Scholarship America I think."

"Not that I know of," he assured her. "I've never heard of that organization, have you Alex?"

Alex was alert now. "No, but I saw that name on something and was going to ask you about it," she told Thomas. "It was on the books from D-Tech. There are regular deposits into some kind of an account. They were fairly substantial. I tried calling the bank, but they wouldn't give me any information. They said it was a restricted access account and only those members listed could gain access. I wasn't listed. They wouldn't even tell me who was on the list. I was planning on bringing it up to you and if you didn't know anything, I was going to get legal on it." Alex said confused.

"Strange," Thomas mused. "I don't know anything. Let's talk to Tom in the morning and see what he can find out."

"I think your parents paid for my college," Sam continued. "Then once I graduated, Luke made sure I had a good job. I think Marlena continued to look out for me. The whole scholarship thing was strange to begin with. I went to live with my grandparents after my family died. They weren't destitute, but they didn't have the means to pay for college either. My grades were okay, but not great. I began applying to colleges, cheap ones, hoping I could get into one and then find a job to pay the bills. One day shortly after I graduated from High School, a man showed up at our door. I have no idea who he was. I've never seen him again. Anyway, he tells me I've been selected to receive a scholarship to the college of my choice. He asked me if I'd considered where I wanted to go yet," she paused. "I remember telling him I wanted to get a good degree in electronics. I was already interested in the topic even back then. The man made a couple suggestions and I told him I could never afford those colleges, even with a scholarship.

He told me it was a full ride. Depending on which college I chose, there might be some money left over for housing and other expenses. Of course I didn't believe him. He said he'd mail me information on the top colleges in the area. I would need to choose one and get back to him right away. A couple days later a packet arrived. I was nervous about it, but I picked the best college on the list. I figured I'd still have to work, but this guy seemed to think the scholarship would pay for most of it. When I checked in at the registrar's office, to make sure everything was in order, I was presented with a check. I couldn't believe it. It was enough to cover my rent and give me food money for the entire semester.

Now I'm sure that was Marlena's doing. She must have convinced Luke to finance my education. I used to think I'd earned my position with your company. I've been proud of that. Now I know it was a gift. It was a way for Aunt Lana to take care of me," Sam frowned, disappointed. The realization was upsetting.

"You earned it," Thomas disagreed. "You wouldn't have had that position if you hadn't." He held up a hand. "No, don't argue with me. If Marlena had wanted to take care of you, sure dad would have found a spot for you somewhere. They may have even inflated your salary to make sure you could live comfortably. It sounds like you chose not to do that anyway, but dad was impressed with you. He honestly believed you were the best around. He gave you challenging and sometimes impossible assignments and you always came through. Yes, they helped you because they were proud of you. But they were proud of you for what you had accomplished on your own. If I remember correctly, you graduated at the top of your class."

"True," Sam said, hoping Thomas was right. She didn't want anything handed to her because of a relationship.

"I didn't know about the connection and I promoted you to Executive Manager. You can't say you didn't earn that one on your own," Alex insisted. "As far as I knew you were just some girl dad hired for the job. Sure we got along, but I get along with a lot of people at the plant. I could have promoted any of them. I chose you because you're good."

"Thank you," Sam took a deep breath. "This is all so strange. It's like a miracle. I always loved Marlena. She was such a wonderful woman and always seemed to care about my wellbeing. Now I find out she was really my Aunt Lana. And you..." she turned to Alex. "Lexie is alive. I've always had good memories about Aunt Lana, but now I can combine them with all the great memories I have of Marlena. Your mother truly was a wonderful, special woman."

"She was," Alex agreed, then shifted gears. "So, you have a wedding coming up. I guess we should wrap this up and let you go shopping."

"Uh..." Sam felt like an idiot, but she didn't know anything about their ceremonies. "Who marries us?" she asked Ty. "I mean, do I need to find a preacher or an elected official in town or something? I don't exactly know how your marriages work."

"Oh," Thomas answered. "Well, Alex could do it. ."

"What?" Alex exclaimed. "I wouldn't know how."

"Or a council member could do it. If you want, Orin is here. We could ask him," Thomas continued. "We also accept human ceremonies. In fact a good friend of ours just got back from St. Lucia."

"What do you think?" Sam asked Ty.

"It might be cool to have Alex marry us," he suggested.

"I really..." Alex began.

Sam spoke over her. "I was hoping Alex would be my bride's maid," she told him hesitantly. "Would you be terribly disappointed if she was in the wedding rather than officiating it?"

"Nope. Orin it is," he turned to Thomas. "Do you want to talk to him or should I? I need to take care of a couple things. I have to arrange for my rascal of a brother to be my best man and I have one other arrangement I need to make but then I could track Orin down."

"I'll handle it," Thomas assured him. He turned to Alex, "Sounds like you need a new dress. Dimitri is going to be thrilled. That usually means new shoes as well."

"Oh stop," Alex elbowed him. "Dimitri doesn't need to know about the shoes."

Thomas opened the door to find Dimitri sitting on the bottom stair. He looked worried. "Go on in. Their talking weddings. By now I assume that's right up your alley," he laughed and headed out the door to find Orin.

Lizza stepped forward and stopped in the doorway to the study. "Samantha, I was wondering if I might have a word with you."

Samantha looked to Ty but got a vacant look. She walked towards the door. "Uh…sure," Sam answered. "How about out on the porch?" she asked, looking around for a quiet place to go.

"That would be great," Lizza said heading for the front door. Once outside she was a little hesitant. "Well, I know your mother passed away some time ago. I don't want you to think I'm trying to take her place or anything, but I was wondering if you would allow an old woman to accompany you to town to pick out your dress." She hurried on, "if that would make you uncomfortable, I understand. It's just I have the two boys, boys I love with all my heart, but that means I miss out on all the wedding stuff. I won't get to help with picking out the dress, arranging for flowers, you know, the stuff the daughters do with their mother. My wedding was so wonderful, I've always hoped when the boys got married their intended wives would let me participate in some way. I expected to be competing with another mother for something to do but…well anyway I was just hoping I could help. I was hoping you would allow me to be involved."

"I'd like that," Sam said softly. "I've asked Alex to be my bridesmaid and we were just trying to figure out how we were going to get into town to find dresses. As the mother of the groom I assume you are going to need a new dress, too."

Lizza smiled. "As a matter of fact, I do. Let me grab the keys from Ken. We'll take the rental. I don't know this area but I'm sure we can find something suitable." She rushed off to locate her husband.

Sam walked into the study, but immediately turned back around. Everyone had left except Alex. Dimitri had joined her and they were deep in discussion. Alex was crying again. This time Samantha was not going to eavesdrop on their private conversation.

Dawn

She slipped out the door and collided with Ty. "Oh," she exclaimed as his arms wrapped around her waist. "You scared me."

Ty smiled. "It looks like you made my mother happy. What did she want?" he leaned in and gave her a gentle kiss. "I'm proud of you for the way you handled everything in there. I wanted to talk to you about it but..."

"I know," Sam assured him. "I understand. They told me when you figured it out. At the time I was beyond difficult so you didn't have a chance. Then Alex and Dimitri ordered you to keep it a secret."

"Well, I don't mean to contradict them but they didn't actually order me," he sobered. "I suppose they told you that to keep me out of trouble. They asked me if it would be okay if Alex was the one to talk to you about it. I agreed, I thought it was a good idea. I still do. I think it was best that Alex broke the news. It seems it was also good for her. Maybe she'll start to remember her past now," he paused. "But back to my mother. What are you two up to?" he quizzed.

"You're mother wants to be a part of the wedding. She wants to help plan it that is," Sam grinned. "It seems having two rambunctious boys instead of a sweet, docile girl like me has deprived her of doing girl things. Things like planning weddings, picking out flowers, that sort of thing. I told her I'd appreciate the help."

"Thanks," Ty said touched by her willingness to include his mother. "That's going to mean a lot to her. She'll never forget it."

"I like your mom. Plus, I have no idea what I'm doing. I can use all the help I can get. If she's willing to step in, that's a huge relief to me," Sam confessed.

Lizza found Ken with Atticus. They were out in the barn with the horses. She explained her need for the car to take the girls shopping. "Here you go," Ken said as he held out the keys. He turned to Atticus, "looks like it's me and you today old friend. Once we finish up here, let's head over to the fort and you can show me around." Lizza slipped out and headed for the car.

The three women shopped for hours. They found the perfect dress for Samantha. It wasn't actually a wedding dress, it was sleek ivory with light beige undertones, perfect for Sam's skin tone and stunning against her deep red hair. It was a long, slimming dinner gown with elegant thin straps. Once she put it on, they all knew it was the dress for her. Alex bought a deep maroon gown that accented her strawberry blond hair. Lizza bought a gorgeous fuchsia gown with a flaring skirt. It was beautiful with her ash blond hair. Lizza also stumbled onto a man's tie that matched her dress almost perfectly.

"Steve and Pearl should arrive first thing in the morning. Steve said he'd grab Ken's black Gucci suit and one of his Armani shirts. They're going to look great with this tie!" she said enthusiastically. "What about Ty?" she asked Samantha. "Does he have something with him?"

"I don't know. Maybe I should call him," Samantha said, worried now. She didn't know anything about Ty's dress habits. While he'd been at the fort he was usually in jeans and a t-shirt. She pulled out her phone and dialed his number. "Hey," she said when he answered.

"Hey yourself," Ty responded. "How's the shopping going?"

"Really good," she said lightly. "Um, your mom is buying a tie for your dad and said your uncle is bringing him a suit. She wanted to know if we needed to get anything for you while we're

Dawn

here. I hope you're not planning on wearing jeans," she teased. She was still so amazed at the connection she had with Ty. It felt like her life had been a little off center for years. Nothing had been quite right since she was twelve. Then, this morning, everything magically clicked back into place. Now her world was back on track and she was exactly where she was meant to be.

"Don't worry," Ty assured her, bringing her back to the conversation. "Dimitri took care of everything. Jake's going to gather up the suits for all of us. He and Marta will be here in the morning. I'm afraid the wedding party is growing. Are you okay with that?" he said concerned.

"Don't worry, Ty. I know you have a lot of people that care about you," she paused. "Just don't make it too big, okay? I was hoping for a small intimate wedding. We're going to run out of space eventually."

Ty laughed. "We'll keep it small. Well, I gotta go. Dad and Atticus need help. See you when you get back," he paused. "I love you."

"Love you too. I'll talk to you soon." She hung up and turned to the two women checking out shoes. "Sounds like they're all covered. Dimitri got a hold of Jake, whoever that is, and he and Marta are bringing suits for all the men. They'll be here in the morning."

"That's wonderful. I'm so glad Jake and Marta will be able to make it. Maybe I can talk Marta into cooking. Your wedding is going to be perfect," Alex grinned. "But only if we get these shoes to go with your dress. What size are you? I'll find a salesman."

"Alex, this all seems so frivolous. I don't need new shoes. When am I ever going to wear these things again?" Sam argued.

She cringed when she saw the price tag. She'd never spent that much on one outfit in her life. Her entire wardrobe hadn't cost her that much.

"I'm buying so don't argue," Lizza beamed.

"Oh, I couldn't..." Sam began.

"I said don't argue. Nobody wins me in an argument," Lizza was so excited. "Please give me this small pleasure. It's not much, but it makes me happy. You don't want to deprive me of a little happiness do you?" she sobered.

"I don't know," Sam hesitated. "I don't want to be labeled one of those hussies that's just after your son's money. Like...what was her name? Valerie," she finally declared.

Alex laughed. "You deserved that," she told Lizza

"Who told you about Valerie?" she asked surprised.

"Gavin," Samantha said simply.

"Figures," Lizza sighed. "There's no controlling that boy. Well anyway I'm buying the dress and the shoes. You have to have the shoes."

The group finished gathering accessories and wedding gowns, moved across the street to the flower shop where Lizza went nuts again, then headed back to the car.

"Oh!" Sam exclaimed. "I don't have a ring for Ty," she said gloomily. "I've got to have a ring."

"We've got plenty of time. Let's drive around, they have to have a jewelry store somewhere around here," Lizza suggested.

Alex pulled out her phone and punched in a few commands. "Found one," she announced.

"What?" Lizza asked. "How did you do that?"

"I have internet on my phone. If you don't have one, you've got to tell Ken to get one for you. They are so handy!" Alex passed her phone to Lizza.

"I'm getting one of these," Lizza declared studying the phone. "As soon as I get home, we're getting one of these. You can't imagine how often I've needed one. It's so hard to keep up with technology. You may not understand that yet, but you will."

"I don't know how I ever managed without it," Alex told her. "Now let's head to the jewelry store. It should be up ahead, looks like the third road to the left."

"You're pretty handy," Lizza grinned. "Maybe we should keep you around."

"I try," Alex shrugged as she pulled the door shut.

An hour later they were headed back to the farm house. Sam had found the perfect ring for Ty. It was simple, but still seemed elegant. She knew it couldn't be large and gaudy, or he wouldn't like it and therefore wouldn't wear it. It needed to be simple, like jeans and a t-shirt.

"I love it," Lizza declared. "It's perfect. It won't get in the way while he's working on the ranch."

"The ranch?" Samantha had asked.

"Uh...yeah," Lizza said hesitantly. "Sounds like the two of you haven't talked about living arrangements."

"No, we haven't gotten that far yet. Ty owns a ranch? In New York?" Sam asked.

"I'm going to let him do the honors," Lizza told her. "But yes, it's just outside New York. I usually call it upper New York, but it's actually in Poughkeepsie. It's within driving distance of the city, just a long drive. He can't always get home with the late nights he spends at Tyson Electronics though. I think he was going to rent an apartment in New York before Dimitri made him move in with Thomas. He needed the space in his apartment complex for his new pilot. He hasn't said what his plans are now. I think that's something the two of you will have to work out."

"Please, just don't tell Dimitri if you're going back to the ranch," Alex begged. "He doesn't need to know until we head home."

"What's wrong with his ranch?" Lizza asked. She loved Ty's place. It was beautiful and peaceful.

"Dimitri doesn't think the security is adequate. Unless Dimitri installs it, nobody's security is adequate," Alex added.

"Oh," Lizza said with understanding. "Dimitri is a perfectionist when it comes to security."

The women pulled into the drive and headed to the house. Everyone was in the study. "Hey, what did you guys bring for dinner?" Gavin called out. "We've been working hard all day. I'm starved."

"It's nice to see you too," Lizza called out sarcastically. "No, don't worry we can take care of unloading the car. But thanks for asking," she turned and headed to her room.

Dawn

Ty walked into the foyer and stood in front of Sam. "Do I get to see the dress?" he asked obviously curious.

"Nope," Alex said, pushing him away. "The groom's not allowed to see the dress until your bride walks down the aisle. Oh! Sam, whose going to walk you down the aisle?" Alex said concerned.

"Uh..." she glanced into the study. "I was thinking maybe I'd ask Thomas. I know he's not a blood relative, but Luke and Marlena took me under their wing. I kind of came to think of them as my extended family."

Alex dropped her bags and pulled Sam into a huge bear hug. "He's going to be so honored. He told me he hopes one day you'll think of him as your cousin, too. I know technically he's not your cousin, but he's my brother in every possible way that truly matters. That makes him your cousin," Alex suggested.

"I think I already do," Sam confessed. "I thought it would be strange, but I've already accepted you as Lexie and Marlena as Lana. It seems natural somehow. It feels right. Along those same lines, Luke always felt like family. Accepting him as my uncle isn't really a stretch, which makes Thomas my cousin. You can't imagine how good it feels to be a part of a real family again. I never thought that was possible."

Alex hugged her again then picked up her belongings. "You get to ask Thomas yourself. I'm going to take care of these so they don't wrinkle," she turned to the study. "Hey, Thomas. Can you come here, Sam needs to talk to you in private." She laughed at the horrified look Sam directed her way.

"What's up?" Thomas asked casually when he stepped into the foyer. Ty took a couple steps backwards then leaned against the wall. He wanted to give these two a little space.

"Uh..." Sam paused. "I was wondering...well, uh...don't hesitate to say no if you don't want to, but I was wondering if you would be willing to give me away tomorrow," she blurted.

Thomas was stunned. He had hoped Samantha would eventually accept him as family. Did this mean she already had? He was touched by her request no matter the reason. "I'd love to," he said quietly. "Thank you for asking me."

Samantha was relieved. "Luke and Marlena always made me feel like I was somehow a part of your family. I think Luke was the closest thing to a father I've had for a long time. I'm so grateful for the time we had together. And Marlena was so caring and somehow protective of me, although at the time I didn't realize she was being protective. Does that make sense?"

"It does to me," Thomas admitted. "She did the same with me. Once she married dad, I instantly thought of her as my mother. It was just a natural transition. Most people wouldn't understand it, but I think you do," he decided.

"Initially I felt like we became friends too," Sam explained. "Later, I guess I also came to think of you as my family as well." She looked to Thomas for a reaction, when he didn't respond she continued. "What I'm trying to say, is I already thought of you as family before all of this. Now that I know about Alex and Marlena, I guess we're actually cousins. So, as one of my few living relatives, I would be honored if you would walk me down the aisle and give me away."

Dawn

"Thank you," he pulled Samantha into a big hug. "I've always felt the same about you. I guess it's the atmosphere dad and Marlena created for us. Then dad, once Marlena was no longer with us. The three of us enjoyed a lot of dinners together during dad's last year. I already love you Samantha. Welcome officially to the family. I would be extremely honored to give you away tomorrow. Ty's a wonderful man. You two are lucky to have each other." He leaned in and gave her a gentle kiss on the forehead. Then he turned and pulled Ty in for a hug. "Looks like we're going to be family now too."

Ty laughed. "Looks like," he paused. "But don't think you can take advantage of me now that we're related. I still want my fair share of the profits when we hit it big on the new simulators."

Thomas grinned. "What simulators?"

Chapter Thirteen

Samantha sat in the small room watching Alex and Lizza fuss. They were doing things to her hair she never knew was possible. Half way through Alex stood and began riffling through a large bag. Moments later she declared she was going to take care of Sam's makeup. Now Samantha's back was to the mirror so she couldn't see what these women were doing to her.

Every few minutes, Lizza would frantically blink her eyes to dissipate the tears that were forming. "You're so beautiful," she exclaimed. "Ty is going to be thrilled when we get finished."

"Does that mean he's not thrilled with me just the way I am?" Sam retorted.

"Of course he is dear," Lizza said casually. "It's just a special day. You need to look the part."

Dawn

Sam glanced at the overpriced dress hanging on the back of the door, then down at the shoes and frowned. It was all such a waste.

"Stop frowning," Alex scolded. "That's necessary too."

"It just seems so frivolous," Sam protested. "When am I ever going to wear something like that again?"

Alex smiled. "That's not frivolous," she disagreed. "My wedding gown is going to be frivolous. There is absolutely no way that I can ever wear the elegant, expensive gown again."

"Oh, I didn't mean..." Sam began.

Alex waved her off. "What I mean is that weddings are made to be frivolous. You on the other hand might find owning that gown convenient when I call you up at the last minute and tell you to go represent D-Tech at a charity event, or a social gathering. John used to have to attend those things all the time. I haven't made you do it because I've had you busy with other things. Don't get used to that. I will be sending you to dinners and all kinds of social events. Gatherings that will require dinner gowns just like that one." Alex smiled at Sam's astonishment. "You better start spending some of that big raise I gave you on other gowns too because I can't have you attending every event in the same dress."

Sam was still reeling from the news she was going to have to spend that kind of money on other outfits when Lizza joined in. "In addition to the stuff Alex sends you to, Ty has to attend functions himself. You're going to need evening wear for those as well. He's the head of a large, successful corporation. His wife is going to need to look the part. You're a corporate wife now."

Sam was dumbfounded. She hadn't thought of that. Alex giggled at Sam's discomfort. "I hate them, too. But, I've been attending them most of my life. Don't worry, you'll get used to it. It's not like you have to dress up every day." She paused as she searched through the makeup bag for just the right color. "Ninety-five percent of the time you and Ty will get away with the jeans and t-shirt look you both seem to love so well. But there will be times in your job when you'll have to dress up. Not just evening gowns, but business suits and business casual socials. Spend some of your money on clothes, Sam. It's not going to kill you."

Lizza had finished with her hair and was watching Alex finish up with the make-up. She wiped away a tear and stood. "I need to go freshen up myself and change into my dress. I'll see you outside." She turned and left the room.

About two minutes later Alex turned the chair around triumphantly. "All finished. What do you think?" she asked expectantly.

Samantha was stunned. She'd never looked that good in her life. "I think you two are miracle workers," she said in awe. "I never could have done this myself. How do you know how to do that?" she asked.

"Mom," Alex said still beaming. "Now, change into that dress and wait here until I come back to collect you. I need to get ready, too. Do not let Ty see you until Thomas is walking you down the aisle. We're looking for the dramatic effect here. It's going to be perfect," she said gleefully as she whirled out of the room.

Sam sat staring in the large mirror. She knew the transformation into a warrior had drastically improved the texture and color of her skin, but she looked amazing. Lizza had clipped a small hair claw at the base of her head to give her hair volume. It was elaborately decorated in diamonds. Sam hoped they were fake. She had matching earrings and a delicate necklace. Her hair was sleek and shiny. Much different from the ponytail look she usually dawned.

She slowly stood and headed for the dress. At least she wouldn't mess up her hair pulling the thing on. She loved the way it looked on her, but she couldn't wear a bra with it which made her feel extremely self-conscious. Once dressed, she walked to the window and stared at the garden. It was elaborately decorated with an arch and tons of flowers. Lizza had outdone herself. All the warriors were standing around visiting. It was a good sized crowd, not too big but not too small. She spotted Ty's father, Ken. He was visiting with a man and a woman. Sam thought they must be his brother and sister. She jumped and swung around when she heard the door open.

Alex had slipped back into the room, beautiful as ever. "I thought you weren't supposed to show up the bride," Sam commented.

"I haven't," Alex assured her. "The bride is the most beautiful woman in attendance today." She joined Samantha by the window. "I think they're ready. Should I fetch Thomas so we can get this show started?"

"I guess I'm as ready as I'll ever be," Sam agreed. She started for the door.

"Nope," Alex stopped her. "You stay here until Thomas leads you down. I need to get everyone seated and make sure Ty's in position before you make your grand entrance."

Sam sighed and turned back to the window. "I can't believe all of this is real," she admitted. "I've had so many wonderful changes in my life over the past couple days. I have to keep pinching myself to make sure I'm not dreaming."

Alex walked back over to Sam. "I am so happy for you." She took Sam's hand in hers. "I know how hard it is to focus when you're world tips upside down. It happened to me a few months ago. Be patient. Everything will get easier, I promise." She hugged Sam then rushed out the door.

Moments later there was a soft knock. "Sam, it's Thomas, can I come in?"

Sam walked to the door, pushing it wide open. "How about I come out," she suggested.

"Alex was right, you're stunning." Thomas smiled and held out his arm, "shall we?"

Sam slid her arm through his and they slowly headed for the stairs.

When Samantha and Thomas stepped onto the back porch the music started. Where had that come from? Lizza had apparently thought of everything. Samantha swallowed hard and took one hesitant step then another. By the time they reached the arch she and Thomas had a rhythm. They glided through and all eyes were on her. Sam's eyes found Ty's and never moved. He looked great in his suit. She briefly noticed Bo and Ace relaxing on the back porch, suddenly they stood and their ears perked up when they saw Samantha. Ty shot a look their way and the two dogs settled back onto their stomachs. Once he was sure the dogs wouldn't move he shifted his gaze back to Sam. Half way there, she thought. If I can just make it to the front of this crowd I won't have to move. She wasn't used to wearing such fancy shoes. The heels weren't high, just tall enough to cause concern. Her worst fear at the moment was showing her inner klutz. She would be so embarrassed if she tripped and fell flat on her face in front of all Ty's family and friends.

Ty knew the moment Samantha stepped onto the porch. He could feel her nervousness. She was doing this for him. He knew that. She really didn't know any of the guests that well except Ariel, Alex and Thomas. She looked like an angel stepping through the archway. She was always beautiful, but today she was stunning. His heart leapt. Soon she would be his wife. He never imagined he could be so happy about something as simple as a wedding. He'd been forced to attend hundreds of ceremonies in the past. At the time, he never understood what the big deal was. Now, looking at the woman he loved, he finally got it.

Sam reached the front of the garden. Thomas smiled at Ty and presented him with Sam's hand. Ty took it anxiously. He put his arm around her waist to help guide her to the podium. He couldn't resist. He leaned over and gave her a quick kiss.

"That part comes later," Orin scolded.

Ty gave him a sly grin, but waited for the cue before he kissed her again. The ceremony was brief, but not too short. Ty slipped a ring on Sam's finger and was surprised when she did the same. He hadn't expected her to buy him a ring. He studied the simple band, then smiled at her. "You seem to know me pretty well," he whispered. "I couldn't have done better myself."

Samantha was staring at the large flat diamond Ty had placed on her finger. It looked old and expensive. She looked at Ty then back to the ring. It was elegant and designed for someone far more sophisticated than she was. She continued to study it and realized she could wear it at work or even hunting and not worry about snagging it. She loved it!

Orin said a few words to the congregation and then the music started again. She knew the warriors were going to bring out food and give everyone time to mingle. It wasn't exactly a reception, but the casual social fit the newly married couple's style. The warriors stood and quickly walked toward the barn. They methodically began pulling out tables and chairs. In no time the seating area was set. The women rushed inside and had mounds of food piled everywhere in no time. Ty watched as Dimitri's puppy, Cane, ran out of the barn and joined his two dogs on the patio. Bo and Ace had already become protective of the small puppy and welcomed his company. Ty thought it was good for the small dog. He was learning how to behave from a couple pros. Hopefully Cane would take some of that back home with him when Dimitri and Alex returned to New York.

He shifted his attention back to Sam and gently pulled her into his arms. "Do you like it okay?" he asked.

Sam knew he was talking about the ring. "I love it!" She smiled at him. "But it looks old and very expensive. I hope you didn't spend too much."

"Actually, my grandmother gave that to me just before she died. She wanted my future wife to have something of hers even if she never got to meet her."

"Oh, then this should stay in your family. It's an heirloom." Sam protested.

"It is staying in the family," Ty corrected. "You are my family now, Sam." He pulled her close and kissed her passionately.

"None of that yet," Gavin complained. "I want to hug my new sister."

Dawn

"Go away," Ty protested but he turned Samantha into Gavin's waiting arms.

"Welcome to the family sis," Gavin said joyfully. "I don't think I've ever seen mom this happy. I just hope she doesn't start with me about finding my own mate now. I plan to spend the next couple hundred years enjoying the single life. So many women, so little time." He laughed as he released her and pulled his brother into a big hug. "I'm happy for you, big brother. She's quite a catch. In fact, I think maybe you married a little out of your league."

"I know I did," Ty grinned at Sam, "I'm just glad she didn't figure that out an hour ago. Now she's stuck with me forever."

Ty's parents were the next to approach them. Lizza pulled Ty into an emotional hug. She held him close as only a mother can. "I'm so proud of you. I hope the two of you will be as happy as your father and I have been all these years. She's a special woman. Take good care of her," she whispered as she stepped back. She turned to Samantha, "Now it's your turn," she pulled her into a big bear hug. "I'm so thrilled you are going to be part of our family."

Each member of the crowd congratulated the couple then they all sat down for a wonderful dinner. The close group visited well into the night. Atticus, Ken and Steve were a hoot. They told old story after story to the younger kids as they put it. They kept referring to their time as the good old days. Victor, Ariel, Breena, Orin, Tony and Megan sat at a table by themselves. They were also having a good time sharing stories. Every once in a while Victor or Orin would join the bigger conversation to correct a story or add some missing detail. She may not be friends with Ariel anymore, but at least all the tension and anger seemed to be gone.

Kylee and Dusty both seemed right at home with the group. She was still amazed at how well Kylee was taking the strange new world she'd accidentally discovered. An outsider looking in would never guess how many species were represented in this small group of friends. Sam was surprised at how quickly all the warriors had accepted her as one of them. She had assumed that was going to take time, but she already felt like she belonged. It was nice. She'd never belonged anywhere before, not since she'd lost her parents. She was so blessed and humbled to be a part of such an amazing partnership. She knew she still had a lot to prove. She wanted to be worthy of this new life she'd been offered. That's how she was starting to think of everything. She had been granted a new beginning. She now had the opportunity to take part in something worthwhile. Ty had given her a special gift in so many ways. She glanced over at her new husband and smiled.

Ty watched the three dogs romping and playing by the barn. He was proud of his two companions. They weren't just playing, they were teaching the small pup. The three friends appeared to be playing tag. The old rope Ty had tied for his dogs the day he arrived back at the farm had been more of a treat for them than he could have imagined. So many things had happened since then. What a contrast between the depression he felt that day and the absolute joy he felt today. He glanced over at Samantha. She was responsible for both. He was still amazed she'd agreed to be his wife. He smiled inwardly, they were going to have the most wonderful life together. He stood. "I'm beat. I'm going to take my lovely bride and call it a night." He held his hand out for Sam to join him.

Sam was grateful. It had been such an emotional day. She was more than ready to go to bed. "Thank you everyone for being here. You made today more special than I ever could have imagined." She placed her hand in Ty's and let him lead her into the house.

Dawn

Ty hesitated and glanced back at the dogs. Dimitri caught it and waved Ty off. "I'll take care of them. Go enjoy the rest of your wedding night."

Once they were in Ty's room he quickly pushed the door shut and maneuvered Sam up against it with his body. Ty moaned softly as he pressed his lips to Sam's. "I have wanted to be alone with you ever since you stepped out on the porch." He lifted her into his arms and walked to the bed. "I have a surprise for you," he whispered softly as he gently set her on the pillow then joined her.

"What's that?" she asked, perfectly content.

"I've made arrangements with Alex and Dimitri for you and me to spend a week all to ourselves," Ty smiled.

"Really? I get a whole week alone with you?" Sam said enthusiastically, she had assumed tomorrow they would need to get back to work.

"Yep," he assured her.

"Do we get to leave or do we have to stick around here?" she asked.

"We can go anywhere you'd like. You pick," he kissed her ear gently.

"Can we go to your ranch?" she asked.

"Do you mean our ranch?" he asked absently. "Now that we're married, what's mine is yours." He smiled when she squirmed then pulled back and looked at her. "What part of that makes you uncomfortable?"

"It's going to take me awhile to get used to the married part. Don't expect me to immediately jump into the multimillion dollar, have whatever I want part. I've already gotten the lecture about buying more evening wear and acting like a corporate wife," Sam paused. "Please just give me a little time to settle."

"You better not act like a corporate wife," Ty said annoyed. "Who told you that?"

"Your mother," she said hesitantly. "But Alex said I have to go to dinner parties and social events for D-Tech, too. I'm just not sure I'm ready for all the changes."

Ty kissed her gently. "I don't want you to change, baby. I love my beautiful, brave, brilliant, stubborn wife just the way you are. I've never wanted a wife that was afraid she'd break a nail if she sneezed."

Samantha slid her hand beneath the pillow self-consciously hiding her short broken nails.

"Oh, no you don't." Ty pulled her hand out and kissed each finger gently. He was now hovering over her, propped up on one elbow. He slowly bent her wrist back and gently kissed her palm. "Please promise me you will never act like a corporate wife. Sure, we have to go to dinner parties and social events, but I spend most of my time in jeans. Mom likes the parties and all that social junk, so I try to humor her a little, but I mostly like to be casual. So do you. Keep the formal obligations in prospective. Don't let mom convince you to buy anything you don't like. Although, I must say..." his gaze moved slowly down her body. "I do love you in this dress."

Samantha laughed. He was such a guy. "So do we get to go to the ranch?"

Dawn

"We can go to the ranch, but not until you call it our ranch," he teased.

"Okay our ranch," she said emphasizing our. "You're mom told me you had one, but she was pretty mysterious about it. I can't wait to see it. Is it big or small?" she asked.

"It's fair sized," he assured her. "Do you need anything from your apartment on the way? We can stop off in New York if we need to."

Samantha wrinkled her nose at the thought. "Absolutely not," she said adamantly. "I hate that place. I'd be embarrassed for you to see it," she confessed. "I'll just go by sometime and grab my things."

"We'll go by sometime and grab your things." He gently kissed her neck, then her earlobe. "We're partners now, Sam. I realize it's going to take time for you to get used to it, but from now on we do things together. That means from the little stuff like gathering up your property to the big ones like hunting vampires. I need you to promise me you won't ever go out hunting alone again." He had sobered and was watching her seriously now.

"I promise," she assured him. "I don't have to anymore. If you're not around I'll get Alex to go with me."

Ty smiled, "Good luck with that one."

"What do you mean?" she asked frowning.

"Alex is the queen," he began. "It's more dangerous for her out there than the rest of us. Dimitri is very protective of the woman he loves," he paused. "So am I." He ignored her grimace. "Oh, Alex still fights and she's good, don't get me wrong. She's better than good, she's amazing. But you two actually planning a night out vampire hunting? That's never going to happen. It shouldn't. It would be reckless of Alex, and you for that matter."

"I keep forgetting she's the queen," Sam admitted. "She's too…"

"Normal?" he provided. "I know, but she can also be stern and forceful and even sophisticated, diplomatic and poised when she needs to be. Wait until you see her in action, you'll know what I mean."

Sam didn't know what to say. She'd seen Alex deal with difficult men at work. She was sure her boss would be just as effective as queen. She was looking forward to learning everything there was to know about her new world. The enormity of her life changes hit her again.

"Now what?" Ty asked, feeling Sam's anxiety. "What's upsetting you?"

"I'm just a bit overwhelmed, that's all." Sam tried to brush it off.

"Overwhelmed about which part?" Ty asked.

"All of it," she admitted. "Being married to you for starters," she paused cautiously. "You've always had money. You're a millionaire, billionaire, I don't even know which one. You told me how you got your start with explosives capping wells in your family's oil industry. Then you moved into construction with your father to do his explosive demolitions. Now, you own the biggest, most successful gaming company around. You've always had money. I never have. I've come from a humble farm out in the country to a rundown apartment in the Bronx. I'm plain and normal and I don't know...homely I guess," she said vulnerably.

Ty laughed. "You are the least homely woman I've ever met. The money only means something because, like you said, you've never had a lot. Warriors, fae, we all live a long time Sam. All of us are rich. It's easy when you live thousands of times longer than a human. Give it a little time and you'll see it's just money. There's always more of it to be made somehow," he studied her. She seemed even more anxious than before. "Now what?" he asked exasperated.

"I just realized I have no idea how old you are. When you were talking about your past that night with the game, I believed you were human. It seemed like a lot for a guy in his thirties to have accomplished. Now I realize you could be several hundred years old. I might have just married an old man!" she said in horror. "How old are you anyway? Please tell me you're less than five hundred. I think that's my breaking point."

Ty rolled his eyes but Sam continued to sit there staring at him in anticipation. "Okay, fine. I'm less than five hundred. And I'm not an old man. Age is relative," Ty shrugged. "In my world I'm still a frisky young colt."

"What does that mean exactly?" Sam asked narrowing her eyes at him. "In your world? How old are you in my world?"

"Well since we now live in the same world, I'm the same age in yours as I am in mine," he teased.

"How old?" she pressed.

"A hundred and sixty four," he admitted. "Can we go to bed yet?" he asked impatiently.

"A hundred and..." Samantha paused. "You're a hundred and twenty nine years older than me," Samantha exclaimed. "You're an old man. I've married an old man!" She said in horror. "How could I have missed this? How could I have let myself get hitched to someone that ancient?" She was teasing now. She buried her head in the palm of her hands.

"I'll show you old man," Ty said grabbing her earlobe with his mouth and biting down gently.

Sam giggled. Ty was right, it was all relative. If they lived several thousand years, what was a hundred and some change when you looked at the bigger picture? She settled in to begin her new life with the man she loved. For the first time since she was twelve, she felt like the luckiest woman in the world.

THE END